I0744702

Love Touched Hearts: A Regency Romance Valentine's Day Collection

Five Delightful Regency Valentine's Stories from

Arietta Richmond

Grace Austen

Isabella Thorne

Katherine Keats

Alyce Healey

Dreamstone Publishing © 2017

www.dreamstonepublishing.com

Copyright © 2017 Dreamstone Publishing, Arietta Richmond, Grace Austen, Isabella Thorne, Katherine Keats and Alyce Healey

All rights reserved.

No parts of this work may be copied without the author's permission.

ISBN: 1925499472

ISBN-13: 978-1-925499-47-6

ARIETTA RICHMOND, GRACE AUSTEN, ISABELLA THORNE,
KATHERINE KEATS, ALYCE HEALEY AND SOPHIA ANSLEY

Disclaimer

These stories are works of fiction.

Names, characters, places and incidents are the product of
the author's imagination and are used fictitiously. Any
resemblance to events, locales or actual persons, living or
dead, is entirely coincidental.

ARIETTA RICHMOND, GRACE AUSTEN, ISABELLA THORNE,
KATHERINE KEATS, ALYCE HEALEY AND SOPHIA ANSLEY

Introduction

We hope you enjoy this Valentine's Day Collection of Regency romance stories. As authors, we each have a different style, but we are brought together by our love for Regency Romance. This collection presents some very different heroes and heroines, but the common theme is that they all find love, despite trials and tribulations along the way, at Valentine's Day.

We have each also given you a bonus, with some previews of our other books. We hope that you love reading these stories as much as we enjoyed writing them, and that you will also go on to enjoy all of our other Regency books!

Thanks for reading 'Love Touched Hearts: A Regency Romance Valentine's Day Collection'!

Arietta Richmond

Grace Austen

Isabella Thorne

Katherine Keats

Alyce Healey

Table of Contents

ARIETTA RICHMOND, GRACE AUSTEN, ISABELLA THORNE,
KATHERINE KEATS, ALYCE HEALEY AND SOPHIA ANSLEY

Number 1 Bestselling Author
Arietta Richmond
Giving a Heart of Lace
His Majesty's Hounds - Book 3
Sweet and Clean Regency Romance

His Majesty's Hounds– Book 3

Sweet and Clean Regency Romance

Giving a Heart of Lace

Arietta Richmond

ARIETTA RICHMOND, GRACE AUSTEN, ISABELLA THORNE,
KATHERINE KEATS AND ALYCE HEALEY

Books by Arietta Richmond

His Majesty's Hounds

Claiming the Heart of a Duke

Intriguing the Viscount

Giving a Heart of Lace (a prequel to Winning the Merchant Earl)

Being Lady Harriet's Hero (coming soon)

Healing Lord Barton (coming soon)

Winning the Merchant Earl (coming soon)

Loving the Bitter Baron (coming soon)

Rescuing the Countess (coming soon)

The Derbyshire Set

A Gift of Love (Prequel short story)

A Devil's Bargain (Prequel short story - coming soon)

The Earl's Unexpected Bride

The Captain's Compromised Heiress

The Viscount's Unsuitable Affair

The Count's Impetuous Seduction

The Rake's Unlikely Redemption

The Marquess' Scandalous Mistress

A Remembered Face (Bonus short story – coming soon)

The Marchioness' Second Chance (coming soon)

A Viscount's Reluctant Passion (coming soon)

Lady Theodora's Christmas Wish

The Duke's Improper Love (coming soon)

Other Books

The Scottish Governess (coming soon)

The Earl's Reluctant Fiancée (coming soon)

The Crew of the Seadragon's Soul Series, (coming soon - a set of 10 linked
novels)

Dedication

For everyone who had the grace to be patient while this book, and the ones before and after it, were coming into existence, who provided cups of tea, and food, when the writing would not let me go, and endured countless times being asked for opinions.

For the other writers in my Regency Romance mastermind group, who inspire me, and ask the kind of questions that make us all learn more about this fascinating period.

For the readers coming to know these characters well, and who inspire me to continue, by buying my books!

For my growing team of beta readers and advance reviewers – it's thanks to you that others can enjoy these books in the best presentation possible!

And for all the writers of Regency Historical Romance, whose books I read, who inspired me to write in this fascinating period.

ARIETTA RICHMOND, GRACE AUSTEN, ISABELLA THORNE,
KATHERINE KEATS AND ALYCE HEALEY

Chapter One

The coal box was empty. The larder contained some cheese, some bread, and very little else. Serafine walked to her room with a heavy heart. In her dresser drawer there was a small metal chest – the sort that, in another life, she might have used as a jewellery box.

She turned the key, and opened the chest. She stared at the contents, as despair gripped her. The box contained only ten pounds. Ten pounds that were their last remaining money. And, carefully wrapped in a scrap of silk, a heart made of lace and ribbon and beads, all sewn onto a piece of parchment.

Lace that was all she had left of her grandmother. Everything else had been sold. Sewing that heart had been just for fun, then – it seemed an eternity ago – before *'the fall'* as she thought of it. Before her fool of a brother had gambled away everything, drawn into a tawdry gaming hell by that demon Pendholm, and bled of everything that had any value in their lives. Before her brother had committed the ultimate betrayal, and killed himself because of it.

Before the *ton* had shunned them for the scandal of a suicide in the family. Before.....

She shut the thoughts away. At least they had the house. It was small, and in a rather unfashionable part of town – not quite respectable at all – but it was her mother's outright, left to her by her aunt, shortly after Serafine's father's death. Although an unheated house, with no servants, and little furniture left was not exactly the most pleasant place to live, at least it was theirs.

She took out two pounds, her finger absently stroking the lace as she did, then shut and locked the chest, hiding it away again. Today, she could buy food and coal. What would she do on the day when there was no longer any money to do so?

~~~~~

Serafine sighed, holding the bag of food close against her. It was heavy, but she treasured the weight – it was the substance of survival, at least for a little longer. The coal would be delivered later in the day – enough for a month, if she was very careful. The food would not last near so long.

Passing the shop on the corner, she paused to look in the window a moment. Once, she would have thought such a shop beneath her – now, what it contained was as far beyond what she could afford as the moon was above the earth. Yet she still liked to look at pretty things. A little collection in one corner of the window caught her eye. A pile of what might be called favours – little cards and items, decorated with ribbons, lace and sometimes paste gems or feathers.
~~~~~

Pretty little nothings that a man might give his mistress, or a woman he was courting.

One, in particular, a little stained on the edges, but still pretty, reminded her of the heart with her grandmother's lace – it was the sort of thing that some called a Valentine. She stared at it for a while, feeling as if it was important, but not knowing why, then shrugged, lifted her bags again, and went home.

~~~~~

The next day was clear and bright, but very cold – they would likely have snow on Christmas Day. Serafine sat at the window of the parlour, sewing. She was nearly finished embellishing the gown for Mrs Johnson, which was a relief, for it meant that she would be paid for the work, but also a worry, for there were no more dresses waiting her attention. And her sewing was their only income –the only way to stretch out what money they had, for a little longer.

The ladies of the merchant classes, who lived all around them, those who had some money, but were not rich enough to ever consider going to a modiste in the heart of London, they were her customers. They found the idea of a Lady born sewing for them somehow satisfying (not that anybody ever called her 'Lady Serafine' any more – that manner of address belonged to *before* – now she was just 'miss' most of the time. And to those who knew her name at all, she was Miss Sera – Serafine had seemed a lovely name to her mother, who was fascinated by old mythology and similar, but now it was simply out of place for her current station in life.).
~~~~~

The merchant ladies appreciated her fine sense of fashion. But more than that, they appreciated her affordable pricing.

She hummed as she worked, her clever fingers sewing beads onto a tracery of lace on the hemline of the dress, but her mind was elsewhere.

Her thoughts kept going back to that sad little pile of favours in the shop window. She wondered if they sold well, and what sort of people bought them. She'd seen a few things like that… *before*… but she'd never thought much of it. She thought of it now. They were such little things, and sewing them was, she suspected, not so different from sewing embellishments onto dresses.

Were they a thing that members of the *ton* might buy? Perhaps – if someone important bought one, or gave one to someone noticeable… if that happened, then others would follow – there were always those who simply copied everything the arbiters of fashion did, or the royal family did. She brought her attention back to sewing the last few beads onto the dress – what a goose she was, dreaming about the royals and the *ton*! They had nothing to do with her world now, nothing at all.

Chapter Two

Mr Raphael Morton was bored. That was a terrible thing to admit, when what he was doing was going over the business ledgers with the man he employed to do his accounts. Mr Manning was excellent at his job, and the ledgers were neat and clear. They showed just how wealthy Raphael was – just how well Morton Empire Imports was doing. Most men would be excited by what they saw – not bored.

But, bored he was. For Raphael, the exciting part was the planning, laying out the path that led to this, that ensured that, if all the steps were followed, the wealth would grow. After years at war, the inactivity of sitting in an office, or walking the warehouse and speaking to customers, was slowly driving him mad. To make it worse, his ship's captains came back not only with cargoes of exotic goods to make him even wealthier, but with tales of distant lands, strange sights and different people.

He envied them. He wanted to see those places himself. No amount of wealth and rich living here could change that. London was a gilded cage.

For, no matter what they had vowed to each other, the world would go as it did – his friends, those who had been closer than family for those long years of war, would be forced away from him. It was simple fact. They were all titled, and he was not. He was, in fact, that worst of things (from the *ton's* point of view), a Cit – a merchant, one tainted by dirtying his hands with trade. No matter that it had made him wealthier than most of them, no matter that they craved the luxuries he imported, he was, to the *ton*, to be disdained for his lower class existence.

How could his friends ever overcome that? He would not wish them shunned by their peers for associating with him. Yet he missed them sorely. Better to travel the world alone, than to live here in luxury, so close, yet never able to see them.

"That will do for today, Manning. Your work is excellent, as usual. Make sure that the Captain of the Morton Venture receives a suitable bonus – he has done far better than I expected with this cargo."

Manning blinked in some surprise, for they were barely half way through the review of the ledgers, then nodded, closed the books, and left the office.

~~~~~

Two hours later, Raphael was still sitting there, thinking. He had reached the rather depressing conclusion that there was no easy answer to his boredom, or to his sense of being trapped. Perhaps it might be more bearable if he had something new and different to do, some new venture?
~~~~~

At least then he could sink himself into the planning, into bringing something new to life, and making it profitable. But what? He had warehouses full of exotic materials, objects, spices and other things – was there some new way that he could use them, something new he could create, that could be cleverly brought to the attention of the most influential of the *ton*, or perhaps even the Prince Regent? Raphael knew that, for something new to become a profitable venture, it would have to draw the attention of those with money to spend.

The idea took hold, it was a puzzle to be solved – what new thing could he create, using goods that he already had, which could take the fashionable people by storm, and make him even wealthier? (not that he cared about the money, he had enough – it was the challenge that mattered...)

He spent the next few days stalking through his warehouses, looking at everything, terrifying his managers and warehouse labourers, who were certain that he must be seeking evidence of wrongdoing on their part. He could feel an idea, an insight, at the edge of his thoughts – but it refused to surface. He went home to toss and turn in restless sleep, dreaming of exotic oddities.

~~~~~

With Mrs Johnson's dress completed and delivered, Serafine took a little of the money that she had been paid, and went to the market. She would add some more food to their supplies while she could, and getting out and walking felt good, after the last few days of sitting and sewing.
~~~~~

At the little shop on the corner she stopped, looking at the items in the window again. Surprised at what she saw, she considered a moment, then turned and entered the shop.

"What can I do for you, Miss?"

The shopkeeper looked at her, obviously assessing her possible wealth from her clothes.

"In the window – those little... favours? I noticed them the other day, and meant to come in earlier – I particularly liked the heart shaped one, but I can't see it now – has it been sold?"

"Oh yes Miss, you've got to be quick to get a nice one of those – they sell all the time, any that I get. The young gents are always looking for tokens to give the girls they're courting. The heart shaped ones go fastest – seems they like it to be obvious what they mean when they put it in the girl's hands. Don't often get a young lady asking about them though."

Serafine thought for a moment, as the shopkeeper waited, his expression curious.

"Where do they come from? I mean, who do you buy them from?"

"Well Miss, it's not always the same. Used to be my old mother made some for me, but she's gone to God now, and m'wife don't like to sew fiddly things. So now it's only when someone brings some in, that they want to sell, that I can get any. Pity, because there's always those as wants to buy 'em."

"How much do you sell them for?"

Serafine waited for the answer, almost holding her breath.

When the shopkeeper, after some time thinking, named a figure, she was pleasantly surprised, even though she suspected he might have inflated the number, because he thought she looked like she could afford more. That idea almost brought a bubble of bitter laughter to her, but she repressed it. An idea was forming – maybe there was a way for her to earn more, to keep them surviving a bit longer.

"What if I had some to sell you? New ones, heart shaped ones with pretty beads or ribbons, not just lace?"

The shopkeeper's eyes narrowed with avarice, and Serafine knew, instantly, that her instinct was right – this *was* a way to earn more.

"Likely I'd be interested in buying... if the price was right..."

Twenty minutes of haggling later, Serafine left the shop, with a bounce in her step that hadn't been there for a long time. They had agreed that she would bring him three as a sample, in a few days' time. For those, he would give her about half of the price he normally sold them for. If they sold well, he would buy more – and give her a better percentage of the price, especially if she made things that he could sell for a higher price to begin with.

By her calculations, she could earn as much from making four or five of the pretty little favours as she could from embellishing a dress – and she would need to use less materials to do so. After a quiet luncheon with her mother, who declared it far too cold to go out, and wanted only to huddle by the fire and read, Serafine went out again – to buy beads and lace, and some heavy paper.

It was time to get to work.

~~~~~

Some hours later, tired but satisfied, she carefully put away the collection of beads, laces and little paste gems that she had bought – the amount it had cost her, even buying mismatched and second-hand (for small favours did not need many beads, unlike dresses!), worried her, for it had taken far more of their money than she was comfortable with, but there really was no choice – she had to earn money somehow, and that meant spending some first.

If these did well, though, she would need to find another source of materials – both to get better quality, and because, with today's purchases, she had quite exhausted the supply from the places she usually shopped.
~~~~~

Chapter Three

Christmas Day arrived with a deep fall of snow overnight, after which the day dawned clear and beautiful, the winter sun making the icicles on the trees and eaves sparkle like decorations. For Seraphine and her mother, it was a day of sadness – their second Christmas since '*the fall*' - and now they were considerably poorer than they had been for the first one. They missed James, her brother – for no matter how much Serafine might curse what he had done, he was still her brother – and his absence hurt.

There was enough coal to warm one room of the house – it had to be enough. And, taking Serafine completely by surprise, Mrs Johnson, and two of the other ladies whose dresses she sewed, had sent their servants to her door bearing a hamper of Christmas food and a bottle of good wine. The simple kindness had brought her to tears.

Between that, and the success of her first few favours, the money would last a little longer, and that was, at least, something to be grateful for.

Curled by the fire, Serafine was thinking about favours. The first few that she had made were Christmassy – in the hope that young men might buy them to give to their sweethearts for the Holiday. She had tried, as much as possible with the cheap materials, to make them look expensive, to make them look like the sort of thing that a member of the *ton* would not be ashamed to give.

It seemed that she had succeeded, for Mr Tanner at the shop had been impressed, and she was sure that he had sold them for even more than he had originally thought he might. She had seen his eyes narrow with avarice again, when she unwrapped them from the box she had brought them in. She might have pushed for more than he had paid her, but she was grateful for what she received – and anyway, if she wanted him to buy more, it was best not to make that too hard for him.

She had gone back two days later to see if any of them had sold, and been startled to discover that they all had – and that he would like more, as soon as she could make them. So she had. And now she had used up almost all of the materials she had bought. The money from those favours would, with care, keep them in coal until the weather got a little warmer. But she would need to make more – Mrs Johnson and her friends only had so many dresses in need of work, and there was nothing else to provide an income.

So she stared into the flames and worried. She worried about what sort of favours she should make next – what holidays or events might there be, that would encourage people to buy favours for their mistresses or for the girls that they courted?

And even more, she worried about where she would get some more suitable materials, without having to use money that they would need for food. Whatever else happened, she would not see her mother starve, after all that they had been through. She dreamed of the sort of shop that she used to buy her ribbons and gloves and bonnets from, before, when she was a Lady, when she had money and no idea of what it was to be poor, or reviled. Oh to have even a tiny bit of the sort of ribbons and lace that could be bought in such a shop!

As her eyes drifted shut in the quiet room, a tiny thought floated through her mind, just before sleep took her:- *'where did those shops get their stock from?'*

~~~~~

For Raphael, Christmas was also strange – there was the joy of actually being there to celebrate it with his mother, sister, and brother, yet the sadness of his father's empty chair. He missed his father with an intensity that had caught him off guard – and he deeply regretted that war had taken him away, when the business had grown so astoundingly in his father's talented care. There was so much that he might have learnt, had he been at his father's side.

There was also the truly odd feeling of not even knowing exactly where the other Hounds were. After more than four years together at war, their tight knit band of specialists, called 'His Majesty's Hounds' by most of the rest of their troops, for their uncanny ability to find and deal with French spies, and to predict French troop movements, they had become almost more family than his family.
~~~~~

Christmas without them seemed somehow wrong, somehow a betrayal of the bond between them.

He felt cast adrift, trying to be a serious merchant, running what had become a vast empire of trade, yet totally unsure of his own place in the world, now that he had to deal with the rules of society. Over the last few weeks, since the day when he had realised just how bored he was, he had repeatedly thought about his wish to travel – and the complete impossibility of doing so. And the puzzle that he had set himself that day, of finding something new to sell, some new way to leverage what he had, still nagged at him. He had no answer. He would find one yet.

"Raphael's not listening, mother. I don't think he heard any of what I just said!" Isabella's voice was somewhere between teasing and petulant, for, after so long of not having Raphael there, she could not truly be angry with him.

Raphael realised, with a start, that he had, indeed been wool-gathering – had been drifting off into his puzzle, oblivious to the conversation around him.

"I wasn't completely ignoring you, Bella. I do know that you were talking about dresses and Balls, and eligible young men, and bemoaning the fact that we are not of the aristocracy, so that you will not be invited to any of the truly fashionable events." The fact that he could not remember anything of exactly what she had said did not prevent his summary from being accurate. She turned her huge dark eyes upon him and proceeded to look like a hurt puppy.

"Well, it isn't fair! We can afford dresses and jewellery just as beautiful as theirs – why should not being titled matter?"

His sister had an alarmingly revolutionary attitude to some things, he thought with chagrin.   Whilst he could rather sympathise with her sentiment, that attitude could make her life somewhat difficult, given the, oh, so rigid, rules of society.

Gabriel was uninterested in his sister's complaints – at 16, he was just growing into himself, with the shape of the handsome man just beginning to emerge from the boy. He was, however, most interested in doing justice to the remarkable Christmas Feast that their chef had produced. Raphael watched him with affection, and prayed that Gabriel need never go to war, need never see any of the things that he had seen, need never know the terrible things that men could do to each other. He hoped that Gabriel would join him in running the business – but that was at least two years off, for he would have the best education possible before then.

Isabella was speaking again, and he had missed part of the conversation... again.

"...quite beautiful – so intricately worked – a little heart, with ribbon and lace and little bells and holly berries on it. It must mean that he truly cares for me, mustn't it, mother?"

What on earth was she talking about? Raphael wondered, as the conversation continued.

"Now my dear, perhaps he does have a *tendre* for you... or perhaps he simply wishes to outdo your other admirers..." Their mother's voice was filled with affection and amusement and she watched her daughter consider that comment.

"No, no, he must really care. You don't understand – I will have to show you!"

Completely ignoring any sort of ladylike behaviour, Isabella rose and ran from the room, to return a few minutes later, with something cradled in her hands.

"You see?" She deposited it on the table for them to examine.

Raphael, curious, scooped it up. It was a piece of heavy, parchment like paper, folded in two so that a message could be written inside, and decorated on the outside with lace, ribbon and gems (which were almost certainly paste), with tiny paste holly berries in a cluster, and two even smaller dangling bells. The whole thing was cut to a heart shape. It was, he had to agree, charming. He had seen things like this before, on the occasion of Saint Valentine's Day, and at other times attached to bouquets and gifts. This was both more elaborate and, strangely, more elegant than any he had seen before.

Just as he went to open it, and see just what message had been written for Bella, she snatched it from his grasp.

"Oh no – that message is for me, it's private. You can't read it!"

"As you wish." Raphael made great show of turning away and becoming uninterested, which only made Isabella make a little huff of expelled breath in exasperation. Tilting her nose up, she turned away.

"I think I shall remove myself to the parlour." He watched her leave the room with a fond smile. But the image of that exquisitely wrought little piece of frivolity stuck in his mind. Why did it seem significant?

Chapter Four

Within a few days, the pristine white snow of Christmas morning had turned to half melted muddy piles of icy slush on London's busy streets. People ventured on their way with care, in boots or with pattens on their feet if they could afford it. Serafine set out that morning in her best remaining winter dress, with the pelisse that was still mostly respectable over it. She had woken from her nap on Christmas Day with the memory of that passing thought. And now she felt compelled to investigate – *where did the shops that sold pretty trifles to the nobility buy their goods?*

She went back towards the more fashionable parts of the city, back towards her past... She sought out the shops that were close to, but not on, the most fashionable streets. Shops that would have been beneath her... before... And therefore, shops where she would not be recognised. She could not bear to face the cut direct from those she had once called friends – she would not allow herself to risk that again.

At least she must have managed to look like a Lady should, for a scruffy crossing sweeper leapt out to sweep the snow and detritus from her path as she crossed the street. She tossed him the smallest coin she had – she could ill afford to, yet she would not see anyone starve – not now that she knew the feel of true hunger herself. She received a few curious looks – a young gentlewoman out without a maid beside her - but she ignored them. Just ahead was exactly the sort of shop she was seeking.

Inside, the shop was small, yet full of many beautiful things. An older woman, well dressed, yet in garments some years out of fashion, was seated behind a small counter. She rose as Serafine entered.

"Good day to you, my Lady, what may I help you with today?"

Serafine almost laughed – it was so long since anyone had called her 'my Lady' that it almost sounded wrong. She looked around, and wandered through the shop, drawn from display to display, with so many beautiful items to explore.

"I am not sure – I would like to simply look for a little – to see what appeals to me most."

"Certainly, my Lady, do ask me if you wish to know about anything, or see anything else." The woman sat again, quietly waiting, and watched her every move.

In the back corner of the shop, jumbled in a little basket on a shelf, she found a collection of scraps of lace, short pieces of ribbon, broken pieces of paste jewellery, little feathers, and other interesting things. She took it to the counter.

The old woman looked at her in surprise, but waited for her to speak.

"This basket of things – how much? I know it may seem strange, but I like to make small things, for my friend's children's dolls, and other little things – all of these pieces are interesting, and I can use tiny amounts like this."

The woman smiled at her, seeming to find the explanation reasonable – for many ladies of the nobility amused themselves with charitable works and most embroidered or sewed small trifles. Waiting for the answer, Serafine ran her fingers through the tangle of items – some pieces were unusual – in colour or texture, or in the shape of small silver or carved stone beads.

"Where do these come from?" She hoped that her question sounded casual enough.

The woman looked at her again, and named a price for the little basket – a remarkably reasonable price, considering the location of the shop. As Serafine produced the money to pay, the woman went on, finally getting to the answer that Serafine really wanted.

"Where do they come from? Things come from all over the world, from India and beyond – China and the East Indies, from Africa, from many places – sometimes materials are brought here, and made into things here, sometimes they are imported complete. The merchant companies get very wealthy finding exotic trinkets to keep the *ton* happy. I buy things from only the better importers – I like to sell quality to the quality!" She gave a small laugh at her own words, and Serafine joined her.

"I've never thought about it before, but when I saw all of these things, and touched them, I couldn't help but wonder." She smiled at the woman, hoping that she might say more.

"You'd be a rare one to think about it. Most of the young Ladies I sell pretty things to don't care where they come from. There're some good merchants now. Now that the war's over, more goods can get here, shipping's safer, they tell me. The good ones even charge a bit less, now there's less risk in their business. For those who've got a taste for the exotic or the unusual, and good quality, I buy from Morton Empire Imports. That's a sad tale though. Old Mr Morton, God rest his soul, the poor man died before his son got home from war – such a sorry thing!"

It seemed that Serafine had unleashed a flood of words. Perhaps the woman rarely had anyone to talk to – anyone who had the slightest interest in her business or her life, that is.

"There's other companies, but Morton is the best of the bunch – never had a faulty shipment from them, not once!"

After letting the woman ramble on for another twenty minutes, Serafine finally extracted herself from the shop, her purchases in hand, and took herself home. Now she not only had some more materials to work with, but a name. What if she could buy materials direct from the importer? Surely that would be cheaper, or at least better quality for the same amount of money. She would have to find out where this Morton Empire Imports had its office.

~~~~~
~~~~~

A few days later, when Serafine delivered the next batch of favours to Mr Tanner's shop, he greeted her with great enthusiasm.

"Good day to you Miss, I do hope that you've got some more of your excellent work for me?"

That was more flattery than usual from him – she wondered why. She didn't have to wonder long – he could hardly contain himself.

"Those last few – the Christmas heart ones – I sold the smallest of them to young Jemmy – works as a groom at the Arbuthnot place – they're the second wealthiest merchants around, don't you know. You'll never guess what happened next! Mr Arbuthnot – Porter his name is, he's the son of the house – saw it, and he liked it so much he actually came here, to buy one for the girl he's sweet on. Now that's the sort of customer I like! He bought the biggest one – that nice one with the little bells - didn't even blink at the price."

Mr Tanner was so excited at the idea of such a wealthy customer that he was almost rubbing his hands together with glee.

"The wealthy merchants' sons, they're always trying to outdo one another – all except Mr Morton that is – he has no need to outdo anyone, he's the wealthiest of the lot. If any of the others hear of this, they'll likely come looking to buy something similar – so I hope you've got some quality work for me."

Silently, Serafine placed her basket on the counter, and lifted out her latest work.

There were 5 favours, each unique, some heart shaped, some not, made using a mixture of ordinary ribbon and lace, and some of the unusual bits and pieces she'd bought from the fashionable shop.

"I think that these would please the most exacting customer. I will have to ask you for a slightly higher price for these, Mr Tanner – for the materials are a bit more expensive – but if you want to tempt the wealthy, the items have to be of a suitable quality."

She waited, outwardly looking calm, serene, but inwardly terrified that he would refuse to pay extra. He looked closely at the favours, obviously wanting them, unconsciously narrowing his eyes in that characteristic expression of avarice. Eventually he looked up.

"I do agree Miss, things need to be obvious quality to sell to the better class of customer. I like these – I'll give you a better price."

Serafine nearly sagged from relief. And so the haggling commenced – for Mr Tanner couldn't agree to anything without some haggling. When they were done, Serafine was happy, for she had secured his agreement to a standard price twenty percent higher than that which he had paid for her previous work. Mr Tanner looked happy too – so she suspected that she could have pushed him for more, and succeeded. But haggling was exhausting – at least they were both happy with this outcome.

Now that she could stop worrying about the money, something of what he had said earlier came back to Serafine.

Surely that richest merchant family he had mentioned –
Morton wasn't it? Surely she'd heard that name recently? Then
it came to her, a clear little bubble of memory in her mind. The
old woman in the other shop – she'd said she bought from
Morton Empire Imports – it had to be owned by the family Mr
Tanner spoke of, for the chances of two wealthy merchant
families of the same name were low. Taking a deep breath, she
spoke as casually as she could.

"This Mr Morton you mentioned – the wealthiest merchant?
What does his business do, that they are so wealthy?"

Mr Tanner was always happy to show off his knowledge of
everyone and everything, and especially when he could make
himself look important by association. He puffed his chest up
with that supposed importance, and launched into a long,
gossipy explanation.

By the time he was done, Serafine knew all about the last
two generations of Mortons, about how sad it was that the old
man had died before his son Raphael returned from the war,
how the son was a war hero, even if he didn't speak of it, how
the mother was Italian, and her three children all strikingly good
looking as a result, how young Mr Arbuthnot was sweet on Miss
Isabella Morton, but Mr Tanner doubted he stood a real chance
there, and she had also been treated to what seemed an
exhaustive list of the sort of products that the firm imported,
from the far reaches of the empire and beyond.

Her face and neck were aching from nodding and smiling as
he talked and Serafine thought, with wry amusement, that she
seemed to have developed rather a talent for gossiping with
shopkeepers.

Taking advantage of a break in his conversation, she thanked him, and, escaped into the cold afternoon.

She was now absolutely certain that she needed to seek out the offices of Morton Empire Imports as soon as possible.

Chapter Five

Rafael rode through the streets, observing as the morning bustle gave way to quiet, the closer he came to Hyde Park. The *ton* did not rise early, unlike the merchants, even the wealthy merchants, who lived nearer his home. He felt the need to let his horse stretch out and shed its excess energy, to feel the wind on his face, to be moving.

His head was full of cobwebs and an ache that came from imbibing a little too much, yet he was happy – happier than he had been for many weeks. The previous evening he had, for the first time since their return, spent time with the rest of the Hounds, who were, with the start of the Season approaching, all in town. It had been wonderful – not just to see them, to feel at home again, in a way that he had deeply missed, but also because it had gone a long way to assuaging his fear of losing them.

He was still very cynical about their ability to continue to associate with him, as, should the *ton* become aware of it they would most certainly show their disapproval pointedly.

But for now, all was well. He reached the park, and gave Foxfire his head. The rush of fresh air blew the last of the effects of the drink away, and the day was beautiful as the soft winter sun lit the frosted grass and trees in a sparkling glitter.

Two hours later, relaxed, and refreshed, he turned to make his way home, ready to tackle the day. He was preoccupied as he rode, still worrying at the challenge he had set himself before Christmas, to find a new project, which would leverage his existing stock, yet be unusual and attractive to the wealthy. It was proving a much bigger challenge than he had expected.

As he reached the Grosvenor gate, he was startled to see, perched on the high seat of a fashionable phaeton, his sister. She was laughing in delight as the young man beside her drove in through the gate at a rather indecorous pace. Who was Isabella with? He had not known that she intended to go out, and an early drive with a young man, with no more chaperonage than a very young looking tiger, who clung with some desperation to the back of the speeding vehicle, was not the sort of behaviour that he expected from her. He would not want her thought fast.

As they came closer, he realised that he knew the young man – it was, surprisingly, Porter Arbuthnot. His family had not been on good terms with the Arbuthnots for many years – not since his father's skilled handing of the business had brought them to wealth and prominence, quite eclipsing the Arbuthnots, who had, hitherto, been acclaimed as the wealthiest of merchants.

He wondered, as he moved aside, unnoticed by Bella and Arbuthnot, if this had been going on for any length of time.

Was Porter Arbuthnot courting Bella, seriously? Or was this merely an amusement to him? Or worse, some attempt at disadvantaging his family through disgracing his sister, in revenge for their mercantile success?

Raphael turned his horse, and followed them, at a distance, keeping amongst the trees and out on the grass, simply watching.

After a half hour or so, they turned back, and Raphael, relieved, followed as they proceeded, at a more sedate pace, through the streets towards his home. He had half expected them to stop in the park, and descend to walk in some secluded spot – which he could not have allowed.

As Arbuthnot deposited Bella at the front door of their home, Raphael slipped quietly into the lane at the rear, and delivered Foxfire to his groom. Striding into the house, he was in time to catch Bella still in the Hall, as she removed her fur pelisse and scarf.

"Is that the first time young Arbuthnot has taken you for a drive?"

Bella startled, her cheeks flushing a charming pink, which could charitably have been attributed to the cold wind outside, but which, to Raphael, more resembled guilt than anything else.

"N..nnooo. It was the third time." Her voice had that edge of defiance that he recognised from many moments in her childhood. Her chin came up, and he could see that she was waiting for a reprimand. Intentionally choosing to disconcert her, he smiled genially.

"I would prefer, in future, that you have a maid with you, should you grant a gentleman the honour of taking you for a drive in the park. I would not have you thought fast, or your reputation called into question."

Obviously surprised, and expecting more, she glared at him for a moment.

"Yes Raphael, if you so insist."

It was too easy an acquiescence.

"Is he courting you? And do you wish it so?"

Bella flushed again, before half shaking her head. She answered with the honesty that was the essence of her, which endeared her to him more.

"I do not truly know. He is flattering, and amusing to be with. He flirts with me, but I am not sure that I would call it courting. I like it well enough, but... I am not sure if I wish it to become more."

Raphael did not allow his face to show the relief that he felt. A sudden insight made him ask, "Was it he who gave you that pretty Christmas favour?"

Bella nodded, blushing again, and said nothing more.

"Be careful Bella – best that you discover his true intentions before things go any further. After all, our families have been on less than friendly terms, ever since father began to do better than they, in business – it seems odd that he should be so friendly now.

She nodded again, and fled to her room to think.

Raphael went in search of a light meal, before turning his attention to the business of the day. Pensively, he considered the conversation with Bella, and, unbidden, the image of that Christmas favour rose in his mind again. He remembered her delight at receiving it, and their mother's admiration for its prettiness, as well as his own recognition, at the time, of the quality of its design.

Now there was a simple thing, which could yet be made in many different designs, which might interest the *ton*, as easily as it did his sister – so long as the quality of materials and manufacture was high enough. For the *ton* loved fripperies and extravagant gestures... the thought led to the very beginning of an idea.

~~~~~

Serafine took a deep breath and pushed open the door, causing a bell attached to it to ring. Inside was a small seating area, and a counter, off to one side. Behind the counter, in an exquisitely constructed glass fronted case, were samples of fabrics, beads, feathers, and a range of other items. As she stood there, feeling nervous and unsure, the door to one side of the counter opened, and two men entered.

The first appeared to be a clerk, well dressed but ordinary. The second was another thing entirely. They were mid conversation as they entered, but stopped immediately upon noticing her presence. The second man turned towards her, taking her in with a single pass of his dark eyes, and she felt suddenly unable to breath, a flush of heat rushing through her entire body.
~~~~~

He was tall, lean and elegant, moving with the fluid economy that spoke of skill with weapons and military experience. His hair was dark, and his skin tanned as if from long exposure to the sun.

She thought that he looked somehow foreign, just a little – perhaps Italian? This must be Mr Morton - hadn't Mr Tanner said his mother was Italian?

She had never seen a man so handsome, so understated in his dress and manner, yet so utterly sure of himself.

He looked like he would have been completely at home in the ballrooms of the *ton* – yet, if he was here, and so obviously in a position of authority, if he was *the* Mr Morton, then he could not be of the nobility.

He waited, eyebrow raised, while she stood there, stunned to silence. When it became obvious that she was not about to speak, he approached her and asked, "Can I help you my Lady?"

She felt a ridiculous sense of relief, that she still looked enough of a Lady for him to grant her that status of address immediately. Would he still think her a Lady when she asked the questions she had come to ask?

"I hope so, Mr....?"

"Mr Raphael Morton, at your service, my Lady."

He swept a courtly bow over her hand, his eyes sparkling with some amusement.

"Welcome to Morton Empire Imports – how can we assist you today?"

Serafine's heart beat harder – she had not imagined the owner of such a large merchant business to be so young and good looking – somehow, she always expected successful merchants to be old, and bent from poring over ledgers.

"I... I would like to ask some questions about the materials that you import – to see if they may be suitable for a project of mine." Sera watched his reaction, hardly daring to breathe.

This was obviously not quite what he had expected her to say, but, being both a consummate gentleman, and a clever merchant, he simply waved her to the seating area and turned to the clerk.

"Jenkins, if you would, some tea and biscuits for Lady.... "

He looked at her enquiringly.

"Lady Serafine Parkington." She managed, just, to keep her voice steady as she spoke, waiting for the condemnation to appear in his eyes – for surely a merchant as wealthy as he would be aware of the gossip of the *ton*, would know of her disgrace.

He simply nodded, and waved Mr Jenkins on his way. She let out the breath that she had not realised she was holding, and lowered herself to a chair, depositing her basket on the floor at her side. He turned back to her.

"So, Lady Serafine, tell me more about your project, ask your questions, and let us see if I can supply what you wish for."

Wickedly, her internal voice suggested that he could supply many things that she wished for, in her most secret thoughts. She pushed it away, and began.

"First, Mr Morton, I must make an admission that may shock you, coming from a well born Lady."

At her words he looked most interested, and raised that enquiring eyebrow once again, but said nothing, waiting for her to continue.

"I… create… things. It began as a hobby of sorts, some years ago, but, in more recent times, it has become more… commercial… in nature. My family are in rather… straightened… circumstances, and I have been forced to supplement our income in small ways."

She waited, again, for an expression of horror or disgust to cross his face – for Ladies were not expected to sully themselves with work. It did not appear. He simply nodded, and she had the most peculiar feeling that, even wealthy as he was, he truly understood what it was to be poor.

At that moment, Jenkins returned with the tea tray, and placed it on a small table before them. She was forced to wait until Jenkins had left, and tea had been poured. It felt strange to have a man pour tea for her, but this was his premises, after all. At last she could continue.

"I am finding that I need more materials for my creations – materials of a better quality than those I have been able to source to date. It seems that there is a demand for my work – but a demand for items of the best materials. I only need very small amounts, as the items I make are quite small, but the materials must be unusual and high quality. I purchased some offcuts and other items from a shop selling trifles to Ladies of Quality, and the proprietress informed me that she purchases such things from your business. Hence my visit."

In her need to get her explanation out, Serafine had quite forgotten to be nervous, somewhere in the middle of speaking – perhaps because he seemed so genuinely interested in what she had to say. There was something about him that made her feel respected, safe, in a way that she had not, since... *before*. He appeared to consider for a moment, then spoke, his voice warm and positive, wrapping around her softly.

"It certainly sounds as if I may be able to assist you – but to do so, I believe that I will need to see an example of these items that you create, to better understand your needs. For I must confess, at this point I am at a loss to guess what they might be."

As he said it, she felt like a complete goose – how had she managed all of that long winded explanation, without ever actually telling him the core of it? She lifted her basket to her lap. Folding the cloth cover back, she lifted out the last of her most recently made favours, and, pushing aside the tea tray, laid them on the small table before them.

A small gasp escaped his lips, and he reached out a hand to lift one up and examine it, touching it as if it were some precious thing. She was not sure that her work deserved such reverence. Silently, she waited until he had completed his examination. When he looked to her again, his face was alight with what appeared to be excitement, with a smile that lit his eyes, and transformed him from merely handsome to utterly breathtaking.

"The perfect solution!" His exclamation confused her, and she waited for him to say more.

"Did you, perchance, make some of these just before Christmas, Lady Serafine? Including one with tiny holly berries and bells?"

She nodded, wondering how on earth he had seen it, when it had been purchased by that other merchant – Arbuthnot, if she remembered Mr Tanner's ramblings aright.

"Excellent! A hopeful swain gave it to my sister, and I was most impressed with its elegance and workmanship when I saw it. So was my mother, whose taste is quite beyond compare."

It was as if he had read her thoughts. She still could not fathom why he was so delighted, for surely the small amounts of materials that she might buy would be but the tiniest pittance compared to what most highborn Ladies might buy from him.

"Lady Serafine, I have a proposition for you." At the look of shock in her eyes, he gave a light laugh and continued, "A business proposition only, let me hasten to assure you, nothing of any impropriety, one which I most sincerely hope will be of monetary profit for both of us."

She found herself laughing with him, and a ridiculous, giddy bubble of hope was fluttering about in her chest. "Please, Mr Morton, you intrigue me – tell me more."

"I have been looking, this past month or more, for a new venture, a new way to use materials that I already have, or import often, to create something new to catch the interest of the *ton*. For the wealthy of Quality love to outdo each other with fripperies, and fads, and I would profit from that shallowness."

She nodded, fully understanding what he meant, for the outrageous fashions taken up by the *ton* had always both fascinated, and repelled, her even whilst she was one of them, and oblivious to how the world truly went on.

"Ever since I saw my sister's Christmas favour, it has niggled at the back of my mind – I felt it important, but did not know why. Now I do. For surely, this sort of thing, created with high quality materials and workmanship, and using exclusive, exotic imported materials would appeal to them. I need only gift a few select pieces to the current arbiters of fashion, or perhaps to the Prince Regent himself, and, should they like them, they will be all the rage overnight, and will be sent to young Ladies as often as hot-house flowers are."

Excitement shot through her, for this was her vision, multiplied tenfold. The thought that one day, a piece made by her hands, her, a shunned and disregarded member of society, might reach the hands of the Prince Regent was both satisfying and sublimely ridiculous. Still she must take care.

"That seems a wondrous concept, Mr Morton, yet… even with the best of materials, I can only make so many, for each takes some time. Should your vision come to pass, I could not keep up with such a demand."

Nervous again, she reached up from habit, tucking the escaped tendrils of her rich dark brown hair back. His eyes followed her movement, and she found herself caught in them. They simply looked at each other, until he broke the spell by speaking again.

"Ah, but I have a solution to that problem too."

Serafine was suddenly utterly conscious of everything around her, in fine detail – the colours of the fabrics on display, the subtle scent of oriental spices that pervaded the place, the pine and leather scent that could only be from Mr Morton himself, the muted sounds of movement in the back rooms of the shop. It was as if her future turned on this moment. She waited.

"It would be possible for you to teach others to make these, would it not?"

She nodded again.

"But... if I should do that, how would that make income for me?"

Perhaps her question sounded greedy, but she had to ask – her mother's survival, and her own, turned upon the answer.

"Because, Lady Serafine, you will not simply be a pair of hands to sew, you will be a business partner with me, and the business that you will own half of, will be a manufactory for these. I have a small building nearby that we can use, and we will employ poorer girls from hereabout, helping their families survive, and you will teach them how to make these to the exacting standards required for us to sell them to the *ton*. You will help me understand exactly how to make them something that the Ladies of the *ton* will crave – for of that world, you have much greater knowledge than I."

His eyes were alight with excitement again, and she found herself caught up in it, swept away by the scale of his idea. This was beyond all her imaginings. There was only one thing that she could do.

"Yes, Mr Morton, I accept your business proposition."

"Wonderful! We will need to move fast, for I believe that our best opportunity to launch this endeavour approaches. In but a month, it will be St. Valentine's Day, and people of all classes will be giving love tokens to those they admire. Can you design some suitable favours, that girls could make, in time for us to have them on sale before then?"

He was sweeping her along, and she felt like a leaf on a torrent, caught in the enthusiasm of his ideas. It was terrifying and exhilarating at once.

"I will most certainly do my best – but there is much to be done, and for some of it, I have no idea where to start, for I find that the education of a gently reared Lady is sadly lacking in the area of setting up a manufactory."

He laughed, delighted at her gentle wit, and reached to take her hands.

"My Lady, I will have a contract drawn up, immediately, so that you can be assured of your security in this enterprise. And I will arrange staff to assist you. If you will return her tomorrow morning at 10, all will be ready – you will have the contract, your staff, and the building at your disposal."

Stunned, she simply nodded, for the heat flowing through her from the touch of his hands quite fuddled her brain, his nearness leaving her more flustered than that of any man, ever before. He looked at her again, as if considering whether he should speak further. Then, apparently, he decided that he should.

"I will understand should you be offended at what I am about to say, but I feel that I must say it, nonetheless."

The old dread curled in her – was she, after such a wonderful few minutes, about to meet the rejection again – had he, perchance, just remembered the scandal attached to her name?

"I sense, Lady Serafine, in what you said, and what you did not say, that your financial position is, at present, very difficult? I must commend you for your initiative in acting to change that, for many young women of the aristocracy would simply retreat into tears and depression, and starve."

She could do nothing but nod, again (he must be beginning to wonder if she had a weak neck, for she had been nodding stupidly through half of this conversation!). She was embarrassed at the truth of his words about her poverty, yet elated to find that he actually respected her for taking action. It was a novel experience for man to regard her that way. When he continued, it was tentative, as if he expected her to push him away. Startled, she realised that he still held her hands.

"Lady Serafine, in recognition of the enormous effort that you have agreed to put in, over the next weeks, before our enterprise will begin to make sales, I wish to offer you an amount now – an amount that I regard as being fair compensation for the licensing of your idea and knowledge, for use in this business. Can you see your way to accept such a thing?"

She understood his concern, for a 'true Lady' would reject such apparent charity with scorn.

She was long past such scruples.

'Mr Morton, that is a more than generous offer, in the light of all that you have already agreed to do, and to contribute to this business. But, I am somewhat embarrassed to admit, you have assessed it correctly. My situation is somewhat dire. So, for my mother's sake, I will most gratefully accept your offer, in the spirit it is made."

"You, Lady Serafine, exhibit great courage and sense, as well as beauty. I cannot imagine a better person as a business partner!"

After a short further conversation, which she barely managed, so dazed was she by the fact that he spoke of her as beautiful, as she was about to turn and leave, he shook her hand, just as if she were another gentleman of business!

Then he drew forth a purse and handed it to her, saying quietly, "An advance, Lady Serafine – I will have a draft on my bank for you tomorrow, along with everything else. But I do not wish to see you in any difficulty. Please, take a hackney home, for your safety - it grows dark."

"Thank you." What more could she possibly say?

All the way home she replayed the afternoon in her mind, hugging it to her as if it might dissolve in the winter rain outside. But the purse was real, as was the scent of Mr Morton, which clung to her hands where he had held them, and seeped, dizzyingly, into her senses.

~~~~~
~~~~~

Raphael watched her leave, feeling at once bemused, confused and more excited and alive than he had since arriving home from the war. She was a stunning woman – rich dark brown hair, thick and a little unruly, curling into tendrils from the winter damp, eyes that were almost golden, that seemed to glow from within when she was caught up in an idea, a figure that no worn and slightly outdated dress could hide, and lips that should, oh definitely should, be kissed.

And she was intelligent, resourceful and loyal. It was a seemingly impossible combination, but, improbable as it was, it existed. His friends might think him mad, but he had no doubts about the decisions he had just so impetuously made. He was quite, quite certain, with the instinct that had kept him alive in Spain, that she was everything she said she was, and that this would work.

And, he had to admit to himself, the thought of days with a woman like that, to create a new venture, was arousing – in more than one way – he would not at all object to spending time working with such a beautiful woman at his side.

Chapter Six

That night, Serafine slept better than she had for months. Her sleep was threaded through with dreams of Mr Raphael Morton, whose handsome face and compelling dark eyes seemed even more so in dreams. The purse he had handed her was under her pillow, and the subtle remnants of his personal scent which clung to it surrounded her.

The money it had contained was safely locked in her little metal box, along with the heart of lace which had begun all of this. She had been astonished, when, upon reaching home, she had dared to investigate just what the purse contained. More than thirty pounds! Enough to keep them, in their current excessively frugal lifestyle, for months! And this was his idea of a small 'advance' on what he intended to pay her for agreeing to join him in a business venture! A venture which would, later, also return her a share of the profits!

It all seemed too good to be true, yet she knew that it was true. She had never felt more certain of a man's honesty and good intentions in her life.

Her mother had been abed when she had returned, and she had not disturbed her. Now, as the weak morning sun shone through her somewhat grimy bedroom window, she rose and dressed, eager to tell her mother of the momentous events of the day before.

In their little breakfast room, they sat to a plain repast of bread, cheese and a little cold meat. Serafine ate, then, unable to wait any longer, she began.

"Mother, I have such news! Wonderful news. News which, it is my hope, will solve our precarious financial situation forever."

Her mother looked up, startled, and was overjoyed to see the light in her daughter's eyes, and the enthusiasm in her expression – neither of which had been present since her brother's death. As Serafine went on to explain, her mother's face showed at first doubt and uncertainty, but swiftly moved to a hope equal to Serafine's. When Sera spoke of the funds already received, her mother's amazement and relief were obvious, although deeply coloured by embarrassment at having their severe financial straits known.

"This Mr Morton sounds a positive paragon – you are quite certain that he is being honest with you? That he will not try to take advantage of you in… inappropriate ways?"

"Quite certain – he is everything a gentleman should be – much more so than many of those young rakes and fops of the *ton*, who panted after me, then were the first to turn away."

"I would meet him. Might I accompany you this morning, to see that all is in order, and set my mind at ease?"

Serafine was most glad of her mother's interest – it had been many months since her mother had set foot outside their house, her depression had been so deep.

"Why certainly mother, if you will not be embarrassed to be seen about without a maid to accompany us."

"As we have no maid, I will have to be content, will I not? You have seemed to do well enough in these circumstances Sera, much though such things might once have horrified me."

Both smiling, they rose from the table and went to prepare for the day.

~~~~~

From the moment she had walked out his door, Raphael had swept into action, summoning his man of business to draw up the contract, arranging staff to be allocated to support of this new project, and sending Jenkins to arrange a cleaning of the building they would use, which had recently come into his possession as payment of a debt from a Lord who was financially embarrassed at present, but whose wife had spent rather excessively on the silks that Raphael imported.

He fell into a deep sleep, late in the night, and woke with the dawn, feeling full of energy. For the first time since his return, there was no trace of boredom in his thoughts. After Garrett had assisted him with dressing (a situation he still found peculiar after years at war, looking after himself), and he had broken his fast, he gathered up his hat and gloves, and slipped on his caped winter coat.
~~~~~

As he turned to the door, Bella came down the stairs, just beginning her day. He went to her and took her hand a moment.

"Bella, dear sister, I must thank you."

She looked at him, startled at this pronouncement.

"You see, dear sister, that pretty Christmas favour you showed me, it has given me a new business idea, which I hope to find most profitable. I shall tell you more this evening, but for now, my thanks."

He swept on his way before she could do anything but smile. It was typical of Raphael, she thought, to leave her with a tiny bit of information, and expect her to wait all day to hear more!

~~~~~

At precisely the hour of ten, the door to Morton Empire Imports opened, and Lady Serafine entered, followed, Raphael was surprised to see, by an older woman. A woman who could only be her mother, he thought, for the resemblance was clear. The older woman's hair was streaked with some grey, but was still thick and shining, and the sharp lines of her high cheekbones were a clear echo of the softer lines of Lady Serafine's face.

Raphael bowed over their hands.

"Lady Serafine. And this is... ?'

"My mother, the Dowager Lady Galwood."
~~~~~

For a moment, as she spoke, fear flickered across Serafine's face, and that of her mother also. More than a year of being treated to the cut direct, as soon as people discovered who they were, had left its mark. Raphael wondered at the fleeting expression, but let that go to think about later.

"Delighted, my Lady. I am Mr Raphael Morton, owner of Morton Empire Imports. Your daughter is most talented and enterprising. I count myself fortunate to have found such a person to be my partner in this business venture."

He waved them to the seating area.

"Please be seated, I will have everything brought momentarily. Might I offer you some refreshment? Some tea, perhaps?"

"Thank you, Mr Morton." Lady Galwood was, suddenly, the elegant aristocratic woman that Sera remembered, rather than the shadow that she had lived with for the last year.

By the time another hour had passed, Serafine was in possession of a signed contract, making her the half owner of a new business, to be called Parkmorton Gifts, a signed bank draft for a remarkable amount of money, a business manager in the form of Mr Jenkins, who had agreed to take on this new challenge, a housekeeper in the form of Mrs Jenkins, who would assist with hiring domestic staff, as well as finding girls to employ in the manufactory, as she was well known in the surrounding area, and an assistant, a Miss Emily Nunn, who would help with identifying suitable materials from the vast stores of exotic items in Morton Empire Imports warehouses.

Once again, she felt like a leaf tossed on the torrent.

It was wonderful, exhilarating and positively the most frightening experience of her life. Her mother appeared to feel the same way, as she watched all of this happen with amazement.

There followed a visit to their new building, which was only a few blocks away, where Sera could barely contain her excitement – for it was large, larger than she had ever imagined, and, whilst still being cleaned after some time unused, was most suitable, with rooms for offices, sitting rooms for meetings, a tidy kitchen, storerooms, and a selection of large rooms with excellent windows where the light would be suitable for girls to sit and do the fine sewing necessary.

There was also a small stable at the rear, where the yard opened onto a lane between the buildings. And… the stable contained a small town carriage, two horses, and a cheerful groom/coachman named Alf. Mr Morton casually informed Sera that they were for her use – she was now an important merchant, and should look the part, apparently.

At the end of the visit, when Mrs Jenkins had arrived and been introduced, Alf drove Lady Galwood and Mrs Jenkins back to Sera's home, to begin on the hiring of staff and the planning there, and Sera returned to Morton Empire Imports office with Mr Morton, and Mr Jenkins, to begin planning in earnest.

By evening she was elated, and exhausted, and still only just beginning to believe that this was real. The sense of unreality was heightened when she reached home (driven by Alf!) and a footman opened the door for her.

Mrs Jenkins greeted her in the hall, and introduced the shy looking young girl standing behind her as, "Polly, your new maid, my Lady."

As she dropped into sleep that night, the thought drifted through her mind that it was incongruous, and rather amusing, that the thing that should give her back something almost like her old life was to 'sully her hands with trade' – that idea most reviled by the nobility. After a year of barely surviving, she would take practical and comfortable over poverty and ridiculous concepts of noble behaviour every time.

~~~~~

Over dinner that evening, Raphael had, as promised, explained his new venture to Bella, and the rest of his family. His mother thought it an excessively clever idea, and praised his astuteness in capturing Lady Serafine's skills before anyone else saw the potential. Gabriel thought it boring – girls sewing fripperies held no interest for him – he would rather listen to the sea captain's tales of exotic lands.

Bella thought it wonderful, and romantic, that making love tokens should transform the life of a woman fallen on difficult times, as well as make what should be the coup, for their own business, of starting a new fashion. Perhaps she would tell Porter Arbuthnot what a wonderful chain of events his gift of the favour had set in motion.

She was still unsure how she felt about him, but she had agreed to another drive tomorrow, albeit insisting that it be in a vehicle where Liza, her maid, could accompany them.
~~~~~

Indulging in a quiet glass of port with his mother, after the meal was done, Raphael was surprised when she spoke, breaking into his thoughts of business.

"Raphael, Lady Serafine… you said that her mother is the Dowager Lady Galwood?"

"Yes, that was the name." He wondered where this conversation was going.

"I seem to remember something about that name. From more than a year ago, whilst you were still at war. Before your father…"

Her voice caught, for she still missed her husband fiercely, although she rarely let that show. He waited, sipping his port, letting the stresses of the hectic day slide away, as she paused, seemingly sifting through memories. Eventually, she spoke again.

"I remember now. There was a scandal, young Viscount Galwood, that would be Lady Serafine's brother, killed himself. Gambling debts, I believe. He had gambled away everything not entailed, and left his family ruined, so he took the coward's way out and killed himself. His mother and sister were cut dead by the *ton*, for the scandal of having a suicide in the family, and the title went to some distant cousin. That would explain their straightened circumstances, and her need to create an income."

"Whilst I cannot see that suicide should ever be a choice for a man of any class with any honour, I also cannot see why the *ton* must cast aside the family of such a man. Surely they suffer enough in losing him, without needing disgrace added to that."

"Raphael, I must agree with that sentiment. The poor women, this last year must have been hell. It does, however, amaze me that this Lady Serafine has the vision and the courage to have even considered working, and going into business – for most members of the *ton* would surely actually starve before they did so!"

"She is, indeed, most unusual." As Raphael spoke, the image of her rose in his mind, as she had been that morning, flushed, excited at what they had begun, golden eyes alight, rich dark hair escaping its pins to lie in tendrils around her face, and full of intelligent questions. She was beautiful in an unconventional kind of way, for he found that her beauty came as much from her keen intelligence as from her fairness of form.

He also remembered, in that instant, the fleeting expression that had crossed both Lady Serafine's and her mother's countenance – could it have been fear? Did they fear that he would act as the *ton* did, and reject them for the actions of her brother, actions over which they, personally, would have had no influence whatsoever?

With him, they had no need for fear, he would never behave that way. But... he wondered, how the other Hounds would respond? They were of the *ton* (although Gerald had only recently risen to such high estate), would they reject her? Or see it as he did? It was the first time that he had ever had to consider a situation where their opinions might be so divided. He did not like the possibility at all.

"Thank you for the information, Mother, I will bear that in mind as we proceed with this."

Soon after, he took himself to bed, to dream of golden eyes and hair the colour of rich mahogany timber from the East Indies.

54

Chapter Seven

Two days later, whilst Serafine and Raphael were immersed in a whirlwind of arranging the manufactory, hiring girls, choosing materials and starting to teach them how to make the favours, Isabella was nervously awaiting the arrival of Mr Porter Arbuthnot, her maid, Liza, standing patiently by her side.

When she saw, peering through the curtains of the front parlour, the small but elegant open carriage draw up outside, Isabella breathed a sigh of relief – she hated waiting – for anything.

A moment later, there was a knock on the door, and the footman ushered Mr Arbuthnot in.

"Miss Isabella, you are beautiful as always." He took her hand, and performed an exaggerated bow, his lips barely brushing her glove. Liza stifled a giggle. Isabella glared at her, sidelong.

"Why thank you sir!"

He offered her his arm, and led her out to the carriage, Liza dutifully following. Once they reached the park, and he could take some of his attention from the task of avoiding collisions, he asked her how she had been, declaring that he had missed her terribly since they had last met. Isabella blushed, not entirely convinced, but certainly flattered.

"Why Mr Arbuthnot, I believe you are gulling me. For, surely, your duties in your father's business must occupy your thoughts the majority of the time?"

"Ah Miss Isabella, nothing can completely distract me from thoughts of you." She was beginning to find his approach rather overdone, now that she considered it. Still, perhaps he was sincere.

"Well... I have mostly been rather bored, for it has been a little too cold for my liking, to walk, or even to visit my friends. Still, I do have one bit of news that may please you. You remember, I am sure, that delightful Christmas favour you gave me?"

He looked at her, puzzled by this turn in the conversation, and nodded.

"Well, it was so beautiful that I showed it to my family at the time. My mother, and my brother, both thought it most elegant and well made – a very nice sentiment. And now I find that it has inspired my brother to a new enterprise. He plans to arrange the making of such things, to sell through our business! Your romantic gesture has resulted in good fortune for us, and for a Lady who has agreed to assist with this venture. Isn't that wonderful!"

Whilst Isabella was enamoured of the romantic nature of the whole concept, it seemed to her that Mr Arbuthnot was not. As she spoke, it had seemed to her, for a moment, that an expression of annoyance, almost anger, had crossed his face – but... surely not? For what was there, in what she had said, that might conceivably annoy him?

After that, for the rest of their drive, whilst he spoke most amiably to her, he seemed a little distracted, and flattered and flirted considerably less than usual – a development that Isabella was not sure she appreciated at all. Still it was a pleasant outing, and she returned home happy enough with the day.

~~~~~

Two sennights later, Sera regarded the shelves of the storeroom with satisfaction. Neatly laid out, each wrapped in a delicate bag of sheerest muslin, the shelves contained the first 200 favours of their manufacture. Ten girls now worked for her each day, and they were proving most adept at learning the required skills to produce very high quality favours.

The selection of exquisite silk ribbons, fine laces, beads of exotic woods and metals and highest quality paste gems which had been chosen from the warehouses of Morton Empire Imports had proved of perfect suitability to bring the designs that she had envisaged to life. Tomorrow, Raphael... Mr Morton, she sternly corrected herself... intended to send a selection of the best favours to the Prince Regent, and one or two of the *ton's* most acknowledged arbiters of fashion.
~~~~~

The thought of it was both immensely satisfying and utterly terrifying – for what if they did not take the fancy of these important people? Then all of this work might be for nought, and, if their venture did not succeed, what would become of her income, or the income that this work now provided for the girls?

Raphael had taken the ones that he had selected to his home, to sit, this evening, and write carefully crafted letters to accompany the gifts. Now, all was quiet. She had sent the girls home, with her enthusiastic thanks for their hard work so far, and was, as she usually did, taking a bit of quiet time to herself, tidying things away, and assuring herself that all was well, and ready for the next day.

She had locked the doors, all but the little one at the rear, and sat, now, appreciating the peace, still astounded at her good fortune, and at how much the last weeks had changed her life. All because one man had chosen to listen to her, had seen the potential in her idea, and, rather than simply stealing it from her, had given her the great gift of treating her as he might another man, and taking her on as a business partner.

He was a remarkable man. She found herself wool-gathering, dreaming of him – his deep dark eyes, his lean elegant face, his strong hard body and his voice that flowed over her like a rich wine. As if that wasn't enough, he was a good and kind person. So much for the disdain that the *ton* held for those of the merchant class! Her experience with Mrs Johnson and the other ladies had begun the change in her view of the world, but Mr Raphael Morton had quite totally turned those views upside down.

If she was completely honest with herself, she was half in love with the man. Which was ridiculous – to him, she was a business partner, nothing more. He insisted on treating her with the full deference due to a Lady of Quality, no matter her circumstances. She felt it like a wall between them – no matter how they might speak of the business, and converse freely and happily, it was as if the invisible barrier of the difference in their birth grew stronger over time, not weaker.

It saddened her, yet she supposed it was the way of the world.

~~~~~

Raphael sat back, shaking the sand from the last carefully penned letter. Leaving it aside for the ink to completely dry, her turned to the small stack of boxes on the side table, and began to pack the favours carefully into each, counting them as he did so. After three checks of his count, he huffed a frustrated breath. There was one too few. He had been a fool, and allowed himself to be distracted by watching the afternoon sun draw deep red lights from Sera's... Lady Serafine's, he corrected himself... beautiful hair and had miscounted when collecting the favours.

There was nothing for it. This had to be perfect.

He locked the door to his study, collected his hat and coat from the footman on duty at his door and set out to walk the moderate distance back to the manufactory, to select the final required favour.
~~~~~

~~~~~

Some sound brought Sera out of her dreaming, and she flushed, a little embarrassed at having been mooning over a man like a love-struck young girl. Glancing around, she realised that more time had passed than she had thought – the windows showed only the deepening dusk outside - her mother would be expecting her home. It was odd, though – normally Alf would have come to find her by now, keen to drive her home before it got too late and cold. She wondered where he was.

A sound came again, and an odd, reddish light tinted the dusk through the window. Alarmed, she stood, and ran to look. From the window she saw, to her horror, the flickering light of flames – she ran to the rear door, and went to open it, but the heat of the metal door handle nearly burnt her palm, and she backed away in fear. She grabbed for her keys and ran to the front of the building, through the small kitchen.

Her skirt caught on the logs waiting near the kitchen hearth, and she was spun by the tug, the keys flying from her hands and down into the grated drain near the washtub under the small window. She froze, staring at where they had disappeared, terror taking hold deep inside her. She had seen what fire could do to houses, had seen people barely rescued in time from a burning building. At that instant, she saw her death before her.

She could hear the fire now, burning the door, and the window frames – she ran, again.
~~~~~

Perhaps she could force open a window at the front, and attract some passer-by's attention. But the windows were all secure, with strong bars – they had put great effort into protecting this property, and their new venture. Despairing, she crumpled to the floor against the front door, then shook herself out of the stupor, and pulled a pin from her hair. She had heard tales of hairpins being used to pick locks – this was the time for her to attempt such a feat, if ever.

~~~~~

Three blocks from the manufactory, a rough looking man stepped out of the shadows, and approached the well-dressed young gentleman who stood in the pool of dim light from a nearby street lantern.

"It be done, just like ye wanted. Ye can see the colour from here." He pointed and, indeed, the red flicker of light from flames was visible on the wall of a tall building some distance away. The rough man held out his hand, and, unspeaking, the young gentleman deposited a heavy purse upon it.

"Always happy to oblige, Mr Porter, if'n ye should need me again." He sketched a parody of a formal bow, turned, and faded into the shadows.

The young gentleman stood a while longer, watching the colour on the wall, then nodded to himself, turned and was gone.

~~~~~

Raphael took the shorter way to the manufactory, ducking through the lanes to the rear, in a hurry to get the favour and get home, to have all in readiness for the morrow. He turned the last corner and stopped in shock for a second, before launching himself forward at a full run. For the back wall of the manufactory was wreathed in flame, and the yellow and red tendrils of it were licking towards the stable.

Surely Sera and Alf were both safe, for by now Alf should be driving her home, but he would not let all of their work be destroyed – not when they were so close to a great success!

He reached the stables and ran inside, grabbing a horse blanket from the rack and soaking it in the horse trough at the door, then used the wet wool to beat out the flames which were just reaching the stable wall, carried on the few wisps of spilled hay and straw that had not been swept up – he thanked the Lord God that they kept a neatly swept yard at all times. As Raphael turned to thrust the blanket into the trough again, he heard a moan from inside the stable.

He glanced at the door, then at the manufactory building – the flames were gaining strength – he had little time, but... if that was Alf, he needed help. And, if that was Alf, could it be that Sera was still inside? His heart beat harder than it ever had in his life, and horror froze him to the spot. Then his battle reflexes took over, and the judgement honed on the field of war took him into a cold calm space where he assessed his options in an instant, and acted.

As Raphael turned to the stable door, Alf staggered out, unsteady on his feet, and clutching his head. His face, already white, turned ashen when he saw the flames.

Alf pointed, shaking, and croaked in a harsh voice "Lady Serafine...."

In that moment, Raphael was utterly grateful for the cold calm of battle, for under it, he felt fear greater than ever before – fear of losing a woman that he had come to care for, well beyond the respect a man might have for a skilled business partner. Despite the difference in their stations in Society, she had, in these last few sennights, become central to his life.

Grabbing the soaked horse blanket, he threw himself at the building like a madman, beating at the flames. Moments later, water splashed past him to land at the base of the flames where grass and straw, and a scatter of refuse reeds from the kitchen floor gave the fire enough fuel to keep it hot on the timber of the door. Alf turned and was soon back with another bucket full.

Raphael beat at the higher flames. Spending all of his effort to stop it spreading further, working along the wall as best he could, and desperately wishing for more hands to help. He kicked aside the neatly piled stack of logs kept for the kitchen fire, scattering them into the icy slush of the yard, satisfied that they would not burn further there. The blanket began to burn, and he ran back to the water trough to soak it again.

As he did, three young men rushed past him into the yard, buckets in hand, and a small spark of hope filled him. With extra hands, they had a chance. A fraught fifteen minutes later, the fire was out. The rear door and window frame were nearly burnt away, the window broken, and all of the mortaring of the stone of the wall would need redoing, but the building stood.

His elegant clothes charred and blackened with soot, Raphael stood a moment, quickly bowed, and thanked the young men, then threw himself at the door, breaking through what remained of the still smouldering timber. His three young assistants looked at Alf quizzically, as if to ask if the man was mad. Alf shook his head, and again, pointed.

"Lady Serafine."

Horrified comprehension spread across the faces of the men.

"No... She give me sister a job there, we'd be close to starving without that – we came to help because a' that. I nivver thought the Lady might be trapped."

Alf just waited, quietly praying. He had faith in Mr Morton. But what if Lady Serafine was hurt... or worse?

Chapter Eight

Sera struggled with the hairpin, but the lock was stubborn, and her fingers began to hurt from the effort of trying. At first, apart from the fear, it was not so bad – this far from the back of the building, there was no heat, but she could hear the flames, hear cracks and thumps as the building suffered its assault. But, after a few minutes, there was a loud cracking noise, and a tinkle of falling glass. The kitchen window must have shattered in the heat.

That was enough to start a flow of air into the building – air laden with thick smoke. As the smoke began to fill the rooms, Sera coughed and struggled to breathe, to concentrate on the lock – surely she could manage to pick it! But it stubbornly refused to open. And she began to feel light headed, her vision blurring as the smoke made her eyes shed continuous tears.

It was no good, she thought despairingly. She had tried so hard. That everything she had worked for should end like this, and her with it, was insupportable. But it was happening.

She sagged against the front door, barely able to breathe any more, and wished desperately that she might see her mother to say goodbye, that she might see Raphael, to tell him how she felt about him – whether it be foolish of her or not. But that was a fever dream – the reality was the darkness closing in and the air no longer supporting her breath.

Just as she slipped into the blackness, she thought she heard a resounding crash – surely her exit from this life was not to be announced with a clash of drums? Then there were arms around her, and she was lifted against a hard chest, which was surely real, for she could feel it move as its owner coughed in the smoke filled room.

Moments later, sweet fresh air filled her lungs, and, subtly underlying it, she recognised the pine and leather scent that could only mean that it was Raphael who held her so tightly against him, even as he staggered a little, passing through the burnt doorway and into the yard. It seemed that her prayer had been answered. He staggered as far as the stable, still holding her, and collapsed on the bench just inside.

Sera opened her eyes, to find his only inches away. A magical stillness overcame them both, and everything else but his eyes seemed to fade away. She had never seen anything so wonderful in her life.

"Sera." His voice was a smoked strained croak, but her name on his lips was sweet nonetheless – for no-one but her mother usually called her Sera, not since James.... And then those lips were upon hers and a sweet heat rushed through her body. She felt alive, intensely so, most especially because, short minutes ago, she had expected death.

After some unfathomable length of time, the kiss stopped, and they found themselves simply gazing at each other.

"Raphael…" her voice was a smoke shattered whisper, but he heard in his heart what she had no voice to say. He pulled her tight against him.

"Alf…"

"Yes, Mr Morton?"

Alf stuck his head around the door, looking pleased when he saw her still in Raphael's arms, but with her eyes open and obviously not badly hurt.

"Please arrange with the helpful young men outside to have a guard mounted on the building until we can arrange repairs tomorrow. They will be amply rewarded. And then, if the horses are alright, please hitch them up – I think that we will need the carriage to take Lady Serafine home."

"Yes, Sir!"

Once Sera was safely settled in the carriage, Raphael stepped back.

"One moment – there is one more thing that I must do, before we are on our way."

He turned and went back into the building, making his way carefully to the storeroom, and selected the one extra favour that he had come for. And a blessing it was that he had miscounted to start with – for had he not, Sera might now be dead, and all their work in ashes. The thought that he might have lost her was a band of agony on his heart.

Climbing into the carriage, and meeting her enquiring expression, he explained, in his roughened voice, just how he had come to be there, to save her.

She was beginning to think that the favours were the signposts of change in her life. What might they bring to her next?

Chapter Nine

For the first time in a very long while, Raphael was nervous. It was an odd sensation, and not a comfortable one. He had seen the carefully and elegantly wrapped boxes, each containing a number of the Saint Valentine's Day themed favours, and a carefully penned letter, dispatched for individual delivery by footmen in his employ, each dressed in new and impressive livery. Now there was nothing but waiting – for the men's return, and then for the reaction of the recipients.

He turned the nervous energy to good effect, and set about arranging the repairs to the building, so that business might go on as before. He had arrived to find that the young men had been true to their word, and diligently guarded the manufactory overnight. He handed each of them a sizeable purse, and sent them off home to rest. They were effusive in their gratitude, but he brushed it aside, assuring them that their efforts in helping him fight the fire, and then as guards, were worth that and more.

As he settled the last of the girls to working, and saw the last of the workmen off to obtain the required repair materials, he was surprised when Sera arrived. He had expected her to spend today recuperating from her experience – but obviously she was made of sterner stuff. He was unreasonably pleased to discover that to be the case.

He was not sure how to approach her – he had kissed her yesterday, and she had most certainly not pushed him aside, yet today, it was as if nothing, and yet everything, had changed between them. Did she regret that kiss now, in the light of a new day? Did she think it presumptuous that he, a merchant, should have kissed a Lady born? He certainly did not regret his actions, and if truth be told, he would happily sweep her into his arms immediately, and kiss her again. But all of his training made him wait to see her reaction, for he was utterly unsure of how she might respond.

So he held himself back, drinking her in with his eyes, seeing just how beautiful she was, and feeling again that sense of how lucky he was not to have lost her. He bowed, allowing himself to take her hand.

"My Lady, I am surprised, and very glad, to see you looking so well today. I had feared that your terrible experience yesterday might have left you less than well today."

A brilliant smile lit her face, and she shook her head.

"Oh no Mr Morton, I will not let such a thing prevent me from being here – for we must not let this stop us. This venture must succeed, and I fully intend to be here to do my utmost to ensure that. Even if my voice is frightfully unmelodic at this point."

It was true that her voice still suffered from the effects of the smoke, but he found the low, slightly roughened tone of it seductive, indeed, almost erotic, rather than unpleasant in any way. She flushed a little, as if suddenly unsure how to go on with him, and turned away, going to each of the girls in turn, to reassure them of their continued employment and to see to their work in progress.

Feeling suddenly unnecessary, Raphael turned away, and took himself home, hoping that his deliveries had, by now, all been made.

~~~~~

All but one of the footmen had returned, and reported that each parcel had been received with curious interest, delivered, as per his instructions, only directly into the hands of the persons he had so carefully selected as his targets. The one who had not yet returned had been tasked to deliver his parcel to the Prince Regent – a challenge which, it was entirely possible, might take him days to achieve.

Raphael could not settle to anything, and found himself prowling the house like a caged tiger, looking for something to distract him from the tension of the waiting. There was no point him going to his offices, for he would only disturb his perfectly efficient shop and warehouse staff, yet simply waiting would drive him quite mad. He entered the parlour, and discovered Bella, curled inelegantly in a chair, a book in her hand – a book it was quite obvious she was not actually reading.
~~~~~

Upon his arrival, Bella heaved a dramatic sigh. Raphael repressed his amusement, and, instead, asked her casually, "What causes you to sigh so, dear sister?"

"Oh Raphael! I am so bored. For this last sennight, Mr Porter Arbuthnot has not seen fit to invite me for a drive. I may not be entirely sure that I desire his interest, but at least he has provided me with some amusing conversation, and the chance to get out. And now he has abandoned me! Not even a message for days!"

"Perhaps, Bella, he feels that you have not shown any great interest in him, and has decided to not press his attentions if you do not wish him to?"

"But... surely any man who truly cared for me would not be so easily discouraged?"

"Perhaps you have simply confused him, then?"

"You are no help at all!" Bella dropped the book onto the table at her side, with rather more force than was seemly. Watching her, amused, yet sympathetic, he decided to act.

"Bella, if you so wish to go for a drive in the park, I shall take you. For I find myself with some free time this afternoon." She spun to him, a smile claiming her face.

"Raphael! That is most kind of you. Yes, I would love to go for a drive, please, may we go now?"

Nodding his agreement, he led her from the room.

When the final footman had returned, it was to report his mission a success – he had actually managed to deliver the parcel into the hands of the Prince Regent himself. It seemed that fortune had favoured him, for, as the footman had made his request for audience, he had been overheard by Cecil Carlisle, Baron Setford, who had, at mention of Raphael's name as the sender, turned back a moment, and whispered something to the Prince Regent. Suddenly, the footman had been waved forward, and given the chance to deliver the elaborately presented favours.

Raphael was elated – for if the favours were a success, orders would follow. He did wonder, in passing, what Setford had said. He had not seen the man since leaving the military, yet he suspected that Setford would be aware of his movements still.

Within the day, the whispers of gossip began to make their way back to him, reported faithfully by his employees and household staff – for many of them had sisters and brothers, or other relatives and friends, working in the houses of the nobility. For a merchant, the gossip was valuable, and allowed him to most effectively supply the desires of his highest paying customers.

But this time, the gossip was newly precious, for it told of the progress of the favours. Being items designed to be given, those he had sent them to were now doing exactly that – giving them to the women they admired. It seemed that Ladies of all stations had received them, from actresses to the daughters of the nobility. And, most pleasing of all, the current most favoured mistress of the Prince Regent

Although this was what Raphael had intended, it was succeeding faster than he had expected. By the following day, he heard of shopkeepers in Bond Street receiving enquiries from members of the *ton*, who were seeking to purchase these newly fashionable favours, in time for the coming Saint Valentine's Day. Raphael, smiling, sent forth messengers again, this time bearing missives to all of the most exclusive shops, offering them the chance to obtain a supply of the favours – for a premium price, of course.

By the end of that day, they were sold out, and had a waiting list.

Chapter Ten

Serafine's life became a whirlwind of hiring and training more girls to make the favours, creating new designs, ensuring that everything was made to the best quality, packed and sent to the right addresses, occasionally remembering to eat, and falling into exhausted sleep each night. The success of the venture astounded her, and she was impressed at the cleverness with which Raphael had brought the favours to the attention of the *ton*.

Each time she saw him, her heart beat harder, her breath came a little short, and the memory of that kiss filled her mind. He was, to her, even more handsome and desirable when tired and somewhat dishevelled; carrying boxes along with his staff, being fully engaged in making sure that their venture was as successful as possible. She could not imagine any other gentleman she had met, of whatever station in Society, willingly doing such work. She certainly did not despise him for it, as convention said she should – indeed, she admired him instead.

After all, Society's mores said that she should also despise herself, for sullying her hands with work and trade. And that, she had long decided, was ridiculous – to have the funds to live in comfort, she was more than willing to work like this. A year of living in fading genteel poverty had impressed that on her, quite thoroughly.

They never touched, beyond the brief moment when he would gallantly greet her by bowing over her hand. She wished for more, but knew no way to breach the gulf that seemed to have opened between them. That kiss almost might not have been real, so distant, so unreachable did he seem now.

She had little time to think of it, however, except in the drifting moments before sleep took her each night, but it left her with a permanent little ache of sadness in her, nonetheless. Perhaps she had dreamed some of it – perhaps her smoke hazed brain had imagined the care in his voice when he had spoken her name, or the tenderness in his eyes when he had kissed her. She no longer knew what was real, beyond his presence every day, and the chaos of attempting to produce as many favours as the *ton* wished to buy.

~~~~~

Raphael ached. Somehow, he was fitting everything into the days – the running of Morton Empire Imports, the coordination of the distribution of the favours, making sure that Serafine was safe, that the building was repaired and guarded, and that everything that should happen, did happen, and nothing else.
~~~~~

He fell into bed each night, slept for not enough hours, and did it all again. He had not slept this little, and felt this worn, since Spain. Yet, at the same time, he revelled in it. For he was not bored, he was much too busy to feel trapped, as he had before, and everything that he did was succeeding, beyond his expectations.

There was, he had to admit, one thing that he was unhappy about. Serafine haunted his dreams, all golden eyes, pale skin and rich dark hair, soft in his arms, and pressing into his kiss. Over and over, he relived that moment in the stable – but only in dreams. He wished, with startling intensity, to make it more than dreams, but saw no way to do so. She was a Lady born, no matter that she chose now to engage herself in trade. He was not of her station. He might do business with her, but he could not expect to ever have her attentions in any other way.

Her family had suffered enough scandal – she did not need it added to, by an association with a merchant, beyond that of an astute investment in business. He would not do that to her. He was not certain, anyway, if she had truly, in any sense welcomed that kiss, or if her reaction at the time had only been the natural relief at finding herself alive, when she must have thought that her death was imminent.

So he watched her, his eyes drinking her in, his mind finding joy in her kindness and cleverness as she worked with the girls in the manufactory, transforming their lives, even as she transformed her own, his body aching to touch her, beyond that single touch he allowed himself each day – the torture of the moment when he greeted her and bowed over her hand.

He would never press his attentions on a woman who did not wish them – he had seen too much of the worst of that at war, so he suffered, not knowing if she even noticed him, beyond his existence as a business partner, and threw himself into the work to dull the pain.

And then, somehow, sennights had passed since the fire, and Saint Valentine's Day was upon them.

~~~~~

The last boxes were settled into the cart, and his delivery man drove off, keen to get them delivered and be done for the day. Raphael turned, wiping a hand across his brow, and stepped back into the building. Sera sat at the little kitchen table, her hands around a mug of slowly cooling tea.

They had sent all of the girls home, with a bonus payment each, and declared that the manufactory would be closed tomorrow. The day after that was Saint Valentine's Day – there was no more time to make and deliver favours for that day's benefit. What they made hereafter would be for other occasions.

Raphael sank into a chair opposite her, a sigh escaping his lips, to echo softly in the empty room. The silence, after so many days of busy work and voices, seemed wrong, deafening in its own way. Their eyes met, and time slowed. They sat, as the afternoon light faded into evening, simply drinking each other in, with no words said. It was a companionship of effort shared, and of words that neither dared speak.
~~~~~

In the end, it was Raphael who broke the spell. He stood, stretching a little, with the same grace and strength that a cat does, and held out his hand.

"Come Lady Serafine, let me drive you home. Your mother will be glad to see you, and the dark circles under your eyes tell me just how much you need to rest."

"Why Mr Morton," she smiled, "how every ungallant. A gentleman should never indicate that a Lady looks anything less than radiantly beautiful." That she had the energy left for even mild repartee after the last month astounded him, and yet was typical of her tenacious character.

But she took his hand, the first true touch they had shared since the kiss after the fire, and rose from the table to accompany him out the door. And he thought, as she did so, that to him, dark circles or no, she would always look radiantly beautiful.

He delivered her to her door, and accompanied her in, greeting Lady Galwood with genuine pleasure, seeing before him a changed woman, a woman restored to her rightful state of health and comfort. A woman who might not say so in words, but whose expression told him just as clearly how much she appreciated what her daughter, and Raphael had done, to transform her circumstances.

"Good Evening Lady Galwood. I fear that Lady Serafine has quite exhausted herself, and needs a day of rest. We have agreed to close the manufactory for tomorrow, so that all can rest after the hard work that has been done."

Lady Galwood nodded approvingly.

"I would like to invite you, Lady Galwood, and Lady Serafine, to a dinner at my home, tomorrow evening, in celebration of our most successful business venture. Will you do me the honour of attending?"

Lady Galwood inclined her head regally, and smiled, drawing Sera to her side.

"We shall be delighted Mr Morton."

"Excellent – I will send Alf to collect you at seven."

He took Sera's hand, and bent to kiss it, his lips lingering longer than usual, as he breathed in the unique scent of her, clean and fresh and touched with something faintly exotic.

"Until then."

"Thank you – for everything, Mr Morton." Sera's voice was soft, thready with exhaustion, rich with sincerity. He wondered if that 'everything' included the kiss.

Chapter Eleven

Sera stood in the foyer with her mother, awaiting Alf's arrival. She smoothed the soft wool fabric of her dress, and settled the silk shawl around her shoulders, her fur pelisse close to hand for when they must step out the door. New clothes, which she might once have barely regarded, were now a thing to treasure and appreciate – a year of poverty had taught her that. The wealth that had come with her business venture had given them back comfort, and dignity – she would never let herself forget the lessons of the last year.

It felt most odd to dress as a Lady for a dinner party, after so long. She wondered what Raphael's family would be like, and if her dress was appropriate. Her mother, it seemed, had no such doubts or questions, she simply stood, elegant as always, and waited, watching her daughter fidget with a fond smile.

There was a tap at the door, and Alf was there, ushering them to the carriage cheerfully, surrounded by a faint but pleasant scent of hay and warm horses.

It was not far, yet she was most glad of the carriage, for the chill of late winter was still sharp as the day closed in. Her fingers closed around the strings of her reticule, reassuring herself that its contents were still secure. Perhaps she was a fool, but perhaps this was the right decision. She would see.

~~~~~

They drew up outside a most impressive residence, considerably larger than their respectable but unfashionable dwelling. The sheer size of it made her nervous, but she pushed that aside. The doors opened onto a marble tiled hall, and a respectful footman took their outer garments. Another ushered them into a parlour.

It was a beautiful room, part panelled in rich inlaid timbers, part papered with a delicate Chinoiserie pattern of birds and bamboo, all in delicate gold tones, with tiny highlights of red. The chaises were covered in gold toned brocades, and a magnificent painting hung above the mantle. It resembled paintings by the Flemish masters, with late afternoon light on golden hills and fields, all under a sky of dramatic storm clouds with just a trace of blue. It was, she suspected, worth a fortune.

The door opened behind her, and she spun, somewhat embarrassed to have been caught gawking at her surroundings like someone who had never seen an elegant room before. Raphael was followed into the room by his mother, sister and brother, but, at first, she did not even see them. He looked as she had never seen him before.
~~~~~

In evening wear of the highest quality, of a cut that was both elegant, and yet displayed his form to perfection, he looked more the gentleman than any man of the *ton* she had ever met. Her lips parted in a little gasp of admiration, and her eyes locked with his, their dark depths drawing her in, the warmth of his gaze unmistakable. He hesitated a moment, then, blinking, looked away.

The rest of the room, and the people with him, came rushing back into focus. His mother was most definitely Italian, and age had in no way diminished her beauty. Sera could see immediately that Raphael's face echoed the elegant lines of hers.

"Mother, may I present the Dowager Lady Galwood, and her daughter, Lady Serafine Parkington."

Sera chose to honour Mrs Morton with a curtsey, although their respective ranks did not demand it. Raphael's eyes glowed with appreciation at her gesture.

"And Lady Galwood, Lady Serafine, may I present my mother, Mrs Sophia Morton, my sister, Miss Isabella Morton, and my brother, Mr Gabriel Morton."

Isabella performed a curtsey to match Sera's, and Gabriel managed a creditable, if slightly wobbly, bow. Gabriel showed all the signs of equalling Raphael's handsomeness in a few years' time, and Isabella was already a beauty – had she been a daughter of the *ton*, she would have quite been the toast of this Season.

There was a moment of silence, into which Lady Galwood smoothly inserted a gracious thanks for their invitation.

Mrs Morton swept forward to capture Lady Galwood's hands, and spoke, the lilt of Italy still in her voice, even after all the years that she had spent in England.

"I am delighted to meet you at last. My son has been full of extravagant praise for your daughter, and I must add my gratitude to you both. For Raphael was quite blue-devilled at first, upon his return to us – feeling the loss of his father, and readjusting to civilian life – this business venture has completely cured him of that state. Now, come, pray be seated, let us be comfortable together."

Sera blinked in some surprise at her words. Extravagant praise? For her? It was a startling concept. She found herself liking this forthright woman – very much. Raphael had, on hearing his mother's words, actually blushed – something she had not thought it possible to see. Perhaps, after all, she had made the right decision – her fingers unconsciously patted gently at her reticule, reassuring herself that its contents were safe.

They fell into comfortable conversation with ease, with Isabella excited to learn about how she had come to have the ideas for such beautiful designs, Gabriel asking slightly wistful questions about how young men of the *ton* spent their time and Mrs Morton setting them completely at ease, with witty and intelligent discussion on an astonishingly wide range of topics, including some rather tart, but accurate commentary on members of the *ton*.

It was a great insight for Sera, into how the merchant class saw the nobility, and on just how much they knew about the lives of the upper ten thousand, just from the goods sold to them.

It was, in fact, rather humbling. The courtesy and good cheer in this house quite outshone that of those of the Quality who had been her supposed friends... *before*... As dinner was announced, and they rose to proceed to the dining room, Sera came to a realisation which left her shaken to the core.

These people knew so much of the life and the gossip of the *ton*, it was impossible that Mrs Morton, at least, was unaware of their family scandal. Yet she had received them with sincere pleasure and grace, and seemed truly happy in their company. The kindness of soul demonstrated here nearly brought her to tears on the instant. For surely, if Italian, it was quite possible that Mrs Morton was of the papist church – who held taking one's own life as an even greater sin than did most. That she could look past that terrible blemish upon their family, and receive them with genuine warmth was a great gift.

As the dinner proceeded, Sera found herself relaxed and enjoying herself, engaged in discussions that ranged from the business plans for the next year to the comparative virtues of different fabrics, or the qualities required in a superior cologne or perfume, to Isabella's wistful desire to attend society Balls, even knowing that she would be looked down on. Although, as had often been commented in Society drawing rooms, *sotto voce*, a merchant's daughter with a very large dowry to accompany her beauty might often be forgiven her birth and seen as a suitable bride for a Lord in need of funds.

Raphael relaxed as the evening went on – he had, at least a little, been concerned that his family might not take to Sera – which would have made him most unhappy – although he did not inspect his reasons for that too closely.

The last course was removed, and the ladies retired to the parlour. As an acknowledgement of his growing maturity, Raphael retired to the library with Gabriel, and provided him with a glass of port. The boys eyes lit up at being treated as an adult, and they sat for a while, talking of horses and vehicles, of boxing and fencing and other 'gentlemanly' topics, and only a little of business.

Eventually, though, the port had its effect, and Gabriel's eyes drooped. Raphael smiled at him, glad to see his brother happy.

"Off to bed with you, Gabriel, before you fall asleep in the chair."

Gabriel started, then placed his near empty glass on the side table with exaggerated care, nodded, and rose.

"I like her, Raphael, and I rather think that you like her more than you say, too. That's good, you should have someone to care about that way. Good night to you." Yawning, he left the room.

Raphael stood, open-mouthed in surprise for a moment, before turning and pouring himself a brandy that he felt a sudden need of.

Epilogue

It was very late, and the enjoyable evening would end soon. If she was going to do this, now was the time.

Sera rose and asked for the direction of the necessary, then quietly exited the room. But she did not follow the directions given. Instead, she made her way down the hall to the slightly ajar door of the room that she had seen Raphael enter, when they left the dining room.

Her heart beat hard, thumping almost painfully in her chest, and her palms felt damp with nerves. But she was determined. He might reject her gesture – if so, at least she would know where she stood. But he might not, and in that case, the future might hold things she had once though lost to her forever. At least there would be a chance.

She pushed the door open gently, stepped in, and just as gently pushed it closed behind her. The soft click of the closing door brought him round, from where he stood staring into the flames of the fire, to gaze instead, at her.

The soft amber colour of her gown made her golden eyes glow more brightly than usual, and the deep red highlights in her hair shone in the lamplight. He waited, bemused, as she walked to him and stopped.

"Raphael…" her voice had the same soft huskiness he had heard in the stable, but this time it was some emotion, not smoke, that had roughened her voice. He shivered at the sound, feeling it deep within him, in the place that had ached for her, all these sennights.

"I… I wanted to give you something." Her voice shook a little, but her smile was breathtaking. She lifted her reticule and undid its strings. Raphael watched, intrigued, waiting. Sera opened the reticule to its fullest extent, reached in, and very carefully withdrew something.

"Your hand, if you please"

Still bemused, he complied, holding out an open palm.

Delicately, as if handling a tiny bird, or something equally fragile, she laid something on his hand.

He dragged his eyes away from her face, and looked. On his hand lay a tiny favour, a heart made from beautiful antique lace, adorned with tiny beads of crystal and ruby, all stiffened by a piece of old, old vellum of the highest quality. If he had thought the favours she made for their business exquisite, then this was a step above and beyond them again.

He raised his eyes to hers, and she smiled, shyly, with uncertainty, but with something in her eyes that he had dreamed of, and barely hoped could ever be real.

"I made this some years ago… *before*… I put all of my wishes and longings into it, all of my memories of my grandmother, and the good things in my life, into this, made with her lace. It was a promise to myself, through all of the bad things. The heart of me. Now, I want to give it to you. It is near midnight. In but a few minutes, it will be Saint Valentine's Day. Please, accept my Valentine."

She stopped, and simply stood, watching his face. She was afraid, shaking, terrified that he would reject this, more vulnerable than she had ever felt in her life, and by her own actions. But she would not presume – she would wait upon his response.

Raphael lifted the tiny thing and studied it. It was imbued with the scent that he had come to know as hers, it was, in its way, as utterly beautiful as she, as much from its simplicity as from its complexity. He brought it to his lips and kissed it gently. Then he slid it carefully into the pocket inside his jacket, close against his heart. Perhaps his dreams had a chance, after all.

"Thank you. This is a gift beyond price. I will treasure it, as I treasure you, always."

He held out his hand again, and this time she placed her own in his. He drew her to him, enfolding her in his arms as he had in the stable, and tilted his face against her hair, the silky softness and the scent of her arousing him, as no other woman had. After a moment, he raised his hand, and tilted her head up. Her eyes sparkled with unshed tears, and something more. Her lips were soft and inviting, reddened where she had nibbled at them in her nervousness.

He bent his head and kissed her, gently at first, his lips exploring the shape of hers, his tongue caressing, and then, after a moment, she responded, her lips opening to him, her body pressing to his, her hands coming up to encircle his neck, to tangle in his hair. The kiss deepened, and everything faded away, but the feel of her in his arms, and the taste of her on his lips.

As the clock gently chimed midnight, and it became Saint Valentine's Day, towards which they had both worked so hard, they explored each other in a kiss that went on, and on, and on. Neither wished to stop, for stopping might require words again. For now, the possibilities for their future, which were contained in touch, taste and scent, were all that they wanted, perhaps all that they would ever need.

The End.

Read more of Raphael and Serafine's story in 'Winning the Merchant Earl' coming in late 2017.

91

About the Author

Arietta Richmond has been a compulsive reader and writer all her life. Whilst her reading has covered an enormous range of topics, history has always fascinated her, and historical novels been amongst her favourite reading.

She has written a wide range of work, from business articles and other non-fiction works (published under a pen name) but fiction has always been a major part of her life. Now, her Regency Historical Romance books are finally being released. The Derbyshire Set is comprised of 10 shorter novels (6 released so far). The 'His Majesty's Hounds' series is comprised of 8 novels, with the third having just been released.

She also has a standalone longer novel shortly to be released, and two other series of novels in development.

She lives in Australia, and when not reading or writing, likes to travel, and to see in person the places where history happened.

Be the first to know about it when Arietta's next book is released!

Sign up to Arietta's newsletter at

http://www.ariettarichmond.com

When you do, you will receive a free copy of the <u>subscriber exclusive</u> novella **'A Gift of Love',** a prequel to the Derbyshire Set series, which ends on the day that 'The Earl's Unexpected Bride' begins

This story is not for sale anywhere – it is absolutely exclusive to newsletter subscribers!

ARIETTA RICHMOND, GRACE AUSTEN, ISABELLA THORNE,
KATHERINE KEATS AND ALYCE HEALEY

Books in the 'His Majesty's Hounds' Series

Redeeming the Marquess (coming
soon)

Healing Lord Barton (coming soon)

Winning the Merchant Earl (coming soon)

Loving the Bitter Baron (coming soon)

Rescuing the Countess (coming soon)

Attracting the Spymaster (coming soon)

ARIETTA RICHMOND, GRACE AUSTEN, ISABELLA THORNE,
KATHERINE KEATS AND ALYCE HEALEY

Here is your preview of

Claiming the Heart of a Duke

His Majesty's Hounds – Book 1

Sweet and Clean Regency Romance

Arietta Richmond

Chapter One

Having broken his fast at the inn that morning, Hunter Barrington, tenth Duke of Melton, had decided that he would ride for the last leg of his journey, because he was heartily sick of the stuffy carriage and of his valet's mournful mien.

This worthy, whom he had hired following his friend Raphael's advice (for it seemed that his business was a source of excellent information, not just imported goods), had vainly tried to turn him into a dandy during their short stay in London. Hunter smiled thinking of Bulwick's dismay when he had flatly refused to use the cane that Bulwick had tried to foist upon him, or to buy the inordinate number of fobs, which it was fashionable to attach to one's watch chain. After years in the field, his taste in dress was so simple that it could be called austere. Not so long ago, a day with clean clothes had been worth savouring, so all of this fuss seemed rather ridiculous to him.

Poor Bulwick had been horrified when he had declared his intention to ride.

"You can't possibly do that, my Lord," he had whispered.

"You will reach Meltonbrook Chase in a dishevelled and mussed condition. You will get a head cold, of a certainty. And, my Lord, if I may presume to comment further, the road is in very bad condition and frozen all over."

"Fustian!"

Hunter had exclaimed, shrugging away his valet's concern.

"It will do me good. Look after my luggage, Felton. I'm off."

The road, in his opinion, was quite good – certainly a vast improvement on trampled battlefields and roads in a war zone!

So, without further ado, he had swung onto his horse, leaving the bewildered valet with his mouth still open in protest.

For the first few miles, the ride had been exhilarating. Warmly clad in his greatcoat, beaver hat and fur lined gloves, astride his dapple grey stallion, he had delighted in the cold wind and in the speed-blurred landscape, as he let the stallion run off his energy.

The feeling of freedom, however, did not last long and had already vanished when Meltonbrook Chase appeared in the distance. It was the first time he had seen his family estate since his father, the late Duke, had purchased a commission for him, as was traditional for a second son.

Hunter could remember, perfectly well, his father's stern admonitions, imparted before sending him on his way to London, and hence to the Peninsular and war.

"Honour first of all, my son. Honour means more than life to our family. Never tarnish it, never demean yourself, never show a streak of the yellow. Remember, an officer and a nobleman must be an example for his men. England must stand against the French tyrant. Your commitment must be wholehearted. Your days as a dissipated and wild young buck have ended. Do you understand?"

'I thought I understood, Father, but I didn't. Only later, I did. Oh, yes, later I understood, all too well, what you meant.' Hunter's thought was wry, and a little sad.

He was so absorbed in his musings that he was barely registering the landscape. It took some time for him to realise that he was inside Meltonbrook Chase's expansive park. He reined in his horse, and stopped to look at the wintry landscape around him.

The silence was profound, broken only by the cawing of a crow, somewhere in the woods, and by the soft murmuring of the nearby brook.

The grounds were immaculate under the heavy pall of snow, the ice-traced tall poplars, which surrounded the lake, shining like silver filigree under the setting sun's slanting rays.

"I'm home." he thought, steeling himself for his first meeting with his family, after so many years.

Riding into the deserted stable yard, it seemed surreal that he was actually here – and even more surreal that his father and brother were gone, that all of this was his now.

He dismounted, the icy gravel crunching under his feet, as a brawny groom, in a leather coat, came running toward him.

"Master Hunter! Master Hunter! Is it you? Is it really you? At long last you're home again!" The man suddenly checked and lowered his head.

"Begging your pardon, Your Grace. I've been overfamiliar, but me happiness made me tongue run away with me, it did, old fool that I am."

"Never you mind, Nick. Master Hunter it is, if you wish it, as long as you keep it just between us. You know how stuffy my mother can be... Now, this is Nuage...." he gestured to the horse, which snuffled curiously at the old groom. "I bought him in France, and a valiant fellow he is. Take good care of him, will you? Go with Nick, my boy, he's a good one."

Nick stroked the horse's silky coat and took the reins.

"Always been a good judge of horseflesh, Master Hunter. Since you was a stripling, you was. Come along Nuage, a good rubdown is what you need right now. And what about some clean straw to lie on and some oats to chew?" Talking to the horse, the head groom disappeared around the corner toward the stable, as the carriage, bearing his valet, and his meagre luggage, drew up before the house.

~~~~~~~~

Nerissa looked at her reflection in the tall mirror and sighed.

She would never be an Incomparable, and that was that. Her colouring was all wrong, she was too tall and her face was too angular. In the pale pastel colours that were deemed fashionable for young ladies, she faded into insignificance.
~~~~~~~~

She sighed again, thinking of her sister Maria, an acknowledged Beauty, who had cut a triumphant swathe through the *ton* during the previous Season. It had been fashionable to be in love with Maria, with her flashing amber eyes, rich auburn hair and flawless creamy complexion.

Thus, Maria had had the opportunity of choosing from amongst a veritable army of suitors and was now betrothed - very advantageously betrothed, to be sure, to a wealthy Earl, to their parents' delight.

Donning her fur lined pelisse and her velvet bonnet, Nerissa crossed the hall and stepped into the carriage with her maid, bound to Meltonbrook Chase, where she was to have tea with her bosom bow Alyse, the Duke of Melton's daughter.

No, not daughter, sister, she amended her thought. Hunter was Duke, now, after the untimely demise of his father and his elder brother.

She blushed. They hoped that Hunter would be home soon, for he had sent his family a message from London, but with the deep snow on the roads, he was likely delayed.

Would he recognise her? She did not think so. He had had scant interest to spare for her, to begin with, when he was a young man just back from his term in Oxford, and she was just a shy ten year old, all angles and elbows and not even a promise of feminine allure.

Nerissa leaned back on the carriage seat, closing her eyes. *'Much good it does me to wool-gather like that'*, she chided herself. *'I'll be lucky if I don't find myself married to some gouty old man before the Season is over.'*

She shivered, and not because of the sharp wind blowing and howling through the naked trees.

~~~~~~~~

As Hunter approached the door, the butler, a delighted expression lighting his usually impassive features, opened it. Immediately regaining his formal demeanour, Jermyn schooled his expression to a more serious face, better suited to the Butler of a great house.

"Welcome home, my lord. The ladies are in the drawing room. Follow me, please."

"No need, Jermyn, I know the way", answered Hunter, secretly amused by the butler's display of self-restraint, and almost ran to the drawing room doors, suddenly unable to wait any longer to see his family.

He opened the doors, and an instant of shocked silence followed his entrance.

Hunter scanned the tableau – a morning visit frozen before him. All of his family were there (although part of his mind still expected to see his father and Richard as well), and there was someone else.

A woman he did not know, a woman who was more beautiful than any he had seen.

She had burnished golden hair, surrounding her face with a profusion of waves and ringlets, a honey and gold complexion; long, almond shaped green gold eyes, fringed by thick burnished golden eyelashes and emphasized by high cheekbones, and a tall, shapely body.
~~~~~~~~

The only feature detracting from perfection, but greatly adding to character, was a rather large, mobile mouth, much more capable of expressing feelings (and temper, he suspected!) than a proper prim little rosebud. He was captivated. Her eyes met his across the room, and for a moment, everything else faded away.

He was brought back to the moment when the silence was broken by his sister Alyse, who cried out: "Hunter! Hunter, you are back! Is it really you, Hunter?" and, without any further ado, threw herself at him. His eye contact with the woman was broken, and he forgot her in the chaos that followed.

Hunter's mother, the Duchess Louisa, half-fainting, reclined on the sofa, fanning herself and calling for her vinaigrette. His sister Sybilla, almost jigged around the table, before forcing herself to behave with greater propriety. His brother, Charles, obviously tried to be the cool gentleman, but could not help but step forward and embrace Hunter, his eyes shining with held back tears.

"At long last, my son," sobbed his mother.

"Come here, and let me look at you. Last time I saw you, you were a boy. Now you are a man. And what a man! Your father, God rest his soul, would be so proud of you..."

Moved despite himself, Hunter gathered his weeping mother into his arms.

"Shush, Mother, I'm here to stay. I'm so sorry I was not here when it would have really mattered. I feel that I have failed you all, yet it was at the time of Waterloo, and I did not even hear the news for months! I'm so sorry..."

The Duchess brushed her tears impatiently aside.

"I'm a foolish old woman, my son. This is not a time for weeping, but a time for rejoicing. God knows, we have been mourning long enough. And look who is here, Hunter. Do you remember Lady Nerissa Loughbridge, Lord Chester's youngest daughter?"

A faint recollection of a meddlesome brat, always trying to follow him around, vaguely stirred in Hunter's memory.

He turned his head and froze again, caught by her appearance.

Brat? She was not a brat anymore, she was a woman, and a very beautiful woman at that, more so because of her unusual colouring.

It was all he could do not to stare at her with his mouth agape. He tried to react in some polite way, and smiled, suddenly recalling one of Nerissa's youthful misdeeds.

"Nerissa? Was it you who hid inside your brother Kevin's portmanteau, because you wanted to come with us when we went to our hunting lodge near Cottesmore? And did we not discover you because you sneezed? Do you remember, Charles?"

Nerissa had not heard a single word.

Hunter's sudden appearance had completely stunned her.

All her childhood emotions flooded back, crowding her mind, amplified with new meaning and significance. A rosy blush washed upon her face as she dared to smile back.

"She's not a child anymore, Hunter," broke in Alyse.

"She is a dear friend to us all, and I really don't know how we would have managed without her. She is a sensible young woman, with a good head on her shoulders, and she gave us invaluable help when Mother was so ill after…" Alyse's voice faltered "…after the accident…"

Hunter looked at his family: his sisters, pretty, vivacious, eager to try out their wings during the London Season, his mother, with her gentle face marked by loss and sorrow, his brother, suddenly scowling and dark browed, and the enchanting stranger in their midst. He felt rather like he had stepped into the centre of a whirlwind.

Suddenly he felt mortally tired, in dire need of rest and solitude.

He went to his mother and kissed her gently on her cheek.

"Will you please excuse me, Mother? I have had a long and tiring journey and I'm much fatigued. I believe that, if you will forgive me, I will have a bath drawn and a tray sent to my room. I am not really up to a formal supper. Tomorrow, we can all begin to catch up."

"But of course, my dear. How thoughtless of me not having foreseen your needs… my happiness at seeing you again quite overwhelmed me. I have not all my wits about me, I'm sure… Jermyn, please, see His Grace to his apartments and make sure that his valet attends him."

"Yes, my lady. Please follow me, Your Grace."

To his chagrin, Jermyn did not lead Hunter to his bachelor's quarters as he had unthinkingly expected, but to his father's apartments.

That was the precise moment at which the full import of his new condition crashed in upon him like a dark and overwhelming wave.

He was the Duke of Melton.

Not his father, nor his elder brother, both now dead after a freak carriage accident. Himself.

He had not wanted it, he had not coveted it, truth to tell, he had no idea how to go about being a Duke, but there it was, with all its implications and obligations, including the need to marry, and to sire heirs to the title.

It was like a bad dream, but it was not going to disappear at dawn.

Get

'Claiming the Heart of a Duke'

to find out what happens next!

ARIETTA RICHMOND, GRACE AUSTEN, ISABELLA THORNE,
KATHERINE KEATS AND ALYCE HEALEY

Regency Romance

Lord Haverly's Valentine Pursuit

A Clean & Wholesome Regency Romance

Grace Austen

ARIETTA RICHMOND, GRACE AUSTEN, ISABELLA THORNE,
KATHERINE KEATS AND ALYCE HEALEY

Copyright © 2017

Tica House Publishing LLC

All Rights Reserved.

No part of this publication may be reproduced in any form or by any means, including scanning, photocopying, or otherwise without prior written permission of the copyright holder.

Dedication

This book is dedicated to you, my readers!

Many warm thanks for your encouragement, emails, and kind reviews! You are what makes my work so special.

ARIETTA RICHMOND, GRACE AUSTEN, ISABELLA THORNE,
KATHERINE KEATS AND ALYCE HEALEY

112

Chapter One

January 28, 1814

"He's dead?" Evelyn asked. She gaped at the doctor and plunked down on the settee by the fireplace. A gulping wave of grief rose in her throat. She no longer felt able to stand, "Are you quite certain?"

"Yes, my lady. I feel dreadful having to be the one to tell you this news," the older man answered quietly.

"But I … I don't understand how this has transpired. How could such a thing fall upon one as healthy as the Earl? He was known far and wide for his good health and excellent constitution. How did this happen?" Her eyes were wide and unflinching as she stared at the doctor.

"I don't know. Although I consider myself to be rather skilled as a physician, I must confess that, in this circumstance, I am beyond my capabilities. Your husband does not appear to have suffered, if that is of any comfort to you."

Evelyn's head was pounding. She could not wrap her senses around such an earth-shattering truth. She clasped her hands in her lap.

"This is too horrible to absorb. My husband lies dead in his bedroom, appearing as though he were asleep, and there is no explanation, no possible conclusion that may be drawn?"

The doctor took a step closer. "How I wish it were otherwise. But you have explained the current state of affairs with thorough understanding."

Evelyn forced down her sorrow and felt her hackles rise.

"My understanding is hardly thorough. You have given me nothing *thorough* to go on. I may be in the position to repeat the facts as stated, but I must be honest. It is incomprehensible to me that my husband, a man of thirty and six years, has been found dead by his valet with no explanation that would bring peace to my troubled mind."

The doctor inhaled deeply.

"My lady, I only wish that you should not have to grieve at all. I bear the full weight of my inability to offer an explanation of the true nature of Lord Montebank's untimely passing. But I fear my humblest apologies are not an accurate replacement for the truth and the answers you seek."

Lady Evelyn Oliver turned away from the doctor and gazed at the flames burning in the fireplace. They lapped hungrily at the wood, consuming it without compunction. Her emotions went cold. She felt as if she had fallen into the icy waters of a northernmost lake in the darkest depths of winter. She began trembling.

It was not possible that her husband, the seventh Earl of Montebank, lay dead in his bedroom.

She raised her chin and bit her lower lip to control the shivering that now spread through her entire body. She simply would not accept the words of the doctor. There was no way that she, at barely three decades, was a widow and that her young son was now the next Earl of Montebank, and he at the tender age of only seven. Not only that, but her daughter was now robbed of the father whom she adored.

The shivering deepened, and her eyes burned. The thought of her darling children without their father, and the grief that they both must bear at ages far too young for such news, was not to be borne. It brought on such paroxysms of grief that she felt utterly wretched.

Doctor Applewhite observed her, and his face registered his growing alarm. One moment the lady seemed perfectly composed as would be expected of one of her rank, regardless of the circumstances. But in only a matter of minutes, he watched as her composure gave way to intense quaking and weeping. The change was so sudden, so rapid, that he could only stare.

And then, he was moved to action. He knelt before her and attempted to offer her comfort and assistance.

"Lady Montebank, you are not well. I fear the news was too much for your delicate constitution. I would never forgive myself if my abrupt announcement and treatment of such terrible news were the cause of any illness. Please, we must get you to bed at once. You *must* rest."

Evelyn's mind grew foggy. She saw the doctor's lips move, but his words seemed far away, as distant as the chilling wind that swept across the moors.

She tried to concentrate on his meaning, but she was unable to ascertain what he was telling her as she slid into the darkness and fainted.

~~~~~

Later that afternoon, Evelyn opened her eyes and found herself in bed. From her vantage point, she could see the red brocade of the bed curtains and the glow of the fire blazing in the fireplace. Her gaze was drawn to the windows, and she watched the snow softly falling outside in the grey afternoon light. She sat up, and with some difficulty, tried to recall the events of the morning that had led her to this state.

"My lady, you are awake. I am glad of that. You gave us quite a scare." A woman slightly older than Evelyn stood up from the ornate chair by the bed. As Lady Evelyn's maid, Charlotte had hardly left her mistress's side since she had fainted.

Evelyn rubbed at her eyes and felt how swollen they were.

"Charlotte, you are here. Please do not fuss. I am well. At least, I believe myself to be. But my thoughts are confused. You may be able to offer assistance in that regard."

"Yes, my lady. I will do anything you ask."

Evelyn sucked in her breath and forged ahead.

"The events of this morning, were they a dreadful vision of the night, a dream half remembered? Or are they the truth? Has tragedy struck this family?"
~~~~~

Charlotte visibly shuddered.

"Lady Evelyn, you must steel yourself. I am sorry to tell you that the events you speak of truly happened. Our gracious master is dead."

Evelyn shook her head, and her throat became tight.

"That cannot be true. Surely, there has been a mistake."

Charlotte's eyes brimmed with tears.

"No, my lady. No mistake."

Evelyn gulped in air.

"Oh, my poor darlings! Have the children been told?"

"Yes, my lady. Please don't be angry. I, Mrs. Bowles, and Mr. Gurley all thought it best to tell the children. They are of the age where it would be difficult to hide such things from them. The governess has told them the sad news that they no longer have a father."

Evelyn pulled at her covers, gripping them tightly.

"I should have preferred to tell them myself. They should have heard such news from their own mother."

"Forgive us, my lady." There was fear in Charlotte's voice.

Evelyn swallowed past the growing lump in her throat. "I cannot be angry at my staff for making a decision that all of you thought was best. I was indisposed, and I am certain that neither you, nor the remainder of the staff, were certain when I would once again be myself. No, it was a decision borne out of the best of thoughts and intentions, and I cannot be vexed in any way."

Charlotte gave an audible gasp of relief.

"Thank you, my lady. We meant no disrespect, and we didn't mean to overstep our place by making a decision that should have been yours alone to make. It was a decision that none of us had ever thought would be left in our hands, but with the young master at his age, we felt it would be impossible to hide the truth from him for very long."

"You have done well. I trust in Miss Edwards' abilities, that she handled it with the grace and compassion it warranted."

"She did. We were all there in the nursery when she told the young Lord and Lady. She did as you would have wished."

"Very well. If the children are able to be brought to me, I wish to see them."

"Yes, my lady, right away."

<div align="center">~~~~~</div>

The arrival of the children brought fresh tears and grief to all parties. Charlotte stood by and witnessed the scene of deep woe and cries of disbelief. Her own eyes were wet with tears as she watched her mistress and children gather in an embrace of sorrow over their mutual loss. It was heartbreaking to behold.

With her children gathered to her, Lady Evelyn made a vow within her own heart — the family would break with the London area and all that they had long associated with their departed father.

The grief and pain of his passing were too much to bear in the halls and rooms which he had so recently filled with his presence.

A departure was just the thing. Evelyn was convinced that it would bring about a timelier end to their mourning. She could not bear to think of her children, her precious son and daughter, sick with grief for one more minute than was necessary.

As she held her children in her arms, she rocked them back and forth, and sang to them a lullaby of faraway places and distant lands. It was there in the words of a child's song that Evelyn found the inspiration for her plan. Her husband had been dead only a few hours, and she was certain that she was overwrought with emotion, but the grief of her children was terrible. As a mother filled with the strongest of maternal devotion, she promised to do whatever she was capable of doing to ease their suffering.

The snow fell as the tears from her own eyes. The heartbreak of the morning moved into an evening of grief and muffled sobs. Evelyn's resignation to the facts of the dreadful day gave her the conviction that she was thinking in a way governed solely by logic. Her plan became more firmly embedded in her will.

As the evening settled into the purple darkness of night, Evelyn became more and more convinced that she would honor her departed husband and keep his memory alive for his son and daughter by changing locations. New surroundings would lessen the pain of their absent father.

They would begin anew in a place that the children did not associate with him. They would be best served by a change of circumstances, a change that would be facilitated as soon as it could be arranged.

Her children fell asleep by her side. Evelyn felt desperately alone. The loss of her husband was a pain that she felt so strongly in her breast that she could scarcely breathe, yet breathe she must. She was compelled by the love of her children to bear the pain and be strong for them. She would grieve in silence and remain stoic. She would appear as a rock; she would be the foundation that her precious children needed as they faced the changes that were to be expected with the sudden death of their father. It would be difficult, and she prayed that she would find the fortitude necessary to face this task.

Chapter Two

February 5, 1814

The funeral of the seventh Earl of Montebank was attended by prominent members of the local gentry and the *ton* — the elite members of society that ruled the upper class of the realm. Evelyn's husband was laid to rest in his family's crypt at the estate in Yorkshire, and a gathering was held at the estate after the ceremony.

It was customary that the widow receive her guests with grace and all the pomp that the Earl of Montebank would have commanded. For Evelyn, this was not the time for tears or expressions of grief; she must be strong and hold her composure. Her guests must be greeted and shown deference, and the traditions of the household must be upheld. It was barbaric to think that the widow be compelled to interact socially with her peers, but it was her duty and it was expected.

To her horror, her son, at his tender age of seven was expected to receive guests as the eighth Earl of Montebank.

The expectations of her own duties were barely civilized, but to expect a boy at such a tender age, who had just lost his father, to receive guests was more than she would allow. She created a slight uproar among the older members of her staff by suggesting that the lad was simply too young to perform his duty.

But Evelyn stood her ground. She was the mistress of everyone now, and she would be obeyed. She told the butler, Mr. Gurley, that it would be permissible to say that the young Lord had taken ill after the carriage ride from London.

The butler surprised her by agreeing. "In all truth, Lady Evelyn, I am pleased that you've made this decision. The tradition is far better suited to an adult inheriting the title than a small child. I do not believe that this one concession will destroy the prestige of the Montebanks. You are a historic family, and others grieve with you."

Evelyn helped make the necessary excuses to the members of society as to the whereabouts of the young Earl. She told anyone who made inquiries that the lad's health and constitution were being closely monitored. She explained that after the sudden death of his father and the carriage ride in the harsh conditions of winter weather, the new Earl's health was far more important than societal institutions. The words of agreement she received were hardly sincere, but Evelyn found that she couldn't be bothered with their reactions at that point in time.

She had other more pressing concerns. There were dreadful rumors circulating among the *ton* as to the circumstances surrounding her husband's death.

It should never have been brought to her attention, yet she was oddly grateful that it had been.

It was a close acquaintance, Lady Georgiana Chatham, who spoke with her privately at the reception, giving her the news. Evelyn could tell that Georgiana's motivation behind the dissemination of such news was not to cause harm or injury.

The woman joined Evelyn by the fireside in the drawing room after the funeral.

She leaned in close and whispered, "Lady Evelyn, I am not at all certain that I should be telling you this, but I would be remiss if I did not give you the opportunity to rectify a situation."

Her words startled Evelyn. Evelyn took her arm.

"My dear Georgiana, please accompany me to the study where we may speak in private without concern of being overheard."

"Yes, that would be best," Georgiana readily agreed.

The ladies made their way to the study. Evelyn was aware that whispers and stares followed her every movement. She wondered what could be the source for such rude behaviour as she passed the well-turned-out members of the *ton*.

Evelyn walked into the study and was temporarily shocked that there was not a fire burning in the fireplace.

The sudden chill of the room was equalled by the stark realization that the staff had neglected to provide a fire in the room because the master was no longer in residence to use it. It was yet another reminder that her husband had passed.

She was tempted to fall right then into the dark pit of grief, but she was entertaining guests and she was in the company of Lady Chatham. She took a deep breath and focused all of her attention on the news that her guest was so eager to share.

"So, what is it?"

"I am embarrassed to even speak about it. It is reprehensible and distasteful in the utmost." Lady Chatham did indeed look ashamed.

"Whatever can you mean? You may speak plainly between us. I will not be offended."

"I am appreciative of your kind reception. I tell you this as a caring gesture and nothing more. If the roles were reversed, I would hope that you would find it in your heart to do the same for me."

Would the woman *ever loosen her tongue?* What could it be? Evelyn wanted to stamp her feet with impatience, but she kept her voice level.

"You have my undivided attention."

"I am sad to say that it concerns the recent passing of your husband. I must be bold in my question, and I do not mean to cause you grief by the asking of it. Has the doctor been forthcoming as to the cause of death?"

Evelyn's eyes grew large in astonishment. She had always considered Lady Chatham to be a reliable woman graced with intelligence and a subtle refinement. To have such a question so blatantly asked at the funeral of her husband was beyond the bounds of decency.

"Oh dear, I can see from your expression that I have offered great insult to you. That was not my intention, not in the least. I only ask such a terrible question because it is the topic of conversation among those who would call themselves our peers. They dare not ask these questions outright for fear of appearing crass or common, but among themselves they have shown no restraint. In London, before I left, it was the only gossip that anyone cared to discuss."

"Lady Chatham, if you do not mind, I must sit down."

"Yes, of course, please do. Is there anything I can do to help you? Shall I ring for your maid or a footman?"

"That will not be necessary. I am well. I just need a few minutes."

Evelyn sat down in a carved wooden chair across from the desk that her husband used to frequent when he was in residence.

She gazed at the empty desk and once again, found her resolve to be strong and mourn in silence sorely tested.

"My dear Evelyn, I offer my apologies. I thought I was doing my duty by you, to tell you of these things."

"You are entirely blameless. It was the action of a true friend. It was selfless to risk my ire when your heart was moved purely by the best of intentions. If you will permit me a few minutes to regain my composure..." Evelyn looked into the caring face of her friend. "But you have not revealed the nature of this gossip."

Georgiana flushed.

"I hesitate… All right, then. There is speculation of, well, copious drink. Also of perhaps, another person… Of someone else involved. Of an unrevealed alliance… I feel horrible about it, and I want you to know that I have defended your husband's honor…"

Evelyn's lips parted. She was incredulous.

"What?"

"I do apologize. Please forgive me. I should not have mentioned anything. I am sure the Earl was most loyal to you."

Anger surged up Evelyn's throat.

"In actuality, you have done me a service."

Georgiana looked puzzled.

"In what way?"

"You have just reinforced a recent decision I have made. Now, may I request a moment to myself…?"

"Of course, I will leave you to a few minutes' peace." Lady Chatham looked relieved to be exiting the study.

The door closed, and Evelyn sat alone in the cold room that once had held the great warmth of her husband's personality. He had spent many hours at the oak desk, and she remembered having tea with him in the afternoons as he answered correspondence or looked over the ledgers of the estate.

Now she was alone, and the cold was piercing.

She looked at the door and was filled with a sudden desire to run out of the room and up the staircase to her chambers.

These people that she had associated with for so many years, these members of the *ton*, were about as compassionate to her plight as buzzards that swarm over a dead rabbit in the field. The news that there was speculation concerning her husband's death and integrity was offensive and the last straw as far as she was concerned.

It was inexcusable that she should be met with whispers and rumours in her time of grief. And how heartless to malign her husband's name. Where was the compassion and the sympathy that was a widow's due? She wondered how she was supposed to face these people who were more interested in the death of the Earl than they were in offering their sincere condolences to his family.

She thought about her vow, her commitment to remove her family from the halls they had known their entire lives, to take them to a place where they would find space and new experiences. With the knowledge that the *ton* was consumed by the gossip of her husband's death, it was one more sign that her decision to make a break with society was warranted.

After a goodly amount of time, she squared her shoulders and left the study. Her intention was to remain stoic and composed and to pay no heed to the whispers and the stares. It would be a trial, but it was one that she was bred to bear. After all, she was the daughter of a Marquis and the wife of an Earl. She was an aristocrat by birth and marriage, and she would not give these people the satisfaction of a display of emotion or cowardice that they so blatantly desired.

Evelyn was halfway across the great hall when she was greeted by her brother-in-law, James Oliver.

James was the younger brother of her husband and a welcome sight at this gathering.

"My dear Evelyn, it is good to see you. I do apologize for my late arrival."

"Your time of arrival is of little consequence to me. I am just glad to have you here at Denningham."

"I received the news upon my return home from a hunting trip and made as hasty a departure as could be arranged. It grieves me that I was not able to see my brother laid to rest."

"I am so sorry that you missed the service." She gave him a sorrowful smile. "You are here now, and I am in dire need of assistance in receiving our guests. I must confess it is difficult, more difficult than I ever dared dream."

"You cannot be expected to bear the weight entirely by yourself. I am here now, and I will receive the guests at your side, if you will have me."

"I am relieved and grateful that you would agree to undertake so gloomy a task."

"My brother would have done the same for me, would you not agree?"

"Yes, and so he would. Shall we go to the drawing room, or would you prefer to freshen up in the guest chambers?"

"No, I have no need for such pleasantries. My valet has brought my trunk and can see to my comfort. In the meantime, I will be found at your side."

"Thank you, James."

"And the children?"

"They are resting in the nursery."

"Very good. I shall greet them later. And young Arthur, the new Earl? He's in the nursery, too."

"Yes, with Mary."

"That is good. And I intend to do my duty to the young Earl. I am happy to be his guide and spokesperson until he is of age."

Evelyn smiled at James and was immensely grateful that he had arrived. She no longer felt alone to face the members of a society that she no longer considered friends. A deep sense of betrayal overtook her heart. She did not share the disturbing rumours with her brother-in-law. She did not want to compound his grief by telling him such disturbing news.

Instead, she resolved to bear the gossip alone and found, to her surprise that, rather than magnifying her grief, it had the opposite effect. It served to strengthen her resolve to leave the closed clique of aristocrats and seek the company of new faces and society.

With her determination thus strengthened, she stood taller and held her head high. Now, when she entered the parlour, the strange looks of pity and curiosity made more sense to her. It seemed that Lady Chatham had been correct with her tidings.

Evelyn was content to let these people whisper behind her back and say what they desired about her and her late husband.

It would not matter to her in the end — not at all.

Chapter Three

February 25, 1814

Less than a month had passed since her husband had died, leaving Evelyn a widow and the mother of the eighth Earl of Montebank.

She sat at the oak desk in the study at Denningham and drank a cup of tea as she perused the endless papers from the office of her husband's solicitor, Mr. Sloan.

She had met with Mr. Sloan and was relieved when the reading of the will had gone well, and there were no surprises. During the same occasion, they had discussed the financial aspects of the estate in great detail.

The accounts were well in order, and no money was owed to creditors or merchants. The Earl had died leaving the estate that he had been entrusted with in better shape than it had been at the time when he inherited it himself.

It was with great relief that Evelyn learned for certain that her son would inherit a title and wealth that would rival any of the richest families in England.

As mother to the young Earl, she was within her rights to continue to live in the residences and properties until such time as the young Earl grew to the age of manhood and accountability. Even then, she would likely be welcome to remain.

Evelyn thought about the many properties and investments that her husband had made during his time as Earl. The papers in the desk were a written record of the many sources of income for the Earl of Montebank. Evelyn only hoped that she would be able to manage it all and leave her son an estate of which he could be proud.

As Evelyn looked over the documents piled high on the corner of the desk, she considered again her promise to herself, and to her children, that they would make a new beginning elsewhere. As Earl, her son was expected to remain in residence, but as he was still a child, she felt that his permanent residency could wait.

It would take money to set up a household in another location, and she wondered as she looked at the towering stack of paper if her husband may have owned a property that would make an ideal destination for what she had in mind.

His investments and properties were numerous and far more extensive than she had realized. It seemed as though logic would dictate that she search the properties owned by the Earl before seeking a situation that would require a significant investment. Feeling a sudden burst of inspiration, she hastily sorted the papers into categories. There was a pile for business ventures, and one for investments in shipping, trade and companies. There was a pile for agriculture and livestock and finally one for properties.

As she perused the properties, nothing in particular came to her attention. The Earl owned a hunting lodge, a country estate, a townhouse, and many small properties that were a source of rental income. With a disappointed sigh, she relinquished her notion that she could simply pick up her family and move into a residence already furnished and ready for inhabitants.

She stood and paced in front of the fireplace. The logs blazed, and the heat they gave out was considerable and stuffy. But still, she paced. She was frustrated and had no solution.

She found it difficult to believe that there was not someplace the Earl owned that they could retire to, perhaps rest for a season or longer, until the children were well over their grief. As she paced and stared back at the desk, a piece of paper caught her eye.

She stopped and looked at the document which sat atop the pile marked agriculture and livestock. She picked it up and read it carefully. By the end of the page, she could not believe that she had somehow managed to overlook it earlier when she was sorting. In her hand was the answer to her problem, the solution for which she had been so desperately searching. She could have danced her delight, but of course, that would have been unseemly, especially for a widow.

Even when no one was watching.

Evelyn sat back down at the desk and poured another cup of tea. As she sipped the steaming amber liquid and felt its hot warmth run down her throat, she read the document once more, carefully this time, to be sure of its meaning.

Reading it thus, she could vaguely recall a conversation that her late husband had with her, at tea one afternoon shortly after their daughter was born. The document in her hand was the direct evidence of that conversation so long ago.

It was as though the Earl had somehow known of his untimely demise and that his family would need a haven, a safe place to weather the storm of their grief. He had provided the answer his widow was so anxious for, and he had surprised her with it when she was in her hour of need. Evelyn knew that she was being overly sentimental to suggest that her late husband had provided for her and the children in such a manner from beyond the grave, but the timing was extraordinary.

The document she had now read for the third time was everything she could have hoped for. The Earl had made an investment in Ireland, in property and agriculture. To Evelyn's way of thinking, it was less agriculture and more of a business venture. In County Meath, her husband had purchased an estate solely for the purpose of raising horses, both racing and draught.

She remembered how he had taken great pains to explain the origin of steeplechase racing in England, and the market for breeding fine race horses. He had also explained that with the tremendous amount of agriculture in the country, draught horses were a source of considerable income. It was remarkable that the details of a conversation held so long ago, now came to her mind as fresh as though it had only taken place yesterday. Now, the memories flooded into the present, and she felt as though fate was stepping in and providing her with a hint that she should take her family to Ireland.

She opened the desk drawer and withdrew paper for a letter. It did not take her long to draft an inquiry to her solicitor asking for more details concerning the property known as Chapel House. She inquired as to its size, its current state of habitation, and the success of the horse raising venture. Ringing for the footman, she asked that he post the letter as soon as possible. She hoped that she would hear from the solicitor quickly. It would be difficult, but she longed for the freedom of a foreign land. If she could arrange travel to Ireland with her children by midsummer, she would be delighted.

ARIETTA RICHMOND, GRACE AUSTEN, ISABELLA THORNE,
KATHERINE KEATS AND ALYCE HEALEY

Chapter Four

March 18, 1814

It was as though fate was pointing Evelyn in the right direction. She was astounded by how quickly all of the details came together for the "Ireland Venture" as she regarded her current scheme. Mr. Sloan had written to inform her that the house in Ireland was smaller than her current residence in the country, but it was habitable and would suit the rank and disposition of the Earl of Montebank.

The estate was quite successful, and the venture was doing well; although it still only represented a fraction of the income that it might one day generate, under the proper management. Mr. Sloan sent the names and current information of the staff at Chapel House and inquired if there was any other way he could be of assistance.

Upon reading his letter, Evelyn did not need any time at all to consider her present circumstances. It was worth the risk to move the household to Ireland, at least for the summer. She wrote to Mr. Sloan, requesting that he make arrangements for passage and staff.

Once the letter was in the post, she felt far better than she had in a great many weeks. It was as though an enormous weight had been lifted from her shoulders.

She left the study and climbed the stairs to the second floor. The children were undoubtedly to be found with their governess in the school room, and she could hardly wait to share such exciting news. Evelyn's arrival in the middle of a math lesson was a welcome surprise to her son and daughter. They immediately raced to her side and were excited to show her what they had been learning.

She listened with great interest as they recounted their sums and multiplication tables. Evelyn smiled at the governess and then made an announcement to her children.

"My dears, how would you like to go on an adventure with your mother?"

"An adventure? Wherever could we be going?" asked Arthur.

"What is adventure?" Mary asked as she climbed into Evelyn's lap.

"An adventure is when you go to a place you have never been before and see things you have never seen before. It is exciting and is like a tale in your books."

"I 'fraid of adventure," said Mary petulantly.

"There, there my darling, there is nothing to be frightened of, not at all. Don't you want to go to a land of emerald hills and fairy folk?"

"Fairy folk? Mama, is there really such a land or is it a story?"
Arthur asked, as he pushed the dark hair out of his eyes.

Her son looked so much like her late husband that it nearly
broke Evelyn's heart to gaze at him. Still, she loved him with all
her heart.

"Arthur, I am proud of you. Your question is quite astute for
a lad in school. In answer to your question, yes, there *is* such a
magical place. It is called Ireland, and we will be traveling there
by midsummer."

"Is it far, this Ireland?"

"We shall have to take a ship to reach it. Won't that be
exciting? A sea voyage?"

"I have dreamed of ships and boats… Yes, it will be exciting,"
Arthur decided.

"I 'fraid of boats," said Mary.

"My dearest girl, there is nothing to be afraid of. If you are
brave and so is your brother, you may both have a horse when
we reach Ireland."

Arthur perked up.

"A horse? Of my own?"

"We shall have lots of horses," Evelyn said with a smile. "But
you may have a special horse all for yourself."

Arthur's grin was wide. "My own horse…"

"Will we be gone forever?" asked Mary.

"No, my love, we will not. Only for a little while. It is healthy to go to new places and meet new people from time to time."

"And sail on ships?" Arthur asked.

"Yes, Arthur, and sail on ships."

"Mama, I want a pony not a horse. Can I have one?" asked Mary.

"Yes, my dearest, you may. We will find you a lovely pony all your own."

"When do we go? Can we go today?" the little girl asked.

Evelyn smiled with relief. Her children were excited about the trip, and so was she. It was just what they all needed, a place where the tragedy and questions surrounding the Earl's death would not haunt them. In truth, she was as excited as her children. She could not wait to board the ship and leave England far behind.

~~~~~

The tender scene in the schoolroom faded to a distant memory in the following weeks as Evelyn oversaw the planning of such a large undertaking. It was decided that the housekeeper, Mrs. Bowls, and the butler, Mr. Gurley, would remain at Denningham. Their leadership and management of the estate would be crucial while Evelyn was away.

Evelyn was disappointed that Governess Edwards would not be joining the family in Ireland, but her reason for not going was above reproach.
~~~~~

Her ailing mother did not live far away from the estate in Yorkshire but it was obviously much too far away from Ireland. With reluctance, Evelyn accepted her resignation. She wrote to the solicitor to find the children a new governess in Ireland that could be engaged as soon as possible. Mr. Sloan made all the necessary long distance arrangements for the family's arrival.

As the day of the family's departure quickly approached, Evelyn was confident that all details were well taken care of by the solicitor and his staff. The excitement of the journey temporarily supplanted any grief that she or her children felt.

And thus, Evelyn was well pleased to see that the trip to Ireland was already having the affect she had hoped to achieve.

~~~~~

June 10, 1814

On the eve of her departure to Chapel House in Ireland, Evelyn's brother-in-law James journeyed to see Evelyn and the children. He shared dinner with her at the estate and expressed his best wishes for their safe journey. He seemed as happy with the arrangement as Evelyn, and she was certain that he was overcome with compassion for all the sadness that she and her children had been through in the past months.

As James toasted her and the newest Earl of Montebank, Evelyn could not have been more content to have a brother-in-law who cared so deeply for her welfare.
~~~~~

"Thank you for handling the young Earl's business while we are away," Evelyn told him for the third time.

She had shunned any contact with her peers since the funeral, except for a very few close friends. She could see now that she had made the right decision. There was no need of social connections with those who would probably judge and discourage her when she had the respect and affection of such a wonderful a man as her brother-in-law.

"It is my most honourable duty," he assured her. "One that I take with great seriousness."

"And you shall contact me if my son needs to do anything personally."

"Never fear. I shall contact you."

As she raised a glass to the journey which was set for the following morning, she was confident that the fortunes of the Oliver family were on the rise.

Chapter Five

June 5, 1815

"Charles, you must allow me to assist you. This is quite clearly providence that has led to your arrival at my estate and this happy circumstance," Lord Seldon remarked, riding his stallion at an agonizingly slow pace.

"You think too highly of providence. I am more inclined to think that a man creates his own luck in this world, and I am determined to change the course of my own," answered his companion.

"You have no secrets from me, Charles. I am well aware that you have been through a rough patch, and I have sworn as your closest friend to do all that is within my power to restore you to better circumstances."

"If it were any man but you with such blatant remarks, I would without a doubt have no choice but to defend my honor. But I know you are not moved by bragging or boasts. Tell me, is it as bad as that? Am I the laughing stock of society?" Charles looked at his friend.

"On the contrary, I am only aware of your particular set of unfortunate circumstances because of my own small investment in the tea company. My solicitor informed me that the civil unrest in the provinces of China has ruined many a noble Lord who invested heavily in that venture. I trust that you will not be the only Lord who suddenly awakens to find his circumstances greatly reduced."

"So, I am not alone. Well, I feel marginally better with that news. Now, you have admitted that you attribute my arrival to providence and to happy circumstance. By your words, I am failing to grasp the meaning of this riddle."

"You have arrived here in County Meath to purchase the finest racing horses that money can buy, am I correct?"

"Yes, I am not destitute yet. With my remaining funds, I have developed a scheme to invest in racing horses and increase my profit by wagers. I intend to make up for my loss in the tea company venture."

"When I tell you about the opportunity that awaits a man as intrepid as yourself, a man who is ready to take destiny in his own two hands, I am certain you will understand my meaning."

The stallion that Charles — Lord Haverly — was riding was having a difficult time maintaining such a slow trot. The stallion, like his owner, was far more inclined to traverse the green hills at a pace that would leave the devil himself frightened. Charles exerted a great amount of control over the powerful animal as he indulged his friend's taste for a slower, leisurely pace.

Charles hid his growing impatience. "Tell me, then. Make me wait no longer."

"The owner of the estate at Chapel House, the same owner of the fastest, prize-winning race horses in the realm, is none other than Lady Evelyn Oliver, Countess Montebank, a widow with a large fortune."

"William, you jest."

"On the contrary, she keeps to herself and is devoted to her children and horses. There is no rumor of her involvement with any gentleman of society."

"There must be a reason she shuns society. Is she old of years or not blessed with a fine countenance?"

"There again, you will find yourself in luck, my friend. She is quite young to be a widow, amicable, and handsome. I am uncertain why she would choose to exile herself to such a lonely place as County Meath, but there you are."

"Young and handsome, surely you are toying with me. That is a well-suited combination for what I require. As long as her estate is profitable, I would find myself content with a crone that looks handsome only on the darkest of nights." Lord Haverly spurred his horse to a gallop.

The animal had been waiting for the spurs to release him from the boredom of the trot. His powerful muscles sprang into action as Lord Haverly gripped the horse with his strong thigh muscles and smiled with a roguish air.

William spurred his own horse to a faster pace as he considered his friend's reckless demeanour.

He hoped that Lady Evelyn Oliver would be the answer to his friend's financial difficulties. Perhaps, she would not only prove to revive his economic status, but also be a settling influence in Charles's life. There was much to be wished for by the introduction of his friend to the wealthy young widow, and William suspected that Lady Evelyn would prove to be quite an asset.

~~~~~

Half hour later, William and Charles were once again riding side-by-side at a trot. Charles's horse was far less rebellious at the slower pace this time around since he'd had the opportunity to run at a full-out pace across several fields. Charles was pleased with the exertion and found his own temperament far more agreeable after the gallop. He patted the horse and was less fractious as his friend described the young widow that they were likely to meet that very afternoon.

"The estate that the widow calls home is not as grand as the estates you are accustomed to seeing in England, but I can assure you, this is not her only address. There is an estate in Yorkshire, a house in London, and more property than she could ever have use of," said William.

"It appears that you have done considerable research on the current status of the widow and her estate. It is a dozen wonders to me that you have not divorced your own wife to marry her."

William snorted.
~~~~~

"You are a character... But make no mistake, my wife came to our marriage quite wealthy, and I could do no better. My interest in the widow is purely driven by business concerns. I had, at one point, decided that I would make her an offer for her horse breeding venture. I was under the impression that she was a poor widow, and that all the property she owned was this simple country house. I am glad now that I did not make a fool of myself by making such an offer. It would have been looked on as an insult, I am certain."

"William, you devil. I believe I am beginning to see the true meaning of your sudden interest in my poor financial status and my present unmarried state. Yes, this is rather providential, is it not? If I were to woo this widow, marry her, and become the guardian of the estate for the young Earl you've told me about, I would be in a position to accept your offer for the sale of the business or accept you as partner in a joint scheme."

William nodded, with a look of pleasant contentment. "As you can tell, it would be advantageous to all parties concerned. You would finally have a wife worthy of your title to provide an heir to your lineage as is your duty as a Viscount. Your financial setbacks would be a distant memory, and I, your closest friend who has treated you as a brother, would finally have ownership of the most successful horse breeding operation in the country."

"And the widow, what would be her advantage?"

William smiled and answered, "Good sir, she would be the wife of a handsome man in society and would find herself unburdened of the tedium of managing an estate. She is a woman, after all. I am sure she finds it all too taxing."

Charles laughed as he considered his friend's well-thought out scheme. Yes, it was a good plan and one that he could make work. He had the reputation of being eligible and notoriously hard to catch among the ladies in London society. Surely in Ireland, a widow would easily succumb to his irresistible charms as had so many ladies before her.

Chapter Six

June 5, 1815

"My lady, there are two gentlemen who would like to have a look at the race horses. Shall I direct them to the stables and have Mr. Cleary show them around?" asked the footman.

Evelyn looked up from the open ledger on the desk in the small study. Ordinarily, she would have agreed, but today, she knew that Mr. Cleary was traveling to County Cork to have a look at a stud from the famed Callahan lineage. If the gentlemen wanted to see the horses that were available, she would have to do it herself.

"Have Liam bring the two stallions to the paddock, and I will meet them there momentarily," she answered as she returned to her ledger.

The door closed, and she was alone with her books and her thoughts. It had been nearly a year since she had arrived in Ireland, and her venture had proven to be better than she could have ever dreamed.

With the expertise of Mr. Cleary and the shrewd business acumen that she scarcely knew she possessed, they had built the reputation of the race horses at Chapel House to be the finest in the land.

This achievement had taken months of hard work and a few well-considered risks, but together, they had created a profitable business. She could not be happier with Mr. Cleary and had made him a part owner in the venture. It did not bother her that he was poorly educated and she was a Lady — his hard work and dedication was the heart of the success, and Evelyn was generous with her gratitude.

The business was successful, and so was her scheme to bring happiness and laughter back into her children's lives. Since they had been in Ireland, both children had benefited from the fresh air, the good, honest people, and the wholesome life on the estate. Her son was becoming a capable rider, and her daughter was showing signs of promise with her equestrian skills. It made Evelyn proud to see how easily her children had adapted to the quiet life of riding, music and their studies.

Back in England, her brother-in-law was handling all matters belonging to her young son. She knew that one day, she would have to return. Her son was titled, and she needed to allow him to grow into it. But not yet.

No, not yet. Things were going too well to disrupt everything by a move back home.

She closed the ledger and locked it in her desk. Soon, they should return to England at least for a visit, but for now, this green patch of Ireland was home.

It pained her to think of ever having to tear her children away from the place they had grown to love.

She left the study and walked through the hall of the Chapel House. It was not as imposing as her other properties. In truth, it reminded her of a hunting lodge and less of a country estate. But she adored her house; it offered her a haven away from the society that had proven so eager to pounce on rumours after her husband's untimely death.

The only complaint she had with her quiet life was the loneliness she felt. It was deep and far-reaching, and she dared not dwell on it for very long. She had several amiable companions, and she enjoyed her conversations with members of the local gentry, but there was a part of her that longed for romance and love. Living through the previous Valentine's Day had been particularly troublesome for her. When she had been courted by her late husband, he had made a big fuss of the holiday, spoiling her with flowers and even a verse he had penned himself. That verse still rested in her desk drawer. She used to read it on occasion after their marriage, but lately, she had not touched it. But the fact that it was there weighed on her. She missed him. But even more than that, she missed the companionship he had offered.

Thus, her first Valentine's Day as a widow was wearisome and difficult for her, the long hours draining her energy. She found herself yearning for things as they had been—which made her impatient with herself. With the success of her business venture and the happiness of her children, she was predisposed to believe that she should be content with what God had already given her and that asking for her own happiness would be far too much.

Greed was not in her nature, and she felt that requesting a new love or a shred of joy that she could call her own was truly risking the anger of God. She did not want to appear ungrateful after all of the blessings that her family had received, so she soldiered on in silence. These thoughts were forced to the recesses of her mind. She was aware of them like a dream that was remembered for a fleeting moment at daylight — she felt the pain of loneliness — but then in a moment, she stashed it away.

She walked to the paddock with these thoughts swirling like storm clouds through her mind. On that particular day, the loneliness was not to be denied as merely a dream. The only explanation she could offer was that it was nearly the anniversary of her arrival in Ireland, and the days that were marked on the calendar for remembrance often proved to be powerful reminders of the past and all that had changed since she'd left her home in England.

Liam, the assistant to Mr. Cleary, was a talented young man and was putting the two stallions through their paces for the gentlemen. Evelyn recognized His Grace, William Church, the Duke of Seldon. He was a pleasant man who owned the estate that bordered her own. He had an interest in horses and on occasion had purchased a racehorse from her.

The gentleman in the company of the Duke of Seldon, she did not recognize. She could not recall seeing him in London or in Ireland. He was dressed in the latest fashion and his carriage suggested a gentleman with an aristocratic upbringing, yet she could not place his face — although she found it to be pleasant and his build to be comely.

She scoffed at herself as she became aware that she was brushing the errant dark strands of her hair into place as she approached the gentlemen. It was the action of a young girl, and she was far too old to be behaving as a maiden just introduced into society.

"Your Grace, it is always good to see you at Chapel House," she greeted the Duke of Seldon.

"Lady Evelyn, as always, the pleasure is all mine. May I have the honor of introducing to you a gentleman I know well? Mr. Charles Harris, the Viscount of Haverly. And Charles, this is Lady Evelyn Oliver, the Countess of Montebank."

"Countess Montebank, it is indeed a pleasure to make your acquaintance," said Charles as he greeted Evelyn with a warm smile.

The Viscount bowed graciously and kissed her hand. It had been far too long since she had felt the lips of a man brush her skin, and she tried to concentrate on what to say next. However, she found her mind filled with thoughts too sensitive to acknowledge as she gazed into the deep blue eyes of the handsome visitor.

"Viscount, the pleasure is all mine," she finally uttered and then felt the color rise to her cheeks as she regretted saying the word *pleasure*. What if she had given him the wrong impression and would now be considered a coquette or a flirt?

"Lady Evelyn, William speaks highly of your horses here at Chapel House. I have always had an interest in racing and would like to make an initial investment in a good stallion or gelding for the steeplechase — a real winner. What is your suggestion?"

"Winners are born to be winners. You must have good breeding in the horse for it to perform admirably. Once you have located a well-bred horse, the training is vital. After the training, it is entirely dependent on the relationship between the rider and the horse. But naturally, if your horse does not have the correct temperament or the ambition to win, then all is lost, and you might as well be purchasing a mule."

Charles grinned with appreciation. "It seems that Lord Seldon was perfectly correct in his praise. You do understand the subtleties necessary for the success of a racing horse. I require a horse that can perform well at Newmarket."

"The two horses Liam has shown you have both proven themselves at the point-to-point races in Cork and Meath. They are both of champion bloodlines and will make fine race horses. I can recommend either horse equally as they are both competitive, and neither horse is prone to nervousness or anxiety."

"You are familiar with the races at Newmarket, Lady Oliver?" asked Charles.

"I am. One of my favorite racehorses, Templeton's Pride, competes there on occasion, always with winning results. He is one of our horses, bred here at Chapel House," she answered with satisfaction.

"I have wagered on Templeton's Pride from time to time, and I find myself never disappointed by his performance. So, he is one of yours, do you say? I am impressed," Charles replied.

Evelyn looked at the Viscount and was overcome with a girlish sense of self-consciousness.

She began to wonder if she had spoken too profusely or was unladylike in her appearance as she gave details about her racehorses. It was not common for a Countess to conduct business and to speak about financial matters like a gentleman; but in Ireland, the rules for polite society were much more relaxed.

Nevertheless, Evelyn felt nervous that he would think her too worldly or too business-like.

She found herself doubting what she was saying, what she was doing, and how she looked while she doing it. It was most inconvenient, and she knew all of it was due to the appearance of the dashing Lord Haverly at Chapel House.

~~~~~

Evelyn was not the only party experiencing an unexpected reaction to the introduction. Charles had expected the widow to be plain, soft-spoken, and easily charmed by his smile and his attentions. He was taken completely by surprise by the confidence that he discovered in abundance in Lady Evelyn Oliver.

Not only did he discover a poised woman, sure of herself and her business, but he discovered a woman so handsome and with such personality that he was captivated.

Her dark curls were pulled back from her face in a bun, with several loose stands framing her heart-shaped face. He longed to reach out and touch the soft curls and gaze into the bewitching green eyes that so coolly assessed his own eyes under dark lashes.
~~~~~

It was rare that he found himself unable to speak or unsure of what to say in the presence of a lady, but Evelyn was in a category entirely all her own. Her quick wit, captivating charm, and stunning emerald eyes were a potent combination, and Charles wondered if love at first sight was truly possible. In the past, he had considered it to be only found in poetry and songs sung by madrigals.

"Your Grace, Lord Haverly, I am confident that you will find either horse suited to your purposes. You may take as long as you require to consider which one you would like to purchase. Liam can answer any of your questions. Until then, I will be in the study."

"Lady Oliver, do you mean to tell me that you intend to leave us? What if I require your expert opinion?" asked the Duke.

"Your Grace, you flatter me. I have no doubt that you know far more about racehorses than I or Liam could ever hope to," she answered.

"What if we asked you to remain with us because we value not only your opinion but your company as well?" asked the Viscount.

"Your Grace, is your companion always so bold in the presence of Ladies?" she asked the Duke, suppressing her smile.

"I am afraid so. Charles does not hold with the conventions of polite society. It is a wonder that I am able to allow him to accompany me at all, as evidenced by his behavior here. I do heartily apologize," the Duke said with light humor.

"I suppose I may make an exception this one time. If you would enjoy the company of an old widow woman, I will be happy to oblige, *if* that will ensure that we have a deal," she answered with a laugh.

"Lady Evelyn, that is one if your best attributes. Your business sense is unrivalled and so is your wit. I only wish that more Ladies in London would act as you," the Duke responded.

"In London, they would consider my behaviour to be unladylike, and I would have to wholeheartedly agree with them. I tried to be a Lady before my husband died, and I found it to be somewhat confining. Now, I am not certain that I would ever be able to go back to a life filled with rules and narrow expectations," she commented in a moment of unexpected candour.

"My compliments, Lady Oliver. I have never met a woman who knew her own mind as well. I believe that you and I have much in common, I find those same rules to be far too narrow for my own liking, and the women in society to be dull and predictable." The Viscount gave her a roguish wink.

~~~~~

Evelyn had surprised herself with her own candour in the presence of the Viscount — a man she found to be irresistibly attractive. He had a devilish smirk, blond hair, and beguiling blue eyes that were as deep as cool pools of water on a summer day. When he spoke, she tried to remember to concentrate on his words and not become lost in the depths of his hypnotic eyes.
~~~~~

She hoped that she had not spoken too honestly and incurred the poor opinion of the Lord Haverly.

~~~~~

June 10, 1815

Any worry that Evelyn may have had concerning the Viscount's opinion of her were laid quickly to rest. In the days that followed their meeting, Lord Haverly paid a call to her every day, and always for the purpose of socializing.

He enjoyed going for long rides, and one afternoon, he had arranged a picnic at the estate of his friend, the Duke of Seldon. Another day, there was a carriage ride to examine the ancient ruins for which County Meath was known. The day after that found them on a promenade in the village and a visit to a church dating back over eight hundred years.

Evelyn discovered his company and companionship to be intoxicating. She had not realized how much she missed the easy conversation of a peer. How refreshing it was to be in the company of a gentleman from whom she did not have to keep at a proper distance, due to differences in class or education. It was invigorating. However, she did wish she was not enjoying the attentions of the Viscount so much, for it would be far more difficult to return to her life of self-exile after his departure.

~~~~~

Lord Haverly enjoyed Evelyn's irreverent humour and intellect. Women of his acquaintance were often beautiful creatures that were accomplished in music and fashion. It was an unexpected surprise to find a Lady living so far away from society, who represented all that was desirable in a proper Lady, plus the independence of a woman who behaved with a certain strength, as if she were not born to the upper classes. All of this resided in Lady Evelyn, and her handsome visage and natural grace gave him more cause to give her attention.

Even if he were not in a dire financial situation, he would have longed to spend time with so handsome a Lady, as well as attempt, through every ploy he knew, to make her fall hopelessly, madly in love with him. His motives that had once been far from admirable, were now only fuelled by the purest of intentions. When she spoke, and especially when she laughed, he could feel his heart slipping farther out of his grasp and beyond his own ability to rein in. It was inconceivable to him, but he was falling desperately in love with the Countess, and it was not motivated by greed.

His friend, the Duke of Seldon, was far more cynical in his assessment of the current state of affairs between the Countess and Charles, and he commented on it frequently and publicly in the good-natured fashion of old friends and brothers.

"I say, Charles, you have done me proud, yes, indeed. A few more weeks of your romantic administrations, and I believe that we will be celebrating your wedding to the lovely Countess, and I will be congratulating myself on my new business venture," remarked William at breakfast one day.

Charles shifted uncomfortably in his chair.

"William, that may have once been the case, but now I find myself driven by other emotions. Such feelings which, I must confess, are difficult to admit."

"You don't have to convince me, my friend. All you have to do is convince Lady Evelyn. I believe she is rather taken with you and is likely to welcome your proposal with gladness and a positive answer."

"That may prove to be true, but I want to win her fairly. She deserves a man who appreciates her intellect and her beauty. She is a remarkable woman, and I want her to know that I admire all that she has accomplished."

"My good man, if you continue speaking like a lovesick fool, you will even have me believing that you love her. I daresay, if you were not a gentleman, you would have made a very impressive actor on the boards."

~~~~~

Nearby, but out of sight, a footman moved unnoticed around the stately house of the Duke. He was always alert, paying attention to the wants and desires of his master, as well as to his words.

The master who believed he had secrets in a house with a full staff was a fool. The men and women who brought the tea and made the beds were always in attendance, and often the only witnesses to conversations that were presumed to be private.
~~~~~

Unfortunately, that was the case on that particular morning, a fact that would reveal itself to be catastrophic in the near future.

ARIETTA RICHMOND, GRACE AUSTEN, ISABELLA THORNE,
KATHERINE KEATS AND ALYCE HEALEY

162

Chapter Seven

August 17, 1815

The summer had gone by quickly, and Evelyn could scarcely believe her good fortune. It was a dream to be in love with a gentleman as accomplished and romantic as the Viscount. He had courted her with a passion not found in youth and only to be appreciated in later years.

There were picnics and quiet dinners, conversations in the garden and the reading of poetry in the library. Evelyn could not remember a time in her life when she felt more alive and loved, even when she had been married to the Earl.

She oft found herself remembering the Earl and her marriage to him, and it did give her room for pause. Her marriage to the Earl had been voluntary, yet it had the feeling of an arrangement.

He had been six years her senior and had proposed to her after meeting with her only three times. She was but a girl of ten and nine when she'd met him, and she was his wife at the age of twenty.

He had been a kind and courteous husband and she loved him, but compared to the feelings that she had for the Viscount, she wondered if her feelings towards the Earl were truly love or solely an amicable companionship. She found some degree of guilt whenever she laughed at the Viscount's jokes and whenever he would steal a kiss from her in their favorite picnic place, by the stream under the shade of an ancient oak tree.

She spoke of her guilt to no-one, yet she had the feeling that the Viscount would understand if she shared the sentiment with him. His feelings and thoughts were so in line with her own thinking that she was sure that all the love stories and lines of poetry she'd ever read and heard were telling the truth.

The change in her disposition had been noticed by her maid, Charlotte, and by her friend, Mr. Cleary. Both were delighted that their mistress had finally found happiness after such tragedy.

As summer was coming to a close, Evelyn dreaded the news that she was certain was inevitable. Lord Haverly would soon be returning to London. He had purchased both of her promising race horses, and during the summer, both she and Mr. Cleary had offered him all possible assistance in the training of them. The horses were fine and capable and would undoubtedly make a remarkable showing at Newmarket. Evelyn almost wished to be there for their debut, but she shunned going back to the society she had been so eager to leave.

~~~~~

The Duke of Seldon was hosting a dinner, on the night of the seventeenth, for the local gentry in the county. It was traditional, and marked the end of the season in Ireland. In the coming months, the Duke would be bound for his hunting lodge in Scotland and then on to London for the winter. Evelyn tried to remain in good spirits, but she knew that her summer of love and romance was rapidly coming to an end, much like the season itself.

That evening, with the assistance of Charlotte, she dressed in her finest evening gown. It had been well over a year since her husband had passed away, and her widow's mourning attire had been retired. She was now able to wear other colors, and select jewelry in good taste. Her gown was a dark midnight blue that gave her ivory skin a glow of alabaster. Charlotte chose silver jewelry and combs that would complement her mistress's dark hair and the dark silk of the gown. The effect was ethereal.

"My lady, you look like a fairy princess, you do. I believe this land agrees with you."

"Oh Charlotte, I think so, too. Tell me, do you miss England?"

"Not so very much. Although, I do confess I miss the fine cooking of Yorkshire. There is no substitute for a good pudding or hot cross bun." She smiled.

"I should say that makes two of us," Evelyn agreed as Charlotte helped with her gloves and wrap.
~~~~~

Evelyn tried to smile despite the feeling that something magical was coming to an end. She walked down the stairs to the carriage waiting outside. She was glad that she was alone on the ride to the estate of her neighbour, the Duke of Seldon. It gave her a moment to compose herself as tears threatened to well up and spill down her cheeks.

Her carriage arrived at half past eight. The sun had set, and the darkness was illuminated by the warm glow of candles in the windows and lanterns held by the footmen in attendance. Her conveyance came to a stop at the steps, and she was helped out by a footman in full livery. He smiled at her, although strictly speaking, he was not supposed to. She recognized him as the younger brother of Mr. Cleary and returned his smile.

She was received in the drawing room by the Duke of Seldon and his wife. The Viscount was soon at her side, and she found that she could let go of her sorrow and apprehension in his presence. He led her to a settee on the opposite side of the room, away from the other guests. There, they could be alone and discuss all their favorite subjects without fear of being overheard. Tonight, the topic was one that was far more serious than their usual subjects.

"Evelyn, I must bring up a regrettable fact, of which I am sure you are already aware. I must return to England soon. The horses must race at Newmarket in September."

Evelyn looked down at the carpet and tried to think of words that would convey the depth of her emotion. She looked at the face of the man she loved and said, "I am grateful for the weeks you have shared with me this summer. It is more than I could have wished for."

His eyes were intent on hers. "It has been more than I could have hoped. I was not expecting to fall in love with you."

At his words, her pulse increased. She leaned toward him. "Nor I with you. I understand that you must return to England. I will always treasure this summer. You made me feel what I had only experienced in the pages of books. I will miss you and always remember you." She turned away to hide her tears. Why was he making no effort to make their relationship permanent? Why didn't he ask for her hand in marriage? Had she misread the depth of his affection?

"Evelyn, I have no desire to be apart from you, but I must return to England in a few days. I have no right to ask this, but I would be honoured if you would consent to become my wife. I am aware that my title is not as prestigious as that of an Earl, but my heart is true, and I believe, so is yours."

Her breath caught in her throat. He had done it. He had asked for her hand in marriage. She smiled at him through her tears. "My dear Charles, I will marry you. I accept your offer with my whole heart."

Charles fairly gleamed. He grabbed her hand and brought it to his lips. Then he pressed her hand to his chest, holding it tightly. "My darling, when I return from England we can be married. Will you promise to wait for me?"

"I will wait for you." She gazed at him lovingly. "Will you return before Christmas?"

"Yes, my darling, you can count on it."

The Viscount brought her hand once more to his lips.

The same electricity that Evelyn had felt when his lips grazed her skin that first time in June was still there and even stronger. Evelyn wanted to throw herself into a wild embrace with him, but she was aware that the drawing room filled with dinner guests would be scandalized by such behaviour.

After his proposal, the remainder of the dinner was a time of quiet bliss. Rather than lamenting the end of summer, Evelyn had the momentous pleasure of dreaming about her coming wedding. The children would be happy with the news as they had both expressed their admiration for the Viscount on several occasions. It felt to Evelyn as though her family had finally found their way out of the darkness.

She owed everything to this beloved man.

After the dinner came to a close, the Viscount escorted her to her waiting carriage. He promised to see her and the children once more before his ship set sail. She would miss him terribly, but the aching was dulled by the tremendous joy of the promise of their future.

Chapter Eight

September 2, 1815

During the days following the dinner, the elation of Evelyn's pending nuptials eased the sorrow of the Viscount's departure. Her optimism and unbridled joy were great. She could recall feeling that way only twice before in her life, and in each instance, it was marked by the birth of her children.

That particular morning had been spent in the happiest of preparations as she and Charlotte sat down with a dressmaker to order a wedding dress suitable for the second marriage of a woman in her very early thirties. It had been a delightful endeavour, and Evelyn carried that pleasure with her as she met later with Mr. Cleary in his office at the stables.

By the strained look on his face, she could tell right away that something was amiss.

"Mr. Cleary, what is wrong? Is your family in good health?"

"My Lady, all of my family are in good health, and before you ask, so are our horses. Never better."

"What seems to be the trouble? You do not appear to be as I know you to be, jovial and in good spirits."

"I regret that I may be the harbinger of ill will to your ladyship."

"I don't see how that is possible unless you tell me that you have an interest in leaving Chapel House."

"No, my lady. Although, you may wish it to be so after speaking with my younger brother."

"Your younger brother? Yes, I remember him. He is a footman with the Duke, is he not?"

"He was. But with the Duke of Seldon returning to England, he has found himself in need of new employment. I suggested inquiring here first."

"There will always be room for another Cleary in my employ."

"That is very good of you, my lady, but he brings news that you will want to hear, but you will not be the happier for it."

"Then where is the man, that he may speak with me?"

"He is helping Liam in the stables. I will fetch him."

Evelyn could not imagine what could be said by a footman employed at her neighbour's estate that would matter to her in the least.

But she decided to listen as she did not want to be rude to any family member of the man she had come to depend on for the successful running of her horse breeding venture.

Mr. Cleary returned to his office accompanied by his brother.

"Go on, Owen. Tell her what you told me. She has a right to hear it from you."

Mr. Cleary's brother, Owen, bowed in her presence and removed his hat.

"My lady."

"Owen Cleary. It is always a pleasure to speak with one of Mr. Cleary's family. I understand that you would like a position here at Chapel House. Is that correct?"

"My Lady, it is. I am trained as a footman, but I can help with the horses if you prefer."

"I could use either. I understand you have news that you believe will be of interest to me."

The man looked at his brother, and Evelyn could see quite clearly that he was not accustomed to speaking candidly to anyone but family.

"Go on, Owen," Mr. Cleary repeated. "She's not like the rest of them. You can tell her what you told me."

Owen nodded his head and looked down at the floor as he began to tell Evelyn of the conversation he had overheard in the breakfast room one day back in June. As he spoke, Evelyn could feel the color drain from her face, and she felt weak. Was it possible that the man she had agreed to marry was only interested in her to improve his grim financial state and to hand her business venture over to the Duke?

It was too horrible to be believed, yet she recalled that the Viscount had seemed eager to return to London to the horse races.

Her legs turned shaky, and she feared she would faint in front of them both.

"I am dreadfully sorry," Mr. Cleary said, his brows drawn together in a frown.

Evelyn inhaled sharply and worked to square her shoulders.

"Thank you, Owen, for bringing this to light." Her voice wavered, but she forged ahead. "I have but one question. Why did you not speak of this to anyone at an earlier date? Why wait until now to reveal such treachery?"

"My lady, I was employed by the Duke of Seldon. I couldn't risk losing my position if it became known that I spoke out of turn regarding my Lord's private affairs. I am telling you now because I regret my earlier silence. You don't deserve such deceit."

Evelyn reached out to brace herself against the wall. She swallowed hard.

"Owen, you have my gratitude. If you will be so kind as to hear the details and salary information from your brother, you may start immediately."

"Thank you, my lady." He gave his brother a sorrowful yet relieved smile and left the office.

Evelyn looked at Mr. Cleary and without having to say a word, he understood what it was she sought.

"My lady, Owen is a good lad, always has been. If he's told you what he heard, I would wager every penny I ever made that it's the truth. I am terribly sorry that you have to hear bad news from my family."

A deep trembling moved through Evelyn's stomach. She felt ready to retch. But she had survived the death of her husband, and she would survive this. She bit her lip until she tasted metal. And then she spoke.

"I would rather hear such ill tidings from those like yourself."

She looked about wildly as if trying to find somewhere to hide. Mr. Cleary looked at her with compassion.

She gazed at him.

"Now, if there's nothing else. I will take my leave," she said, her voice forced.

"No, my lady, there is nothing that cannot wait. I only wish your well-being. Even I was taken in by the gentleman, and I pride myself on spotting the ne'er do wells."

Evelyn gave him a shaky nod and returned to the house. She slowly walked up the stairs to her bedroom, and with each step, her legs felt heavier. She threw herself on her bed and sobbed into her pillow. How could this be true? It *couldn't* be, could it?

She shouldn't simply believe what one person shared with her. She should check into it further. Wasn't this just gossip? And didn't she detest gossip and all it entailed?

Charlotte knocked on her door, and Evelyn feigned a headache and expressed a wish to remain alone in the solitude of her room. Charlotte acquiesced and left her.

Evelyn sat up and wiped her eyes. All she wanted to do was to face the Viscount. Ask him for herself. Force him to reveal his true character. Maybe, there was a mistake. Maybe the lad had misheard.

But somewhere, deep in her heart of hearts, she knew he hadn't. Young Owen Cleary had reported exactly what he had heard.

It was early evening when Evelyn decided she was strong enough to do what had to be done. It was time to write a letter to the Viscount which would certainly extinguish all hope for her future happiness. She sat down at her writing desk and with quill to paper, she composed a heartfelt letter detailing her feelings and the betrayal that she felt at the hands of the Viscount and his friend, the Duke. Never again, she vowed, would she entertain thoughts of romance or friendship with someone she hardly knew.

She closed the letter with her seal and rang for Charlotte. Her heart was broken and the pain she felt was so striking, so horrible to endure, that she swore it would serve as a reminder to never look to her own happiness again.

The children would have to be told something, and she vowed to confess the loss of the Viscount in due time, but for the present, she would wait as long as was possible.

Chapter Nine

December 6, 1815

It had been nearly three months since Evelyn penned the letter to the Viscount, expressing her feelings of betrayal and bitter disappointment. There were several letters that came to her in response in the weeks that followed, but she never once opened them to read the contents. She had no interest in the empty flattery and easy lies of a man so gifted in the art of deceit. His letters had all ended up in the fire, where they went up in smoke and turned to ash.

As dreadful as she felt, she was glad on one account. He had *not* succeeded in marrying her and ruining the life she had worked so very hard to build in Ireland. She decided that it would have been far worse to have been the victim of such betrayal after she was married and could not legally speak up for herself or her business venture.

She wrote to her solicitor in England for the assurance that all was well with the estate, the properties, and the investments.

It was with glad tidings that she received his letter on the feast of St. Nicholas. He assured her that all was better than could be expected. The estate was sound, and her son's inheritance was secure.

Evelyn had heard from her brother-in-law and knew that she had to schedule a visit back home soon. Her son needed some time with his uncle to begin learning his duties as Earl. But she pushed the thought away, as she had done so frequently of late. She wasn't ready to face life in England.

The staff spent the better part of the holiday attending church and preparing the dining room for the feast. This was the traditional beginning of the Christmas, and Evelyn had given the staff permission to have their own feast in the servants' hall after her family had enjoyed a feast of their own.

In the three months that had passed since she last saw the Viscount, she had learned to live with the dull ache that never left her heart. She tried in vain to shed the anger that lit like a flame at the mention of Charles's name or anything about him. The love she had once felt for him was pushed aside. She shrivelled from humiliation at being taken in by so talented a cad. It was as his friend had said - he would be suited for a life on the boards, where he could charm many a female patron from her riches.

That night, she invited Mr. Cleary and his family to join her and the children. Mr. Cleary often behaved more like a brother to her and an uncle to her children, Arthur and Mary. The Cleary family arrived after sundown, and she was glad to have their company so that she would not have to spend a dinner alone with only her children while her heart still ached, and her nerves were still raw and on edge.

The Cleary family was cheerful and made good company, and Evelyn smiled, despite the pain she felt.

After dinner, Evelyn, her children, and their guests assembled in the drawing room. Evelyn had made certain that her guests had presents to open, and her children were positively enamoured of the gifts she had chosen for them — a new doll for Mary and a wooden boat and atlas for Arthur. Mrs. Cleary had just given Evelyn the gift of a piece of personally made lace, when the footman appeared in the drawing room and announced the arrival of an unexpected guest.

Evelyn sucked in her breath when the Viscount darkened the doorway. Arthur and Mary ran to him and greeted him in the innocent way that children do, without suspicion and with an exuberance only equaled by Evelyn's mortification. She had never told her children the particulars about why the Viscount was no longer to be part of the family.

Mr. Cleary looked at Evelyn and seemed to be waiting for her to give him a sign, an indication of what action he should perform. Evelyn shook her head and stood. She walked to the Viscount and in a voice trembling with indignation, she spoke, "Viscount. What are you doing here?"

"I have tried to send letters to you, and you have not replied to a single one. I suppose I deserve that," he said quietly.

"You deserve far worse," she said, a hiss in her voice.

Mr. Cleary cleared his throat, his fists at the ready.

Evelyn looked at her children and her guests.

"If you will excuse me and my unexpected guest, I will return shortly."

Evelyn left the drawing room, and she could hear Charles's footsteps behind her. She led him to her small study and closed the door before she completely lost her composure. She whirled around, facing him, her anger burning through her stomach.

"What is the meaning of this outrage? Was betraying me and my business not enough? You now come here to my house during the feast of St. Nicholas to offer me more insult?"

"I cannot deny that is how it appears, but it is not the truth." Charles's voice was solid, and he gazed at her steadily, without falter.

"How can you offer me proof otherwise? You were going to rob my son of his fortune, and your friend was going to rob me and Mr. Cleary of our business. You've already robbed me of my heart and destroyed my faith in you. What is now left? To break the hearts of my children?"

An urgency covered his face. "Please, Evelyn if you would only listen to me... If you had only read one letter that I sent to you, you would understand. Much to my shame, I can't deny my original devilish plan, but in time, I grew to love you. I could no longer go through with so reprehensible an action."

But Evelyn hardly heard him. "You must have lost what little remains of your fortune if you have the nerve to come to me now. Or you must believe me incapable of denying my feelings. Well, you underestimate me. I am acquainted with tragedy and heartbreak, and I've proven myself strong. I ask you to leave. You are no longer welcome in my home."

"Evelyn, I have something for you, something you ought to see, before you make a pronouncement of such gravity."

"What could possibly interest me? What could you possess that I would care to observe?" But she felt herself weakening, such was the effect this man had on her. She trembled and stiffened her back.

"This," he said as he handed her a document.

She snatched it from him and walked to the fireside. She read the words and figures on the page. The document had been prepared by her very own solicitor. It proved that the Viscount had paid his debts in full. There was another letter proving that the winnings he had incurred at Newmarket had been considerable to say the least. It appeared that Charles was no longer destitute, but was in fact, rather wealthy. Tears burned the back of her eyes as she read the words.

She gaped at him.

"What does this mean? You must know that I will be sending a letter to Mr. Sloan requesting confirmation of these claims."

"You're welcome to do so. What it means is that your horses are famous, and that I no longer need your money. Yet, here I am in Ireland on St. Nicholas Day to once again ask you to reconsider my offer of marriage."

Her nostrils flared, and her chest tightened.

"How am I ever to trust you? How can I marry you when you intend to give my business to the Duke?"

Charles drew in a long breath. His eyes didn't leave her face.

"I have a proposal created by your own Mr. Sloan as to that regard. Should we marry… you would remain the guardian of all of your property. It would be in trust for your son and would never be touched by me. *Ever.* Mr. Sloan will attest to my wishes not to take even one scrap of property or money from you."

Tears spilled down Evelyn's cheeks. Was he telling her the truth? Could she believe him?

"I want to trust you," she muttered, feeling suddenly dizzy with indecision. Oh, how she wanted to trust him. She sniffed and wiped at her eyes.

"I still love you." She paused. "But I don't know how I will ever see you in the way I did before."

"You do not have to." His brows drew together. "I am so sorry. So very, very sorry. Just say you will marry me — that you will give me a chance… And then give me an opportunity to earn your trust once more. If I must wait a month or a year, I will wait for you. I will endeavour each and every day to create trust born from my actions and my devotion. If and when you say yes on that long-awaited day in the church, there will be no uncertainty, but only the assurance of my love for you."

He walked to the fireside and stood before her, bowing his head. "I humbly apologize and ask for your forgiveness."

He looked up then and took her hand in his. "Lady Evelyn Oliver, will you deign to be my wife, to allow me to earn your trust with acts of chivalry and honor, to win your love now and every day of our lives together?"

Evelyn looked at the face of the man she had tried so desperately to purge from her heart and her mind. Dare she try again? He was offering to prove his love for her. And there seemed to be no reason he would lie anymore.

She would make him earn her hand, make him deserve her. Unexpectedly, she felt sure it would come. And so, on that evening, she bestowed upon him the single best Christmas gift that she had the power to give.

She answered him, "Yes. Lord Haverly, I will marry you. I cannot deny my love for you. I offer you my hand and my promise that I will marry you — but only after you have proven your devotion."

Lord Haverly gathered her in his arms. His lips found hers, and his kiss was warm and sweet. As he held her tightly in his arms, tears of joy hovered on her lashes.

Lord Haverly kissed them away and whispered, "I love you, dear Evelyn. You have given me the greatest present I could ever hope to receive. I promise that I will earn your love every day of the rest of our lives."

Her eyes misted over once again.

"I have hopes of winning you by Valentine's Day. Wouldn't it be lovely to be joined together then? On the most romantic day of the year?"

She stared into his deep blue eyes. How had he known how much Valentine's Day meant to her? He couldn't have known. But there he was - offering his love and devotion and commitment to her on Valentine's Day.

Evelyn closed her eyes and relaxed fully into his arms. It was not as she had dreamed it would be, but standing in his embrace was far better than any book or poem or Valentine's verse. It was real, and it was true. She tilted her head up to his, and they kissed once again.

The End

Thank you for reading *Lord Haverly's Valentine Pursuit*! **Are you wondering what to read next?**

Why not read *The Duke's Unwilling Bride?*

You'll find a preview just after the 'About the Author' section.

About the Author

Grace Austen loves everything Regency. Sometimes, she feels she was born in the wrong century! When she fell in love with Greg Austen and took his last name in marriage, she was delighted and honoured to be sharing the name of the most famous Regency author of all.

Immersing herself in the world of Regency Romance is Grace's favorite thing to do. In her "real" life, she loves to spend time with her husband and three children. They have a little Malti-poo puppy who enjoys a good cuddle on anyone's lap - she's not fussy!

When not writing and caring for her family, Grace loves to explore antique shops, garden, talk long walks by the sea, and read! She loves to watch movies and munch on popcorn with her husband, and she would never turn away a piece of dark chocolate! Visit her at: http://www.GraceAusten.com

Or on Facebook at :

https://www.facebook.com/AuthorGraceAusten/

Get the News First!

If you **love Regency Romance**, go to:

http://www.GraceAusten.com

to hear about all **New Grace Austen Romance Releases!**
I will let you know as soon as they become available!

Thank you, Friends! I appreciate your kind support. You are my motivation.

Much love,

Grace Austen

Other Books from Grace Austen

Four Captivated Hearts!

Romance Bonanza!

Regency Romances, sweet, clean and inspirational!

GET ALL FOUR Romances at a Nice Discount! Friends, Get these 4 COMPLETE romances in one volume. And at one great bargain price!

Escaping the Vicar

Amelia's father was in trouble. To save him from ruin, she agrees to be courted by the odious vicar, Mister Prior. Dutifully, she shoves aside her love for Mister Halberd, sacrificing everything for her family. The vicar swoops in like a vulture to claim his prize, but he doesn't count on Mister Halberd's plan to rescue Amelia. But Mister Halberd's time is running out, and Amelia's engagement seems written in stone. And then, there is still the matter of her father's secret debts...

The Duke's Daughter's Portrait

Amelia Gale has one purpose: Find a rich husband. She dons the finest gowns and makes herself available at every society ball. And she is miserable. Escaping into side rooms becomes normal. One evening, the Duke of Reinbrook is lurking near the fireplace with his own dark secret. The two spar. Fate takes over, and Amelia ends up painting his young daughter's portrait. Watching Amelia deal with his motherless daughter brings a salve to the Duke's heart. When Amelia's father makes a devastating arrangement for her future, she finds herself in need of the Duke to rescue her. But, will he?

Teaching the Earl's Daughter

After her father's devastating investment, Prudence feels compelled to take the position of music instructor to The Earl of Pembroke's daughter, Annabel. While Prudence grows to love her young charge, she has continual clashes with The Earl. He is insufferable, and Prudence decides she must leave. When Annabel grows deathly ill, she puts off her resignation. In the turmoil, she discovers the true reason for The Earl's harsh treatment. Will the truth free Prudence to see The Earl for who he is?

Lord Henry's Missing Fiancé

Lady Teresa's banishment to America has ended. On the ship back to Devonshire, she meets Lord Henry. Sparks fly, but unfortunately, he's engaged to Lady Eleanor. Teresa's father forces her into a courtship with the odious Colonel Wertford. When Lord Henry's fiancé goes missing, both Lord Henry and Lady Teresa find much more than either of them bargained for.

Rejecting the Earl

Margaret Cooper will stop at nothing to marry The Earl of Canark. His wealth and title will secure her family's future. However, she doesn't foresee the attentions of Mr. Fitzgerald, the lowly son of a knight. The man infuriates her with his bold and cunning wit. When the Earl disappears, Margaret risks everything to find him. Mr. Fitzgerald interferes. She finds out the shocking truth, and it's not what she thought it was...

Vexing the Earl

Dorothy Evans sails to England to claim her inheritance of the lavish estate of Moorway. She discovers a journal and reads of her aunt's doomed love affair with the Earl of Wainright. When Dorothy meets his son, she determines to seek revenge. But she doesn't count on the young Earl's dashing good looks and maddening charm. Will her revenge ruin every chance for happiness and love?

The Duke's Dangerous Love

In this clean and wholesome Regency Romance, Amy Chippering is plunged into the dark world of Kall Signon, the future Duke of Kent. Innocent of what his ominous secret really means, she allows herself to be swept away with his gorgeous good looks... Is there anyone to save her?

ARIETTA RICHMOND, GRACE AUSTEN, ISABELLA THORNE,
KATHERINE KEATS AND ALYCE HEALEY

Regency Romance

Here is Your Preview of

The Duke's Unwilling Bride

Stella Moorland is disenchanted with social privilege. Harbouring noble, if misguided, notions, she falls in love with a servant. Oslo Riley, a young Duke, tries to warn her away, claiming he knows the servant's true character. But Stella will not be swayed. She is certain the Duke is simply flaunting his privilege...

Stella Moorland was one year shy of twenty years old when she found herself the last of her sisters as yet unwed. She was the fourth of four girls in the family, and her sisters were all happily married to titled men. Stella loved her sisters dearly and held them in the highest esteem, but she could never quite see eye-to-eye with them. She did not relish the idea of marrying a man simply because he was "suitable" as their mother would say.

"But Stella," her sister Beth said to her right after she became affianced. "A title is merely a product of birth. It does not mean you cannot love your husband. Robert means everything to me. You saw our courtship and how tender he was. The cold fact of his title does not take away from his genuine affection, or mine."

"What if I were to feel genuine affection for a servant boy or a boot black?"

Her sister gasped, obviously hoping very much that Stella was making a joke. "Stella, you don't mean…?"

"No, sister, there is no one special in mind. I only meant it as a hypothetical, but your horror is answer enough. Oh Beth, I do love you, but I'm afraid we are not of the same mind."

"At least, you can give the men that mother picks out for you a chance, Stella. Promise me that much. Swear to give them a chance into your heart. That is all I can ask of you."

"I will give them a chance," Stella said, but deep inside, she wasn't sure that she would.

In truth, Stella had walled-off her heart to any man who did not meet her exaggerated idea of worth.

She liked to think of herself as an open-minded woman, but she had an intense prejudice against her own kind. Stella spent a great deal of time reading novels, and in nearly all of them, she came upon hard truths about her class of people—they were often the villains. It was the servants and the schoolteachers who were kindly and good people.

Stella suspected she was taking this to heart in a way that was unhealthy, but she allowed her fantasy to continue. She liked to think she was a person who saw all of her fellow humans in an equal manner, but this was distinctly untrue. However, not in the way one would think.

Stella saw her societal lessers in a brighter, better light than those who were of the landed gentry. What Stella did not consider — what she refused to consider — was that she was not doing those "common" folks any favor.

In her assumption of their innocence and purity, Stella was attributing an identity to the working class that was not their own and was not a sweeping truth in any sense of the word.

In her own way, Stella was acting in the same manner as those of her own class who so infuriated her.

In her glossing over of the common humanity of servants and cooks, she was no better than those who looked down on them as subhuman. Stella dehumanized the working class by imagining them as some kind of celestially-perfect beings.

Of course, as a young lady of ten-and-nine years, Stella could perhaps be forgiven for her false notions of the world, but that did not prevent her from learning things the hard way.

"You will, of course, need to attend," Lady Moorland said to Stella calmly as she stirred milk into her tea.

"Mother?"

"The Ball. Have you not been listening to me?"

No, Stella had not been listening to her mother at all. Her mind was still fully within the pages of the Fielding novel she had been reading in her window nook behind her bedroom curtains.

"Must I?"

"Stella, do you want to live here with your father and me forever? We must find you a suitable match, and the way to do that is through social means. You are a beautiful young woman, but not so beautiful that you put off a beacon. You must be seen, dear. You must have the eyes of young men rest upon you for them to fall in love with you. It is simply the reality of the world."

"Can I not wait to fall in love myself?"

"Oh, daughter of mine. You have so much to learn. It is the men who fall in love first. That is how it is done. A man will fall desperately in love with you, offer for your hand, and then take you down the aisle. The woman's turn does not come until later. After you have married and spent some time under the same roof as your new husband, that is when the woman's love comes. A man's love is fast, but a woman's is more delicate. It takes more time to blossom. Women learn to love. Men are mired in it with their appetites and their basal nature."

Stella did not argue with her mother because there was nothing to be gained by it, but it sounded to her like her mother was suggesting that she settle — settle for much less than true love and to reconcile herself to whatever situation she found herself in.

That was what the Lady Moorland was suggesting to her youngest daughter, which made Stella enormously sad. Again, Stella's mind wandered to those noble under-classes, allowed to marry for love as they pleased, their marriage beds unsullied by the shame of unfulfilled yearnings and forced love.

Stella was so very young.

"I understand, Mother."

"Good. Good. The ball will be lovely, dear. Simply lovely. It is the very ball at which your sister Melinda met Lord Rucker two years past."

Lady Moorland took the final sip of her tea and stood to take her leave of her daughter. She moved around the small table and placed a soft kiss on Stella's forehead.

"Ah, Stella," Lady Moorland whispered. "You hold such a special place in my heart. I was once much like you, an idealistic, young woman. I only hope that you avoid the same mistakes I have made. Idealism is most unwise in an eligible young lady."

Stella looked up at her mother, surprised by such a revelation. What exactly was her mother admitting?

As Lady Moorland left the room, Stella thought she heard her utter, "It only leads to pain."

Continue Reading

'The Duke's Unwilling Bride'

at:

https://www.amazon.com/dp/B01M3UO064/

ARIETTA RICHMOND, GRACE AUSTEN, ISABELLA THORNE,
KATHERINE KEATS AND ALYCE HEALEY

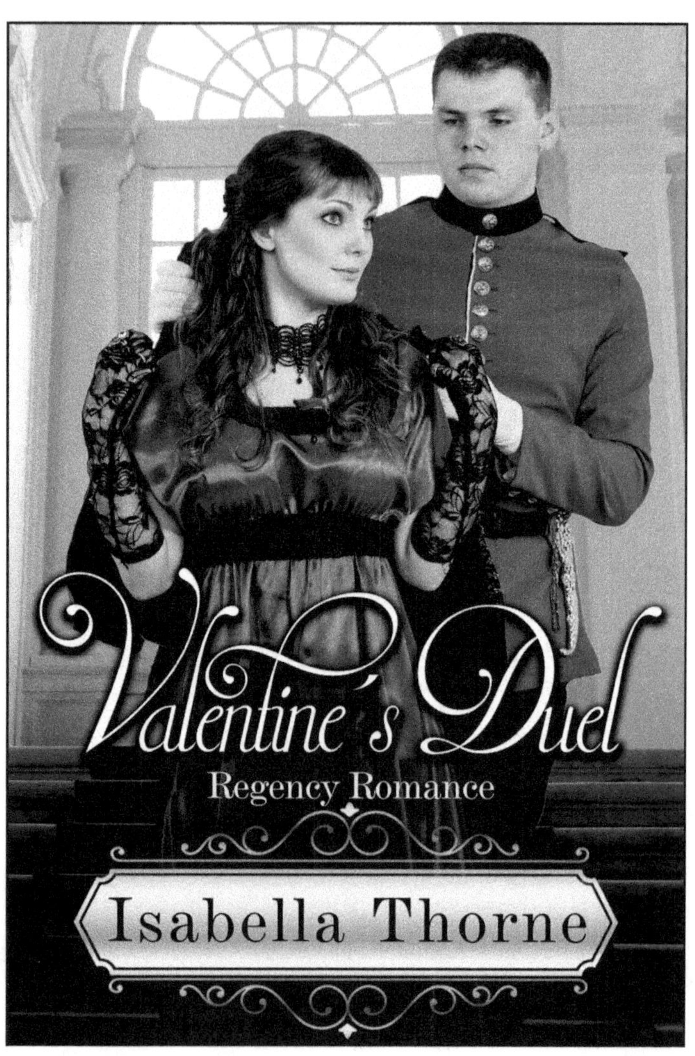

Regency Romance

Valentine's Duel

Isabella Thorne

ARIETTA RICHMOND, GRACE AUSTEN, ISABELLA THORNE,
KATHERINE KEATS AND ALYCE HEALEY

All rights reserved

Copyright © 2017 by Isabella Thorne

Please visit Isabella's website at www.isabellathorne.com

All Rights Reserved.

No part of this publication may be reproduced in any form or by any means, including scanning, photocopying, or otherwise without prior written permission of the copyright holder.

Chapter One

Mary Highland heard the sharp clang of metal upon metal and her heart fluttered beneath her ample bosom. The sound was quick and repeated often, causing Mary to tilt her head and look to the open window nearby. She sat in the parlour, sitting across a small card table from her youngest sister Josephine. Jo smiled and groaned good-naturedly as she shook her head from side to side.

"He's here, and off you'll go like a hound called forth with raw meat."

Mary stifled a laugh into the back of her hand and then knit her eyebrows in an approximation of a cross face.

"I am no hound," she said.

"You would be if he asked it of you," Jo said. Jo was only fourteen, thin and tall like their mother. Her face was sharp, her nose pointed, but still she was beautiful, the way a bird was beautiful.

Mary took after their father. He was handsome, but dark, giving her the appearance of having gone out in the sun once or twice too much without a parasol. Whereas Jo, and Mary's other sister, Helen, and their mother, were all blonde and light skinned, like fairy princesses, Mary had a natural tan and dark hair which fell in coiled curls past her shoulders. Her lips were plump, her breasts and hips round and much larger than her mother's. She had begun to form as such at Jo's age, and had caught the attention of men ever since. Her father was anxious to marry her off.

But Mary's heart belonged to just one man, and he belonged to another. Jo sighed and glanced to the cards she held fanned out in her thin fingers, and then she tossed them to the table, knowing their game was forfeited.

"Go on," Jo said good-naturedly. "I know your mind is not on the game. I would have won, you know," she said.

Mary laughed.

"You always do dear sister."

The younger sister watched as the older sister stood up.

"He's due to be married, you know," Jo called after Mary, "They announced last week."

Mary pretended not to hear her as she swept from the parlour, the skirts of her blue gown held aloft by nervous fingers. The gown was one of Mary's favourites; the blue was the color of the sky in the morning, not when the sun was so low that the clouds were shot with orange and purples, but before it was so high that the blue was washed out with white.

That blue, of a day full of promises and wonder. Mary never knew when the man she loved would visit, so it was pure luck if he ever called when she was dressed in her best gown, like today.

As she hurried through the corridor, she nearly ran into her sister Helen.

"Watch where you are going," Mary snapped. As usual, Helen's nose was in a book.

If she had tried at all, Helen could have been the one to marry a title, but she was such a blue-stocking no one wanted her. Privately Mary thought that her sister was like to be an old maid if she didn't soon change her ways.

"Sorry," Helen muttered without looking up from her book. As she walked, one of those lacy Valentine's letters fell from the book. Helen with a Valentine? Mary was shocked.

"You dropped this," Mary began, but Helen didn't hear her, so engrossed in the book was she. Mary sighed and hurried on, following the sound of clanking metal.

Her heeled boots clicked upon the hard floor of the hall as she went towards the rear door of Greenbriar Manor. The home was large and impressive, her father's grandfather having made a fortune in trade, the same as her own father was doing now. The main house was atop a small hill, the grounds sloping slightly as one moved away from the house, but masterfully and beautifully maintained and landscaped. They had everything money could buy; only they did not have a title. That task would be up to Mary.

The rear door opened up into a garden perfect for reading, which Mary did often. She was partial to novels, her favourites being Miss Jane Austen's. She liked to read, perched upon one of the numerous benches, usually near the fountain in the center of the flower bed. She so loved the smell of roses and hyacinths in the spring. Mary's brother Thomas found another use for the garden, actually several uses, but Mary was not supposed to know about the baser ones. Today he was fencing.

Thomas was an avid fencer, and, while his father preferred him to use the newly appropriated athletics hall or better yet retire to Bond Street to practice, Thomas usually made use of the garden. Mary saw him first as she stepped through the door. Her brother was tall and broad shouldered, very strong, with the same dark hair and skin and eyes that she had. It was not such a terrible thing to be plagued with the perpetual vulgarity of a suntan if you were a man. He wore a thick doublet and held a thin rapier in his hand. As she watched, he stepped forward and thrust and Mary let her eyes travel down his arm and along the blade to the man whom he attempted to strike.

Captain Victor Darten was the most handsome man Mary had ever seen. The worst part of it all was also the best. He had the confidence of ten men, and heads turned when he walked into the room.

He was keenly aware of the fact that he was a handsome man. Although his hair was also dark, his jaw seemed to be chiselled from white stone, as if he was a statue chipped slowly out of marble, somewhat as she imagined the statues which the sculptor Michelangelo had made.

Victor's eyes were shining deep blue, and his smile was so rarely seen, and so dazzling, that it made Mary weak in the knees whenever she coaxed it out of him. He was much more like to scowl, but not at her. Mary was sure he scowled less at her than any other, including his bride to be.

As Mary watched, Victor easily knocked her brother's strike to the side and then thrust forward with his own. His blade landed and he grinned, a fleeting look upon his face.

"Point for me," he said, and then his eyes flickered to the side and he took in Mary. "We have an audience, it seems," he said, and then raised the hand, which held his blade, towards Mary and bowed. "Your lovely sister, Mary."

Thomas turned and frowned.

"Mary, we are training."

"I came to read," Mary lied quickly. "It is a garden; not a fencing school."

Thomas seemed to accept that, but of course Victor would not allow it. He was too quick of wit and he seemingly loved to torment Mary. He knew she liked him; he knew she was attracted to him, and he never let a moment go by without reminding her that he knew, as if he could coax a blush from her olive skin. He usually could. He had visited at their home long before he went to the war with France which had put such a permanent scowl on his face. Mary longed to rub the lines from his brow and bring him happiness.

"You've forgotten your book," he said, and Mary felt the heat rise in her cheeks and was for one moment glad she did not have the pale skin of her sisters.

Victor was four years her senior, twenty-one, and a captain in his Majesty's Royal Navy. He had toured France, fighting the petite Frenchman and his evil henchmen. She liked to think of him in his dashing red coat, freeing the people from the tyranny of the little dictator, but his time in service was at an end.

The war was over, and Napoleon was captured. The Royal Navy sailed home. Victor's father worked with Mary's own father in trade, and he was planning retirement to his country home.

Mary thought he would make a fine country gentleman, although something of war seemed to settle about him lately. He and Thomas had been friends since childhood, but he was no longer that carefree lad. Victor was present so often, as Mary was growing up, that she once considered Victor a second brother. That was no longer so, she thought with a blush.

Embarrassment took hold and Mary spun without a word. She rushed back inside. When she found that Jo had left the parlour, Mary went to her room. She sat on the edge of her bed, cursing herself in her head.

She was such a foolish girl. Victor was going to marry another. It was all arranged, and their marriage was set for the summer, only months away. Why she felt the need to torture herself she would never know.

An hour passed as she sat alone with her dark thoughts, and then her door opened so swiftly she cried out in alarm. It was Victor. He had taken off his doublet, leaving him in a tie and jacket. His face was red, his temples slick with sweat.

"Forgive my appearance," he said as he stepped inside and shut the door behind him with a soft click. She gasped, thinking that she should stop this right now. She should tell him to get out, but he had apologized, she thought stupidly. Mary didn't know exactly what he was apologizing for. Did he mean his appearance and the toll the physical exertion had taken on him, or the fact that he was in her room at all.

No man save her father and brother had ever been in her room, and they were very infrequent guests to say the least. In fact, since the room had been converted from a nursery, she couldn't think of a single time her male relatives had visited; certainly this was most improper. She must speak - it would not matter to the *ton* why he was here. If he was found, she would be ruined.

"You cannot be here," Mary said and she rose, but Victor strode forward and took her by the arm, pulling her back down as he sat on the bed himself. Mary's heart beat within her chest, and she feared it was so loud that the man she loved would think a war was being waged inside her body. In a way it was. She wanted to tell him to leave, but she wanted him to stay. She turned and looked at him, expecting him to talk, but instead he leaned over and pressed his lips suddenly to hers.

He tasted salty and somewhat sweet from the sweat of the match. It was not the taste she expected. It was nothing she expected. She knew that lips pressed upon lips became a kiss, and she wanted to be kissed regardless of the impropriety. Mary closed her eyes. It was everything she imagined and nothing she imagined. Her lips parted of their own accord, and his tongue was in her mouth. His tongue!

She knew she should not allow such liberties, but instead, she gripped him tighter. She felt his hand on her arm, and it slid down and switched to her waist. His fingers were strong, and they caught the material of her dress for a moment and she felt the strength of them and lost her own. The thought terrified her, and yet she knew she would give herself to him, fully, no matter how frightening she found the idea of being bedded by a man, but only if she were his wife. Only then...

But it was not to be. He broke the kiss, and then stood up. He smiled down upon her — that dazzling, heart stopping smile.

"I wanted to apologize for teasing you," he said. "And now, I must apologize for kissing you."

Mary nodded. She could not speak. She brought a hand up to touch her lips. She could almost feel him still there, kissing her. Somehow his words felt as though he was still teasing her. He was to be married after all. He couldn't come into another girl's room, he couldn't kiss her. He shouldn't, at the very least. But he had, and then he turned and left, tossing one more smile over his shoulder before his face clouded into a scowl. He exited the room and pulled the door shut behind him. Mary watched him go, her mind awash in confusion.

Her first kiss, and it had been nothing like how she had imagined it. She felt her cheeks redden again, and she fell backward, throwing her hands over her face as she fought the urge to scream. Maybe she should have allowed him take liberties with her, she thought. If they were found together, yes, she would be ruined, but wouldn't he have to offer for her?

Wouldn't such an action destroy all of her father's prettily laid plans to marry her to a titled gentleman? She, who was usually so logical, couldn't puzzle it out. She felt as if her head were filled with wool. She closed her eyes, trying to recapture the dream of his lips on hers.

As she rolled over on the bed, she realized that the paper lace of the Valentine was crumpled beneath her. This was the letter her sister Helen had dropped. Mary stared at it. It was, in her mind, a cheap counterfeit of poetry, but Helen had never appreciated works of poetry. Her wont tended much more towards mathematics and the sciences. Who would write such a thing for Helen, she wondered.

Then shall we meet in warmth and sun

Telling surely I shall come

Your thoughts and figures straight and worn

For Oft to you, my love is sworn

Where in thy arms I am undone

She turned the paper over, looking for a signature. There was no signature, but there was a strange little drawing of a figure, with a bell pull and tiny lines above it, and some numbers. Well, that told her more than anything that the love note belonged to Helen. It made no sense.

She should turn the note over to her mother straight away, but today, right now, she could not do it.

In this moment, she believed in love, and even such a creature as Helen was welcome to it. She placed the note in her bureau, thinking to give it to Helen later.

Chapter Two

When Mary left the room she felt as though she could walk on air, though she kept to the floor as she made her way down the curving staircase. Mary heard Helen speaking with her mother in the nearby drawing room, arguing really, although their voices were not raised. Disagreement was present in the tone.

As usual, Helen was seeking permission to go to some boring lecture on mathematics or science. Mary could not, for the life of her, figure out why she would want to sit through such a thing, but then she thought of the Valentine. Was it possible that Helen was deceiving her parents? No. Mary shook her head. Not Helen. She was not the type for a clandestine tryst. But it was puzzling. Mary shook her head. Since Mary was hoping to find Jo, she slid silently by without disturbing Helen or her mother.

Helen was the middle sister, older than Jo, but younger than Mary. Helen and Mary were as different as sisters had ever been, and had never gotten along.

She was of course, her sister, but Mary found herself much more devoted to Jo. Jo was the baby of the family, and everyone seemed to dote upon her. Everyone but Helen, and this was another source of contention between the two older girls. In Mary's opinion, Helen was quite selfish. She thought only of her own pursuits and not of the good of the family.

Jo was in the kitchen, trying to sneak morsels from the cooks as they prepared supper. Jo was stick thin, but ate like no one Mary had ever known.

"Wait until you have to pick at morsels on a plate," she said. "It's not lady-like to eat too much."

"I was hungry," Jo countered.

"I should have known I would find you here," Mary teased. Jo grinned at her older sister as she popped a piece of yeast roll into her mouth. Being around Jo always made Mary feel young again, though at only seventeen, she supposed she was indeed young. She no longer ran through the manor in stockinged feet, giggling and hiding and causing trouble, but when she was around her sister Jo, she felt like doing such things. She felt like the weight of obtaining a title for the family was not so daunting when she was with Jo.

"I have to speak with you," Mary said, and Jo saw something in her sister's face which led to her easily abandoning her food related quest and walking with Mary to the garden. They sat on the bench nearest the fountain and Jo waited for Mary to fill her in.

"Victor ...she started, and she covered her face. She spoke between her fingers. "The Captain. He did something."

"What?"

"He embarrassed me."

Jo laughed.

"Dear sister, I think it more likely you embarrassed yourself."

Mary shook her head.

"I told them I came out to read, he pointed out that I had no book. Wasn't that cruel of him?"

"Why shake your head? It looks as though I was right."

Mary slapped playfully at her sister's shoulder.

"It would do you well to be nice to me," she said. "Or I shan't let you visit me in my manor when I marry."

Jo giggled.

"He kissed me," Mary said suddenly. She could hold it in no longer. Her sister's eyes went wide.

"The captain?" she whispered.

Mary nodded.

"He kissed you?" Jo repeated.

"He did."

"Here?"

Mary shook her head. "In my bedroom."

Jo gasped. "You took him into your bedroom?" Jo asked, her face that of one who was thoroughly scandalized.

"No!" Mary insisted. "I had gone up after her had teased me. He came in and apologized. He sat down on my bed and kissed me.

"He kissed you?"

"Yes!" Mary said.

"In your bedroom," Jo repeated at a whisper, her eyes wide. "No one must find out. You will be ruined."

"No one will find out," Mary said. "Who would tell?"

Jo sucked in her breath.

"He is to be married," Jo said, trying to reason it out in her own head.

"Believe me, I remember," Mary said somewhat bitterly.

"I can't believe this," Jo said. "What could it mean? Did he wish to ruin you? That's cruel. Many have called him a rake. But Mary, I have never known him to be cruel."

Mary did not have an answer for that. Her shoulders simply rose and fell, and the two girls were silent for some time. She was not thinking of cruelty when he kissed her.

"Did you kiss him back?" Jo asked suddenly.

"What do you mean?" Mary asked.

"It's something I've heard women say. Kissing back. Did you do it?"

"I don't know; I think so. I didn't mind the kiss," Mary said her heart fluttering. "It was…" She paused thinking she should not be discussing this with a fourteen year old, but who could she tell?

"But you need to figure out if you kissed him back. That's important," Mary's younger sister said.

"What do you know of kissing? You are but a child yet." Mary said.

"I know that if you kissed him back," Jo stuttered to a stop, crossing her arms over the front of her dress. "If you kissed him back, that would be very good, or very bad indeed."

"You are the romance master," Mary conceded, teasing her sister.

"What are you going to do?" Jo couldn't hide a smile, and both girls jumped when a voice barked at them from across the garden.

"Mary, my office if you please," the voice said. It was deep, demanding.

"Father knows," Jo hissed.

Mary felt the blood drain from her face.

"Surely not," she said, but her heart was all aflutter and her mouth dry.

The girls' father, Mr. Highland, was a stern man, but he loved his family very much. His moustache was large and bushy, the hair on his head gray and thinning. Mary looked him over when she went into his office. Sometimes he looked so old when she saw him, a way he had not looked until the last year or so. He was standing behind a mahogany desk - he was often working, even at home.

"Yes, Father," Mary said demurely.

"Sit please my dear," he said and Mary did so, perched on the edge of the seat. Her day dress was not so corseted as to cause her discomfort, but she still sat straight backed as if ready to bolt. Her father sat as well, the desk between father and daughter.

Mary felt nervous, she wondered if her father had heard her and Jo speaking about Victor. She knew full well how her father would react if he knew that the man had come into her bedchamber and kissed her. She watched as he smiled at her, and she knew he had heard nothing. He wasn't angry, he seemed… sad? No, that wasn't quite right, though it looked as though tears were forming in his eyes, threatening to spill over his bottom eyelid. He reached forward for her hands and she gave them to him.

"I will be brief."

"Is everything alright?" Mary asked.

"It is splendid," her father replied. "You are to be married."

"Married?" Mary asked. Her insides ran suddenly cold.

"The Baron of Millersmit," he said. "He is a bit older than I was planning for you, but you will have a good life. He is a kind man and his manor is not far from here. Visiting will be an easy matter. His Manor is in a bit of disrepair, but well, that is where our funds will come in.

Normally she would have been ecstatic to hear such news, but it was just half an hour since Victor had kissed her, and the news was bitter.

"I don't know him…"

"Nonsense,"

"Not well, I meant," Mary tried.

"He is a kind man and titled. He will take good care of you, and best of all, for your mother at least, you will be close."

Mary was speechless. She nodded.

"You are to be a Baroness," her father added. She could see the excitement in her father's eyes, mixing with the tears of joy. He was confident that he had done well by his daughter. If he had told her yesterday, she would have thrown her arms around her father's beefy neck and planted kiss after kiss on his cheek, but today... today she could only think of Victor.

Victor had kissed her. It probably meant nothing. As Jo had reminded her, Victor was considered to be somewhat of a rake. But not with her, she thought. Surely not. She could not force herself to see reason. The kiss meant nothing to him. No. It meant something. Perhaps it meant he loved her, and he was willing to be with her instead of his bride to be. But now... it was all ruined, she was promised to another.

Her father mistook her own tears for ones of joy, much like his own.

ARIETTA RICHMOND, GRACE AUSTEN, ISABELLA THORNE,
KATHERINE KEATS AND ALYCE HEALEY

Chapter Three

Helen spent the better part of a week in her room. She would rise and dress, and then sit on the end of her bed trying to figure out the sums. They were correct. She was sure of it, but she wanted to share the discovery.... to speak of it. He had not communicated with her in some time. She was worried. Had some awful accident befallen him? She could not relax. Sometimes, she would venture out to break her fast, or perhaps eat supper, but often she skipped meals, opting instead to work. She would not speak to anyone who came calling.

He had not written. She was worried that he had forgotten all about her. She understood that he could have forgotten about her, but not her mathematics. He could not forget that.

That evening she had a bath drawn, and, as she slipped into the steaming water, Helen lay staring at the ceiling and calculating the number of buckets in the tub. It would work, she told herself. It had to work. When the water cooled, she resolved to herself to get over the matter.

There was absolutely nothing she could do. If he took her calculations as his own, no one would believe that she was indeed the brains behind them. She was, after all, only a woman. What mattered was not credit, but that the design was made. Still, it galled her that he would leave her behind. Nonetheless, she was pouting like a small child. There was nothing she could do if he took the design for his own. Nothing. She was a woman, and no one would believe the design was hers. She could pout about the injustice or she could so something about it. She decided on the later.

She was a mathematician! She was more than a woman, at least in this modern society. She was not fairer, or weaker than a man. She could do everything anyone else could; and she would.

And so, after her bath Helen dressed and left her room. She went downstairs, surprising her father and mother in the dining room as they broke their fast. They were getting on in age, both of them with greying hair, her father a strong man with a thick neck and a long nose, her mother slight and dainty. She loved them both, even though they did not understand her.

"Helen," her mother said as she came in.

"Mother, father, I've come for breakfast."

"I can see that, and glad of it I am," her father said with a smile. He picked up a small silver bell from near his plate and shook it. A serving woman entered the room before the chime faded completely.

"Bring Helen a plate please, it will not be needed in her room," her father said. "She will eat here."

The woman bowed her head and exited.

"I am pleased to see you up and about," her mother said.

"I am prepared to live my life, and go on in my pursuits," Helen said.

"Good. Good," her father said. "As soon as we get your sister settled, it will be your turn. Perhaps we can entertain a season for you."

"With your sister's match, we should be able to acquire some invitations," her mother added thoughtfully.

Mary burst into tears, and excused herself. In a moment Jo followed her.

Helen pursed her lips.

"I will not marry. My pursuits are more scholarly than that. I have designed..."

Her mother sighed, but her father let anger take him quickly. His face grew red and he balled his fist before sending it slamming into the tabletop, just as a plate of food was brought in and set before Helen, causing it to shake and clatter.

"These damned scholarly pursuits," her father said. "Enough of the mathematics you foolish girl!"

"I am no girl, I am a woman grown!"

"Yes, you are grown, and then some!" her father argued. "That is the problem my headstrong daughter. Your sisters had, and have, no problem living in this society as they are expected, but you... it's simply too much to ask for you to find a man, and be married."

"Then why has Mary left the table in tears — again," she asked.

"She is just high strung," mother commented. "Perhaps she has a bit of the hysteria. She should take the waters."

Helen rubbed her forehead. Dare she voice her ideas and inventions? She thought not.

"I do not want to marry. I want to study mathematics. I have worked hard and already figured out…" she said, but her father interrupted.

"You still rebel, preferring your bluestocking ways. You are a most unnatural woman," he spat disgustedly.

Helen did not know what to say. She felt the stinging pain of tears in her eyes, but she blinked them away, banishing sadness. She would not give in to her father. She would not cry. She did not know what to say, and so she did not say a thing. She picked up her fork and knife, and began to eat. She blinked back the tears when they came.

Her father had been spoiling for a fight, and he would not let her off that easily.

"We will send a note to the Baron and you will apologize for your rudeness. Perhaps he will let you stay with your sister for the season."

"I will not!" Helen said, her father becoming too much for her vow of silence to take. She slammed her fork and knife down next to her plate. "And I don't want a season."

"You will do as I say."

"I shan't."

"You do not grow younger, my dear," her father said. "You are already labelled a blue-stocking."

"I don't care. There is more to life than marrying," Helen argued.

"What?" said her mother.

"Not for you!" her father roared, and Helen knew the argument was then over. She looked to her mother, wanting some sort of support, but her mother was looking down at her plate, as though she wished to be anywhere else in the world, and Helen knew she would get no support from her.

"As you wish," Helen said finally, and she began to eat again.

~~~~~

The tap on Mary's door caused her to sit up in bed. She sniffed and brushed back tears.

"A moment," she said, trying to get herself in order.

"Mary?" The voice was Helen's. "May I come in? I would have a word."

"Yes," Mary said.

Helen sat on her bed and consoled her.

"You do not have to marry this Baron," she told Mary. "You can choose your own man to love."

"I cannot," Mary cried. "The man I love is about to be married to another." She broke into sobs.
~~~~~

"The Captain," Helen surmised.

Mary nodded miserably. "How did you know?"

"Oh, Mary. You have been quite transparent," she said.

"And you?" Mary asked. "Will you truly not marry at all?"

"I will not give up my brain to marry," she said. "Perhaps if, one day, I find a man who understands... But I think that is unlikely. For a while I considered Mr. Feetham although he is not of an age...."

"Oh," Mary said suddenly. "I've forgotten. She went to her bureau and took out the crumpled Valentine. "You dropped this the other day."

"Yes," she said. "When my books came in the post."

"Is it?" Mary hesitated uncertain how to continue. "Someone," she said. "A lover? Is that why you do not wish to marry?"

"Oh, no!" Helen laughed aloud. "No. It is another mathematician. Mother kept throwing away his drawings, so we decided to correspond in another way. We were working to improve upon the shower bath.

Mary shivered. "I have no desire to dump cold water over my body."

"Exactly," Helen said. Mr. Feetham and I were working on the engineering of the thing. He owns the ironworks in London. He came to the country to speak to me, and Mother would not let me speak to him. We had to make other arrangements.

"You are serious about these mathematics, are you not?" Mary said.

"Very much so. Mr. Feetham has convinced me that I should not let the fact that I am a woman stand in my way."

Mary wondered when on earth Helen had managed to speak unchaperoned with the man, but she did not voice her musings.

"So you shan't," Mary said. "I will help you get word to Mr. Feetham."

"And I will help you speak to the Captain."

"I have spoken," Mary said. "It is hopeless."

"I do not think so," Helen said.

Mary begged her sister to tell her what she meant, but Helen would not speak.

"Not until I speak to Charlotte," she said.

"Charlotte?" Mary questioned. "The Captain's fiancé?"

"The very one," Helen agreed.

"Have you met?" Mary asked.

"She is the daughter of the banker who we hoped to finance our shower bath," she said.

Mary opened her mouth and shut it again.

ARIETTA RICHMOND, GRACE AUSTEN, ISABELLA THORNE,
KATHERINE KEATS AND ALYCE HEALEY

224

Chapter Four

Victor took a deep breath before he raised a fist to the door and knocked. He did not want to be here, he did not want to have the conversation he was about to have, but he knew he needed to. He loved Mary, and after they had parted the day before, he needed to break off his engagement. His knock lingered in the air for a moment, and then, just as he was about to knock again, the door before him was opened.

"Good morning," the butler said. Victor inclined his head. He could not for the life of him, remember the man's name. Carrow? Carroll? Carrot? Oh bother. He nodded noncommittally and said,

"Good Morning. I've come to call upon Charlotte. Is she at home?"

"I will see, Captain Darten," the butler said, taking Darten's calling card. "You may wait in the drawing room, Sir." He gestured and Victor, tense, wandered around the room. He was too nervous to sit. He paced.

A moment later, the butler returned.

"She will see you," he said.   "She is tending to her horses." She asks that you come around.

"I will do that," Victor said with a smile, waving his hand towards the side of the house. The man bowed and shut the door, and Victor stepped away from it, and walked across the well-kept lawn, around the corner of the large home and down the lane to the stables.

Charlotte was the youngest daughter of Benjamin Bailey, a man who had started work at the London Bank long ago, as a young man, and had worked his way up to position of the Bank's director. His first wife had given him one boy and two girls. Though she had passed away half a decade ago and he had remarried two years past that, his new wife had not borne him any children. The son was due to take over the Bank, and the father wanted to settle his daughters sooner rather than later, especially after he walked in on Victor and Charlotte kissing. She was not a titled Lady, but her father seemed not to notice the lack.

Charlotte was adored by her father, and the man was rather protective of her. It had taken him a long time to warm up to Victor, given the man's gambling problems were not secret and his reputation with the ladies didn't help his suit. Still, Victor was charming and kind, and the old man had eventually been pleased to accept Victor's request for Charlotte's hand in marriage — right after he caught Victor with his hands in Charlotte's elaborate up do, and his mouth on hers - at least they were in the drawing room and not in the bedroom.

Had they been, Victor was quite sure there would have been a funeral instead of a wedding, but when Victor had offered for Charlotte the man calmed down and accepted.

Victor, after all, had the expectation of a title, minor though it was. His father's cousin was a Baron, and had never had children, nor had he now any living siblings, which meant that when the old man died, the title would pass to Victor. He had not given the title much thought, but it did turn Charlotte's father's head and allowed him to accept the marriage proposal.

And Victor had been pleased as well. He did enjoy Charlotte, even if he did not love her. She was beautiful, and kind, and would make an excellent wife. More than that, her father had more money than he knew what to do with. Victor could think of many uses for that money. He was sure he would come to love her, it would simply take time. He had always been taken with Mary, but he knew he could not soften her father's resolve, the way he had that of Charlotte's father. And so he had proposed to Charlotte. Now, he wondered if he was wrong. The taste of Mary's lips on his would simply not go away.

Mary had pursued him. He was flattered. He should have been appalled; she was acting the hoyden, and her father would certainly not approve. Then he had kissed Mary, her lips so sweet and chaste under his, and in that moment he had realized that he was playing with fire. He had no intention of marrying Mary, and being found in her bedroom, of all places, would ruin her. With him already betrothed to Charlotte, he would not be able to offer for her.

She was the little sister of his best friend. She was chaste and beautiful and... then he wondered just why he had offered for Charlotte. Charlotte, of course was more biddable. She would not scold him for gambling, but neither would she excite him so.

He sighed. When Mary's sister Helen had suggested that perhaps Mary's father would let her choose who she married, whether he liked the man or not, everything had been upended. The largest problem, of course, was Charlotte's feelings.

She was a kind girl, and Victor knew she would be immeasurably hurt when Victor told her that he was calling off the engagement. She was a wonderful person — his friend. They had thought they could make a marriage, but he knew it was not so — not when he could only remember Mary's lips when he kissed Charlotte. He paused looking for her.

There was a grand stable behind Charlotte's home, and it was here that her father housed his horses. She had always loved the beasts; it was something she and Victor had in common, though he lived to bet on them more than he loved to ride them.

The girl was turned away from the entrance, pulling a brush through one horse's coat, and Victor paused to watch her. Her hair was auburn and peeking out from her hat in damp curls. She wore a beautiful dress of light blue, and her skin was kissed by the sun. She spent as much time outside as she could, and she had a smattering of freckles across her nose. They were pale and easily covered with powder, but her mother fretted about her time in the sun.

She had taken off her jacket in the warmth, and her arms were bare, below the short sleeves of her dress, except for the riding gloves protecting her hands.

"Charlotte," Victor said softly, as he strode forward.

"Captain!" The girl said, and she went to him. "I thought you had perhaps run away from me, it has been so long since you called."

Victor tried to smile as he held her gloved hands. He did not lay a kiss upon her cheek. She was just eighteen, and as sweet a woman as Victor had ever known.

Even though he had not seen or attempted correspondence in two weeks or more, she refused to even consider that things were not well in their relationship. He looked into her soft blue eyes and spoke.

"I need to speak with you, and frankly," Victor said.

"Then speak, so that we may put our lips to more enjoyable uses after," Charlotte said leaning in to him, Victor couldn't help but laugh.

As sweet as she was, the young woman was often forward, and she made no attempt to hide the fact that she was attracted to Victor.

"I fear that you will not want to set your lips to any action with mine once I have spoken to you," Victor started.

He paused then, and the woman opened her mouth, but he rushed ahead, intending to get out what he had to say without her stopping him.

"I must call off our engagement," he said. "I am sorry, I truly am, but my heart lies with another. I know it must sting, to hear such a thing, and I know you will not wish to speak to me past this day, but I am sorry, I cannot live a lie. I care too much for you to tie you to a loveless marriage."

Victor stopped then; hardly able to look the young woman in the eye. He did so, and he was surprised to see that she was not crying, as he had expected. Instead her eyes were filled with something close to relief.

"Oh, thank goodness," the young woman said.

"Thank goodness?"

"I did not know how to tell you, but I have fallen in love with another man as well."

"I have not fallen in love with a man!" Victor stuttered, and the girl laughed, brushing a curl from her face with the back of her hand and marring her nose with a bit of dirt from the curry brush.

"Of course not, I only meant, I have fallen in love with another."

The news should have been a relief, but he felt a pang of jealousy mixed with anger assault his heart.

"Who?" he asked?"

The girl laughed.

"Does it matter? Do not torture yourself with such things."

"Why not tell me? Break off the engagement yourself?"

The young woman let her shoulders rise and fall. He noticed that she had a bit of light freckling on her shoulder. In days gone by, he would have kissed each of them. Now he held himself still.

"Why would you wait if you wanted to break the engagement?"

"I was afraid," she said simply.

"Afraid of what? Surely not me."

"No, of course not."

"Your father?"

She took a deep breath and expelled it. She turned back to the horse she was brushing and ran a hand along the mare's neck.

"Is he a good man?" Victor asked.

"He is." She turned to look at him again, her eyes wide and liquid. "Is she a good woman?"

"She is," Victor said.

"Then we will wish each other well, and can remain friends," Charlotte said firmly.

Victor smiled and nodded, though he still felt a strange mixture of emotions inside. He was hurt, that the woman didn't want him any longer, and truthfully, he could count on one hand the number of women who did not find him charming. It strangely hurt that she did not want him though he had gone to tell her that exact same thing.

"Are you alright?" she asked, and he nodded again, quickly.

"Confused," the man admitted.

"About what?"

"You spoke of kissing me, just now, and you don't even love me anymore?"

"I don't know if I ever loved you," the girl said truthfully. "I was playing a role. I... know of your money troubles, but still, you are a man my father was proud to have as a son, once we were married. I did not want to disappoint him, and we are friends. I hoped to make it work. But if you are the one to break up the marriage, then there is nothing I can do, right? You seem upset."

"The woman I was to marry told me she fell in love with another man!" Victor said heatedly. When Charlotte laughed, it only caused him to grow angrier.

"You just told me the same!" she argued. "Why do you care?"

"I've had enough of this conversation," Victor said, and he turned to leave.

"Captain."

He turned to look at her.

"I enjoy your company, but I think we would not do well to be married." the young woman said, reaching for, and stopping Victor by placing her hand on his shoulder. "My father is a jealous man. I want you to know that."

"Good day," Victor said, and he walked away wondering what on earth her father's jealousy had to do with anything.

Chapter Five

"I must confess, I have little to offer in terms of guidance when it comes to the fairer sex. I am, myself, in a bit of a spot with a woman, or women I should say."

His uncle, the Baron Millersmit grinned. "I will not ask."

"And I thank you for that," Victor said. "All I can offer is advice on what to do next."

"And what should I do next?"

"Drink," Victor said, and the two men laughed, and each drained a glass. "Or gamble," Victor added.

"I do not gamble, but perhaps you are somewhere near the mark," the Baron said. "I need a spot of fun, and perhaps you would be so good as to accompany me."

"What did you have in mind?" the man asked.

"Perhaps we need to get away from these damnable women," The Baron said.

"I must agree. The lot of them make my head ache."

"Hunting?" the Baron said with a quirk of his brow.

Victor had never gone hunting, it was not a pastime his father had ever enjoyed, and so it was not passed down to him, the way it had been to the Baron.

But still he told his uncle that he would go, and, three days later, they found themselves atop horses, riding together into the woods.

"There is a cottage ahead, I have invited some others to join us," the Baron said. "We will spend the weekend here."

"I look forward to it," Victor said. He had a rifle, one of the new styles which could be fired more safely in wet weather, slung over his shoulder. The Baron had his two hounds loping after him and his horse.

The cottage was large and would sleep eight comfortably, though the hunting party consisted of only six. The groom settled their horses in a nearby stable, made of the same wood as the cottage, while the Baron squared his hounds away in a kennel built alongside the cottage.

Inside, four men were waiting for them, though Victor's face blanched when he saw two of them. The Baron introduced Victor to the men.

"A long-time friend, his father is a Squire, Mr. Fredrick Grouse; next to him, his cousin, Lord Richard Ashcroft. And then father and son here, Mr. Benjamin Bailey, the lead director of the Bank of London, and his son, Thomas Bailey."

"We know Captain Darten here," Mr. Bailey said, and his son spoke up.

"He recently broke my youngest sister's heart."

An uncomfortable silence fell over the group, but the Baron worked to quickly wash it away. The men had dinner.

"We hunt rabbits at first light," the Baron said, as he sucked on a quail bone after the meal.

"How hard can it be to kill a rabbit?" Victor asked, and the other men laughed, though Victor saw that Thomas Bailey was still rather cold to him.

"They are wily and fast," the Baron told his friend. "Do not expect this to be an easy hunt. They hide in the underbrush, and dash when you are not looking."

"You've never hunted?" Lord Ashcroft asked Victor.

"I have not, at least not like this," he said thinking of prowling along the coast of France in his ship, looking for spies.

"Your father owned some land. It has been well within your right."

"Yes, it is simply not something I've ever tried, but I am here now."

"He's enjoyed betting away all of his father's hard earned fortune instead," Thomas said. He was two years younger than Victor, but speaking to him as though he were twenty years older.

"Thomas," his father said, lifting a hand up. "Let it go."

"My sister has cried and cried," the younger Bailey said. "I will not let it go."

"Cried and cried?" Victor asked. "But she..." he stopped himself, wondering if it was appropriate to tell her father and brother that she had a lover.

She had never actually said she had a lover, but it had always seemed that she was up to something, and after her declaration the other day, he had assumed that perhaps it had been a lover all along.. He decided it was not appropriate to share her peculiar behaviour. Still, if she was crying, it did not match up with what had happened when Victor had gone to break off the engagement.

"Let us leave the women problems with the women," the Baron tried, and after that, the night passed with amicable conversation, and more than a few glasses of brandy. Victor and the Baron were the last two up, as they enjoyed one last brandy by a roaring fire.

"I'm sorry. I did not know you knew Mr. Bailey and his son. I knew you were engaged, but I did not know to whom. And of course I knew that you would be calling it off for Mary's sake."

Victor shrugged his shoulders.

"It is of little consequence, I am a man who ruined his family fortune, I am used to people having low opinions of me."

The Baron laughed.

"Oh. Since I am your family, I don't think the situation is that dire. You needed some cooling off time after France. If being loose with your purse was the worst of your crimes, I would not worry."

"Least of my crimes," Victor repeated.

"He seems to think you wronged his sister," the Baron said.

"I did not," Victor protested, but inside he was hurt, and confused.

The girl had said she was in love with someone else. She had not cried, or been upset. Why did her brother claim otherwise? He would need to speak to her when he returned home; that was all there was to it.

The next morning, all of the men were up with the sunlight, and they broke their fast on eggs cooked in a skillet over the fire, and sausages fried alongside it. They dressed for the hunt, in tall boots and sporting coats. They would travel on foot, a horse did more harm than good when it came to hunting rabbits. Three of the men took a dog with them, the Baron two of his, and the Bailey's each one of their own. The dogs got along about as well with each other, as Victor did with Bailey. Victor waved off his friend's offer to borrow one of his dogs. He didn't want to worry about the snarling things attacking each other instead of chasing rabbits.

"I'll kill my own rabbit thank you," Victor had teased, "I don't need a dog to do it." And the men had all laughed, save Thomas, of course.

They broke into pairs, with Victor and the Baron going together, once they had all reached a small stream.

"Keep your guns steady," the Baron said. "It won't do any of us good to be shot out here."

Victor had begun to laugh, but the other men nodded solemnly, and he quickly stifled it.

"Two years ago some of us were out here when Charles Fox had his gun explode on him. It almost killed him, so far were we from a doctor," the Baron said.

Victor looked at the gun in his hands.

He was used to cannon on his ship. They were manned by others, but they were not likely to explode. "Are these likely to explode?" he asked.

The Baron laughed. "I hope not," he said, and they walked on.

As the day wore on it grew hotter and hotter, and Victor was uncomfortable in his coat, but he found himself enjoying the hunt. His companion had killed three rabbits, which he hung on a rope by their feet, which he then slung over his shoulder. Victor had taken a few shots at a rabbit or two, but had so far come up empty.

"Let us turn back," the Baron said, after they watched a startled rabbit spring from under a bush ahead.

"No, you go, let me go after this one," Victor said. "I do not want to come back empty handed. Then I will be the man who broke Thomas' sister heart, and came back with no rabbits."

The Baron laughed. "Alright nephew. Let's go together."

Victor stalked after the rabbit. He did not come across the animal again, but he did step into a small clearing and come face to face with Mr. Bailey and his son.

"Victor, how goes it?" the elder Bailey asked.

"You speak to him like a friend?" Thomas snarled.

"Oh Thomas, you cannot protect your sister forever. I am sorry it ended of course, but I am sure that the Captain here had his reasons.

"Thank you sir," Victor said.

"I have heard her, night after night, crying and crying. She says you love someone else."

"Thomas, I do not wish to quarrel," Victor said, lifting his free hand.

"And then let us end the quarrel quickly," the younger man said, "I call you out. I will have satisfaction."

Victor laughed aloud. He had never thought he would be challenged to a duel on dry land. On a ship, where tempers were high and men were confined, it was a usual way to settle differences, but here, on land, it seemed ridiculous. Anyway, duels were illegal on land and at sea. He had defused the situation before it actually came to a duel in most cases on his own ship. He did not think such a thing could happen on land.

"Do not be ridiculous. Duels are illegal, and you are no gentleman…"

"So they are," Thomas spat and before Victor could register what was happening, Thomas had placed the butt of his rifle against his shoulder and aimed the barrel at Victor. "A hunting accident it is…"

"What are you doing?" his father demanded, but it did not deter the deranged younger man. He smiled a twisted smile as he pulled the trigger. "For my sister's honor," he said.

There was a flash of light and the blur of clothing as the Baron came from out of nowhere, tackling the man as the shot went off.

Victor was falling backwards, though he wasn't sure why. Nothing on his body hurt, indeed, it almost felt as though he wasn't in his body at all.

He hit the grassy ground of the clearing and then the pain shot through him, centred in his right breast. He yelled out.

He could hear commotion around him, near his feet, and then he saw Thomas, falling forward, the Baron atop him.

"Come help!" the elder Bailey yelled into the woods, and then Victor's world went black.

Chapter Six

Mary had not left Victor's side since he had been returned to London, and she had heard what had happened to him. A parade of faceless chaperones had sat with her, but her eyes were only for him.

Both Jo and her mother tried to convince her to come home and rest, but she could not. He was in a hospital in London, and the doctors had worked tirelessly to keep him alive. At least he was that, alive, though he had not woken once since being brought to the city.

"How is he?" a voice called behind her, and Mary spun. It had been four days, and she was tired and uncomfortable. Helen stood in the doorway, a handkerchief pressed over her mouth and nose. The smell of the hospital was unpleasant, but Mary had long ago grown accustomed to it.

"He is unwell, but alive," Mary said, and then, before she could think better of it, she rushed to her sister and hugged her. "Thank you for coming," she said.

"I am sorry it took me so long to do so," Helen said. . "Let me know what you need, right this second.

"I need nothing besides the man I love to wake."

"Nonsense, you look as though you've lost weight, and there are bags beneath your eyes. You need food, and rest."

"I cannot leave."

"Fine, I'll bring something to you," Helen said, and she stepped away from her sister and left.

It was more than hour before she returned, though when she did the maid who accompanied her had a basket hanging over her arm.

She set it down on a nearby table and set out a small spread of food. Bread and jam, butter as well. Some salted beef. She also had brought a flagon of water. She forced Mary to sit.

"He will not die without you hovering over his bedside," Helen said.

Finally, Mary nodded.

Helen watched her eat, and no words passed between them. When Mary had her fill she made to stand again, but Helen placed a hand on her shoulder and gently pushed her back down.

"Sit for a while," Helen said. "And tell me, what happened? Victor was shot, that is all I know. Jo told me a jumbled account." Mary hesitated a moment before speaking, not sure if she should mention the Baron, but in the end she wanted to tell her friend the whole truth of the matter.

"He went hunting with the Baron," Mary said. "Other men joined them, including the father and brother of Charlotte, Victor's fiancée. Ex fiancée I should rectify. He ended things with her, and that upset the brother."

"Surely he did not shoot him because of that?" Helen asked, easily deducing where the story was headed.

"Indeed he did," Mary said, nodding solemnly. "He sits in prison now. The Baron and his own father wrestled him to the ground."

"My word!" Helen said, placing her hand over her mouth. "I had thought the father must certainly be the culprit! It was the brother?"

"It was." Mary confirmed.

"How horrid," Helen said. "Shot in the chest?"

"Yes. The right side, away from his heart. He would have been killed if it was otherwise. Still, he might be," Mary said, and as she spoke the last words, her voice grew tight, and she sobbed. "We can only pray that there will be no putrification."

Helen knelt before her sister and placed both of her hands upon hers.

"He will be fine; he is a strong man who is in love with a wonderful woman. He would not think to leave her. He will live. I know it."

"The Baron visits often," Mary said. "He is as worried as I am."

"Your fiancé," Helen added.

"He has not spoken of it, or our marriage plans."

"Well, they have become close friends as well as family, it would seem. And Victor is such a charmer. I would assume he has many looking after his health."

"That is true enough. There has been a parade of well-wishers."

"I know. I sent his little sister home after hours here. She is young and needs rest. His mother comes and just weeps. . Also the father comes..." She broke off.

"His father?"

Mary shook her head. "Not his farther. Benjamin Bailey. He has not even visited his own son in prison, from what he says. He cannot face him. He's so ashamed; he cannot believe his son would act in such a way, but he comes and sits here. Him and Lord Ashcroft."

"Ashcroft," Helen repeated with a blush to her pale porcelain skin.

"What is it?" Mary asked.

"Nothing," Helen said. "Only he had an interest in the bathing shower.

"You spoke with him?"

"Jo was with us the whole time," Helen assured her. "And it was strictly a business matter."

"You did not blush when Mr. Feetham left you the Valentine," Mary said pointedly. "I think this may be more than business."

She gave her sister a shrewd look, and Helen blushed again and changed the subject.

"Surely Mr. Bailey knows it is not his fault that Victor was shot He cannot be blamed for the actions of his son," Helen said.

Mary let her shoulders rise and then drop.

"To be honest, though he is nothing but worried, I wish he would not come here. I am mad at his son, but I am mad at him as well."

"Why though? He fought his son, kept him from running, or doing more damage."

"I do not know, it is simply how I feel. Do you ever do that? Feel something, Helen? Feel something for someone instead of your cold mathematics?"

Helen was stung by the barbed question, but she tried not to let it show.

"Of course I do."

Mary sighed and stood. This time Helen did not try to force her to sit back down.

"I'm sorry," Mary said. "I did not mean for that to come out that way, I only meant, I feel things, right now, that I do not understand. I do not know why. This hospital, these people, Victor. It all just... I just feel things."

Helen smiled and took the seat she had just vacated, watching as her sister made her way back to her beloved's bedside.

"I understand, more than you will ever know," Helen said.

"I am glad you've come," Mary said, looking across the room to her sister. "It means a great deal to me."

"And that is why I have come," Helen said.

The two women passed some time together, much of it in comfortable silence. It was an hour after Helen left and Victor's sister Beth came that Victor finally woke.

~~~~~

"A thirst," he mumbled. Mary was sitting beside his bed, her eyes closed. They snapped open, and her face split into a massive grin when she saw his open eyes.

"Victor!" the woman practically shouted.

"Thirst," he said again, and Mary nodded, rising from her chair and pouring him water from a pitcher near the bed. She handed the cup to him and he took it with shaky hands, tipping it to his lips. She helped him hold it.

"What happened?" he asked when he finally pulled the cup away from his mouth.

"You were shot," Mary said. "Do you not remember?"

"I do not," Victor said. "I was in the woods. Hunting. The Baron was there, and that is all I remember. It was an accident?"

"No, Jonathan Bailey attempted to kill you. He is locked up for the horrid crime as we speak." Victor started at that news.
~~~~~

"He tried to kill me? Oh yes, his sister. He was upset because I had called things off. He challenged me to a duel."

"It was a duel?" Mary said surprised.

"Of course not. Duels are illegal."

"Right," Mary said. "It is of little consequence now."

"Little consequence? I have been shot."

"I only mean do not let it rattle your brain just yet. I must go and fetch a doctor. They will want to know that you are awake."

"Do so," Victor encouraged, and he watched the girl leave. His younger sister took his hand. "We thought we had lost you, my brother," she said.

When Mary came back, a doctor was with her, a tall man of some age with piercing green eyes and a large moustache.

"Glad to see you awake," the doctor said.

"Glad to be awake," Victor said, but he groaned in pain as the doctor checked his wound. It was an uncomfortable half an hour, but when the older man was satisfied that Victor would not suddenly shuffle off the mortal coil, he left.

"How are you?" he asked, and Mary couldn't help but laugh.

"How am I?" she asked. "You were shot, and you ask how I am?"

"You look tired," Victor said, and Mary could only laugh again.

"She has not left your side," Beth said.

"Go home," Victor said. "Sleep. I will not die while you are gone. I promise."

With much reluctance, Mary went home to sleep. When she returned, the Baron was sitting with his nephew. He smiled and stood as Mary and Jo entered.

"I am sorry," he said.

"Sorry?" Mary was confused.

"Victor and I have been talking. I am sorry it took my nephew getting shot before I realized the love between you. I will step aside."

Mary looked at him startled. "My Lord?" she said.

"I know we have marriage plans in the making, but I have learned the mettle of this man in the last few days." He gestured to Victor. "I am happy knowing that the Barony will pass to him. If you wish it, your father will have the title he wishes and you will have the man you love. I am sure your being by his side will speed my nephew's way to recovery."

"Are you sure, my Lord?" Mary asked unable to quite believe her good fortune. "I am grateful, but I... do hold you in high regard."

"As an uncle perhaps," he said. "Not as a husband."

Mary had to agree that was preferable.

"I do not think either of us is anxious to be Baron and Baroness. It is only my father's wishes."

"He wishes to see his daughters settled," the Baron surmised. "I understand, even though I have no daughters."

"Yes. If you could see to it that Jo could have a season," Mary said tentatively.

"We could come out together," Beth exclaimed, happy with the thought.

"And Helen?" the Baron asked.

"I think she would be happy with her mathematics," Mary added, "but I am not sure. Perhaps a formal introduction to Lord Ashcroft..." She bit her lip.

"Ashcroft!" Victor exclaimed.

The Baron chuckled. That I can do," he said. "But I do think I would rather give the duties of the Barony over to Victor. The more I think about it, the more I like the thought of it. He will have it in the end, he might as well start dealing with it now."

"But what will you do?" Mary asked.

"Exactly what I have been doing... hunting a little in between managing the estate. Of course, once my nephew is up to snuff I will be able to pass on the managing of the estate to him." The Baron winked at her, while Victor struggled to get out of bed.

"What are you doing?" Mary asked, alarmed.

"I am asking you to marry me," he said as he sat on the side of the bed. "As soon as the dizziness passes and I can get down on one knee."

"Yes," she shouted. "Yes. I'll marry you. Now you get back in that bed and rest right now."

"Far be it from me to argue when my bride demands I get into bed," Victor teased her. Mary felt her olive skin heat, but knew she would not be bright red. Victor's sister Beth, however, had no such camouflage. Mary crossed her arms over her chest. "Captain, how dare you speak so!"

"I will dare much, Mary Highland. For you, I will dare much." He caught her hand and kissed it. "I love you."

The End

You'll find a preview of another of Isabella Thorne's books, just after the 'About the Author' section!

About the Author

Isabella Thorne is an author of Regency and Georgian Romance. The first grown-up books she read were historical, authored by Georgette Heyer, Victoria Holt and Anna Seton. Unfortunately, for her own daughters, the beauty and hallmark of Regency Romance, witty dialogue and the manners of the time, have been over-shadowed by explicit books instead of true Regency Romance.

With a return to romance, Isabella Thorne hopes you will enjoy her light, fun books. You can share them with your daughters with the guarantee that, although there is romance aplenty, and a bit of sexual tension and a kiss, there is nothing explicit in her books.

They are clean and wholesome reads with lots of humour and upbeat "fun poking" at the English mannerisms of the time.

Because Isabella loves the pageantry of the period, she loves to include true events or set stories during a war -- the English were involved in so many of them at this time!

You will find bits of history scattered through the books and an occasional historical figure, but these books are FICTION and not intended to be a definitive history. None of the Peerage mentioned in them, of any land, actually existed.

Isabella hopes that all the British and the die-hard historical readers will please forgive this passionate American if she makes any mistakes, and, if you find one, send an email off to isabellathorne58@yahoo.com so that she can make corrections.

Stop by her website, www.isabellathorne.com for a free story and a notification of special sales.

If you love her books, PLEASE REVIEW and SHARE, so that others can come to love them too!

ARIETTA RICHMOND, GRACE AUSTEN, ISABELLA THORNE,
KATHERINE KEATS AND ALYCE HEALEY

Other Books By Isabella Thorne

The Duke's Wicked Wager Series

Promise Me a Handful of Horses

Promise Me Daring

Promise Me This Dance

Promise Me Your Heart

Mischief, Mayhem and Murder: A
Marquis of Evermont Regency Romance

The Georgette Quinby Series

The Mad Heiress Meets the Duke

The Mad Heiress and the Search for a Spy

The Mad Heiress Visits Vauxhall

The Mad Heiress and the Rose Room Rout

The Mad Heiress' Cousin and the Hunt

Georgette Quinby Boxed Set

Other Books by Isabella Thorne

Colonial Cressida and the Secret Duke

Mistletoe and Masquerade.

Just One Christmas Kiss

New Year's Masquerade

Mistletoe and Masquerade Collection

To find more Regency Romance stories, please visit my
website

www.isabellathorne.com

Please Like Isabella Thorne on Facebook

https://www.facebook.com/Isabella-Thorne-Author-
1737782389810565/

Share or comment on an Isabella Thorne Facebook post for
a chance to win an Amazon gift card

ARIETTA RICHMOND, GRACE AUSTEN, ISABELLA THORNE,
KATHERINE KEATS AND ALYCE HEALEY

Here is Your Preview of

The Mad Heiress

Meets the Duke

Book 1: The Georgette Quinby Series

Georgette had escaped to the garden. Even in winter, the green and growing things gave her comfort. She breathed slowly through her nose. Her breath puffed out like a little cloud. No doubt the tongues would be wagging. The *ton* would think her even crazier than normal to come out here in the cold, but she needed a moment - just a moment - to herself, in the cold winter air. Some time to gather her wits about her, to take some deep breaths. To remember who she was and how it had once been; how she had once been so blindingly happy, and then to remember how it was now. Breathe, she told herself as she pressed her gloved hands together over her stomacher. In. Out. Well, in as far as her corset allowed and then out.

The ballroom had been stifling - an absolute crush, packed with bodies and warring perfumes. And all of them turning their catty faces to her - looking at her with distain. She couldn't bear it for one moment longer.

"Look, it's the Mad Heiress," one of the young ladies had said tittering like a ninny.

"Is it really? I thought she'd killed herself." Her friend fanned herself as she looked slyly over the accessory at Georgette.

"No, you were misinformed," another said, craning her bejewelled neck. "I heard she flung herself off a parapet, after Lord Falks threw her over for Lady Julia."

"I heard it was a cliff," the first one said.

"I'm certain it was a parapet. But no matter. The point is, she survived."

"Poor thing. I'd rather be dead," said the first woman fanning herself quite vigorously.

"It was stairs," Georgette had said to the open air, once she had fled to the garden. "Stairs. If one must gossip, at the very least one should get the facts straight. I flung myself down some stairs."

She should probably stop talking to herself, she thought. She was already known as the Mad Heiress, and she hadn't done anything exciting for almost ten years. Lud, if the *ton* heard her grumbling to herself about stairs she would never rest in peace.

But honestly - a cliff? If it had been a cliff, she might have had some success. Instead, she had woken up in her bed, a few days later, with a sore head and a broken hip, like an old woman. And a fiancé who did not love her. She must not forget that.

Oh, Sebastien. Why?

Ten years ago she had been slipping out of ballrooms to meet him in the garden, the stolen kisses sweet on her lips: Escaping the candlelight and the weak punch and her stifling mother, hoping for a stolen moment with her beloved.

Ten years, and no one forgot. No one ever forgot. She clenched her fists. She would forever be the Mad Heiress. No matter that she had been but seventeen when Sebastien had informed her that his heart belonged to another.

No matter that she was twenty-six-years old now, and a chaperone, a spinster, firmly on the shelf.

No matter that she could not conceive of the sensibility and passion that had driven her up those stairs. She could not remember, but everyone else still remembered.

Deep breaths, she reminded herself as she rubbed her gloved hands over her cooling arms. Breathe in, breathe out. Or, rather, breathe in as deeply as one's corset allows, and breathe out. In, and out, through the nose.

Georgette froze. She sniffed the air. Someone was smoking a cigar.

Oh, bother.

She swallowed. Perhaps the gentleman would not realize she'd entered the gardens. She could surreptitiously sneak back into the ballroom. She made to turn back into the house.

He stood right in front of her. Grey flecked through his hair. She knew his eyes were dark blue, but the darkness of the gardens made them almost black. He peered at her with them, over a royal, aquiline nose.

The Duke of Eversley.

"I beg your pardon," he said. "I did not realize there was a Lady in the garden. I will snuff my cigar."

"Please don't on my account, Your Grace," she said, giving a curtsey. "I was just about to re-enter the ballroom."

He blinked at her. "I know you," he said. He tilted his head and looked at her, no doubt attempting to place her.

Georgette opened her mouth and then closed it again. Did he truly not recognize her?

"Ah, yes, Your Grace," she said. "I do believe we crossed paths several years ago, when I was newly out."

He continued to look at her curiously.

"I was engaged to your dear friend, Lord Sebastien Falks."

"Sebastien? But you can't have been engaged to Sebastien, he married my..."

She knew the moment he pieced it together, the moment he remembered. He colored, though it was difficult to tell in the darkness, and gave a small cough.

"I beg your pardon," he said. "I forgot, you see. It was all so long ago."

She couldn't help herself: she laughed. He stared at her for a moment as if she was demented.

Continue Reading

'The Mad Heiress Meets the Duke'

at:

https://www.amazon.com/dp/B01ICEAT4W/

Regency Romance
Isabella Thorne

ARIETTA RICHMOND, GRACE AUSTEN, ISABELLA THORNE, KATHERINE KEATS AND ALYCE HEALEY

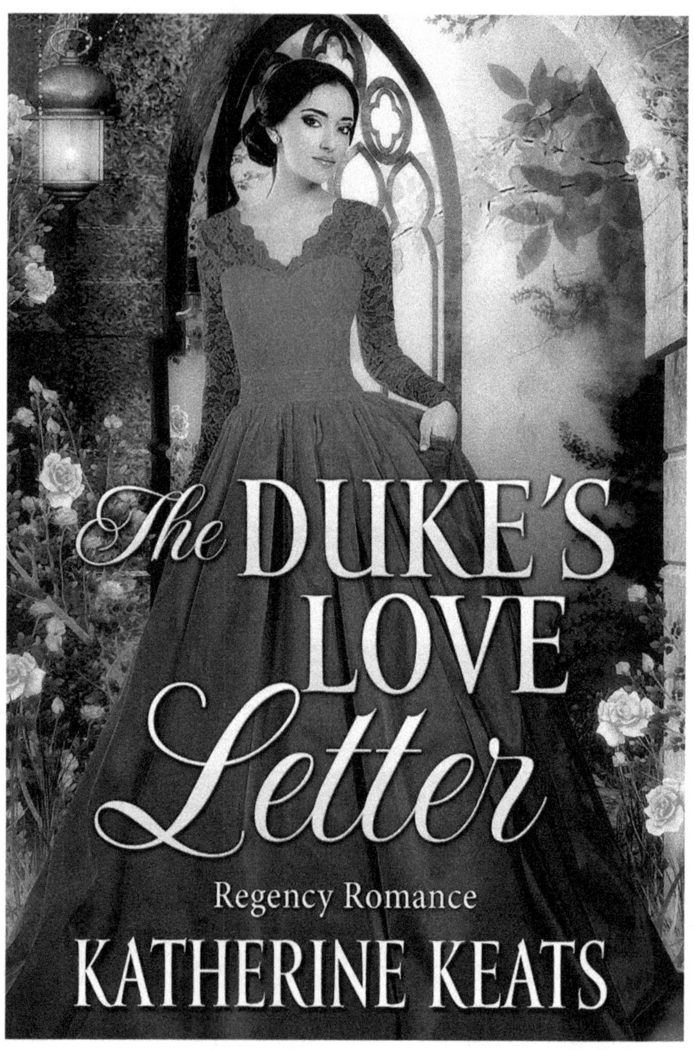

Regency Romance

The Duke's Love Letter

Katherine Keats

ARIETTA RICHMOND, GRACE AUSTEN, ISABELLA THORNE,
KATHERINE KEATS AND ALYCE HEALEY

All Rights Reserved. No part of this publication may be reproduced in any form or by any means, including scanning, photocopying, or otherwise without prior written permission of the copyright holder. Copyright © 2017

Chapter One

David Stanton, Duke of Mowbray, let out a discontented sigh and pursed his lips as he looked across the room at Miss Fairchild. There were surely many virtues and facets of her being that he could draw on as choice material for his Valentine's message. He could perhaps comment on how her hair flowed like a river of molten gold from her head. No. He didn't like the word molten; it was far too harsh and he doubted any woman would wish to be compared to a volcano.

He reflected that he might say something about her eyes. He gazed at those two orbs but, with the distance with which she sat from him, he could not clearly decide what colour they were. It left him feeling ashamed, a fraud. He should surely know the eye colour of the woman he was planning to make his bride.

A smug smile near Miss Fairchild served to distract the Duke further from his mental task and he raised his eyebrow at his brother. "Is something amusing you John?" He spoke in a dignified and disinterested voice.

John's grin only seemed to grow and he stood from his seat, stretching out like a cat after some long nap.

"Only a little joke I was told by a friend the other afternoon. I will tell it to you later, but I have just remembered some business we really need to discuss, if you can spare me a moment alone?"

A light chuckle came from Felicity and she shot her husband a suspicious but playful glare.

"I do not believe you want to talk business for a moment. You never care one jot about business. I would wager, Miss Fairchild, my rogue of a husband just wishes to talk about us behind our backs."

John smiled and leaned down, kissing his wife. He was not the sort to be bashful in company and his lips clung to hers for a long moment, seeming to take her breath away and blunting her sharp wit.

"I promise, my dear, that I only ever say good things about you."

Felicity smiled, apparently satisfied, and John escorted his brother away to the far side of the room. They looked out of the window, staring out at the grounds that had been their family home for generations.

John put an arm about his brother and gave one last look back to the ladies, making sure that they were not studying him too closely.

Once satisfied, he leaned in and began to talk in a hushed voice.

"You know that I have been watching you for half an hour. From where I've been sitting, you've been giving boundless entertainment with the faces you've been pulling. If I didn't know better, I'd say you had a bad case of the cramps."

"You know John, I am glad you weren't born the eldest. Your irreverence would have been a discredit to the family name." The Duke liked to criticise his brother, even if he privately enjoyed John's honest jests.

"You have been studying the beautiful Miss Fairchild and trying to compose some sonnet or something of that sort to gift her for Valentine's." John grinned and shook his head. "I suppose I am to blame for this struggle you face. The words I have composed for my dear Fliss over the last three years have been truly sublime in their genius. Why, I dare say the brightest poets in London would weep and give up the pen if they were to read them."

The Duke snorted and shook his head.

"I wouldn't use quite those words, but I will confess I was impressed to read one or two of the cards you have gifted your wife. I will admit that Felicity is a very rare and wonderful creature, but I would love to know how you gained the gift of writing such beautiful sentiments."

John looked to his brother with an expression that the Duke took for sympathy. "Look, our father was a military man through and through. With our mother dying before I had even learned to talk, there was little hope of either of us learning much of how to woo a woman. I guarantee if we did not have our father's title and money behind us we would be thoroughly unmarriageable."

"So then, what is the secret? How did you unlock your inner poet to help you woo Felicity?" The Duke looked desperately at his brother, pleading for him not to toy with him on the matter.

"If I tell you, you have to swear on your honour you will not breathe a word of it to anyone. I am serious about this David, not a word."

The Duke frowned, surprised to see his brother suddenly so defensive.

"I can't see why I would. Still, if it means that much to you, you have my word."

For one last time John looked back to the women and then whispered in his brother's ear.

"I do not write the cards at all."

"What?" David had to struggle to contain his voice. "Did you just steal someone else's letters, or copy those of a friend?" There was an air of disdain in the Duke's voice.

"Nothing so crass, and do not be so high and mighty with me. Many people do exactly the same thing and less. I at least make sure to personalise what is written in the cards I send."

"What do you mean personalise?" David asked in confusion.

"It's very simple. There is a woman I see who makes the cards I gift for Felicity. Every year we sit down and she asks me about the types of things I want to express. I tell her anecdotal stories of what Fliss and I have shared: experiences, or the things I love most about her and so forth."

John's expression was earnest as he went on.

"Once we have worked out the kind of thing I want to say to her, this woman then goes through her notes and sets it on paper in a more poetic and artful style. So, you see, it is still my words reaching her. All this woman does is to give my words a more delicate presentation."

David pursed his lips as he mulled over the moral implications of letting someone else write a personal Valentine on another's behalf. He did not have long to think though, as John was already wandering back to the women and taking his place by his wife's side.

"Good chat dear?" Felicity moved her body closer to John and rested her head on his shoulder. She seemed to let out a contented sigh as her fingers wound about his. John, in turn, kissed her forehead. David desperately wanted that kind of happiness for himself and could not deny the envy he felt, seeing his brother so settled and happy.

His eyes fell on Miss Fairchild who offered a coy smile before tearing her eyes away. She had been a regular visitor to his estate ever since the Duke had fallen into the company of her father. Still, David knew that he had been tarrying and dragging his heels in the matter of forming a courtship with her. He did not know what caused him to be so hesitant, but he suspected it was nervousness. Soon, if he made no definite intimation to Miss Fairchild that he was considering her as a potential bride, she would lose interest in waiting for him, and her father would send her into the paths of other young men.

Letting out a sigh, David found his moral qualms defeated.

"About what we just spoke of, John… Could you remember to write down the name of your associate for me, and I will be sure to write to them in due course?"

John gave a triumphant grin that was almost enough to make David rethink his course.

"I'll be sure to write down their address before we leave today. I guarantee it will be worth your time."

Felicity's eye shot between the two brothers.

"I would think that my incorrigible husband was trying to get you into trouble, except that I know you are far too sensible to listen to anything he says." Even as she brazenly teased him, John's smile simply continued to grow.

Miss Fairchild looked about her, not comprehending the subtle familial jokes passing between the others. David felt sorry for her, but imagined she would come to understand the nuances of his family's ways in time. For now, he offered her a reassuring smile as the maid came in with fresh tea.

Chapter Two

Standing outside the tailors, Henrietta frowned at the limited selection she could see from the window. She desperately needed more red ribbon to incorporate into her cards for the upcoming feast of St Valentine's.

She had become popular in the last years. Word of mouth from a few good clients had seen demand for her particular skills grow to the point where she almost couldn't keep up. There was another man she was to meet today, who was in need of her particular talents.

The Duke of Mowbray was a step up from the usual type of client she worked for, and she was sure he would have great expectations of her. She only hoped that the man would have a solid idea of what he was looking to say, to whichever girl had been lucky enough to capture his heart.

Looking again at the shabby material on offer in the window, Henrietta stamped her foot in frustration. A bell from the local church tolled the hour of eleven. The Duke was due at her home just after midday.

She didn't have time to trawl through the shop's contents in the hope of finding something worthwhile. If she was to find a good length of high quality ribbon that was not faded in colour or frayed at the edges she would have to go all the way out to Newmarket. How she was to have everything ready and delivered to her clients in time was beyond her.

With a brisk step, Henrietta rushed for home, trying to flee from the worries and concerns that hounded her. There were her client's expectations, the deadlines and, of course, the words themselves. To all of this though, there was added another worry that plagued her. She was becoming tired. All the letters of love and heartfelt devotion she wrote to women whom she neither knew, nor cared for, was becoming tedious.

So many of the men that she dealt with came to her with such bland opinions of their loved ones. Only a precious few like John Stanton showed genuine devotion and interest in their wives and paramours. Some of her worst clients even had the gall to complain about the time she took to interview them and learn of the women she would be writing too.

The most boorish of her customers even refused to spare her more than a few minutes to get the information she needed to create a sonnet or missive that was personal to their lady.

With luck and effort, Henrietta managed to keep one step ahead of the fears that gnawed at her heels. She managed to make it back to her home with over fifteen minutes to spare before the Duke's arrival. It was just enough time to set the kettle over the fire and to tidy away some of the papers and half-finished crafts she had left scattered about.

Her home was small, consisting of only one downstairs and one upstairs room. As a single woman with no money to speak of, except the modest income her writing made her, Henrietta was lucky even to have this place to call her own. If it were not for the fact that the owner of the property was good friends with her late father and mother she would likely have never been able to afford to pay for even this place.

Grabbing all of the spare twists of ribbon, card and paper, Henrietta hurriedly started to move all of her work up to her bedroom, laying the pieces out on her bed with little care. Hurtling back downstairs, Henrietta looked about her. There was still much she should do in order to make her home acceptable to a Duke's eyes, but she was fast running out of time. Setting a few threadbare cushions on her best chair, she made a place for the Duke to sit. A fresh sheet of paper was put out on the table where she ate, and her pen and ink were placed neatly beside it. Taking a deep breath, Henrietta satisfied herself that she was now ready to receive her guest.

When the knock came, Henrietta was practically standing by the door ready to answer. She took a quick moment to smooth out the creases in her dull cream dress and cast one last eye about the room to ensure that there was not something glaringly obvious she had forgotten to tidy away. Satisfied, she turned and opened the door.

The Duke of Mowbray was peculiarly handsome. That was the first thought that entered Henrietta's head as she met the eyes of the man outside her door. It was strange that she should find herself so moved, as he looked much like his brother John in most respects.

Still, subtle differences forced her to admit that he was far more pleasing to her eye than the younger brother she had come to know over the last few years.

The Duke had green eyes like his brother, but the Duke's eyes shone far more, like emeralds. They practically glistened in the low light of the sun and were by far his most arresting and captivating quality. They carried an intensity and weight to them and, as the man looked back at her, his eyes betrayed the great complexity of thought hidden within his mind.

His hair was short and dark, practical, and suited to a man whose family had served for so many generations in His Majesty's Army. Meanwhile, the Duke's skin was rugged, touched and weathered by years of toil and hardship. To some women, this might have been a disappointment, but to Henrietta it made the man seem powerful, wise and well-travelled, despite his young years.

"Are you Miss Hart?" The Duke looked uncertain for a moment, and Henrietta blushed to realise that she had forgotten to say a word as her eyes had studied and mapped his face.

"Do excuse me, yes." Henrietta gave a hasty curtsey. "You must forgive me, I was... I was working on some new material shortly before you arrived and my head was elsewhere."

The Duke smiled. It was a polite smile, somewhat awkward, but it did not appear un-genuine. By the way he stood so stiffly, Henrietta could tell at once that something about her had bothered him.

"I am sorry if my home is a little plain and not suited to company such as yourself."

She made the apology as a stab in the dark, trying to guess just what about her, or her home, had set the Duke on edge.

"No, please do not apologise, it is quite a charming little home you have, and impressive that you are able to own it for yourself. You must forgive me; my brother told me that you were unmarried, and made your own way in the world. It is admirable and intriguing to see."

"Well, thank you. I do what I can with the place." Henrietta tilted her head, her lips spreading into a slight smile. It was rare for her to be complimented, by a stranger, for the life she lived. Most looked upon her spinsterhood as something to be treated with sympathy. Some men had even apologised for it in the past and made her offers of introduction to bachelors, or widowed older men, who might consider taking her.

It did not take long to settle the Duke into the chair she had put aside for him. As soon as he was comfortable, Henrietta quickly set to the task of making tea for them both. Even as she worked though, she noticed that the Duke continued to seem ill at ease and wondered if he might need to drink something a little stronger. She bit her lip, trying to keep her thoughts to herself, but she had always been a curious creature by habit.

"Is everything well your Grace? If you will pardon my rudeness, you seem a little... ill at ease. Is there anything I can fetch you to make you more comfortable?"

The Duke gave another nervous smile which seemed quite strange for a man she would have thought severe and emotionally detached.

"I am sorry, no. If I seem nervous it is only because I have been somewhat dreading this visit for the last few days."

Henrietta turned her head to look at the Duke, a puzzled look on her face. She might have felt offended, but it was quite refreshing to have client who was so candid.

"Dreaded, Your Grace? Might I ask what it is about me you fear?" She gave a slightly teasing smile, but this quickly faded when she saw the look of genuine concern and embarrassment that knotted the man's face.

"It is not you, and it is not a fear," the Duke insisted. "It is more the meeting itself that has me set a little on edge. I will confess, I was surprised to learn that my brother hired a relative stranger to write the romantic missives he gives to his wife every Valentine's and Christmas. I do not wish to appear rude or judgemental of what you do... but I cannot shake the worry that this is a horrible deception he is playing on his wife, and I am not overly sure if I should be following his example."

Henrietta straightened up, and silently brought over a cup of tea for the Duke to take. She let herself study his face for a moment longer, thoroughly fascinated by this oddity of a man, who was so unlike any other client she had seen before. It was curious to hear him address concerns which she herself had battled with in the past, when considering the value of the service she provided.

"I can assure you now, Your Grace, that your honesty does you much credit. If nothing else, it shows your good character that you are so concerned for your Lady. I can understand that you do not wish to trick or deceive her in any way."

Sitting down at the table, Henrietta took a sip from her drink. "I can assure you, that I to share your concerns and I would never consciously write anything that I didn't feel was true and meaningful for your Lady. This meeting is an opportunity and chance for us to explore how you feel for Miss... Miss?" Henrietta's face flushed red as she struggled to remember the name of the Lady the Duke was courting.

"Miss Fairchild." The Duke did not seem at all concerned with Henrietta's forgetfulness.

"Well, we will use this time we have now to discuss your feelings for Miss Fairchild in depth. You might, for example, tell me what you admire most about her. Feel free to express anything you wish. A cherished memory of her, or a facet of her physical beauty that captivates you. I will take down everything you say and from there we will work to present your true feelings as a card, sonnet or song. I promise you, what we create here will be entirely your work. All I do, is help express your feelings with the best possible words."

The Duke nodded, but Henrietta suspected he still did not feel wholly at ease.

"Well, Miss Hart, I shall try my best."

ARIETTA RICHMOND, GRACE AUSTEN, ISABELLA THORNE,
KATHERINE KEATS AND ALYCE HEALEY

Chapter Three

Henrietta looked at the clock and tried to stop herself from letting out a wistful sigh. Things were not going well. Although she admired the Duke of Mowbray's persistence in trying, it was clear that he was uncomfortable expressing his feelings to her and the notes she had made on Miss Fairchild consisted only of uninteresting facts about her. Glancing over the sheet, she scanned everything she knew about the lady so far.

Long blonde hair.

Green but possibly brown eyes – Duke uncertain on this.

Very pale skin – Duke's own words.

First met at Miss Fairchild's home when the Duke was invited to dine there by her father...

Miss Fairchild is shy and retiring in most situations (much like the Duke it seems)

Henrietta stopped reading. The rest of her notes were all quite similar.

They gave her information but didn't help in painting any kind of concrete picture of the woman or the kind of relationship she shared with the Duke. Though she didn't say so out loud, Henrietta wondered if the Duke had ever even really talked to the mysterious Miss Fairchild at all. He seemed to know almost nothing about her likes and passions.

The Duke had been silent for a few minutes now. His head hung low and he carried a look of defeat and dejection. It made Henrietta sad. He obviously wished to say and express more. He seemed positively ashamed that he had contributed so little in such a long span of time. The silence between them was almost deafening and he looked almost like he was awaiting some kind of scolding from her, or perhaps her admission that she could not work with the scant material he had been able to provide her.

Henrietta bit her bottom lip, eyes narrowing as she tried to settle on a course of action. A part of her was telling her to give up. She had enough orders for cards and poignant love letters to keep her busy right up to Saint Valentine's Day itself. Although the Duke represented by far the most lucrative business, it was clear that she would have her work cut out making anything even the slightest bit personal for the man.

He had already expressed his discomfort about her business and no doubt this was, at least in part, what was making the process so difficult for him. Perhaps he was simply not inclined to speak candidly to a stranger about his feelings. If this was the case, how was she ever going to be able to get anything useful out of him.

Henrietta knew, that, if she had any sense at all, she should politely inform the Duke that he did not really want her service and suggest that he work his hardest to write something, himself, for the mysteriously unknowable Miss Fairchild. This was the most sensible path for both of them. Still, something prevented her from giving up on him so easily.

She could not fully explain it, but Henrietta found something noble about the Duke. Even if he had been unable to conjure up any useful information about Miss Fairchild, he had worked his hardest for over two hours to do so. She had watched him suffer moments of awkwardness, embarrassment and frustration as he tried to create the romantic sentiments necessary for a Valentine's missive. At no point over the course of their time together had he given up. She had watched him pace about the room, watched him close his eyes to try and form a mental picture of his beloved. He had put in so much effort that Henrietta found that she just did not have the stone-cold heart necessary to turn him away.

"I am sorry." The Duke's voice was quiet and almost inaudible. The apology was followed by a great sigh, and Henrietta could see his shoulders rise and fall dramatically as he took that great, dissatisfied breath. "This is exactly why I needed to come here. I am thoroughly useless in these matters, to the point where I cannot even talk through my feelings. I can tell from that awkward expression you're wearing that I haven't given you nearly enough about Miss Fairchild for you to write about her."

Henrietta felt her heart ache a little for the Duke's plight.

She tried to put on a braver face for him, banishing the pursed lips and furrowed brow she had let herself adopt.

"Please, do not be so hard on yourself. You have just spent two hours trying to express yourself. I will not lie to you, I do feel that we need more to work with than what you have given me here. That does not mean, though, that you have in anyway failed."

She hesitated for a moment, wondering if it was poor manners to talk about her other clients with the Duke.

"I likely shouldn't admit to this. Many of the men who come to me do so much less than you have done. They enter in and give me sweeping statements about the radiance of their lover's hair, their perfect porcelain skin or some other trite phrases that they imagine to be entirely original. They do not care to waste their time trying to capture the true essence of their lady properly. I will confess, I would like it if we had more to go on, but I am genuinely touched by how persistent you are."

The Duke gave a wan smile.

It was not much, but it was something.

"I thank you for your kindness Miss Hart. Even so, I imagine that you are going to have to decline this particular assignment. I cannot blame you for it. Were you to try and create anything out of what I have given you it would either be a gigantic falsehood, or would otherwise read terribly."

Henrietta clenched her fists. She was determined not to fail the Duke.

Something about him had made her warm to him and she did not wish to let him leave in defeat.

"No; there are other options still before us. One option could be to let me see Miss Fairchild for myself. Perhaps, if you were to invite me to dine with you and her, I could get a better idea of the Lady and your feelings for her simply by watching the two of you interact."

"You mean, tell her that I am having you write a Valentine for her?" The Duke's eyes widened and he shifted uncomfortably in his chair.

"No, not at all. You will merely invite me as a friend of your family. After all, I already know your brother. You would not have to lie to her about our acquaintance, just omit certain details of how and why we have come to know each other."

Henrietta was not sure about this plan.

Even as she suggested it, and assured the Duke that he would not have to lie, she knew that it would not be so simple as she had implied. From the uneasy expression he wore, she thought he would reject the notion out of hand.

"I suppose it is our best chance." The Duke nodded and bit his lip as he contemplated Henrietta's plan. "I am in the habit of entertaining guests often on my estate, and there is in fact a small party which I am holding this weekend. There will be several families in attendance, so it should afford you the opportunity to mingle without being asked too many questions. Miss Fairchild does not yet know my full set of acquaintances and will think nothing of your presence there."

Henrietta nodded.

"Then it is settled. I will come to your estate on Saturday and observe Miss Fairchild for myself. I am sure that, from this, we can create something truly beautiful for your Valentine."

Even as she spoke she wished that she had not made such assurances. She did not know why, but a worry and a doubt was already taking root in the corner of her mind. Still, she had to remain positive and give the Duke hope.

Chapter Four

It had been a bad week. After the almost disastrous meeting with the Duke of Mowbray, Henrietta had found herself becoming consumed by thoughts of him, and of the Valentine she would have to create for him. It drove her to distraction, eclipsing any other thought and making it all but impossible to work on the other Valentine's Day messages which she had already started for other gentlemen.

She did not know quite what it was that drove her, but she was determined to create the right message for the Duke, to help him to express his feelings for the mysterious Miss Fairchild. Perhaps it stemmed from the warm impression the Duke had made on her. It had been quite some time since she had met a man so handsome, in both physical aspect and demeanour. His polite affability and willingness to do whatever it took to make a Valentine's that was worthy of his Lady made Henrietta almost ashamed to write for the other gentlemen, who paid her to write for them simply because they were too lazy to do so themselves.

On Friday, as Henrietta struggled to keep her mind on her work and not on the impending party at the Duke's estate, a knock at the door came as a welcome distraction from her endeavours. Putting down her pen, she stretched and went to the door. Still caught up in thoughts of her work, she took a moment to look her visitor up and down. She was surprised to find him to be a rather smartly dressed footman. By his somewhat expensive clothes, the servant had to be from the Duke's estate. Henrietta wondered just what the man's purpose was, and, even more intriguing, what was the meaning of the large beautifully wrapped box that was held in the man's hands?

"Hello? Can I help you?" Henrietta puzzled over the footman as she waited for him to speak.

"His Grace the Duke of Mowbray bids you a good day and hopes that you are still able to attend his home tomorrow for dinner." The servant spoke very eloquently and to the point.

"Yes, I am still intent on attending the Duke's party, you can tell him not to worry about that."

The servant nodded and then stretched out his arms, offering Henrietta the large ribbon-tied box that he held.

"The Duke will send his own carriage to take you to his estate. You can expect it to arrive at three o'clock tomorrow afternoon."

"Thank you. Might I ask what this package is about?" Henrietta ran her hands over the ribbon.

The servant's face lit with a more natural smile.

"I believe his Grace has left a note inside that should explain everything. Now, if you'll excuse me, I must return to my duties."

Henrietta nodded and bade the servant farewell. She did not watch him leave, her eyes remaining on the mysterious item she had been left with. Wandering back indoors, she laid the box out on the table and carefully slid off the ribbon - it was good quality silk and she would be sure to keep it for use in one of her cards or craft pieces.

Opening the lid, Henrietta gasped at the opulent gown that lay within. It was a cream dress made of fine taffeta and adorned with bobbin-lace frills about the sleeves. The dress was square cut about the chest, with further bobbin-lace rising up to the neck as a kind of collar.

Added to this were a pair of long sleeved gloves and a choker of white silk, adorned with what looked to be a single sapphire in its centre. It was a most exquisite ensemble and Henrietta felt a thrill run through her at the prospect of being able to wear such finery.

She had been quite concerned that even her best dress would be not really suitable for an event at the home of a Duke. As she held the dress up against her, she wondered just where the Duke had obtained such an outfit.

It might, she guessed, be an heirloom of his mother's, lent to her so that she would not appear out of place at his party.

Reverently resting the gown over the back of a chair, Henrietta turned her attention to the note that accompanied the outfit.

"I do hope that this gown is to your liking. I have purchased it directly from the modiste, with the help of my brother (he has a better eye for women's fashion than I). Please accept this gift as thanks for the extra effort which you are going to, on my behalf. I do hope that you do not find yourself having to make too many alterations to the fit of the dress."

Henrietta's mouth dropped open at the realisation that the gown, the gloves and the choker were actually meant as a present for her. It came as such a shock that she was almost unable to process the very idea of it.

Often given to working with various expensive materials, she was able to hazard a guess as to how much the whole outfit must have cost the Duke. Looking over the gown again with a more critical eye she knew instinctively that, were she to sell the dress, she would likely make enough money to live without working for a year or more.

Chapter Five

Stepping out of the carriage with the aid of a footman, Henrietta smiled to find the Duke of Mowbray standing at the door waiting for her. Immediately, she gave a polite curtsey and could not resist giving a little spin on the spot to show off how she looked in the gown he had bought for her. The action brought a smile to the man's face and he began to walk towards her.

"Miss Hart, I am very glad that you find yourself able to attend"

Henrietta blushed as she found herself unable to meet the Duke's eyes. Instead her gaze seemed to fall to his chest and she spoke to his fine gold trimmed waistcoat. "Your Grace, I cannot tell you how astounded I was to receive your gift. It was extremely thoughtful, not to mention extravagant, of you. I hope that you are not considering paying me any more for the meagre service I am giving you."

The Duke smiled and waved his hand.

"I will not hear of it. I intend to pay you properly for the services you are giving me. This is just a token of my appreciation for you having gone above and beyond your remit. I can't imagine you've ever had to do this much work for any of your clients in the past."

Henrietta nodded and bit her lip, willing her cheeks not to redden any more at the Duke's kind words and actions.

"I just hope that I am able to create something for Miss Fairchild that will be worthy of the kindness you have already shown me. At the very least, I can say, without hesitation, that the lady is lucky to have you as an admirer."

The Duke put out an arm for Henrietta. She took a deep breath and placed her hand on the offered arm.. She could not explain it, but there was something wonderfully pleasant about being escorted by this man. She told herself it was nothing more than gratitude that she was feeling, but she could not help smiling as the Duke took her up the stairs and into his home. Then, work began. As soon as Henrietta set foot in the Duke's drawing room, and was introduced to the other guests, she had to focus on her task. As much as she might wish it otherwise, she was not here just as the Duke's guest.

Looking at the sea of faces around her, it was easy enough to discover which among them was the enigmatic Miss Fairchild. There was only one woman in the room with truly blonde hair and Henrietta was, at once, impressed by her beauty. Miss Fairchild had hair that was like a waterfall reflecting the yellow amber of morning sunlight.

Her skin was not pale, but porcelain. Complimented by her small round face, her complexion made her look much like a china doll. She was a perfectly exquisite creature, perfectly suited to the lavish surroundings she found herself in.

However, these were only physical aspects of her beauty and Henrietta knew that she would need to dig deeper in order to learn anything of meaning about her.

For almost half an hour the Duke escorted Henrietta about the room, introducing her to his friends and acquaintances, occasionally giving some history of the estate and of the various pictures and sentimental items that lined the walls and mantelpiece. It was very pleasant to be escorted this way and

it came as something of a disappointment to Henrietta when she remembered that he should be placing his attentions elsewhere.

"Do you think you might want to attend to Miss Fairchild now? I know enough names now to mingle with your other guests and am quite comfortable. I am not going to have much chance to study you with her if you spend all of your evening seeing to my comfort."

The Duke looked over to Miss Fairchild and then back to Henrietta. For a moment, she thought she detected a reluctance in his eyes.

"Are you nervous about being watched by me? I promise, I am not expecting anything grand. I do not wish to see you reciting a poem or declaring your love for her on one knee. Just talk to her as you would normally."

The Duke nodded and his body seemed to straighten up, making him appear more nervous and awkward than he had seemed a moment before.

"Very well. I shall check on your progress later Miss Hart."

After nearly an hour of watching the Duke of Mowbray and Miss Fairchild, Henrietta thought that she was beginning to understand just why the Duke had such difficulty in describing the lady's qualities.

The more she studied Miss Fairchild, the more she realised that the lady didn't seem to actually possess any qualities at all.

Her doll like features seemed to mask a doll like personality, and Henrietta wondered what, if anything, went on inside the girl's head.

No conversation was made between her and the Duke which the Duke did not start up himself.

Miss Fairchild smiled and seemed to nod along to everything that the Duke said, but at no point did she seem to want to take charge of the conversation or make any remarks of her own.

From time to time, Miss Fairchild would pay a compliment to the Duke, remarking on his clothes or some aspect of his features that she liked, but Henrietta thought that she detected, in these compliments, the hint of disinterest.

It was as if Miss Fairchild had a list of phrases in her head that she knew she should say, from time to time, in order to flatter a man.

Henrietta could not tell if this stemmed from any clever artifice on the part of Miss Fairchild, or if the girl was simply very dull and didn't know what else to say in any given situation.

Whatever the truth, Henrietta saw, with mounting dismay, that all of the effort in conversation and attention seemed to come from the Duke - it made her sad. He deserved a woman who would be as attentive and warm as he was.

Eventually, Henrietta put Miss Fairchild from her mind altogether and found herself instead admiring the Duke more and more. She watched as he took the time to talk to each of his guests and make sure that they felt at ease and wanted.

Whenever she caught snippets of conversation it seemed that someone was always thanking him for some good deed he had done, or some gift he had made to them. It turned out that gestures like those he had already shown her were commonplace for the Duke, and his friends all had cause to be grateful and glad of the man's friendship.

It was warming to see, but also made Henrietta wonder how the man could not have found a better woman than the blank canvas that was Miss Fairchild.

After an enjoyable dinner, the Duke's guests were escorted into the ballroom. Their company was not large enough to fill the space, but the Duke had brought in musicians to play so that his guests might enjoy a small, intimate dance.

There were also tables where those less inclined to dance could watch, play cards or talk over drinks.

Henrietta sat alone for the first country dance, watching as the Duke danced with Miss Fairchild. Mowbray was a fine dancer, though perhaps a little stiff in his movements. Miss Fairchild, by contrast, was much more confident and fluid in her steps but held that same disinterested, fake smile that made the whole affair seem like nothing at all.

As the first dance was brought to a close, the Duke escorted Miss Fairchild from the floor, at which point she excused herself and went in search of the ladies retiring room.

The Duke was left alone standing to the side of the floor, a sight which brought a slight pang to Henrietta's heart. As his eyes alighted on her she offered a consoling smile, one which grew fuller as she realised he was walking toward her.

"Would you do me the honour of dancing the next set with me Miss Hart?" The Duke stretched out his hand and gave a reassuring smile which Henrietta could not help but admire.

"It would be my pleasure, so long as Miss Fairchild would not object." Henrietta cast an eye towards the lady in question, who had just returned to the room.. It was immediately obvious that the Lady had no interest in who else the Duke chose to dance with. She did not even seem to be looking in their general direction.

Standing, Henrietta felt like she was floating through a strange kind of dream as the Duke led her out onto the dance floor. She was almost oblivious to the other couples, even to the musicians. It was as if the music just came out of heaven because she had wished it to. She did, however, with a start of pleasure, realise that it was a waltz.

As the dance began, Henrietta noticed the way her hand looked in the Duke's. His fingers were slightly rough but not in a way that she disliked. Her hand looked delicate and tiny against his and he seemed to wrap her fingers up protectively as they began to move in time with the music. Time became an abstract and Henrietta felt herself being led by the Duke through the hazy dream world she now existed in.

Thoughts of her work, Miss Fairchild, or of her own life in a tiny and quiet house, seemed to melt away, so that only the present moment remained. Meanwhile, the Duke's emerald eyes remained locked on her and his smile remained constant and alluring as they spun and moved about in the dance. Then, almost as suddenly as the moment had begun, it abruptly ended.

Henrietta felt dazed as she returned to the world, noticing once more the other guests. She was not even sure what had come over her in that moment, but it frightened her as much as it thrilled and intrigued. Her cheeks were flushed red and the Duke's easy going smile only continued to fluster her. It was clear from his expression that he had not noticed the change he had inspired in her. This brought its own mixed bag of emotions as she simultaneously felt relieved and disappointed.

"Thank you, Your Grace. I must return now to my seat. Lest we forget, I am still making my notes for your gift to Miss Fairchild."

Henrietta could not tell if it was wishful thinking working on her excited imagination, but for a moment she thought she spied a reluctance in the Duke.

Ultimately, he seemed to obey her and walked back towards Miss Fairchild. By the looks of things, the Lady had not even noticed that the Duke had stood up with another woman, a woman previously unknown to her. Henrietta would have expected the lady to show more interest.

Chapter Six

Henrietta groaned and let her head fall unceremoniously onto the table top. She was exhausted. There were now only ten days left until Saint Valentine's Day, and she was beginning to fall into a panic. Whilst she had grown her small enterprise massively over the years, she knew that it could all be undone in a moment. Were she to produce second rate work or, worse still, nothing at all, the backlash from her customers would be enough to see her put out of business for good.

If such an eventuality were to come to pass, she would have to consider new options for her future. Mostly likely, she would end up as a governess to some rich family's children. She would have to leave her property and live out her days as nothing more than a servant, an extension of another's property.

It was not a future that she wanted for herself and, every time she thought of it, the fear helped to galvanise her to work for a few extra hours.

Heavy, grey bags had formed under her eyes and her hair was a mess of loose strands from where she had not washed and brushed properly. From time to time, Henrietta felt her stomach churning as it demanded to be fed. She had not eaten a proper warm meal in days. She just did not have the time to cook anything. Instead, she had grown dependent on cheese, bread and anything else that could be eaten cold without any preparation.

With enormous effort, she lifted her head from the table top and looked down at the words she had strained out on to the page. She was currently writing a long and un-eloquent letter for Mrs Pierce. She did not know the woman and, from Mr Pierce's testimony, she should be glad that she had been spared the acquaintance. Mr Pierce had little good to say about his wife, but he knew exactly what she wanted to hear. She thought her prettiest feature was her nose which was small and delicately formed.

She was extremely fastidious and made sure that their home was at all times in the perfect condition to receive visitors. This, Henrietta suspected, must make the woman a terror to her maids. Forthright in her opinions and always wanting to be heard in any matters of decision making, Mrs Pierce seemed to rule her house like some kind of tyrant. It was a difficulty to sum the woman up in a way that would appear pleasing on paper, but Mr Pierce insisted Henrietta try as his wife had high expectations of him to deliver a perfect Valentine's Day gift.

It dismayed Henrietta to think that she had written cards to Mrs Pierce when she was still Miss Meadon.

In those days, Mr Pierce had been far kinder in his words towards his wife and practically oozed affection for her. It was disheartening to consider how three years had altered his opinion. It made her wonder if Mr Pierce had not been duped by the lady into thinking her something other than what she was. Or, maybe time had simply cooled his affection for her and he had lost the ability to appreciate the good things she did for him. Whatever the reason, writing Mrs Pierce's Valentine was a slow and torturous affair, and Henrietta could not have been more grateful when a knock at the door gave her an excuse to cast the work aside.

She did not know why, but Henrietta was not surprised to find the Duke of Mowbray at her door. Even though she had not seen him since the party at his home the previous weekend, she knew instinctively that he would call on her again. She wished the sight of him could have brought a smile to her face, but it didn't. His arrival only served as a reminder of all of the work she still had to do. Even this worry, though, was as nothing to the other feelings that the party had stirred up in her. Something about the Duke's kindness and nature had drawn her in to the point that she found herself almost jealous of Miss Fairchild. It was hardly ideal, especially when Henrietta was meant to be writing a heartfelt Valentine for the Lady who inspired so much dislike in her.

"Your Grace, what a pleasant surprise."

Henrietta conjured up the most enthusiastic smile she could muster, but she could tell by the Duke's concerned frown that she had not succeeded in fooling him.

"Miss Hart, I am bound to say you look quite terrible. Are you well?" The Duke moved a few steps closer and Henrietta retreated an equal number of steps, turning her body about in embarrassment.

"Please do not mind me; it is my lot this time of year. There is a lot to do in order to make my orders on time. I have just about finished the designs for each card – including your own - and am now working through the actual messages themselves. It is hard work, and I have consequently had little in the way of sleep over the last few days. But please do not trouble yourself; I am not ill." Henrietta walked over to the fire and looked to putting on the kettle.

"You design and create the cards themselves before you write the messages to go in them?" The Duke seemed stunned by this admission. "I would have thought that you would want it the other way around. If the worst comes to pass and you cannot finish an order in time, I would think a gentleman would more desire to have the words ready for him than a blank card: no matter how elegantly designed the card may be."

Henrietta's face bunched up in annoyance. "Well, yes. Normally, I would do it the other way around, but this year I just found myself more inclined to design the cards first." There was a loud clamour as she forced the lid of the kettle on and left it to boil. As she turned back around, she noticed again the concerned look on the Duke's face. "I am sorry. I do not mean to come across as irritated with you. It has been a very trying few days getting all of these orders done. Over half of the poems and letters I have written I am unhappy with in some way, and the other half I have not even begun work on."

The Duke nodded and offered a sympathetic smile.

"I will not torture you by asking on which half my own Valentine lies."

Henrietta took a deep breath, relieved that the Duke had spared her.

"Will you take a seat Your Grace? The tea should be ready shortly, and I am sure that my mind is in need of a break. Right now I am filled with a thousand different compliments, sweet words and passionate pledges. It would do me good to rest my mind for a while."

The Duke nodded and bade her to sit down. "You make yourself comfortable Miss Hart. I will attend to the tea. I remember well enough where everything is from the last time I was here."

Henrietta wanted to deny him. Being of so superior a station, it beggared belief to think of the Duke serving her tea. However, exhaustion overcame all of her resistance and Henrietta simply nodded in thanks as she sat down.

While the Duke made tea, Henrietta found herself speaking to him of the problems that she was having with the letters, using Mrs Pierce as her main example. As she poured out her frustrations, the Duke listened with a patient and attentive ear, never seeming to judge her, or to try to interrupt her with his own thoughts.

From time to time he would nod or sip from his cup. Only when Henrietta had finished did the Duke move to speak. As he did, Henrietta was surprised to notice that she had been complaining to him for almost half an hour.

"I hope you will not think me rude Miss Hart, but it occurs to me that you are not altogether happy with this work you have fallen into. I have seen your craftsmanship many times over the years, in the cards you have designed for my brother John. It is difficult to believe that words of such beauty, expressing such true love, could be written by someone who seems so dispassionate about her work. If I may be bold and venture a little further, it is equally surprising that a woman who could write so well of love has not been given the opportunity of possessing it for herself. I know it is really none of my business, but has no man ever offered their hand to you?"

Henrietta's eyes fell to the floor and she began to fidget. Her fingers began to tent and she bit her lip as if holding something in, restraining a long-held secret. For a moment, she thought that she still had the memory locked firmly away. Yet, somehow, the Duke again inspired her to speech, and she found herself confessing something which she had never thought to ever repeat to another soul.

Chapter Seven

"I have always written, ever since I was a little girl. My first stories I would recite out loud to my mother, and she would write the words for me on paper. She taught me to read by transcribing my stories and having me read them back to her. By the age of eleven, I had a whole shelf full of stacked papers that were my stories. Mother stopped writing the stories for me by my sixth birthday. By my eighth, I suspect she was becoming a little tired of even hearing them. Still, I never managed to lose my passion for stories and I would add new sheets of paper to my stack of tales every new day. "

Henrietta was surprised at how easy he was to talk to – the words came pouring out of her.

"At first I wrote nonsense stories about myself and my mother and father. I would have us go on adventures into the village only for us to discover that the village had been captured by the French and soldiers from the militia had to come and rescue us. Those were the stories my mother liked to hear and laugh at when I was a little girl."

Henrietta looked at the Duke, noticing the smile on his face.

He seemed thoroughly engrossed listening to her, apparently enjoying the thought of her quietly writing in her room every evening. She braced herself, knowing that his smile would not remain for long.

"By the age of eleven, I was writing what might be, charitably, deemed fairy tales. They had far more structure than the old stories I used to write and usually had some point to them. However, after I turned twelve, the subjects of my writing began to change, when I met a young man by the name of Isaac Combes."

"Isaac Combes." The Duke's smile, as she had guessed it would, suddenly disappeared. "Was he a friend of yours, or someone you just happened to admire?"

Henrietta bit her lip, and forced herself to continue.

"Isaac was two years older than me, and moved into the house next door to my family when our old neighbours moved to London. I was immediately fascinated by the boy, and he, in turn, spent a great deal of time with me. I remember always thinking about how smart and clever he was. He knew a great many tricks and liked to show off to me by climbing the fruit trees in my father's orchard. I do not think my parents ever realised, but he was actually able to come all the way to my bedroom window, by climbing the apple tree near the house, and to enter my room. Looking back, I should have reprimanded him for such behaviour. Back then, I took it as a compliment that he was willing to risk so much in order to see me alone. "

The Duke watched her face as she spoke – it was obvious that she was lost in the memory.

"At this time, though I did not realise it, my stories took on a more romantic aspect and nearly all of the characters were paper thin parodies of myself and Isaac. I lived out a thousand and one fantasies of us one day marrying. He would whisk me away, to far off London, then we would travel across the ocean on a tour of the Mediterranean. In my head, we had enough romantic adventures to last several life times. As the years went by, I began to write less and less and instead tried to live out the romantic fantasy I had created with Isaac. By my sixteenth birthday he had declared his love for me in secret, and swore that he would marry me the day that I turned twenty-one."

At that moment, Henrietta noticed how her story had set the Duke on edge. He seemed to squirm in his chair awkwardly. He was good enough not to make any comments or judgements, but she felt that she needed to reassure him a little.

"I am relieved to say that we never did anything together that might sully my honour to a husband, however, on more than one occasion he crept through my bedroom window to see me when my parents had refused to admit him. I... I hope you do not think worse of me for this." Henrietta blushed as a fear took her. She wanted the Duke to think well of her, but she could not lie about her past either.

"I will admit I am a little stunned, but please do not worry. I would hold this Mr Combes to blame, not you. Being older, he should have had more care about how his actions could have hurt you if his nightly visits had been discovered."

Henrietta smiled. It was a weak smile and she drank the remainder of her tea in one quick gulp before she continued her tale.

"Several times over the following years, I tried to convince Isaac to ask for my hand early. I was convinced that my parents would gladly let me wed him, but he always acted as though my father had taken a dislike to him. At first, I didn't believe him. I even teased him for being so scared of my father until I realised how irritable this made him. After a few months, I began to believe what Isaac said and really thought that my parents disliked him and did not wish to see us together. I began harbouring a secret resentment toward my father for this. From time to time I suggested to Isaac that we might run away to Gretna Green to be wed, but even this was not acceptable to him. He just kept telling me to wait until I was twenty-one and able to choose my own husband.

At eighteen, I began to notice that Isaac was spending less time with me and that the time he did spend was becoming increasingly awkward for us both. He had become fixated on the idea that we should give in to the urges of our bodies and not wait until we had married to create a union between us. Though I was sure that I loved him, and wanted to please him more than anything, I refused him. I had built up a perfect picture in my head of how our lives would be and, no matter how he tried to tempt me, I would not cross that threshold he so desperately wanted me to. Whenever he became particularly amorous in his attentions, I would once more remind him that I would happily run away with him to Gretna to marry him. The mere mention always seemed to calm him and he would become sullen."

"I hate to say it, but I get the distinct impression that Mr Combes perhaps did not have the intention of marrying you for love." The Duke had a serious expression, his brow knotted and his eyes fallen to the floor.

Henrietta did not bother to answer him. She was coming to the crux of her tale and, were she to stop now, she was not sure that she could finish the story.

"Things became easier when Isaac began to work. He took a job, which saw him move to London, and he would write to me often. His letters were always filled with the sweetest of sentiments and made me truly believe that the day I turned twenty-one he would come to claim me as a bride. However, other men were becoming interested in me at this time, as I was now eighteen. More than one young man came asking my father if they might attempt to court me. I couldn't understand it, but father seemed perfectly happy to let these men meet with me to try winning my affection. I roundly rebuffed the advances of four different gentlemen before my father sat me down to ask me why I was so resistant to the idea of marrying.

I remember to this day how I laid into my father. I shouted and screamed at him that I was only in love with Isaac and it was my father's stubborn refusal to accept the man that kept us both apart. I revealed the promise I had made, to marry Isaac the day I turned twenty-one, and assured him that there was nothing he could do to make me consider another man as a husband. It was then that my father revealed to me that he had harboured no ill will towards Mr Combes and could not think of any reason why Isaac would think otherwise. He assured me, if my heart was set to marry Isaac, that he'd happily welcome the union."

Henrietta took a deep breath and continued.

"I felt foolish for having thought my father so against me having the happiness that I wanted, and I wrote, straight away, to Isaac with the wonderful news that my father would consent to our union. I never received a reply. After sending that letter, I heard and saw nothing of Isaac for five months. Even his father, who was still our neighbour, was left in the dark as to what had become of his son. By and by, it was decided that he and my father would make an expedition to London in order to find Isaac. We all assumed that he must have fallen ill, or else some worse fate had taken him. Why else would he suddenly fall so silent?"

Henrietta was aware of how her body had begun to shake and the Duke leaned forward, a look of grave concern on his face.

"Miss Hart, I can see that this memory is clearly distressing to you. Please do not feel that you have to continue."

Henrietta shook her head and took a few deep breaths to try and calm her nerves.

"No. I know it may not seem it, from the way that I am reacting, but it is good to speak of this to you. I can finish." She wiped her eyes with a patch of cloth and prepared herself to continue.

"I still remember the grave look upon my father's face when he returned from that venture. The second that I laid eyes on him I burst into tears, fearing that my love had been killed or carried off by illness before we had the chance to join our hearts together. As it turns out, the truth was far harder to swallow.

I was not the only girl who Isaac had tried to seduce with his honeyed words. In London, other women had fallen for his charms, and some of these were far more amenable to forgetting the sanctity of marriage in order to satiate their desires than I had been. It transpired that one such woman had fallen pregnant with Isaac's child, and her father had to track Isaac down with a group of other men in order to force him to wed the girl.

When Isaac was found, he was hiding out in the house of another lady, a young widow who also had claimed to be his lover. Were it not for a desire to see his grandchild born legitimate, I suspect that the father who had gone out hunting for Isaac might have drowned him in the Thames. Instead, they had the boy dragged to an altar and made him say his vows alongside the girl he had left heavily pregnant.

It's funny to think of but, compared to the other girls he had cheated and conned with his artful ways, I was relatively lucky. However, the event had burned me and I took a long time to recover.

My father and mother were patient with me and never tried to rush me into opening my heart to other men. By this time though, I had already ruined my chances of a good marriage. I had gained a reputation among the men of the village for turning suitors away. Few knew the truth of what I had been through and would joke about my soul being a stone from which no light or warmth could be struck."

The shaking had subsided a little, but Henrietta's eyes welled with unshed tears, as she remembered the cruel words that had been spoken.

"I stayed living with my parents in the town where I grew up for another four years, until my twenty fourth birthday. That year, my father died in the winter, and my mother followed shortly after. I resolved to move somewhere new. I found this house, which I now dwell in, through pleading with an old acquaintance who owned the property and who was quite fond of my father. I had a notion that I might be able to make a new start for myself, to find a husband. However, with no family and little income, I was hardly in a position to make the acquaintance of any eligible young men.

I started my business, using the word skills I had learned through years of writing stories and letters to Isaac. It was enough to help me make a small living alongside the little money I was left with after my parents' deaths. Which brings us more or less up to date. I am sorry, Your Grace, if I have burdened you heavily with my story. I could have answered more simply, but it seems I had a need to tell this in its entirety. I am a little embarrassed to say it, but you are the first person I have been able to speak of my past to... and this is after four years of living here."

Chapter Eight

The Duke took a moment to digest all that had been said to him. Throughout Henrietta's confession he had remained relatively silent, body leant forward and listening intently. He shook his head.

His hands occasionally seemed to move forward as though he wanted to entwine them with Henrietta's. If this were the case, something made him hold back and he remained rooted to his chair.

"I will admit, I have never heard a story of such villainy before. This man, who you fell in love with, and who treated your love like some amusing toy, all through your youth... It is to your great credit that you could take the pain of all of this and turn it into something so noble and good."

Henrietta blinked in surprise, not having expected that the Duke would use her tragic past as a means to compliment her.

"I beg your pardon; I do not follow you?"

"I mean to say, you have been treated so harshly in love by someone – who, I am bound to say, does not deserve someone as good as you – and yet, rather than be bitter about it or complain, you have, instead, worked to help bring joy and happiness into other people's lives through your gift of words."

Henrietta looked at the Duke. She tried to smile, but found that she could not. She hung her head low again.

"I do not know if I believe you on that. More often than not I feel like a fraud."

The Duke had a look of concern in his eye and moved his chair closer to hers. Silently he held her hand in his, stroking her knuckles tenderly with his finger.

"Why would you say that about yourself?" His question was asked gently. Henrietta could see, from the intensity of his expression, his desire to understand and help her in any way that he could.

"I feel like a fraud because I am becoming just like Isaac. I use my words to craft letters of love for people. I care nothing for the women I write for and do not pay much heed to the kinds of men I write on behalf of. While there are those, such as your brother, who I genuinely enjoy writing for, there are many more men who I craft Valentines for, while worrying that I am misleading the women in their lives. With each passing year, I get more and more requests for work from men who seem to care nothing at all for the women they are courting. They treat me less as an aide who helps them express their true emotions, and more as a convenient time saver that frees them from having to put in any effort whatsoever."

The Duke squeezed Henrietta's hand a little harder and lowered his head to her level, trying to coax her to look him in the eye.

"No matter how others might misinterpret what you are trying to do, what is important is that you clearly care. If I had experienced the kind of things you have in your life, I am sure that I would have become cynical of love. But it is obvious to me that you still care. If you did not, you would not agonise over your clients the way that you do. Certainly, you would not have let me sit for two hours as I struggled to describe Miss Fairchild to you, nor come to my estate in order to gain a better understanding of her."

Henrietta nodded. She could feel tears forming in the corner of her eyes and drew back her hands from the Duke in order to wipe them. Before she could, she found he had drawn out a handkerchief from his pocket and was already moving to wipe away the tears for her. Though a simple action, the sensation of the Duke dabbing away her tears made Henrietta feel safe and accepted, in a way she had not felt in years. For a moment, all of the worries of the cards she was designing, the letters she had to write, even the dark secrets of her past, seemed to fall away into nothing.

As the tears ceased, Henrietta felt her breathing coming harder. She tried to calm her mind, but her heart was beating rapidly in her chest as she allowed herself to become fully aware of the close proximity of the Duke. He had dropped to his knees before her, his good breeches no doubt becoming stained by her grubby floor. The Duke did not seem to notice this though: his whole attention was focussed on her.

In that moment, she felt that she understood why she had confided in him about her past, why she was facing such a crisis of conscience over her entire enterprise. She had first felt it when she had danced with him at his estate and now she was feeling it again.

Henrietta felt her lip begin to quiver and her breath stuck in her throat. She did not know if she was imagining it or not, but the Duke seemed to be moving closer to her. Closing her eyes, she felt his fingers moving through her hair, stroking through the plain brown strands in a way that sent a shudder down her spine. She could feel his forehead press against hers, and she opened her eyes to look on him. The Duke's eyes were closed. He seemed once again to be resisting something and his face seemed to contort and twist as though pained. Henrietta wished that she had the strength to put her own hands about him and press her lips to his, but she couldn't. Instead she sighed and closed her eyes, committing this moment of closeness to memory before the Duke pulled away.

There was a sound of creaking and the warm pleasant scent of the Duke left Henrietta. She opened her eyes and watched as he quietly stood up and moved away from her, giving them the space appropriate for two people who were still only acquaintances in the eyes of society. She felt like she should apologise. She was meant to be working to help him come closer to Miss Fairchild, but was instead wishing to kiss him. She opened her mouth to try to offer an apology, but found that she could utter no sound.

The Duke ran a hand through his hair and his cheeks flushed with embarrassment.

"Forgive me, Miss Hart. I should... I think it would be best if..." The Duke was struggling for words and Henrietta feared the worst as he straightened up and took a deep breath. "I think, Miss Hart, it might be best if I look to manage my affairs with Miss Fairchild myself from here on. Please do not worry about your fee, I shall still pay you for the trouble that you have taken on my behalf." The Duke tried to offer a rallying smile. "At least with my order out the way you can devote more time to your other clients. For now, I shall leave you to get back to your work."

Henrietta felt like crying in that moment. She had shared a moment with the Duke of the like which she had not thought herself able to experience again in her lifetime. Of all the people she could possibly have developed feelings for, why did it have to be a client who already had his mind set on another woman? She tried not to dwell on it, instead rising to her feet.

"Yes, Your Grace... Perhaps it is for the best. I am... sorry if I have disappointed or let you down. Please believe me, of all the clients that I have worked for over the last few years, you are the one I would most wish to see happy in love; you deserve that much."

For a moment, the Duke of Mowbray stood and looked at her, his body seeming to waver between leaving and remaining. Finally, he summoned up the willpower to move and made his way to the door. Henrietta did not go to the window to watch. It would be too cruel a thing to torment herself with. Instead, she moved over to the letter she had been writing for Mr Pierce.

Wiping her eyes free of the fresh tears that insisted on falling, she read over the drivel she had written for the man. Without hesitation, she gripped the paper in both hands and tore it down the middle.

Chapter Nine

The sound of a cockerel woke Henrietta from a strange and painful dream. On the cusp of sleep and wakefulness, she could not recall quite what had passed through her mind in the caprices of sleep, but she knew that the Duke had featured in it. Every time she cast her mind to the Duke, the only client she had ever failed to deliver for, it felt like a lodestone had been put about her heart and threatened to drag her into some deep impenetrable abyss.

Rolling onto her back, Henrietta wondered if perhaps she ought to get out of bed. There was no real reason to; the busy season was over. For the rest of the year she would make her money through selling poems she wrote in little handmade pamphlets, or in her needle work. Little odd jobs would keep her from destitution until Christmas came around and people would once again require her services to make ornate cards and sentimental messages.

In the half dark, Henrietta tried to conjure up a feeling of relaxation.

For the last few years, Saint Valentine's Day, to her, had meant a day of freedom and rest after busy and frantic work. As this had been far and away her busiest year of business, she felt cheated that she could not enjoy the sensation of having a cleared schedule with no commitments or impending deadlines.

All her mind could think of was the array of women who would be waking up with delighted expectation of a card from their husband or lover. She pictured John Stanton. With his playful attitude and teasing nature, Henrietta could imagine him pretending to have outright forgotten about the feast of Saint Valentine. He would probably feign ignorance until some time after breakfast when his wife would finally cajole him into giving her the card which Henrietta had written and designed on his behalf.

Mrs Pierce, Henrietta imagined, would want to find her card on the breakfast table when she woke up and would ask questions of Mr Pierce at once if she did not immediately see it. She would then peruse the contents carefully before giving her verdict on her husband's efforts. This was all assuming that Mrs Pierce really was the domestic terror that Mr Pierce had privately described to Henrietta in their meeting for that year.

There were many other couples to consider too. Like counting sheep, Henrietta whispered quietly to herself the names of all of those, for whom she had written over the last few weeks, trying to imagine how each lady would react to their lover's gifts. She then thought about how each man would feign that the words of devotion in the letters and poems were wholly their own.

It was strange picturing so many couples this way. It unsettled Henrietta enough that she was forced to give up on the notion of returning to sleep.

Extracting herself from the bed, she groaned as cold air wrapped about her body. The house was draughty at the best of times. With the winter chill still very much in evidence, getting out of bed in the morning was like some kind of physical torture for her to go through.

In the quiet of her empty house, she made her way down the stairs and began to start a fire. It took a while to coax life from the kindling but, after a few attempts, the fire stuck and Henrietta was able to turn her attention to making tea. She drew her chair up very close to the flames for warmth, staring at the black metal kettle as it quietly rested over the hearth.

This was her life now. It had never bothered Henrietta much until recently, but this was how she was likely to spend the rest of her remaining days: alone, watching her kettle boil, with no hope of visitors save for those who had need of the odd services she could provide. It was a bleak future to think on. Somehow, the thought of it made her feel colder despite her nearness to the hearth.

Reluctantly, Henrietta's mind turned to the reason for her current discontent. She wondered just what the Duke would be doing on this Saint Valentine's Day for Miss Fairchild. Would he have managed to write something of his own for the lady, or perhaps he had merely used his money to buy her some lavish token of his admiration? Both scenarios seemed equally unlikely to Henrietta. Whatever the truth, she reminded herself, she would likely never discover the answer.

She was sure that the Duke would not try to make use of her services in the future, and the only other person, who might be able to give her news of the Duke, she would not now see until next year.

As she poured tea into a cup, Henrietta reiterated her promise to concentrate on the moment and put the Duke, Miss Fairchild and everything else behind her. Walking to the single window that looked out onto the street, she observed the birds that were flying about between the chimney pots of the houses. She noticed as the shaggy old dog, which guarded the butcher's shop, was let out by the owner. There was also, Henrietta noticed, a rather ornate carriage parked on the far side of the street. The black lacquer wood marked it as belonging to a person of some social eminence, and she felt her chest tightening as realisation dawned that she had ridden in that carriage not more than a few days previous.

Certain that the carriage was the very same that the Duke of Mowbray had sent for her on the night of his party, Henrietta hurried back upstairs and found her boots. She did not bother to dress properly, and quickly threw on a dress over her night clothes. She feared at any moment the silent, black carriage would disappear and, as she attempted to pull her clothes on, she took frantic looks out onto the street to ensure it had not left.

After five minutes of frantic scurrying, Henrietta was dressed, at least to the point where she would not appear indecent when stepping outside. Hurtling down her stairs, she made for the front door. She did not even bother to lock up behind her, but immediately ran out into the street and to the carriage.

The driver spied her straight away and tapped three times on the roof of the carriage to gain the attention of whoever was inside.

Henrietta trembled as she stood by the carriage door. She could not fathom at all why the Duke would have sent his carriage here, but the opportunity to see him again, even if only to make fuller amends with him, was an opportunity Henrietta just couldn't pass up. The carriage door opened and Henrietta's eyes lit up in shock and confusion.

"Your Grace!" Henrietta practically shouted the words, so great was her shock at seeing the Duke sitting quietly inside his carriage. "Your Grace, it is only just gone seven in the morning; what do you mean by loitering in your carriage outside my home at this hour?"

A thought suddenly entered her head and Henrietta quickly added, "If you wish me to look over something you have written for Miss Fairchild, I fear I will be unable to help you."

The Duke gave a smile that seemed quite out of place, given the manner in which he had last left her. "I can assure you, I have no such intention. In truth, I am here to see you, but realised that I might have come a little too early, so I had my man wait here and thought to knock on your door at a more godly hour."

Henrietta frowned, thoroughly confused as to what the Duke was about. The only other reason she could think of, for his being here, would be to pay her for the work she had done for him. But this would not require the Duke to make the trip personally, and certainly not at so early a time in the day.

"Would you perhaps like to step into the carriage, or perhaps I might be invited into your home; I am not sure which is warmer?" The Duke's emerald eyes seemed to sparkle and his singular ease and affability were at total odds with how Henrietta had ever imagined he might be, were he to see her again.

"I suppose you might wish to come inside then, Your Grace. I have not long boiled water, so I can make you something to drink, if you are cold perhaps?"

Henrietta pinched herself as she led the Duke into her home. If this were not a continuation of her dreams, then perhaps her constant thinking of the Duke had created the delusion of his being here with her. Still, her senses all confirmed that she was, indeed, awake and that the Duke was really standing in her house waiting on a cup of tea. Rather than question the reality of things, Henrietta decided to ask a more pertinent question.

"If I may ask Your Grace, what is so important that you decided to come to my home before first light? I am racking my brain trying to think of a reason, but none is forthcoming. If anything, you should be on your way to Miss Fairchild's home to give her whatever gift you were able to create for her in honour of the day."

The Duke nodded and began to pace the floor near the fire as Henrietta poured him his drink. "Yes, I can see why you might jump to that conclusion. In truth though, it has been a while now since I last thought on Miss Fairchild. I am embarrassed to say that I have been thinking of her less and less, since first my brother told me of you."

Henrietta handed the Duke his cup, her brow knotted in confusion as she listened silently. "After the revelation of your past, I found myself reflecting on my feelings for Miss Fairchild in a new light. What I found in my meditation was that my affections toward her were not as strong as they should have been and, in turn, her opinion of me was similarly lacking. There is nothing at all cold or calculating about the lady, but I came to realise that she showed me kindness and affection for her father's sake, rather than her own. Because he wished to see his daughter marry a man with a title, she acted to fulfil his wishes and thought it would bring her own happiness in the process. I had overlooked this simple fact until now simply because I wished to be loved.

I know it might sound silly to say, but I am turning thirty this year. Seeing my younger brother so lucky and happy in love has long·made me feel like I was overdue to find love for myself. I felt that there was a rush, and a need to find someone who would accept me. Believing myself somehow incompetent in the ways of love, I did not rate my chances highly and settled on the first woman to show me the merest hint of interest. However, I have come to understand, through meeting you and hearing your story, that I do not want the kind of love that someone like Miss Fairchild could offer. Hearing the depth of affection and feeling you felt, even if it were for a man who did not deserve it... it inspired me and made me see that there was a truer love in the world. I did not, and do not, know if such a love can be mine, but I decided that I should at least give myself the chance to find it. So, I have chosen to abandon my dalliance with Miss Fairchild. I do not think the loss of me will weigh much on her mind."

Henrietta nodded. She could not deny that she was glad to hear that the Duke had come to his senses about Miss Fairchild. Still, she could not help thinking that there was something else.

"Is that all you came here to tell me, Your Grace?" She held her breath for a moment, her heart beginning to skip a little as a hopeful anticipation filled her.

"No. I will confess that there was one other matter that drew me here today. This, more than anything else, was the cause for my early arrival, as I was rather impatient to deliver it."

As he spoke, the Duke reached into the inside pocket of his coat. He pulled out a small envelope with a red wax seal and held it in his hand for a moment. For the first time, Henrietta noticed that he was trembling. The letter seemed to swish in his hands and his lips too were vibrating slightly as though the Duke had been overcome by a sudden chill. "This feels like a fools move. To try and write a Valentine for someone who has made a successful business of writing Valentines for others, I fear I will likely embarrass myself with the contents."

Henrietta could not help herself. She put her hands to her face to suppress a gasp and then found that she had to attend to her eyes as she felt them overflow with tears. She tried to speak, but found that her words were silenced by the rush of emotion that filled her.

The Duke put the letter on the table and wrapped his arms about Henrietta. For a long moment he cradled her in his arms. His fingers wound through her hair as they had the last time she had seen him, only this time he did not move away.

This did not stop Henrietta from fearing that he might let go though, and she clung to the lapels of his coat, fiercely holding on to him like he was a lifeline that kept her from sinking below dark waters.

It took some time for the tears to stop flowing and, when they did, the Duke whispered softly in Henrietta's ear.

"If you would like, I can read the letter for you. As I said already, it is nothing compared to your work, so please do not judge me harshly."

Henrietta laughed, rubbing her eyes with the back of her hand as she reluctantly took a step back from the Duke.

"I will be sure not to criticise you too harshly."

Reaching over to the table, the Duke took the envelope and pulled at the seal. Opened up, the letter did not look to be much at all. Even so, Henrietta could imagine that the Duke had likely found himself agonising over every word, writing and rewriting it until it was as good as he could make it.

"Dear Miss Henrietta Hart.

When my brother first gave up the secret of how he wrote such eloquent Valentine's messages for his wife, year after year, he did so because he wished to see me in love with a woman as much as he is in love with his wife. Growing up in a family of strong men, I have always found it difficult to express those emotions and feelings that are so often coveted in these kinds of messages and felt that it was this inability that kept me from gaining the love of the woman I was attempting, so miserably, to court.

What I did not understand then was how powerful love is, or how suddenly it can come into your world. It is not a thing you can just conjure up through the use of pretty words. It is a thing that you must look for while being prepared to wait patiently to find.

I feel now that, though my brother did not mean for things to transpire quite as they have, his pointing me to you has indeed helped me to find the love I was seeking. However, it is you, yourself, that has inspired these feelings. From the dance we shared in my home, to hearing the story of your life, I have been slowly falling under your spell, every day since I first came to your door asking you to help me write a Valentine.

Instead, I now offer you a Valentine of your own. I hope that you will accept it. I hope that you will accept me and that we can discover a future bound up together. If you'll do me the honour of agreeing to accompany me on this journey, then I will faithfully promise to write you a Valentine every year and improve my skill in expression until I write something truly worthy of a woman as precious and beautiful as you."

The Duke lowered the letter and took a few deep breaths. His nerves were getting the better of him again.

"I signed off the letter rather formally I'm afraid. I don't know why I did that."

Henrietta laughed and shook her head.

In the next instant, she near threw herself into the Duke's arms, running her hands through his hair and letting out a contented sigh as she felt him return her embrace in kind.

"I actually thought it was very lovely, possibly the best Valentine a woman has ever received."

The Duke blushed and laughed.

"I am sure that you are exaggerating."

Henrietta smiled, her lips slowly moving closer to his.

"Exaggeration is what good writers do."

Her words were silenced once again and her body tensed with excitement as she felt the Duke's lips brush against hers. He was shy in his ministrations, his kisses delicate. Still, he showed no inclination to part from her. For her part, Henrietta took every kiss gratefully.

The Duke was not as artful in his way as Isaac Combes, her old beau, had been. Even so, the Duke was superior in every way and she relished the thought of being with him forever. As she melted into his arms she was simply giddy with euphoria and dumbfounded at this blissful Valentine's Day which she could never have imagined. Not even in her wildest dreams.

The End

Thank you for reading! I truly hope you enjoyed ***The Duke's Love letter!*** If you have any questions or comments I'd be happy to hear from you. Feel free to contact me – Katherine Keats at KatherineKeatsBooks@gmail.com .

About the Author

Katherine Keats writes sweet and clean Regency Romance. She's a hopeless romantic who loves music, dancing, and long walks on the beach. She enjoys writing stories of true love that defy all odds.

You can connect with Katherine on her Facebook page at:

https://www.facebook.com/KatherineKeatsAuthor/

Or follow her on her author page at:

https://www.amazon.com/Katherine-Keats/e/B01N3R8L65/

Get in touch at:

KatherineKeatsBooks@gmail.com

You may also receive updates and advanced notice of upcoming releases. I look forward to hearing from you!

ARIETTA RICHMOND, GRACE AUSTEN, ISABELLA THORNE,
KATHERINE KEATS AND ALYCE HEALEY

Other Books by Katherine Keats

Clean Regency Romance

The Duke's Unlikely Bride

The Duke's Dangerous Dilemma

Rescuing the Earl

The Duke and the Dressmaker

If you enjoyed reading **The Duke's Love Letter** then I'm certain you will also enjoy my other recent releases : _You can pick them up now for FREE on Kindle Unlimited.

As a special thank you for reading I'm including a preview here for you to enjoy. Turn the page for your preview of 'The Duke's Unforgettable Kiss'

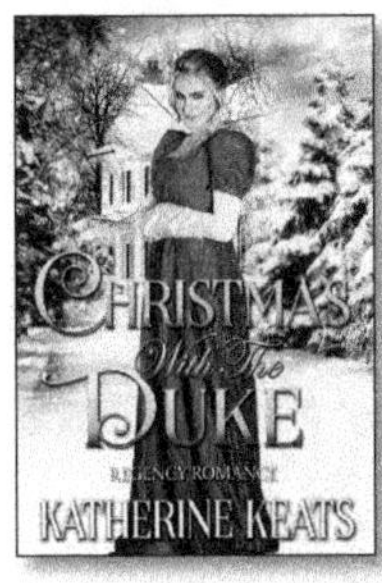

Christmas with the Duke

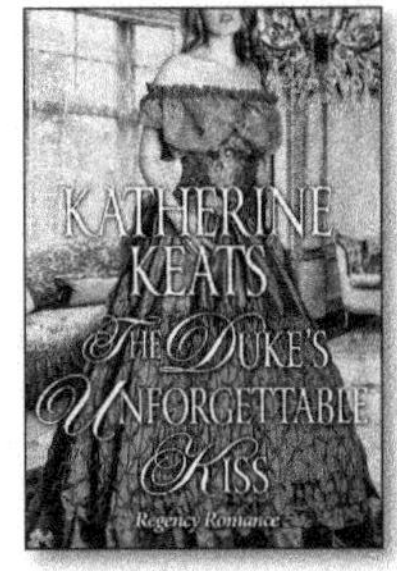

The Duke's Unforgettable Kiss

A Christmas Surprise

A Gentleman's Gamble

ARIETTA RICHMOND, GRACE AUSTEN, ISABELLA THORNE,
KATHERINE KEATS AND ALYCE HEALEY

Here is Your Preview of

The Duke's Unforgettable Kiss

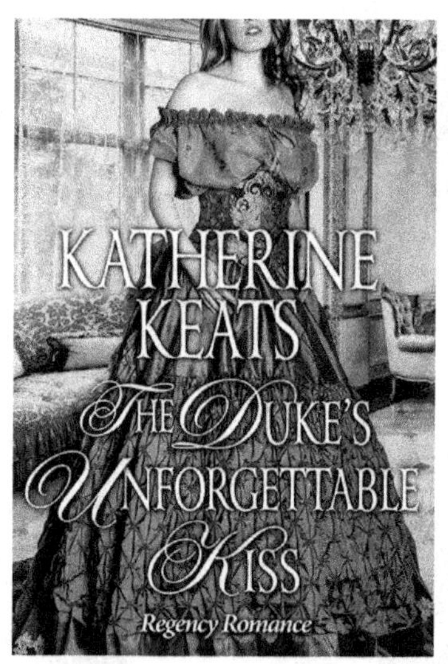

Katherine Keats

Chapter One

She had held the rope for a good fifteen minutes. It was something of a courtesy from her husband, to let her tie the noose around her own neck. It was the smallest of kindnesses that quite failed to excuse the indignity of what he was about to force on her. Unwilling to focus on the true horror that lay ahead, Eleanor let her mind dwell on the coarseness of the rope, fearing how it might chafe on her neck when finally she made the noose for herself. She was delaying the inevitable, and every second that passed only added to her sense of fear and impending dread.

When the bells from the local parish church rang out, proclaiming the hour of eight, she knew that she could delay no more. Marching to the mirror, Eleanor checked herself. She wore her best gown, a pale cream dress with a fetching v shaped neckline and green trim. It was fashionable without being overly elegant. She had been denied a shawl or coat, Mr Barnett saying that she needed to show off her skin a little to the crowds who would be gathering.

She had been permitted to wear jewellery, but Eleanor had chosen only to wear a silver hair pin that held her long mahogany hair in a curled pile high on her head. She was a picture of beauty and sophistication, quite above the horrid fate that was about to be hers. The reminder of that fate remained in her hands, quietly waiting to be tied about her neck.

A knock at the door once again reminded Eleanor of the time and, after almost an hour of cradling the long coil of rope, she flung it in haste about her neck and began to tie a knot. Just as she drew the noose to hang like an ugly necklace about her throat, Mr Barnett came in.

"Come now Eleanor, are you still not ready? Look at that knot; you could at least have tied it properly. What would we do if it became loose on the way?"

Eleanor pursed her lips, holding back a thousand or more choice words she had for her husband in that moment.

"It is not as though I might run. If the rope comes loose, I will just retie it again. Don't think me so foolish as to think I can escape from this." Though her words were not uncivil, she could not help a dose of venom dripping into her tone of voice.

Mr Barnett drew close and began to tighten the rope until it pressed against her neck like a choker. It prickled against her delicate skin and she knew that it would leave a sore. Then, as though to add insurance, Mr Barnett tied a second knot over the first, tugging on the rope several times until satisfied that the knot would hold.

"Right, time to leave. I have your things already on the cart and Leah is waiting outside."

Eleanor raised an eyebrow. She knew that her husband was eager to move his mistress into the house, but she had not thought he would be so quick off the mark. She could imagine Leah's face, the smugness that would spread across her round, fat cheeks. She would be very sure to ignore the woman when she stepped outside, give her no recognition or interest. Eleanor was determined to salvage as much dignity as she could from this situation.

Stepping out into the cold morning air, Eleanor at once felt her skin prickling into goose bumps from the autumnal wind. She suppressed an urge to shudder, and walked behind her husband with deliberate, measured steps, the same kind that she had used when she had walked down the aisle to marry him no more than a year ago. She noticed Leah lurking in the garden, sitting amidst a clutter of her belongings, as she waited to fill the space in the house that Eleanor was leaving behind.

Mr Barnett hoisted himself up into the cart and checked that Eleanor was standing ready. She was not permitted to ride with him, although there was ample room for her. To do so would send the wrong signals, both to Leah, and to the passers-by who would see her being led down the road to the village square.

The walk of a mile and half felt longer and harder when made to keep pace with the cart horse. From time to time, Mr Barnett pulled on the rope, forcing Eleanor to increase her pace or risk a fall onto the frozen mud. She could not fathom why he was being so ghastly. He wanted her in good and perfect condition for the public, so why now was he risking her safety, risking her arriving bloodied and stained in mud?

She could only assume that this was further revenge for her perceived failings as wife.

In the village, the square was already filling with farmers and traders. Cows, sheep, pigs, and fowl were made to stand for the inspection of the villagers, as their owners tried to secure a sale. These animals complained far more about their lot than Eleanor, who remained silent and composed as she garnered the eyes of neighbours and passing strangers. She held her chin high, and feigned disinterest in everything and everyone. Were it not for the rope about her neck, anyone might assume her to be stepping out to attend a summer Ball.

Mr Barnett stopped the cart at a spot where the morning traders were less thickly huddled. He did not bother dismounting, instead choosing to stand on the cart, so that he was high above the throng. Already a few faces had turned to regard him, interested to see just what wares he might be peddling. He looked down at Eleanor and gave a nod of his head, a signal for her to step up onto the cart with him.

Eleanor took a deep breath and hauled herself up next to her husband, ignoring his offered hand as she struggled up to his side. She brushed down her skirt, to try and flick away the few specks of dirt that she had picked up on the walk, and drew her back as straight as she could manage. She kept her eyes dead ahead, but she could already see the faces looking up at her, and a crowd already forming near her.

Mr Barnett picked up a bell from the cart and began to ring loudly upon it, his voice imitative of some pompous town crier.

"Wife for sale! Wife for sale!"

Chapter Two

It was not long before the entire market had shuffled over to inspect Mr Barnett's cart and the single item he offered to the discerning buyer. Even some of the other traders had abandoned their stalls in order to get a closer look at the woman in the cart. Though she had promised herself not to look, Eleanor could not help but cast nervous glances, now and then, at the leering throng.

"What's wrong with her?" One boy of about seventeen asked. He had, obviously, no interest in making a purchase, only wanting to score a laugh from his friends.

Mr Barnett pursed his lips.

"I can assure you there is nothing wrong with my wife, she is a fine and model example of womanhood and..."

"...Then why are you giving her up then?" shouted another man.

Eleanor looked to her husband, momentarily enjoying the pressure he was being brought under.

She was surprised that he had not expected to face questioning and she wondered if he might be forced to admit the existence of his mistress who was waiting for him back at home.

"I... I am embarrassed to say that my situation no longer enables me to look after my wife in the way a husband ought." Another tremor of laughter erupted from the crowd as a few men made jokes and speculations regarding the particular way in which Mr Barnett was unable to fulfil his role as a husband.

Eleanor could not help but smile to see her husband humiliate himself. It was a welcome balm to the wounds he was inflicting on her.

"What I mean to say, good people, is that I can no longer afford to keep my Eleanor under my roof. Selling her is a kindness, you see." The blatant lie was not easily swallowed, especially by those in the crowd who knew of Mr Barnett's marriage. As much as he liked to imagine himself a master of intrigue and discretion, his affair with the widowed Leah had not gone unnoticed.

"I am sure that you would not have the money to keep two women under your roof."

"Good people, please, let us not pick at the particulars of why I am selling my wife. That business is entirely my own and of no importance to you. All that should matter to you is the quality of woman Eleanor is. As you can see, she still has the charms of youth on her. She is a comely-looking country girl and I have never had cause to complain of her domestic capabilities."

"And what of her capabilities in the bed chamber?"

Eleanor closed her eyes and tried to blot out the unsavoury comment. Not so many folks deigned to laugh at this latest jape and it almost seemed to create a new quiet amongst the crowd. The time for jokes at the Barnett's expense was ended and now only the matter at hand remained.

"If we are done with the jokes, perhaps we can start the bidding," Mr Barnett said. "If, however, you are determined to make fools of yourselves, perhaps I might just ride out to Merrystone."

The threat of moving on to a different market seemed to do the trick, and the men in the crowd began to regard Eleanor properly, each calculating how much coin her "comely-country looks" were worth to them.

"I'll take her off your hands, if you'll give me a farthing for her!" Once again, it was the insolent boy who spoke up and this time he had outstayed his welcome. The serious bidders, as well as a few sympathetic women, began to boo and jostle the youth until he was forced to move along and stop wasting the crowd's time.

"I'll start you at a shilling." The first bid came from a farmer who had abandoned his own cattle to look at the auction. He was a hard-faced man with a weather beaten and wrinkling face: easily twice Eleanor's age.

Once the first bid was made, the others came in quickly. Eleanor's face fell to dismay as her husband's grew to an ecstatic grin. In less than five minutes he was already up to two shillings and fourpence. It was a good sale, easily worth the time and degradation Mr Barnett had been made to suffer by the hecklers.

As new bids began to decline and the advancement of the offers began to slow, Eleanor took a look at the two men who stood in contention for her. Though she was eager to be rid of her worthless husband, Eleanor had no desire to go off with either of the men vying for her. She looked about the crowd, willing some of the more desirable men, and those she liked, to risk bidding a little higher.

The high bidder, a quite rotund merchant from out of town, looked quite safe in his victory and his lips curled into a haughty smile as he began to dole out the correct coin into his palm.

"Hold! We have a new bid for a whole pound!" The sudden increase in the bid came as a surprise to all, and an audible, collective gasp came from the crowd as they attempted to locate the source of the new bid.

A man in a red tailcoat and silver wig came forward, money already held smartly in his white gloved hand. He was clearly a servant, though a servant for a man of greater importance than any assembled in the market. The servant held the money aloft, eyes darting to his competitors, as if to challenge them to make further advances. None dared.

Eleanor bit her bottom lip. She liked the look of this impeccably dressed servant, but she did not like the idea of being sold to a man she had not even seen. Although she had determined not to speak, except when necessary, she could not resist asking the question on her mind.

"Where is your master? The law declares that a woman has a right to object to a sale should she have grave objections to the person she is to be sold to."

The servant nodded and a smile spread across his face. "I think that you should have no objection to accepting my master's offer. He is not looking to purchase you to fulfil any base desires or to take you as a mistress. My master's only requirement of you is that you agree to work as a maid on his estate. Beyond this, there are to be no expectations of you. You may have that in writing if you require it."

Mr Barnett seemed beyond caring. His eyes were latched onto the pound held in the servant's hand. Eleanor knew he would not care if the mysterious buyer wanted to have her head mounted as a trophy on his wall.

She studied the servant once more, looking for any trace of a lie or deceit in his look. There was none. Smiling as cordially as she could manage, she gave a nod to her husband.

"Come now; you're not going to get a better offer than this, and by the looks of it neither am I. If you have any consideration for my wellbeing for the future, you'll let me go with this man and live my days as a servant instead of some man's 'other' wife.

Mr Barnett nodded then and handed the rope that bound Eleanor to the servant.

The smartly dressed man held the cord with uncertainty and then handed it to Eleanor to hold.

"I think I can trust you to follow me to my master's carriage without having to lead you like a pack mule?"

Eleanor nodded, relieved to see the servant's manners and courtesy continuing. She hoped that the man's attitude would prove a direct reflection of his master's.

Gathering the rope into one hand, she struggled to undo the tight knot about her neck, not bothering to spare any more words for Mr Barnett as she followed the man who would lead her into her new, and hopefully better, life.

Tucked away in a side alley lay a grand carriage that barely fit into the narrow space in which it was nestled. In order to enter, Eleanor was forced to hug the wall and shimmy along until she reached the carriage door. The door could only open a few inches and Eleanor had to squeeze herself into the plush interior.

Once inside, it was as if she had crossed into a different world entirely. This world was one of a grandeur and splendour that neither her family, Mr Barnett, nor any of her acquaintance could even dream of.

The seats were lined with red velvet cushioning, and the windows were curtained with matching drapes that were drawn closed, creating an eerie sense of twilight in the closed vehicle.

The man who sat in the opulent space was no less impressive than the carriage itself. He was dressed in a black suit that looked to be brand new, shoes that had been buffed to a mirror shine, a top hat that was decorated with a white ribbon of silk, and a shirt, so white and pure that angels themselves must have laundered it with their heavenly tears in order to create such perfect whiteness.

The man to which all of these things belonged was older than Eleanor, perhaps in his mid to late thirties. Still, he kept himself very well indeed and he had a degree of handsomeness to his face that Eleanor was pleased with.

Most importantly, his smile seemed benevolent and kind.

"Forgive my not having come out to bid for you personally, but I did not wish to create a scene. As I do not approve of the practice of wife selling, I do not wish to bring my name into discredit by being seen to have made a bid in such a sale."

Eleanor blushed, feeling like a bad penny in the man's pocket.

"I am sorry if I am an embarrassment to you, Sir," she said, not really knowing how to react to his words.

"You have nothing to apologise for. I made the decision to buy you because you so obviously did not intend to be on that stage. Most wife sales I see seem to take the form of a direct swap of wives and husbands, to allow lovers to be together in a more legitimate capacity. So, tell me, and please do not feel a need to give your husband any undue credit, just why were you on that stage?"

Eleanor sat straight on the luxurious seat and took a moment to compose herself.

She did not exactly feel comfortable in the stranger's company, and wondered just how open she should really be.

"My husband and I were joined at the behest of both our parents, who were eager to see our families joined from a young age. My father and Mr Barnett's father owned stretches of field close together and wished to see our families join so that we might become a single farm."

"I see, so the marriage was not to either of your liking?"

"I did my duty to my family as was only right. My parents have always been good to me and I had no reason to object to Mr Barnett when I met him. However, it seems he was already in love with another woman and engaged in a secret relationship with her. Her own husband was of a sickly disposition and unable to keep a weather eye on her. He died as we came close to our first anniversary as husband and wife, at which point the woman made her intentions, of being more than a discreet mistress to my husband, known."

"So, he decided to sell you. And you made no objection."

The man narrowed his eyes leaving Eleanor feeling uncomfortably judged.

"I did not agree to be sold because of any meekness if that is what you are implying Sir. There was no love between Mr Barnett and myself and I knew things would only become worse between us if I tried to get in the way of him and Miss Leah. It is hard to fight for something when you have no desire to hold on to the thing you have to lose. I knew being sold would be a gamble, but I considered it a calculated risk: there was not much chance of my being sold into a worse situation than I was already in."

The man nodded. "Well, I hope that you will find, in time, that you made the right choice in permitting yourself be sold to me. As my servant may have intimated, I do not intend to make any advances to you, or to treat you like a bought mistress or bawdy plaything."

Eleanor tried to smile, knowing she should show her gratitude. "Yes, your man said you intended to keep me as a servant in your household."

"That's right. Under me, you will have a room to call your own, meals every day and I will not treat you as a slave. I will pay you as I would any other member of my household."

"You are exceedingly generous Sir... Might I ask what I should call you?"

"My name is Mormont, Baron Gilbert Mormont."

Eleanor blushed to have been using the incorrect address to her rescuer for so long.

"Forgive me, My Lord, I did not realise your status was so grand."

The man waved a hand.

"It is no matter. Now perhaps we should be off. I would like to be home before dark and I am sure that you will wish to see your new home too."

At that, the Baron took his cane, which lay by his side, and rapped on the roof of the carriage two times. In a moment, the box lurched and began to move off, its trundling wheels taking Eleanor away to a new and hopefully better life.

Continue reading...

ARIETTA RICHMOND, GRACE AUSTEN, ISABELLA THORNE,
KATHERINE KEATS AND ALYCE HEALEY

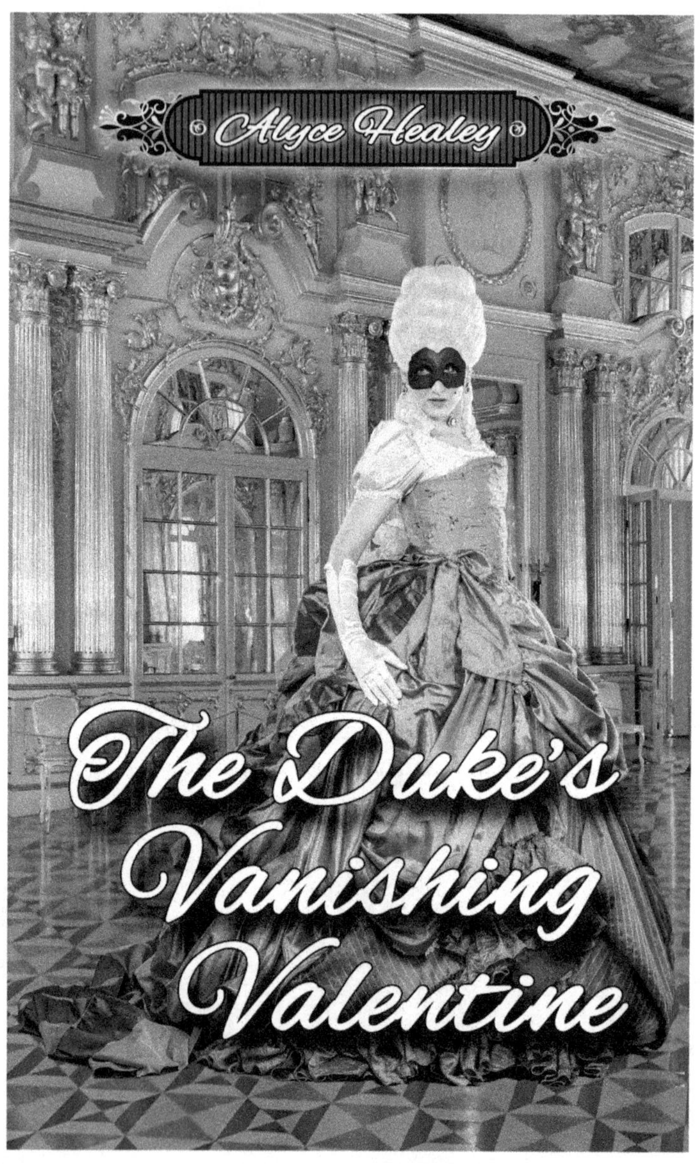

The Duke's Vanishing Valentine

Alyce Healey

ARIETTA RICHMOND, GRACE AUSTEN, ISABELLA THORNE,
KATHERINE KEATS AND ALYCE HEALEY

The Duke's Vanishing Valentine

Copyright 2017

LifeSpark Publishing and Alyce Healey

All Rights Reserved

www.alycehealey.com

Chapter One

"Personally I never cared much for wars," said Selina Notley, Lady Langmere, wife of Felton Notley, Earl of Langmere. "I think that your father demonstrated heroic bravery, but I was glad when he returned home and Napoleon was sent away on permanent holiday. There were not many parties during the war years, and ever since Waterloo it feels like the nation is making up for lost time." She addressed the words to her daughter, Lady Margaret Notley, a pretty, auburn-haired woman of twenty-four. Together with Alice, the lady's maid, they were in Margaret's bed-chamber, putting the finishing touches on the costume which Margaret would be wearing to the Valentine's Masquerade Ball two days hence.

"As you know, I didn't attend many balls when I was younger," said Margaret in a regretful tone. "For as far back as I can remember it seemed like talk of the war consumed everything. Perhaps it was different in other places, but, here at least, every spare shilling was given to our gallant soldiers. If a regiment happened to be stationed nearby, that was different, of course—"

"Like the Ball we threw here at Eastdale Hall that Christmas when the Duke returned on furlough," said Selina with a misty look. Duncan Livingston, Duke of Middleford, was two years Margaret's junior and had been Margaret's close friend and bosom companion for much of her youth. Margaret and her mother were expecting him to call at the house within the next hour or two.

"Yes, how different it all felt back then," said Margaret. "Of course, now it seems obvious that he was going to survive the war and return home, but none of us knew it at the time. When he asked me to dance, I stood there for a whole minute crying into my nankeen handkerchief before I offered him my hand."

"And when he finally did come home for good," said Selina, "his own father had died." The death of Edward Livingston had come as a great shock to his friends and close relations; one morning he had gone into his study complaining of a chest pain and never came out again. "He was so young. If anyone was going to die, I thought it would have been Duncan. He was the one out fighting Napoleon."

"Oh Mama, you make it sound so dramatic," said Margaret, edging her rocking chair closer to the hearth where a small fire was blazing. "It's not as if he and Napoleon had some personal quarrel. In fact, they were never stationed in the same country. Duncan spent most of the war in Portugal and had, to be sure, a miserable time of it. But he only got shot at once, and the bullet went right through his hat."

"Still," said Selina with a significant look, "it was a close thing. Not everyone who went to Portugal came home again."

Margaret wanted to object but something, perhaps the memory of all the nights she had cried herself to sleep worrying about him, kept her in check.

"Please, don't let's talk about it, Madam," said Alice gently. "The war is over now and our boys aren't going away again. They're safe."

She herself had experienced the worry of a mother whose son had been sent off to battle, but in her case, thankfully, he had returned. She spoke the words as much for Selina's sake as for Margaret's. There had been moments when she suspected the prospect of Duncan's death weighed on them both equally. Because Margaret and Duncan had been so close, Selina had treated him like one of her own sons. He had spent nearly as many nights beneath her roof, growing up, as he had under his own.

Selina had long ago — along with Duncan's mother — resolved to see Margaret and Duncan married to one another before their own deaths. In terms of money, things could hardly have worked out better — the sudden death of the Duke two years before had placed Duncan securely in possession of wealth and title.

If things went as planned, Margaret would become his Duchess. Yet Selina's motivations were not purely mercenary. They were the considerations of a devoted mother who had spent countless hours brooding over her daughter's companions, hoping to find the one that held the key to her heart.

In this respect, as well, it certainly seemed that there was no better candidate than the Duke of Middleford.

Yet the very qualities that made him an ideal partner — the years he and her daughter had spent together, the mutual respect and understanding that had arisen between them — also made a relationship unlikely. Having grown up treating him as a brother, it was hard now for Margaret to conceive of him in any other way. In his eyes he had never viewed her as anything other than a best friend. She was the woman whose house he continued to call on with some regularity. It was she in whom he confided all his close-kept secrets, and with whom he frequently attended Balls, soirees and public and family dinners.

However, if there was even a spark of romantic passion lurking in his breast, he had never shown it. Even now Selina found her hopes more and more frustrated. Would her daughter ever have her future ensured with the Duke?

The costume being nearly ready, Selina and Alice induced Margaret to try it on. "The Duke will be here soon," said Selina, "and you might not have another opportunity."

"Why not just wait until he gets here?" Margaret asked.

Her mother shook her head vehemently.

"No, you will spoil it. You want him to be utterly and completely surprised when he sees you for the first time. With any luck, he will not even know it is you!"

Margaret bit her lip thoughtfully.

"I suppose I could do that," she said to herself. "But would it work..."

She seemed to be having a private conversation with herself, from which her mother and Alice were excluded.

"At any rate, My Lady," said Alice, drawing her out of her reverie, "he'll be here in moments, so if you're going to try it on, you'd better do it quickly."

A few moments later Margaret had removed her gown, and with the help of the other two had replaced it with the voluminous dress that was part of her costume.

"Here, try on the mask as well, My Lady," Alice said excitedly. "It will cover half your face, including your cheekbones. Let me help you on with the elegant wig. That will complete the disguise."

With the wig and mask firmly in place Margaret performed a perfect pirouette and waited for a reaction.

The rapt expressions of the two older women as they stood looking at her seemed to answer some unspoken question of her own. "You mean you don't recognize me at all?" she asked with a broad smile.

Alice shook her head. "I've known you from when you was a wee babe," she said, "and even I couldn't tell if you hadn't told me."

Selina nodded. "If I had not raised you, I would think you were some stranger's child."

Margaret was now clearly in an excited state. "What if I talked like *this*?" she said in a gruff voice, like a prime minister with a fondness for pipe-smoking. Alice let out a shriek of delight and surprise. "Or *this*?" Margaret added in a high voice.

"Margaret, I never knew you to be such an excellent mimic," said Selina, picking a piece of lint off the fabric.

"I've had years of practice," said Margaret proudly. "Once when we were very young, Duncan was wandering through the woods by himself. When I saw him coming, I hid myself behind a tree and with a deep voice persuaded him that I was a thief and a robber who was going to cut off his ring finger and send it to his father for ransom. Of course, when he found out who it *really* was, he didn't speak to me for a week!"

"And who should blame him, My Lady," said Alice, and Selina nodded.

At that moment there came a knock at the door. When invited to come in, a footman in red livery entered the room. Taken somewhat aback by the strange woman in costume, he turned and bowed stiffly to Lady Langmere, and said, "The Duke of Middleford is here, My Lady."

"*Where* is he, Jack?" asked Selina, exchanging anxious glances with Alice.

"In the foyer, My Lady," said the footman, finally recognizing the costumed woman as Margaret. "If you would like, I can hold him there until you're ready."

"Take him to the front sitting room and keep him entertained," said Selina. "Play the penny-whistle, or… or do that curious thing you do where you pretend to swallow a guinea, only to have it appear in the sleeve of his jacket. We will be ready in a minute."

The footman bowed and left the room. The moment he was gone, Alice and Selina scrambled to get Margaret out of her costume. She appeared a moment later with her hair in tangles, her gown of fine cambric ruffled as though she had just slept in it.

Her mother hastened to smooth out the wrinkles while Alice combed her hair.

This done, Alice excused herself, clutching the costume in a box under her arm. Duncan saw her scurrying through the hallway outside the sitting room and called out to her.

"I say, Alice!" he called out. She stopped momentarily, still clutching the cumbersome box.

"Good afternoon, Your Grace," she replied. "I trust you're feeling well."

Duncan nodded, all the time wondering what could be in that mysterious container.

"Sorry to keep you waiting," said Margaret a few minutes later, entering the sitting room and looking a bit flushed as she smoothed down her hair. She was holding something behind her back with her left hand.

"Not a problem," said Duncan as he stood. He grinned, his natural good humour enhancing his rugged good looks. He was a handsomely built man with an elegant nose, a square jaw and sandy-colored hair. Glancing behind him, he added, "Jack was trying to entertain me. Poor fool, he thinks I can still be amazed by that one trick of his where he makes a guinea appear in the sleeve of my jacket. As if it was 1799 and I was still five years old!"

Margaret's father entered the room and coughed slightly. Duncan turned and bowed.

"Good afternoon, Langmere. I hope you are in good spirits this day."

Felton Notley smiled at Duncan. "Yes, Middleford, and my wishes are the same for you. I heard that you had stopped by, and just wanted to make sure that you have received your invitation to the next month's fox hunt."

"Yes I have," Duncan replied. "I certainly hope the weather will be conducive for the event. By the way, Townshend, your Master of the Hunt did a superb job during the January hunt."

"He does rather well at that," the Earl said. After a short but awkward pause he said, "Well, I must say I am pleased the two of you are planning to attend the Valentine's Masquerade Ball together. I am sure you have a lot to catch up on," he said as he strode to the door, "so I think I will leave you to yourselves. Talk as long as you want — do not hold back. Youth does not last forever, you know."

His voice trailed off as he left the room, leaving the doors open.

"What's *he* on about?" asked Duncan once he had gone.

"Oh, the same thing as ever," said Margaret, now scowling. "Both of my parents want us to be married and won't take no for an answer. But please, let's not talk about that. The Ball is in two days and I want to know all about your costume!"

Chapter Two

"First things first," said Duncan, smiling broadly and pulling out a large envelope which he handed to Margaret. "Happy Valentine's Day."

"And the same to you, good sir," she said with a grin, as she handed him the envelope she had been concealing behind her.

Each opened their envelope and removed the Valentine's card.

"'To the one man who knows all my quirks and still loves me,'" he quoted aloud. "Yes, I have certainly grown up seeing all aspects of you — and you know I will always love you."

Margaret sat down and carefully examined the card he had given her. It was also hand-made, undoubtedly by Duncan. Although not designed by an artisan, the thought was genuine. It said, "To the woman who brightens every one of my days with her infectious laughter."

Margaret rose and walked to where Duncan was standing. She smiled and gently kissed him on the cheek.

"Now, as to your costume?" she said, bringing the conversation back around.

"You wouldn't believe how long it took me to find the right costume," said Duncan, seating himself on the velvet divan beside her. Salmon-paste sandwiches and a bronze kettle sat on a glass table in front of them.

"You ought to have asked Simon," said Margaret, referring to Duncan's younger brother. "He's brilliant at costumes."

"I always told him he should have gone into the theatre," said Duncan, stretching his legs easily. "He suggested that I dress up as a medieval plague doctor, but we had a remarkably hard time finding the right nose for the part. Then I considered going as a character in one of Mr. Shakespeare's plays — Hamlet with skull in hand, Lear with beard and matted hair, even Viola was suggested — or a Roman senator. None of those seemed to suit me, though. And then I hit on an idea."

"What was it?" asked Margaret, instinctively leaning toward him.

"I was in an inn drinking with some veterans of the recent war, whom I had just met," said Duncan. "One of them mentioned having marched through Bordeaux, and having awakened once in the middle of the night to see what he felt sure must have been the Musketeers of the Guard riding through the center of town. No one believed him, of course — Musketeers in this day and age, and in Bordeaux of all places! But he insisted on it, against all reason."

There was a rushed, ad-libbed quality to this story, as though he was making it up as he went along.

Once or twice he peered into Margaret's face to see if she had noticed, but her face betrayed no suspicion. Emboldened, he went on.

"Just before having that conversation, Simon and I had been discussing what I was going to wear to the Valentine's Day ball. He wanted me to go as a Jinn out of the Arabian Nights, and had even bought the turbans, sandals, and golden armbands to go with the outfit. I was tempted to do it — it was a close thing, I assure you."

"You would have been magnificent," said Margaret, sitting down on the divan and reaching for the tea kettle.

Duncan smiled.

"But when I heard the old man's story, my mind was made up. I resolved there and then to dress as Henri, Seigneur d'Aramitz, Musketeer of the Guard!"

He paused with a triumphant expression and his arm raised and fist clenched, as though expecting Margaret to burst into applause. Instead she said, "Who?"

Duncan's face fell slightly.

"Have you never heard of him? The most famous and storied of all of the King's Musketeers."

Margaret frowned and shook her head.

"You'll have to forgive me. Not everyone is as versed as you in the subtleties of French history. Some of us haven't even been to France!"

"But you know what a Musketeer is?"

"Of course."

"Then you can imagine how excellent this costume is. A scarlet uniform bedecked with blue ribbons, a white-plumed hat of purest velvet, a belt fringed with gold and a golden sword! You simply must see it, it's magnificent." Duncan had placed so much energy into imagining this fictional costume that he forgot, for the moment, that he wasn't planning on wearing it, and that, in fact, it did not exist. However, his story had fooled Margaret, who smiled at his boyish enthusiasm.

"And I'm sure it will look splendid on you," she said, "but you really ought to have consulted me, or your mother, or *someone* other than Simon before choosing a costume like that."

"Why?" asked Duncan, raising a cup to his lips.

"I know this might be hard for you to hear, but wearing a French military costume, so soon after the war, is going to be seen by many as a shocking breach of manners and good taste."

"But we're not talking about the French Legions," said Duncan, looking flustered. "These are the King's royal guards. Their office was abolished when the monarchy itself was abolished in the Revolution."

"I know, but I can assure you not everyone will see it that way. They're likely to take offense at anything that reminds them of France."

"Well, we didn't fight a war against the Musketeers," said Duncan. "And if they had fought in the war, they would have been on our side!"

"You're probably right," said Margaret in a conciliatory tone. "I just don't think it wise. I'm sure you've heard the story of the young man who wore a scarlet coat into an inn in Devonshire. He was beaten badly, I suppose because it stirred memories of the war in France. Never mind that the young man in question had actually fought in the war and been badly wounded at Trafalgar. There's no reasoning with some people."

Nothing of the kind had ever happened, of course, but Margaret thought it worth inventing a cautionary fiction if it kept Duncan out of trouble. Duncan, who hadn't planned on wearing the costume of a Musketeer in any case, smiled wanly.

"Well, never mind all that," he said, setting his empty cup down on the glass table. "We've spent entirely too much time talking about me. Now I want to hear about *your* costume."

Margaret laughed lightly with the look of someone who hoped to avoid answering a question. "I've already got mine," she said. "It's all sewn together and ready to wear. I was just trying it on, in fact, before you arrived."

"Is that why you kept me busy here in the sitting-room while Jack performed his sportive tricks?" asked Duncan with an inscrutable smile.

"Well, there was no way I was going to let you come in there and *see* me," said Margaret. (Duncan couldn't help noticing that she had been staring rigidly at the glass table ever since the conversation turned to her). "It would spoil all the fun of the party."

"*Au contraire,*" Duncan replied. "It would have made the prospect of going to the party infinitely more exciting."

Margaret didn't see how that followed. "You know this about me," she said. "There are some things that I prefer to keep secret until the time is right. Remember the infamous hay festival incident?"

"How you dressed as a reaper and frightened half the children and their parents? I don't think that example works to your advantage. If you had told anyone you were going to dress like that, they might at least have talked you out of wielding the scythe."

"Which is why I'm very glad I did not tell them," said Margaret. "In any case, Alice and Mama both know how I'm dressing. They helped make the costume and have both seen me in it."

"And what was their objective opinion?"

"They loved it, of course," she replied. "Neither of them could recognize me."

"That would, I think, make the costume hard to love," said Duncan.

Margaret laughed. Duncan had a strange way of flirting without really flirting that he had acquired over many years of being her friend. By now she accepted that he was always going to be coquettish and complimentary, without thinking anything of it. It was so habitual an instinct that by now Duncan himself hardly seemed to mean anything by it.

"Anyway," said Duncan, "you ought to show me, since I've already described my costume to you in full."

"Yes, but I haven't *seen* it yet," said Margaret, rising from the divan and beginning to pace the room with a mischievous smile. "And I can't show mine to you, because it's already boxed and put away. It was carried out of the room in that nondescript box Alice was carrying."

"If I had only known," said Duncan with a theatrical air, "I would have wrenched the box open and drawn the costume from its depths!"

"And you would have spoiled the entire party for yourself," said Margaret, "so be thankful that no one told you."

"I don't see how I can get through the next two days without knowing."

"You will, though," she replied. "You'll see me when I arrive at the Ball."

Duncan looked at her thoughtfully for a moment. "I have just one question," he said, raising a single finger in the air.

"Yes?"

"How am I to know who you are," he asked slowly, "if I can't recognize you?"

Margaret laughed merrily. "You won't!" she said, clapping her hands with delight. "That's the beauty of it. I shall be escorted to the Ball in the company of another gentleman, and you won't know who it is. And, to keep you from discovering who I am, I'll disguise my voice and even change my personality by playing a role."

"It all sounds dreadfully complicated," moaned Duncan.

"It will be up to you to find the costumed girl whom you think to be me," said Margaret, ignoring his lament. "Whether it really is me or not, you won't know until midnight and we all remove our masks. You're going to be quite surprised, I assure you, when the clock strikes twelve and you realize you chose the wrong woman!"

"One of us will be surprised, alright," said Duncan, though he smiled in spite of himself at Margaret's enthusiasm.

Chapter Three

The following morning Duncan and his brother, Simon Livingston, sat in the breakfast-room at their home, Woolton Manor. As he sat eating kippers and buttered toast, Duncan told Simon about his conversation with Margaret the afternoon before. "Of course she refused to tell me what she intends to wear to the Ball," he said with a forlorn sigh. "Even the years of anxiously waiting for me to come home haven't cured her of her innate tendency toward secrecy and mischief."

"It was ever thus with Margaret," said Simon, who, though fully two years younger than his brother, was considerably larger and broader of shoulder — so much so, in fact, that his body seemed to spill out of his chair and fill the whole room. "The very first memory I have of her is back when I was five and she found a toad in the well behind our barn. She claimed she could hear it talking, but when I bent down to listen I heard only a loud croak. Undeterred, she proceeded to translate the croaks for me as though she could hear them in perfect English. I spent years thinking she could actually talk to toads."

"A sad story," said Duncan, using the last of his toast to mop the oil from his plate.

"Trickery runs in her family, though," said Simon, dabbing at the corners of his mouth with a cloth napkin. "She picked it up from her mother, who's been engaged in schemes of one kind or another for as long as I can remember."

"Most of them involving me in some capacity," said Duncan. He recalled that during the war Selina had written to him in the Peninsula informing him that Margaret had another beau, a statement seemingly intended to arouse his jealousy. Duncan returned home at Christmas to find her as single and unattached as ever. "There are moments when I'm really tempted to marry Margaret, just so they'll leave us alone."

Simon scoffed. "If you think they're going to leave you alone after you're married," he said, "you're going to be sorely disappointed."

Duncan granted that this was probably true. He rose to close the north-facing window, which was open slightly and letting in a chill draft.

"But Margaret has given me every indication that she intends to go on tricking me during the Ball tomorrow night," he said as he resumed his seat at the table. "I think we're going to have to come up with a trick or two of our own."

Simon looked up at him in surprise, a smile playing at the corners of his mouth. "There's the old Livingston fighting spirit," he said with a proud gleam in his eyes. "What did you have in mind?"

"I told her I'm going to wear a Musketeer costume," said Duncan, "but I have no intention of honouring that commitment."

"That's probably wise," said Simon. "You might get beaten."

"So I've been told. But I was thinking, if I wanted to play a joke on her — and maybe even embarrass her a little — what better way to do it than to wear *a clown costume?*"

Simon eyed his brother quizzically. "Are you serious?"

"But not just any clown costume," Duncan went on, undaunted by the dubious look on his brother's face. Rising from the table he began walking in the direction of the sitting room. Simon rose and followed him automatically.

Duncan came to a halt in front of an ormolu pier table that stood between two windows. On top of the table stood a white box, identical to the white box that Margaret's lady's maid had sneaked out of their sitting room the day before. With a grand gesture he pulled the lid off of the box and produced its contents, holding them up to the light.

"Ah, the commedia d'ell arte!" Simon exclaimed.

It was a brightly colored costume, possibly the brightest object in the room. The large red and green diamond-shaped patches formed a striking contrast with the grey stone walls and the grey six-paned windows. Duncan held up the black mask to his face for a second so that Simon could get an idea of how he would look once he put it on. The mask covered his whole face except for his eyes, which peeped out of two narrow slits.

"She's going to have a hard time working out whether it's really you under there," said Simon with an approving look.

"Especially if I play my part well," said Duncan, holding the costume at arm's length and giving it an admiring look. "I don't just want to *dress* as the Harlequin, you know. I want to *become* him! I want my gestures, my mannerisms, the way I walk and talk, to be so completely transformed that even a close relation would be hard-pressed to know it was me."

"And how do you plan to accomplish that?" asked Simon.

Duncan smiled a small smile.

"I've never told anyone this," he said quietly, "but I was in an amateur theatrical troupe during the war. When we were stationed overseas there were whole weeks when we sat around waiting, half-hoping the French would attack us. To stave off boredom, some thespians in our unit started putting on classes, teaching the fundamentals of acting. Eventually we put on a production of *As You like It*."

"But that's fantastic!" said Simon. "I had no idea you had training in comedy. Though, to be quite honest, I did think you had gotten funnier after you returned home."

"Not the sort of effect you were expecting the war to have on me, was it?"

Simon shook his head.

"I figured there's just something about staring death in the face that makes a man naturally comedic."

Duncan reluctantly returned the costume to its box.

"But if I can accomplish this feat," he said in a breathy voice, "if I can transform myself so completely that she doesn't recognize me, she'll never suspect it's me she's dancing with, again and again, throughout the night."

"But how will you know it's her?"

Duncan dismissed the question with a wave of his hand.

"I'm not even worried about it. I'll figure it out easily, but I'll let her think I'm being fooled, right up until the fatal moment."

Simon was about to ask another question when the door opened and their mother, Louisa, the Dowager Duchess, entered the room. She was a strikingly tall woman with a taut face and prominent cheekbones that gave her, fairly or not, a forbidding aspect.

"I'm very glad to hear that your preparations for the Ball are coming along well," she said to Duncan. "I just returned from Eastdale Hall. Lady Langmere could not be more excited about it."

"That's rather unfortunate," said Duncan, "given that she isn't planning to attend."

"Nor am I," said Louisa, "but surely you would not begrudge us our vicarious pleasures. But what is this I hear about you allowing another young gentleman to escort Margaret to the Ball instead of yourself?"

Duncan laughed, which only served to irritate his mother further.

"It's nothing, Mama," he said, seeing the sceptical look on her face. "Margaret actually insisted on it. She hopes, in this way, to deceive me by forcing me to guess which of the costumed women is really her."

Now that he had said it aloud to his mother, it didn't sound half as interesting as when he had explained it to Simon. "Well," said Louisa, drawing her shawl tight around her, "let us hope you do not deceive yourselves into the wrong marriage."

The air of perfect sobriety with which she spoke these last words was lost on her two sons, for Duncan winked at Simon, and when the door closed behind her both men broke into riotous laughter.

Chapter Four

Duncan arrived at Moorwike Hall on the following night, just as the sun was setting. A couple of footmen bearing torches led his carriage up the long drive toward the stables while another pair escorted him across the rain-soaked lawn toward the house.

Ensconced in his Harlequin costume, Duncan sweated uncomfortably. Outside it was a cold February night, but inside the fireplaces were all ablaze, and his body was already sticky with perspiration by the time he reached the foyer. Yet he was so busy looking around, peering into the faces of the people he passed on his way through the hallway, that he hardly noticed his discomfort.

A crowd was already gathered in the drawing room wearing all manner of colourful costumes. Although announced by Jennings, the butler, he was unacknowledged by most of the other guests. Duncan strode over to the side of the room where a bowl full of shelled almonds stood on a pier table next to a hand-carved oak bookshelf.

Helping himself to a handful of almonds, he stood there with an air of supreme confidence, awaiting the moment when he could walk up to Margaret and claim victory.

Yet the evening wore on and Margaret did not appear. Jennings announced each person as they arrived, yet none of them bore a resemblance to the woman he had known since childhood.

Duncan began to feel increasingly frustrated, and was relieved when Simon arrived at his side a few minutes later.

He was dressed in the powdered wig and fur-lined jacket of a man twice his age.

Sizing him up, Duncan felt sure he must be dressed as a Member of Parliament. He suggested as much to Simon, who merely laughed.

"I suppose I might as well be," he said, handing Duncan a cup full of mead from which Duncan drank without hesitation. "I don't blame you for not knowing, but I was supposed to be an old Russian Prince."

"Perhaps, if I saw you seated in your library, a samovar at your right hand, being tended by an elderly babushka in a sparkling winter gown, I might have guessed that," said Duncan. "But as it is, you look just like an MP."

"Yes, and sadly, elderly babushkas are in shockingly short supply in this part of England," said Simon with a wry smile.

"If you intended to be an old man," said Duncan, "you failed badly at it. You're much closer in age to Wellington. If anyone asks, that's what you must say."

Simon nodded in the affirmative; but this plan was undercut a second later by the announcement of three young men who were all identically clad in the grey pelisse coat, cocked hat, and rubber boots of Lord Wellington.

"Anyway," said Simon, choosing not to acknowledge these new arrivals, "have you spotted Margaret yet?"

"I *haven't*," said Duncan in a tone of disappointment. "I have to give her credit. Either she has not yet arrived, or she's better at concealing herself than I anticipated. I have a feeling the solution is really obvious and that I'm just overlooking it." He put down his cup a bit more sharply than needed.

"At midnight," said Simon drolly, "I'll take off my Simon costume and you'll realize it was Margaret *this whole time.*"

Duncan laughed and clapped his hands in delight. Yet he kept his eyes fixed on the entrance.

But though more women continued to enter the room, he felt sure none of them could be Margaret. He spied women dressed in the tall wigs and gaudy dresses of the pre-war French aristocracy, robed women in sandals like figures out of the Bible, women in loose flowing dresses wearing burqas and bedlas, and women clad in the bulky cloaks and knitted long johns of shepherds.

But Margaret was nowhere to be seen.

Just as the dancing was beginning, Simon nudged Duncan in the ribs and motioned to the front entrance. A man and woman had just entered the room, walking arm in arm, and their costumes were the most elaborate he had yet seen.

"Ladies and gentlemen," said Jennings in a commanding voice, "allow me to introduce Her Majesty Marie Antoinette, Queen of France, and her escort... Mr 'Denny the Dosser'."

A slender fellow, he was playing a mendicant dressed in rags, sporting an utterly convincing pair of fake yellow teeth, and covered in a grimy substance that looked very much like soot. He wore a small cap on the top of his head and a threadbare black and grey vest that seemed to have been half-eaten by moths. There might have once been buttons on his shirt, but they had all been torn or fallen off.

It was an appalling sight, but it served only to heighten, by contrast, the loveliness of the woman beside him.

She was wearing the *robe a la polonaise*, a billowy dress with a bosom-enhancing bodice that had indeed been worn by Marie Antoinette. Given this and the extraordinary size of her pouf, Duncan immediately found himself convinced that she actually might *be* Marie Antoinette.

As she gracefully glided through the room, bowing demurely and scattering French phrases like a child casts crumbs to a goose, Duncan watched her, entranced. Although she was wearing a black mask over much of her face, he could tell by her silhouette alone that she was an improvement over the real-life queen with her unsightly square jaw.

Duncan suspected, from the moment she entered the room, that it was Margaret, transfigured by her clothes to a new plane of existence. She was the same height and of roughly the same proportions with her thin waist and wide hips.

"It's her," he said to Simon, handing back the cup of mead and preparing to venture out onto the dance floor. "It's her, I'm almost sure of it."

"Go up to her and say something," said Simon.

But just as Duncan began walking in her direction, she was led onto the floor by her mendicant escort. "That *Gilbert*," he muttered in disgust under his breath — for he felt sure this was her cousin, Gilbert Johnson. With a forlorn feeling he returned to the edge of the room and, once again grabbing the mead out of Simon's hands, took a long, unhappy swig.

The dance finally ended and she was left standing alone. Sensing his opportunity, Duncan wiped his mouth and strode confidently into the center of the room. But it wasn't until she stepped into the light and he saw a hint of her auburn hair, which she hadn't perfectly concealed under her white wig, that he knew for certain this was Margaret. The words of Shakespeare rose all unbidden into his mind:

Did my heart love till now? Foreswear it, sight! For I ne'er saw true beauty till this night.

Only, those words had been spoken of a stranger, and this was a woman he had known — or thought he had known — all of his life.

"May I have the honor of the next dance?" he asked.

She smiled coquettishly. "You may."

"And you are Her Majesty Marie Antoinette?"

"I am. I surmise that you are the Harlequin?"

Duncan smiled at the lie in the way one would smile at a child pretending to be a magician. But as the orchestra began to play and he led her out onto the dance floor, she kept up the pretence. True to her promise, she was altering the timbre of her voice, and she was speaking with a French accent that, although not completely genuine, seemed so to his ear.

I'll play along with this, he thought to himself. To that end he modified his own voice, speaking in a register slightly lower than normal. If he could just fool Margaret with this disguise, it would be all the more fun.

When he asked where she was from, she replied she had been born in Austria to the Empress Maria Theresa but that early on her parents had arranged for her to marry the future King of France.

"It must feel strange to know from a young age that one day you're going to become the Queen of France," mused Duncan.

"*Non, monsieur,* I had time to prepare," said Marie, "My siblings had all gone on to do great things. Maria Christina and Maria Amalia both became Duchesses, and Maria Carolina became Queen of Naples. Why should I be any different?"

Duncan couldn't help gawking. It was fortunate that he was wearing a mask, for he knew his surprise was plain on his face, and it embarrassed him. He had badly underestimated the extent of Margaret's preparation and her level of commitment to her performance. As the dance went on and she continued to rattle off various facts about her life in France and Austria, he became determined to trip her up.

"What was the King like at home?" he asked.

"Serene and attentive, always," said Marie with a faraway look. "Perhaps too serene for a Head of State. In a better world we might have lived together in a small cottage in Bordeaux, he reading Fenelon and me frolicking through the woods with my dogs. But Providence had other plans for us."

"You loved him, though," said Duncan. "Marrying him had to have been the best moment of your life."

He could see the faintest outline of a smile from behind her mask. "Second best," she said quietly.

"And what was the best moment?"

"On my way to France from Austria," she said, "when I was made to undress in the middle of the Rhine and my Austrian garments were exchanged for French ones. Then I was led into Strasbourg, where the church bells rang and the cannons roared and the people shouted their approval. I was only fourteen." She paused and looked away. "I would never be that happy again."

She spoke these last melancholy words with such an air of conviction that Duncan looked her at in alarm. Her performance was so persuasive that he found himself half-believing that she was the real Marie Antoinette. No doubt after the Ball she would ask him to escort her home, only to leap out of the carriage as they passed the cemetery and vanish into thin air. He wondered if Marie Antoinette's body was buried in England. Somehow he doubted it.

"Stay close to me," he said as their third dance ended. "I have an eerie premonition that you are going to disappear if I let you out of my sight for even a moment."

"Do not worry, Monsieur Harlequin," she said with a laugh. "I will not go anywhere you cannot find me."

Chapter Five

They continued to dance at intervals throughout the night. With each fresh encounter Duncan found himself even more deeply entranced by the beauty and brilliance of this woman he had known most of his life. She carried herself with the confidence and dignity of a French royal, not like the slightly slouching Margaret of yore. When they danced, she floated over the floor with the stateliness and solemnity of a beautiful, gliding ghost. Her conversation, though entertaining as always, was of a level of brilliance and wit heretofore unknown to him. Duncan determined that Gilbert, dressed in filthy rags, would not be permitted another dance with this enchanting creature.

It was just after eleven-thirty that he excused himself for a moment to go and find Simon.

"Do not go anywhere," he said, as if afraid that she might not be entirely real. "I will be right back."

She smiled and gently tilted her head. *"A tout à l'heure,"* she said.

Duncan smiled in return. He had no idea what the mysterious woman had just said, his knowledge of French being nearly non-existent, with the exception of a handful of common phrases he had memorized during the war. He found Simon still standing near the mead bowl, having apparently not moved from that position the entire night. But now the alcohol was heavy on Simon's breath and he swayed slightly.

"Did you see that, were you watching?" Duncan asked. "I just want to make sure it wasn't all a dream. For all I know, I could have been dancing with the empty air."

But Duncan's astonishment was entirely incomprehensible to Simon. "I saw you dancing with a Lady," he said. "I saw other men dancing with other Ladies. I saw them dancing with your Lady. It's an ordinary party, in other words."

"No," said Duncan vehemently. "There was nothing ordinary about her. Not tonight, anyway. I now realize that it's true what they say about long familiarity dulling your senses to the glories of others. What I needed was to be shaken out of my complacency with respect to Margaret, and by heaven she's done it." He paused for a moment. "I find myself truly falling in love for the first time ever, with a 'Margaret' I have never known."

Simon, who had long been accustomed to Duncan's extravagant flights of fancy, nodded sleepily. "You had better get hold of her slipper," he said, "or you won't be able to find her again."

Duncan smiled. "Luckily I know just where she lives. So when her carriage returns to its vegetable state at midnight, I'll make my way over there post-haste."

"You'd better be quick," said Simon, "or some other Duke or Prince is liable to snatch her up. Women like that don't hang around forever waiting for indolent young men to find their courage. Faint heart, as they say, never won fair lady."

"You really think we could get on well together? Margaret and I?"

Simon shrugged.

"She's human, like any other woman. Though she seems to have charmed you into thinking otherwise."

Duncan flattered himself that his long acquaintance with Margaret would give him the edge over any other men who competed for her affections. She had been his for nearly every dance of the evening, laughing at his ridiculous jokes and smiling at his mangled attempts at French. With the conceitedness of youth, Duncan imagined that he really was as interesting and clever and funny as she seemed to think he was. Before tonight he had always felt a little awkward and stupid in the company of his peers. But now, buoyed by her attentions, he stalked through the room like a Prince.

Great was his surprise, then, on returning to the center of the room, to find that "Marie" and "Denny" were nowhere to be seen.

Thinking that she must have just slipped out, he spent some minutes wandering through the kitchens and gardens with a lost look. Occasionally he would interrupt conversations to ask if anyone present had seen where a beautiful woman dressed like Marie Antoinette had gone. But no one had. *She had simply vanished.*

The quiet unease that had gripped him throughout the evening began to feel like a premonition. She had slipped away as easily as if she had never been there. Another line from Shakespeare, less pleasant than the first, rose to his mind:

The earth hath bubbles, as the water has, and these are of them! Whither are they vanished?

Duncan had suspected she was magic, and here was the proof. Margaret had vanished, like the three witches, the second his eyes had turned elsewhere.

~~~~~

The next morning Simon was recovering from his hangover. After breakfast Duncan found him seated at the pianoforte in the sitting room, practicing his scales. A pair of French windows was letting a shaft of brilliant sunlight into the room, and off in the distance Duncan could hear the tinkling of a cow's bell.

"Did you ever manage to find her?" asked Simon, sensing that Duncan had come into the room to discuss this very subject.

Duncan shook his head sadly as he sank down onto the divan facing the window.

"She disappeared without saying goodbye. I feel lied to, in a way — just before she left, she spoke some words in French—"

"What were they?"
~~~~~

Duncan struggled to remember. "A-toot d'alaire? I don't know, something along those lines. You know I never did well with our French lessons — and I have forgotten what little I learned. The few common phrases I picked up while stationed overseas don't help in this situation. Last night I asked Jennings, the butler, about it. He said it means something like 'I'll see you in a little while.'"

"Well, perhaps she's planning to make an appearance today. If you hang around here long enough, she may show up."

This was a pleasant notion, although Duncan doubted it. Grasping a handful of raisins, hazel nuts, and almonds from a bowl on a nearby table, he leaned his head back on the divan with a gloomy expression.

"Maybe, although knowing Margaret she'll want to keep me in suspense for as long as possible. Her instinct for mischief has no rival, as she proved last night."

"She comes over here at least once a week anyway," said Simon. "Invite her to dinner next week, and then you can question her at your leisure."

"I think I just might."

He fell silent, continuing to brood over the events of the night before. It looked like he wanted to say something but was hesitating. Sensing this, Simon paused in his scales and turned to face his brother. "What's wrong?"

Duncan scratched the back of his neck nervously. His clothes and hair had the unkempt appearance of a man who had spent the entire night pacing his room in restless agitation.

"Well, it's this," he said. He leaned forward on the divan and carefully scanned the view through the window, as if afraid there might be spies stationed in the hedges waiting to report his every word to Margaret. Returning to the divan, he said, "Something happened last night that I have no explanation for."

"You mean you fell in love," said Simon.

Duncan laughed in surprise.

"No, not that — although heaven knows that might have happened. No, something strange and inexplicable that's plunged me, against my will, into complete mystery."

Simon's eyes met his brother's with a look that encouraged him to continue.

"Last night, after Margaret and Gilbert vanished, I spent about an hour looking for them until I proved, to my own satisfaction, that they were both gone. Having done this, I went up to Jennings — who I know had seen us together, just as surely as you did — and asked him if he knew where she had gone. 'The woman who was with me,' I said, 'Marie Antoinette, where is she?'

"He looked at me in confusion and at first I thought he was going to deny ever having seen her. But he said, 'The young lady sends her apologies; she had to leave suddenly.'

"I asked him, 'What happened?'"

"He said, 'She just received word that her younger brother was the victim of an accident, and she had to return home at once. It could not be helped, of course. She felt sure you would understand.'"

Duncan ended his story and gazed at his brother intently, as if the meaning was obvious and Simon was obligated to share his surprise.

Instead, Simon shrugged in confusion.

"So she had to go home and see her brother. You've been acting like it was some huge mystery, when this whole time you knew where she was."

Duncan stood up and began pacing in front of the window. He looked slightly deranged with his uncombed hair and his wild eyes.

"There's just one problem," he said. "As you are undoubtedly aware, Margaret doesn't *have* a brother!"

Simon reared back, looking lost.

"What on earth—"

"Yes, exactly! And, what's more, Margaret knows very well that I know she has no brother. So why would she lie to me, Simon? Why would she lie to me?"

"I'm sure there's a perfectly good explanation," said Simon. "You know yourself she likes to play pranks. This is probably just one of those."

Duncan blinked rapidly with the look of someone who was unconvinced.

"You need to calm down," said Simon, returning to the piano. "You're working yourself into a panic. Just give it a day or two and it will undoubtedly sort itself out."

But the end of their conversation only plunged Duncan into deeper mystery.

Feeling frustrated and irritable, he left the room and was on his way into the kitchen when there came a knock at the front door.

Simon rose and walked toward the door, but Duncan reached it first.

A footman in livery was standing on the front steps holding a large envelope in the crook of one arm. When he saw the two men, he pulled it out with the air of a highway robber producing a pistol.

"A message, Your Grace," he said, "from Eastdale Hall."

Duncan took the envelope eagerly, tore it open, and read out loud the letter it contained.

Dearest Duncan,

I wanted to apologize for my absence last night. I know I promised you I would come, but I fell terribly ill on account of the coq au vin that Collette made on Wednesday night. Half the family is sick because of it and none of us are able to travel at present. As soon as I'm able, I'll come see you again. Or, if you would prefer, you can come here. If you can't cure my sickness, you can at least remedy my boredom while I wait for this to pass. I remain

Yours steadfastly and forever,

Margaret

Duncan read the letter over several more times to himself before thanking the footman and sending him on his way.

"Well, that explains it, doesn't it?" said Simon. "She was sick and couldn't attend."

"Yes, it explains a great many things," said Duncan. "She must have purposefully left the Ball before she could be unmasked at midnight, and now she's sent this letter as a prank. We'll see how sick she is when I show up at Eastdale tonight unannounced!"

ARIETTA RICHMOND, GRACE AUSTEN, ISABELLA THORNE,
KATHERINE KEATS AND ALYCE HEALEY

Chapter Six

Duncan found Margaret lying on the four-poster in her bed-chamber.

Pillows had been piled up around her to make her as comfortable as possible. Her face burned scarlet and was warm to the touch. Her maid hovered nearby.

"My head aches, my stomach aches, my whole body aches," she said to Duncan when he entered the room around sundown. Dusky sunlight was slanting in through an open window. "This isn't the first time Collette has tried to cook something and only succeeded in poisoning us. If it doesn't get better soon, she may find herself out of a job."

"Perhaps in the future she could be forbidden to cook," said Duncan. "Remember when she told you she was cooking chicken, but it turned out to be frog legs?"

"That's the danger with hiring these French maids," said Margaret.

"When she arrived she could barely speak a word of English, and she wasn't much to look at. But in the last year she's blossomed into something truly magnificent—just last week, during Candlemas, the miller's son and one of the altar boys came to blows over her. I'm afraid it's gone to her head a little, and now she hardly pays attention to her work."

Duncan nodded, half-listening. It hadn't occurred to him until just now that Margaret had a maid who had grown up in France.

This explained how Margaret had learned so many French phrases, and how she had acquired such an extensive knowledge of the French Revolution and its aftermath. It was the sort of information one could easily pick up living with a Frenchwoman.

He felt more certain than ever that it had been Margaret behind that black mask on the previous night. Yet at the same time it seemed clear that she had really been here, really sick, the whole night. How could anyone be in two places at once?

Seeing that he was going through some difficulty, Margaret said to him, "Forgive my lack of hospitality. We've talked about nothing but me and my troubles since you came into the room. How was the party last night? Did you fall in love?"

She could tell by his hesitant smile that her last question had struck close to the truth.

"I want to know everything!" she said, sitting up a little too quickly.

Duncan handed her the glass of water that stood on the oak nightstand beside the bed.

"It's an awkward thing to discuss," he said, "since I was fully convinced until about three minutes ago that we had been together the whole night."

Margaret smiled in spite of her discomfort.

"Then perhaps," she said, "I was successful after all. Do tell."

Duncan told her everything, beginning with his arrival at Moorwike and ending with the letter he had received from her that afternoon.

"Even then I thought you were trying to mislead me," he said. "But I don't think you could be faking your illness. Your theatrical gifts are formidable, but they extend only so far."

Margaret took a sip, then shook her head and handed the glass back to Duncan.

"At this point I would have *told* you if we had been together all night. While it would have been entertaining for as long as the party lasted, it would be cruel to keep you in permanent suspense."

Duncan searched her face as she talked. He had learned by long habit how to tell when Margaret was lying, and there was no trace of cunning or deception in her eyes.

"Then the whole time," he said quietly, "I was dancing with a stranger. She was witty and knowledgeable, played the part of Marie Antoinette to perfection. She was beautiful, charming, well-mannered and yet exciting. Is it any wonder I thought it was my best friend, come into her true self?"

"I must tell you that I didn't plan to go as Marie Antoinette," she replied.

"The costume in the box you saw was that of Little Bo-peep. My cousin Gilbert was to accompany me, disguised as Lord Wellington."

Seeing the look of despair on his face, Margaret took pity on him. He had the withdrawn, defeated look of Romeo after Rosalinda rejected him. She didn't even have to ask whether he had fallen in love.

"If you don't believe me," she said, "ask anyone you wish. They'll tell you where I was last night."

Duncan shook his head and turned to the window. "It's not that," he said. "If you say you were laid up in bed last night, I believe you. Besides, I had never met anyone quite like that woman." In a pained tone, he added, "She was so — so *different* from anyone else I've known."

"Well, if it means that much to you," said Margaret, shifting uncomfortably, "I'll help you find her. We'll look for her together. You won't have to spend your life pining after this girl."

Duncan turned to face her. There was a feverish look in his eyes.

"Could you really help me?" he asked. "Would you do that for me, dear Maggie?"

Margaret nodded. There was a lump in her throat and a pained look in her eye which Duncan ascribed to the sickness.

"Of course I will," she said faintly. "Through everything we've always wanted what's best for each other. Anything I can do for you I will do happily, my dearest."

"And I for you," he responded. He looked at her hopefully as if half-expecting her to leap out of bed at that moment and put her traveling cloak on. "So where do we begin?"

"Well, first," she said, "you'll have to talk to the other guests and find out if any of them know her, know where she lives, or anything about her or her escort. Second, we've held a few Balls, and I can tell you that the hostess always has a guest list. Her name is bound to be on it."

"I don't know how much good that will do me," he said, "given that I don't know her name, and she was in costume. There were about a dozen women there dressed in French fashion. If I go up to them and say, 'Who was the French girl I spent the night dancing with?', I doubt they'll know anything."

"Well, you have to start somewhere. Try not to be too obvious about the fact that you're pining after this woman. Say she left something of hers in your possession and you want to return it — maybe a bracelet or a glass slipper. Just any plausible reason."

"The entire county's going to know I'm in love with this woman before I even know her name," Duncan said sadly.

"They'll know you're in love with *a* woman. They won't know *who*, any more than you do."

Duncan rolled his eyes. This was small consolation given the embarrassment he was about to inflict upon himself.

ARIETTA RICHMOND, GRACE AUSTEN, ISABELLA THORNE,
KATHERINE KEATS AND ALYCE HEALEY

Chapter Seven

Early the next morning Duncan returned to Moorwike Hall. There he inquired among the staff about the guests at the Valentine's Day Ball.

As he had predicted, none of them knew much more than he did.

"What I really need to know," he told Jennings as they walked down a long hallway together, "is whether you know anything about this woman or her escort. I — understand that her brother was in a serious accident, and I wish to convey my condolences. But the fact that I have no idea who she is or where she lives makes that difficult."

"I do not know what to tell you, Your Grace," said Jennings. "Although I was in charge of welcoming the guests and was careful to spend a few minutes conferring with each of them during the Ball, some of their names eluded me."

"How can that be?" asked Duncan with a growing feeling of hopelessness and frustration.

"Well, it happens as one gets older, My Lord. But also because the guest list I read from," he said in an embarrassed tone, "listed only the name of the character they were portraying. Real names and titles were not mentioned. So unless the woman's real name is 'Marie Antoinette', I am sorry to say that I do not see how that helps you."

Duncan was equally sorry to admit that it didn't help him much.

"But you are sure you do not remember the woman I speak of?" he asked, with an insistence that he felt sure must be annoying to Jennings. "Exquisitely beautiful, dressed in the finest French fashions of twenty or thirty years ago, with a white pillar of wig towering over every other wig in the room..."

"Unfortunately for your quest," said Jennings, "there were at least twelve other women arrayed in the fine fashions of France."

"Yes, but this one excelled them all," said Duncan. "She was heavily perfumed and wore white gloves and a jade bracelet on one wrist. Her dress was a beautiful creation of rose with ruffles, with a bit of white on her shoulders."

Jennings looked at him dubiously, as if suspecting the story about an injured brother might have been completely made up.

"And," Duncan concluded, "she wore a black mask that covered much of her face. She had a beauty mark on her left cheek."

The mention of the mark stirred something in Jennings' memory. "Now that you mention it," he said, "I do remember a woman matching that description. She danced most of the evening with a certain gentleman in a Harlequin costume."

"Yes, me," said Duncan excitedly. "That was me!"

"There was something unusual about that woman," said Jennings. Duncan looked at him in surprise. "Oh, I do not mean that she was exceptional in any particular way that I noticed. I just mean that, while most of the guests arrived with specific invitations, she appeared at the door with a written pass good for attendance at all dances held during the season."

"Do you often see passes like that?"

"On rare occasions, My Lord," said Jennings. "Frequently as a reward for services rendered to the family, although they can also be purchased. So perhaps she had a wealthy uncle who contributed money to the building of the library, and he died. In that case we would have given her a season's pass to express our appreciation and condolences."

"Then you must surely remember why you gave a pass to this particular woman?" asked Duncan, feeling like the object of his quest was both drawing nearer and receding into the distance.

To his immense frustration, Jennings only shook his head.

"No, I cannot say I do, My Lord."

"But there must have been a name on the ticket. Surely you remember the name!"

"I might have known it at one point, Your Grace, but now it eludes me. She, of course, retained the pass for the next Ball, so I do not have access to it." Jennings frowned thoughtfully. "The name may come to me, probably as you are driving away. If I do remember and we happen to run into each other again, I will let you know."

"Please make sure you do," Duncan said.

~~~~~

"I won't say I told you so," he told Margaret as he seated himself on the velvet divan in the sitting room of Eastdale Hall on the following morning. In the two days since his last visit she had fully recovered from her illness and now looked as fresh and hale as ever. "Every time I think I'm getting close to finding this woman, she slips away again. It's maddening!"

"Maybe you're fretting too much about it," said Margaret, seated on the opposite end of the divan with her legs curled up beneath her, twining her hair with one finger. "If it's meant to be, it will happen. If not, then heaven will see to it that you marry the right woman. *All things work together for good.* Remember that."

But Duncan was in no mood to be lectured, as the irritated look on his face plainly demonstrated.

"It just feels like the whole world is conspiring to keep us apart. First the accident with her brother which prevented her from revealing herself at the end of the Ball. Then the fact that *no one* who was present at the Ball seems to know who she was, not even the staff of the host."
~~~~~

"I can see how that would be frustrating. On the other hand, maybe this is just one of those obstacles on the path to true love. You remember how, in *The Tempest*, when Ferdinand and Miranda meet and begin falling in love, Prospero contrives ways of keeping them separated because he wants to increase their longing for each other — *lest too light winning make the prize seem light.*"

"So you think maybe heaven is conspiring to separate us that I might love her the more deeply when we finally meet," said Duncan sceptically. "You know that I have often expressed the opinion that I might not be capable of a genuinely romantic relationship."

Margaret shrugged.

"'The course of true love never did run smooth,' is all I'm saying." But these speculations, while interesting, were bringing them no closer to solving the mystery of the masked woman's identity.

"There must be some way of finding out," said Duncan, "beyond what we've done already. No one can be this elusive for more than a few days, not in a small county like ours."

Margaret rested her hand on her chin with a thoughtful look. "There is one thing we can do," she said.

"What's that?"

"Jennings told you that he remembered this woman being given a pass to attend all of the Balls of the season. Well, if that's the case, then it's unlikely she's going to attend only one Ball. If we keep getting invited to Balls, we're bound to run into her again sooner or later."

It surprised Duncan that this hadn't occurred to him sooner. "These passes he spoke of, are they valid only for events at Moorwike Hall, or could they be used for any Ball of the season?"

"The way it normally works," said Margaret, "at least in my experience, is that the members of the various families coordinate with each other and decide to sell passes. Those passes are then valid for all events held during a given season by the group of families."

"That's brilliant!" said Duncan, clapping his hands together loudly. "Then all we have to do is attend the next Balls—"

"And we'll find her!" said Margaret. "I'm sure of it!"

Duncan was reminded why he loved being friends with Margaret. Given enough time, she could concoct an ingenious solution for anything.

"What about my mother and your parents, though?" he asked. "If they find out I'm pursuing some mystery woman — someone other than you, they will be extremely vocal in their disappointment. After all, in their own minds, they already have us married."

"That's easily managed," said Margaret, looking alert and excited. She was so pleased with herself for having devised a solution to their mystery that she felt she could solve any problem. "I'll accompany you to all the remaining Balls. Our parents won't suspect a thing — in fact, they'll congratulate themselves on their success in getting us to socialize together more often. In the meantime you'll be out there interviewing the suspects, chasing down the woman of your dreams—"

"And I'm going to find her!" He could feel hope returning. All was not lost, not as long as he and Margaret were working together. "Between the two of us, one way or another, we'll find this mystery woman."

ARIETTA RICHMOND, GRACE AUSTEN, ISABELLA THORNE,
KATHERINE KEATS AND ALYCE HEALEY

Chapter Eight

In the next two weeks Margaret and Duncan put their plan into action.

Having learned that a Ball was scheduled to take place at Nether Harbeck at the end of February, Duncan secured a promise from Margaret that she would accompany him.

"The Poles who live at Nether Harbeck are old family friends," said Margaret. "Long ago they became wealthy as a result of their ties to the King of Spain. Alice's father spends at least part of every summer on holiday in Gibraltar."

"But Gibraltar is owned by the British," Duncan pointed out.

"And after that Ball," said Margaret, ignoring his remark but peering at him through a pair of opera glasses that made her eyes oddly large, "what are our plans for the rest of the season?"

"After that Ball," said Duncan, "we get a reprieve for a week until the next Ball at Harcaster Hall. It's a wonderfully frightening old Manor House looking out over a windswept moor, presumably haunted by the ghosts of several small children who died there centuries ago."

"How thrilling," said Margaret, who had put down the opera glasses and was now peering through a telescope. "I'm going to be disappointed when we get there and it turns out to be just a normal old country house."

"Try to keep your expectations low," said Duncan. "Remember what happened when we stayed with the Glossops in Derbyshire. You stayed up the entire night listening to a moaning in the attic which you felt sure was the whisper of a ghostly child vowing to be avenged on her murderers. The attic was searched and—"

"I remember what happened," said Margaret with a dismissive wave of her hand. "No need to remind me of my youthful mistakes. What happens after Harcaster?"

"The week after Harcaster, we attend a Ball at Langmarsh. I must confess I've never been to Langmarsh."

"Nor have I," said Margaret. "I hope they're not hiding any terrible secrets."

"The only secrets I hope they're hiding are good ones," said Duncan. He didn't say anything more, but he didn't have to.

The mysterious woman continued to exert a fascination over Duncan. Again and again he had pored over the details of their evening together in his memory until they had attained a near-mythical status.

Her every action, from the way that she had entered the room after the other guests had already arrived, to her abrupt manner of departure, seemed calculated to emblazon herself on his memory.

Not knowing who she was, yet not being able put her out of his mind, Duncan found himself sleepwalking through life. Things no longer had meaning in themselves, but only in relation to her. Once in the village he passed a shop window displaying a wig identical to the one that she had worn that night. Entering the shop, he inquired of the owners whether they had ever met a woman matching her description, but because she had been costumed and masked, he gave them little to go on — only her general height and build, and the true color of her hair.

"Sometimes it feels like I'm going mad," he told Margaret. "That would explain it, wouldn't it? Perhaps she wasn't real to begin with, and I just imagined her."

"You mustn't doubt yourself, and besides, you know for a fact that Simon saw her as well. Somewhere out there, there's a real woman you really danced with. If you keep building her up in your mind, you're just going to be disappointed when the reality fails to live up to your memories. There are better things than being perfect."

"Like what?" Duncan asked sceptically.

Margaret smiled a small smile. "Like being human."

Duncan gave no outward appearance of having heeded her wisdom, but he kept her words in mind as they prepared for the late winter Ball at Nether Harbeck in the last weekend of February.

The last thing he wanted was to spend the entire ball pining after a woman who wasn't there. In a way he was glad Margaret would be there to hold him accountable.

~~~~~

The week passed slowly for Duncan, but he finally found himself at Nether Harbeck with Margaret at his side, following a long carriage ride. Knowing that she expected him to station himself in a corner of the room and sulk there for the rest of the night, Duncan was careful to surprise her by dancing with many women.

He particularly enjoyed the company of a young woman named Amelia Fitzgerald, a flighty brunette who danced as if enchanted by some spell. However, her conversation couldn't measure up to the conversation he had had with the masked woman at Moorwike. She insisted on telling stories about sisters and cousins and uncles he had never met — or even heard of — and which could only have been interesting to those who knew them.

"How was it," he asked Margaret on their return trip after the Ball, "that the Marie Antoinette girl managed to be so interesting when describing events that she hadn't even personally experienced?"

"Are we still obsessed with her?" asked Margaret in a disappointed tone. The carriage was chilly and she pulled the warming robe tighter around her body.
~~~~~

"I liked Amelia well enough," he replied. "But I spent half the evening listening to her prattle on about a brother-in-law in Warwickshire who lost his right leg fighting in the Battle of Trafalgar, and a boy-cousin named Owen who recently broke his leg and went about pretending he had lost it in the war. You would think losing a limb was the most heroic thing a man could ever do in the service of his country."

"So we know she's not the girl. Did you meet anyone else who struck your fancy?"

Duncan shook his head.

"Amelia was certainly the best of the lot. I wanted to apologize, by the way, for ignoring you for much of the evening. Though the few times I looked over there, you seemed to be enjoying yourself."

Margaret smiled, though Duncan couldn't see her in the darkness of the carriage.

"I enjoyed myself very much, thank you. I was asked to dance by several men." They continued to discuss the various people who had been at the Ball, and Duncan kept the banter light, teasing her about her conquests.

~~~~~

If waiting for the week to pass before attending Nether Harbeck had seemed long, the wait for the Ball at Harcaster Hall seemed never-ending. The wait turned out to be worthwhile, however, as both investigators fared better.
~~~~~

Margaret danced with a couple of gentlemen previously unknown to her. One was a thin but handsome, fun-loving man named Walter who claimed to have been a spy during the war and to have made a daring raid behind enemy lines. Of course there was no way of proving whether or not this story was true, but she enjoyed hearing it immensely.

The other was a devilish-looking red-faced young man named Cecil, who expressed his jealousy of the first man by circling around him and Margaret, whenever they were together, practically brandishing a hot poker in one hand. Margaret, enjoying the attention they both gave her, refused to favor one over the other.

Duncan, too, luxuriated in the company of two women. The first was a young woman named Lucy-Anne Honeyfield "whose dark brown hair," as he later told Simon, "encircled her lovely face and accentuated her deep azure eyes."

Lucy-Anne spoke no more than a few words the entire night, and every time Duncan looked at her, she was staring at him as though enraptured. One might have thought he was a Prince, given the shyness that came over her whenever he asked her to dance. But as she was an excellent dancer, Duncan didn't mind too much.

The other was a young, green-eyed blonde named Juliet. From the beginning she proved more conversational than Lucy-Anne, although not so conversational that he found himself dreaming of escape. Duncan warmed to her immediately and by the second dance they were already talking like old friends.

"I must say, I am enjoying myself thoroughly," he said during a break between dances. "I do not remember seeing you at any of these Balls before. I thought I knew just about everyone in the county. By the way, I do not believe I caught your surname."

"It is Lockhart, Your Grace. Lady Juliet Lockhart," she replied. "And the reason you have not seen me is that I have only recently moved here. My father, Ernest Lockhart, became Earl of Keldby a few months ago, on the death of his brother, and he inherited the estate near where we were living, located some two counties from here."

"So what brings you here, then, Lady Juliet?"

"Unfortunately, the estate had not been maintained for some time and it needed extensive repairs before my father felt it safe for the family to occupy. So it was happily decided that my siblings and I would come to stay for a year's time with a cousin who lives in this area."

"I trust that you are having an enjoyable visit."

"Personally, I am finding it quite delightful," she said. "Everyone in my family seems to have been granted a devilish sense of humour, and we are constantly playing tricks upon one another."

Duncan was immediately reminded of his relationship with Margaret, and a broad smile spread across his face.

The music having resumed, Duncan offered his arm and led Juliet back onto the dance floor.

"You dance well, Your Grace," she told him. "I sometimes think it is a relief that we do not live in fifteenth-century Vienna, and that you are not risking your life by asking me to dance."

Duncan smiled in spite of himself.

"How did such an odd notion come into your head?"

"I was just looking at Edward Harcourt," she said, referring to the owner of Harcaster Hall, "and thinking how much more difficult it would be to meet a suitable beau if our families were at war with each other. We would have to contrive various scenarios for seeing each other without being caught by our parents or my mouthy old nurse."

"Actually I think that would be quite thrilling," said Duncan. "I could be Romeo and you — well, you could be my Juliet."

Juliet shook her head sadly.

"It could only end in tragedy."

Duncan had to take care not to laugh at the feigned solemnity with which she said this. "I have worn disguises to a Ball before, just as Romeo did," he said. "But not because I was caught in a war between two feuding houses." He looked at her closely to gauge her reaction.

"How disappointing," said Juliet. "I tend to think nothing is worth doing unless it carries the risk of death."

It was hard to tell whether or not she was being serious. As far as he could tell, she was one of those people for whom nothing is ever said in seriousness. In that respect she again reminded him of himself and Margaret.

"It was almost as exciting as nearly dying, I can assure you," said Duncan. "It was a Valentine's Day Ball, and I went as the Harlequin."

"Oh." She paused for a moment. "And did you fall in love there?"

"I beg your pardon?" he asked, taken aback.

Juliet's gaze was steady and unwavering.

"Did you fall in love, Your Grace? People do at such Balls, I am told."

Duncan glanced thoughtfully into the middle distance, where a young man and woman were talking and laughing much as he and the mysterious woman had done on that fateful night.

"She was the Queen of France. And yes," he said. "Yes, I suppose I did."

"Then you ought to tell her so," said Juliet. "If you have not yet."

"I will someday." He smiled sadly. "If ever I find her again."

ARIETTA RICHMOND, GRACE AUSTEN, ISABELLA THORNE,
KATHERINE KEATS AND ALYCE HEALEY

Chapter Nine

Duncan returned home that evening with a barely concealed feeling of disappointment. He found Simon playing the clavichord in the drawing room.

"Did you see your one true love tonight?" Simon asked as Duncan hung up his coat and hat and threw himself down on the divan.

"Sadly, no," said Duncan, curling up into a tight ball with his feet resting on the edge of the cushions. His eyes were just barely visible. "I'm beginning to think I won't ever see her again. She hasn't shown up at a single one of the Balls I've attended since Saint Valentine's Day, and at this point I'm close to giving up."

"On the bright side," said Simon, "at least you have a girl to pine for — somewhere."

"Small consolation when I don't even know her name," said Duncan, "and when I'm increasingly doubtful she even exists."

Simon played a single reverberating chord on the clavichord. "Maybe it was the real Marie Antoinette."

"Don't think that hasn't occurred to me."

Rising from the bench, Simon walked over to a bar at the edge of the room. Using a silver ladle, he scooped a few ounces of ratafia into a white porcelain mug. This done, he stood there stirring it for some moments, occasionally sipping it, as though brooding over what he wanted to say.

"I think," he said at last, "it might be time to give up on the dream."

Duncan uncurled himself and rose slightly.

"What do you mean?"

"I mean," said Simon, "that you've spent long enough pining over this girl. You spent one evening together and it was certainly magical, but now your nostalgia is preventing you from moving forward with your life. If you keep your eyes open, eventually you'll find an equally lovely woman who will mean even more to you than this fantasy ever could. But if you continue to cling to the past, you're just going to be lonely."

Simon's words had the force of truth behind them, although it was a truth Duncan wasn't sure he was ready to hear. "Simon," he said, "if you had only seen this woman—"

"No," said Simon. "You know what? I don't even think this is really about her anymore. It's about the legend you've created around her." Seeing the sceptical look on Duncan's face, he added, "I'll prove it to you. What did you and she talk about on the night of the Ball?"

Duncan paused. He felt sure he could have answered this question in depth right up until the moment it was asked. But suddenly his memories were cloudy.

"I—"

"Anything?" Simon challenged. "Name just one thing."

Duncan sat there in silence for several minutes feeling tense and sweaty and increasingly panicked. He had relived that night a thousand times, both waking and sleeping. How was it now so hard to remember the most basic details?

"Maybe I should have written it all down," he said at last, looking defeated.

"I'm glad you didn't. You would have clung to it forever, every word she said, while the real woman moved on with her life and forgot about you. Then in twenty years you'd have met her at a party, completely changed from what she was, from what you remembered. And you would wonder why you wasted so much of your life chasing after dreams."

Duncan half-hated Simon for saying this — and yet Margaret had been saying essentially the same thing. He had always been able to rely on at least one of them to tell him the hard truths.

"I think," he said slowly, but with growing conviction—"you might well be right. I think it might be time to let go and move on with my life."

~~~~~
~~~~~

Two weeks later another Ball was held at Langmarsh Hall, a stately Manor House with stone balustrades lining the upstairs terraces and a sweeping spiral staircase carved out of ancient oak. For the first part of the evening Duncan was so preoccupied with exploring its broad halls and outdoor courtyards that he hardly noticed the other guests.

There was no one present at this Ball he hadn't met before. Half of the small number of guests had attended the first Ball at Moorwike Hall and the other half had attended the third Ball at Harcaster House. Juliet Lockhart numbered among this second group. Because Miss Honeyfield had not come, he found himself gravitating more and more toward Juliet as the night wore on. Because there were so few guests, they were obliged to dance together repeatedly. He was surprised to find that he didn't mind.

"This old house is wonderfully creepy," Juliet said during their third or fourth dance. (After a certain point Duncan had lost count of how many times they had danced). "I would not be surprised if there was a vast system of tunnels running underneath it for miles and miles, probably with stone catacombs where evil men with moustaches torture innocent nuns and conspire to take over England."

"What do you have against moustaches?" asked Duncan, smiling.

"Nothing, in themselves," said Juliet in a low voice. "They just always seem to be worn by the worst sorts of people."

"I knew a lieutenant in the army whose moustache must have covered half his face," said Duncan, "like a stone wall that had been overtaken by weeds and brambles."

"Was he awful?"

"Dreadful. He would have personally executed all of our prisoners of war if he could have gotten away with it. He was an adulterer, and a thief, and he played the guitar very badly."

"He should have shaved his moustache then," Juliet said with a sad shake of her head. When pressed, however, she declined to expound on this enigmatic statement.

Years of absurd conversations with Margaret and his brother had prepared Duncan for Juliet's whimsical perspective. Although at first he had dismissed her as an eccentric, she gradually won him over with the cleverness of her satire and her habit of freely intermingling fantasy and reality.

In fact, there was never any knowing what she would say next, and this made their interactions a source of perpetual surprise. He had never laughed so hard at another person's jokes, not even Simon's — and the fact that Juliet always responded by standing there stone-faced, blinking rapidly, as if she couldn't understand what was so funny about what she had just said, just made him laugh even harder.

He liked her ability to move gracefully with him around the floor. Her hand was delicate and already familiar as it fitted so perfectly into his own. At the end of that evening he surprised himself with a question he blurted out without thought ahead of time.

"Lady Juliet," he said, "would you do me the honor of accompanying me on a carriage ride, perhaps sometime next week?"

Although her heart seemed to skip a number of beats she managed to maintain perfect control. "Yes, Your Grace," she said. "I would enjoy that very much."

"I would be very pleased if you would call me by my given name," he said. "Duncan."

"Then you must simply call me 'Juliet'."

The carriage ride was a notable success, the conversation flowed freely, covering subjects ranging from the latest topics discussed in Parliament to the particular flowers blooming as they passed them on their way. Seated next to her in the carriage he found a sense of comfort. There was also a bit of a frisson when his leg brushed hers. Her hand on his arm made him feel tall and elegant.

Over the next several weeks they began spending more and more time together, walking, enjoying each other's company as they rode through the countryside, or just sitting and discussing the events of the day.

There came a day when Duncan woke up anticipating another opportunity to walk with Juliet before teatime, but he noticed that his breath was rapid and his heart was beating quickly. That afternoon, while expecting a response to a bit of witty repartee, Duncan gazed into Juliet's soft green eyes and finally realized he had fallen deeply in love with her. This was more than attraction. He suddenly realized that his life could not be complete without Juliet. He almost broke into poetry and laughed at his own whimsy.

~~~~~
~~~~~

"I wanted to apologize for neglecting you these last several weeks," he told Margaret when he returned to Eastdale Hall after a long absence. "Not being able to offer any excuses, all I can ask is your forgiveness."

"I would gladly give it," said Margaret with a shrewd smile, "if there was anything to forgive. However, no apologies are necessary because you haven't done anything wrong."

"Dear Maggie!" cried Duncan. "Guiding star of my life. As always, you're too good for me."

"And, as always, you think too highly of me. Though, if I'm not mistaken, you've had a very good reason for being elsewhere. Your attentions, as I gather, have been wholly focused on another."

"Yes," he replied. "She is Lady Juliet Lockhart, daughter of the Earl of Keldby." Duncan's face reddened, stung as he was by the perceived accusation in Margaret's voice. Yet when he looked into her eyes there was no reproach there, only kindness and a deep understanding.

"You need not feel guilty," she said, "and you need not apologize for being in love. It was bound to happen to one or both of us, sooner or later. And now you know for certain that you are truly capable of the genuine feeling of romantic love."

Duncan stared at Margaret for the better part of a minute, studying her face. She appeared different somehow, perhaps a little older, perhaps a bit more settled, and yet more animated than he remembered. He couldn't decide which. For a moment she looked as though she wanted to say more, but then, apparently thinking better of it, she shook her head and sighed.

"You've changed in some way," he said. "I can't quite work out what it is, but something is transpiring that I need to know about." He flashed a wry smile at his friend.

"Well, if you must know, while you have been running around the countryside courting your lady, I have been pursued by one of the gentlemen I met while attending the Balls. He is Lord Ashburn." She studied Duncan's face, looking for his reaction to this news.

His eyes opened wide.

"Is it serious?"

"*Very serious,* I'm pleased to say," she said, almost giggling with delight.

"I must say," said Duncan, "that is wonderful news!"

"How does your mother feel about all of this?

"Oh, she is not entirely overjoyed by the prospect of my relationship with Juliet. I do think, though, that she has come to terms with it. It's just that she so had her heart set on you and me becoming engaged and keeping the relationship 'in the family' so to speak."

"I understand," said Margaret, her lips pursed. "My father and mother have always wished me to marry well, and you being Duke of Middleford — and a long-time friend — that just seemed so ideal to them. But I tell them that now, even if I wanted to encourage such a pairing, that ship has already sailed."

Duncan rose from the divan and took Margaret's hand in his. "*Do* you wish to talk me out of my situation?" he asked.

Margaret shook her head emphatically.

"No, of course not," she replied. "Nothing could please me more than to see you this happy. I expect and hope that you and Lady Juliet will share a long and joyful life together."

"I'm planning on it," said Duncan with a faraway look. "Preparations are even now under way to make that a reality. Yet I must wait but a little while until I make certain the Lady feels the way I do."

Margaret smiled as if to say she wasn't the least bit surprised.

"I'm very glad to hear it. But, Duncan—if you don't mind my asking, whatever happened to the intense search for Marie Antoinette?"

Duncan smiled slyly. "Marie who?"

~~~~~

Each time Duncan came to escort Juliet on an outing it was like seeing her for the first time. He could only describe the lift he felt in his heart as a feeling of coming home.

On an afternoon in late June, Duncan and Juliet took another ride in his carriage. The air was warm and drowsy, the blue sky filled with huge white, fluffy clouds. By now they were very comfortable in each other's presence. They did not need to talk, yet they could talk for hours without provocation.

On this afternoon they drove down a stone lane running near a wheat field.
~~~~~

Duncan wanted nothing more than to recline with his head against the side of the willow tree rising up over a brook to their right, and to nap for an hour or two in the indolent haze of early summer.

How he would sleep with the excitement of his purpose in mind he did not know. He only knew that he was at peace with this woman, and he simply had to know if she was truly his.

Duncan grabbed a blanket and a basket from the carriage and then helped Juliet step down to the ground.

Together they walked closer to the brook, where the earthy aroma of its fresh rushing water spoke of the peace of a beautiful summer's day.

He carefully laid the carriage blanket on the ground under the willow, then he placed the luncheon basket on the edge of the blanket. Kissing her hand, Duncan whispered,

"Wait here, my love." A minute later he returned from the carriage, carrying pillows and a small stool. After helping her to seat herself on the stool, which he placed near the trunk of the tree, he knelt at her feet.

"Juliet, you have come to mean the world to me," he began. "You are witty, beautiful and quite beguiling. I need to know if you find yourself full of affection for me, or you only enjoy matching wits and taking carriage rides."

Blinking at him, Juliet smiled a shy smile which seemed quite out of character for the witty woman with a penchant for mixing fantasy with reality.

"Duncan, you are a delightful change from any man I have ever known. You charmed me from the moment we first danced together. In truth I enjoy your company and your wit. My affection for you has grown steadily throughout our association."

He had reached the end of his reserve, and the question that burned in his heart demanded an answer.

"Juliet — do not torture me!" He fixed his eyes on hers and said, "I love you more than life itself. Do you also feel thus?"

"I love you also," she said, gazing straight across to him serenely with her dreamy green eyes. "Now and forever."

Only the nearness of the tree trunk kept Juliet on her stool as Duncan embraced her, kissing her enthusiastically. She gently pushed him away and laughed.

"Wasn't there something else you wished to say?" she said.

His senses muddled from their first kiss, it took him a moment to respond.

"Yes, my darling Juliet," he said finally. "I have with me our family heirloom engagement ring, passed from mother to son through many generations. Will you do me the honor of wearing it and becoming my Duchess — my wife?"

"Yes, Duncan," she replied, a broad smile infusing her voice with joy. "Of course. Nothing could please me more."

Clasping her left hand in his, he reached into his vest pocket, and finding it empty, began a frantic search through all of his pockets.

More than a little embarrassed he looked once again at the love of his life and said,

"It seems I must have left the ring in the leather pouch in the carriage." Without breaking eye contact he stood up. "I will be right back."

Looking deeply into his eyes, Juliet smiled and gently tilted her head. *"A tout à l'heure,"* she whispered.

Epilogue

Banns were published in late summer, and Duncan and Juliet were married at the local parish church one morning in early fall. Most of the guests were family and friends, including some who worked on either the Duke's estate or the estate of Juliet's father. Even Alice, Margaret's lady's maid was in attendance.

Simon and Margaret beamed at the couple and seemed almost as happy as did the wedded pair. Margaret's and Duncan's parents had finally realized that this wedding was a perfect love match and their pressured manipulations would not have led either of their children to a life of happiness.

With all of the extended families in attendance, there were enough titles to please and placate the *ton*, while keeping the gathering pleasant and without pretence.

A row of maple trees lined the walk leading up to the church on either side, their fallen leaves carpeting the lawn in vibrant reds and golds.

As Juliet and Duncan were walking out of the church together at the end of the ceremony, Juliet took off her shoes and went running through the grass, laughing and kicking up leaves as she went. Duncan followed closely behind. Having recovered from their initial surprise, the onlookers roared their approval.

Breakfast consisted of blueberry muffins, toast, eggs, ham, tea, chocolate — and of course, a wedding cake — and was held in a walled stone garden covered with vines that stood at the back of the church. When they had finished eating, Juliet took Duncan's hand in hers and led him to the edge of the enclosure. There, leaning against a pillar, stood a thin man with chestnut-colored hair and bright, almond-shaped eyes, watching the proceedings with a look of deep satisfaction. A cool autumn breeze ruffled his hair.

"Duncan," said Juliet, "I would like you to meet my brother, Walter."

Walter removed his silk top hat and placed it to his chest. "How do you do, Your Grace?" he replied. Then, waiting for a response, he added, "Pleased to finally make your acquaintance."

"Juliet has spoken of you often," said Duncan. "But I've never had the pleasure of meeting you until now."

"That's because he was never around when you came calling," said a grinning Juliet. "He was always away, pursuing the love of his own life."

Politeness dictated that Duncan enquire who this woman was, and if he could meet her.

But before he had a chance to speak, the woman in question came up and stood demurely by Walter's side. It was Margaret.

"I see you have already made the acquaintance of Lord Ashburn," she said with just a bit of pride in her voice.

"It was *you*," Duncan exclaimed, gesturing animatedly at Walter. "*You* were the man who escorted Juliet to the Valentine's Masquerade Ball — the threadbare mendicant!"

"Guilty, Your Grace," said Walter with an air of perfect self-possession. Motioning to his sister, he said, "Our cousin Dorothy and I convinced Juliet to attend the Masquerade Ball. But it was cousin Amelia who had the clever idea, a handful of weeks prior, to color Juliet's blonde hair with a solution of henna to turn it red. Juliet hated how she looked with that hair, and decided to masquerade as Marie Antoinette so that she could completely cover the hair with a large wig. I made such sport of Juliet's hair that she dared me to attend the ball with her, dressed as a common beggar. And, because everyone in our family loves a good joke, I agreed."

Duncan felt the sensation he had had only two or three times before in his life, that he was finally getting to the bottom of a great mystery.

"But what about the season pass for the Balls?" he asked.

To his surprise, it was Margaret who spoke next.

"May I answer that?" she asked. Receiving a nod from Juliet and Walter, she continued.

"The way Walter explained it to me, the season pass was good for two people. Walter and Juliet agreed to attend the Masquerade together. When it came time for the next Ball, Juliet's hair had only partially reverted to its original color, so she would have been truly embarrassed to go out in public. So she refused to go, and Amelia attended in her place, with Walter as her escort."

Duncan looked wildly back and forth from Juliet, to Walter, to Margaret. It was as if he had just awakened from a long dream in which they were the main characters.

Walter was beaming as he turned to face Margaret.

"And I had the pleasure of dancing so many times with this lady," he said, "that it has become a habit!"

Just then a boy of about eight came charging through the crowd, holding a half-eaten blueberry muffin in one hand and chasing two barking black-and-white dogs as if his very life depended upon catching up with them.

"Owen!" shouted Juliet. "How many times do I have to tell you to act like a gentleman in public?

"Oooh," she said, shaking her head in disgust as she turned to the others. "God preserve us from little brothers!"

Everyone present laughed heartily.

A little more than a year later, the dream of Louisa's heart was finally realized when the Duke and Duchess of Middleford added a baby boy — and heir apparent — to the family line. More children would soon follow, both boys and girls.

Walter and Margaret were married one morning the following spring, in the same parish church.

Some eight years later, Walter's father, Ernest Lockhart, succumbed to a heart condition, and Walter and Margaret became Lord and Lady Keldby. The new Earl and his Countess were thrilled to add their third child the month of the funeral to ease their mixed emotions at the old Earl's passing.

Both families remained fast friends for many happy years.

The End

**If you enjoyed this book, you'll love
'The Duke's Nerveless Nemesis'
– you'll find a preview just after the
'About the Author' section!**

About the Author

Some say that Alyce Healey was likely born with a book in one hand and a pen in the other. She has always loved reading, and began to write stories when she was about six years old.

A romantic at heart, she adores the richness of the Regency era and the strong romantic appeal it offers both writer and reader, an opportunity for both to "get lost" in a world much simpler, much purer than the one we experience on a daily basis. "Love *must* conquer all" is Alyce's guiding principle for all her stories. Forgiveness, redemption and the realization that all things work together for good are the natural by-products of that principle.

Yet falling in love is never a perfect process, and that is reflected in Alyce's stories which frequently involve adventure and intrigue, entertaining plot twists and a surprise or two.

So, Dear Reader, come along and enjoy Alyce's delightful tales of life and love, Regency style!

Connect with Alyce at http://www.alycehealey.com

ARIETTA RICHMOND, GRACE AUSTEN, ISABELLA THORNE,
KATHERINE KEATS AND ALYCE HEALEY

Here is Your Preview of
The Duke's Nerveless Nemesis

Alyce Healey

Chapter One

"As much as I am dreading the ride back to Pennley," said James Beaumont, "there is one thing I dread even more."

"What's that, My Lord?" asked Michael, his manservant.

"Actually getting there."

Michael said nothing and a silence fell between them as the chaise rattled its way across the stone streets. Both men were unusually gloomy, now that their long stay in London was coming to an end. Their friends and relations had warned them that the city was a stable of filth and corruption, and that no one who had any money would choose to stay there during the summer. Yet compared to life at Pennley, since James's father had died, it was positively idyllic.

James had never expected to hate his own home so much and to miss it so little. He and his father, the former Duke of Engleton, had spent countless hours hunting for game in its woodlands when he was younger. Its orchards and lakes stocked with fish were the envy of every well-to-do family in five counties.

Each year at the annual Midsummer's Eve Ball *he* was the envy of every young man, including his slightly older and considerably less handsome brother Frederick.

But then Frederick had taken control of the estate, and everything had changed.

If the late Duke of Engleton could have chosen his own successor, there was no question that he would have chosen James. At twenty-five, he was universally admired. His bright eyes and shy smile betrayed an air of profound innocence. The single stray lock of brown hair that was perpetually falling into his eyes, threatening to obscure his vision, was talked about and sighed over and fought over by half the women in London. Had the succession been put to a vote, every manservant, maidservant, groundskeeper, ostler, groom and herbalist at Pennley would have voted to confer the Dukedom on James Beaumont.

But Dukedoms are not decided by election, and upon their father's death the title was bestowed on Frederick.

The moment Frederick became the Duke of Engleton, he began working to consolidate his rule over the vast estate. Old servants who had been with the family for decades were removed from their positions. (One particularly aged and venerable butler named Bulstrode, who had retired some years before, and been made honorary groundskeeper, was thrown into the street, where he would soon have died of starvation and exposure had the local vicar not taken him in.)

Pretty young girls were given positions better suited to women twice their age and with twice their skill.

Parties were thrown at least once a fortnight, lavish parties that threatened to bankrupt Pennley — curiously mirthless parties where scarcely anyone laughed and few could be enjoined to dance. Staff who questioned the wisdom of this excess were summarily dismissed, and those who remained dared not speak against the new Duke and his rule.

Faced with the choice between staying at Pennley and being lorded over by his brother, or studying agriculture in London, James had decided that perhaps now was the right time for an extended trip.

Michael regarded the serious look on James' countenance. He had become his manservant when James was twelve and Michael but eighteen. Through the years he had become a confidant, almost the older brother James desired.

(In fact, they resembled brothers in every way – more so than James and his true brother, Frederick.)

Because of their close relationship, Michael was allowed to delve into subjects of the most personal nature.

"It amazes me that there could be so many women in London to attract the eye, My Lord," said Michael, "and yet your eye remained singularly undistracted."

James watched with disgust and pity as a young boy, his feet covered in rags, crossed the narrow street carrying a broom in one hand while humming the tune to a filthy song.

"I didn't come here to get married," he said. "I came here to learn. I came here to begin the journey of becoming a man of importance."

"And do you think you were successful, My Lord?" asked Michael.

James frowned, as if not liking the question.

"Only time can tell."

It was a remarkably hot afternoon. The heat had affected the horses, making them sleepy and sluggish. Shimmering mirages of water rose up out of the street in front of them. A woman of no older than twenty with a long neck like a giraffe's passed them on the sidewalk, her white muslin gown splotched with dark patches of sweat.

"Your brother hasn't answered a single one of your letters since we left," said Michael, wiping his brow with the back of his hand. Only six years James' senior, he was a passably handsome man. With no ambition to wed until he stumbled upon the perfect woman, Michael was unconcerned with his appearance. Neat and clean and not at all fancy, he was content to serve his friend. A bit more broad, muscular and not run to fat, only close scrutiny would show him to be a servant and not one of the *ton*.

"More likely he's not even read them," said James. "There's not much I can do about it, but I have been writing to the servants in secret. They're expecting us tomorrow night at nightfall."

"And what will you do when you get there, My Lord?"

"What will I *do*?" said James. "Continue to live there, I suppose. He can't interfere with that. I've a right to live there as much as he."

This wasn't strictly true, as they both knew. Frederick, being a Duke, had the right to turn his younger brother off his property whenever the mood struck him. It was only the threat of a popular outcry in the neighboring towns and villages that prevented him from doing so. Frederick would have been universally disgraced. He couldn't risk it, and they both knew it. Otherwise James might have stayed in London indefinitely.

"But what do you hope to accomplish?" asked Michael.

James chewed his upper lip thoughtfully. "It can't be a secret to you that the servants were displeased with our departure," he said at last.

"They've written to me of nothing else since we left."

"Apparently it was seen as an act of betrayal in some quarters. I hope to rectify that. If Frederick is determined to continue on his present course, there's not much we can do to gainsay the destruction. But we can be a bulwark and moral support, if nothing else. A refuge."

"Your brother won't be pleased with that," said Michael.

"I'm counting on it," said James. "There will be discord. But the people of Pennley need to know they're not alone anymore. If no one else will fight for them, I will fight for them. For the staff, and for my sister."

~~~~~

Young Susan Mowatt sat in her father's library, gingerly holding a cup of tea in both hands above a double-flapped mahogany table.
~~~~~

Her father sat across from her on the velvet chaise lounge reading the *Edinburgh Review* and studiously choosing to ignore the vexed look on her face. The scowl did not serve her well.

"Why is the world so set on being difficult for women?" she said in a raised voice. "Why can't I make my fortune as any man would, through a splendid inheritance or some astonishing display of genius? Why can I not be idle as they are?"

"Because that is the nature of things," said Benjamin. "You will have to earn your own way in the world."

Susan took off her bonnet and set it on the table, allowing her brown hair to flow freely. "I wish I were free," she said, "as these hairs are free." Indeed her hair tumbled down her back in a most becoming manner. Her father thought it set off her sparkling hazel eyes. Surely some fine gentleman would find her irresistible despite a lack of dowry.

"You mustn't talk nonsense," her father replied. "You're eighteen years old and an adult now, and there's no shame in teaching voice lessons. I do it to support us, but also because I love doing it. Once you've gotten settled, you'll find it's not as bad as you think."

Susan folded her arms across her bodice and let out a loud, "Harrumph!"

Benjamin Mowatt had been patiently enduring these outbursts of defiance since Susan was old enough to express herself in words. At first they had angered him; then, as he had matured, they had been an occasional nuisance.

Now, in middle age, he found them entertaining. He had little time for entertainment, finding his own meager living as tutor to the spoiled rich a major exercise in patience and long suffering. His paunchy figure testified to the fact that he did not miss many meals. He supposed he had little to complain about. Since his dear wife had passed on, he'd taken no interest in finding a step-mother for Susan.

Truth be told he realized that he was not a particularly great catch for any admirable woman. His lack of physical exercise due to his penchant for reading, when he wasn't composing or teaching, left him with a less than muscular frame. His thinning hair and spectacles made him resemble a man more elderly than his actual years. No matter, he had Susan, the bright star he loved without reserve. He tried not to despair of her future, even as he saw her potential linked to his own meager status.

For the past three months Susan had been giving vocal lessons to Caroline Beaumont, a girl of thirteen who lived on her brother's estate at Pennley. Susan had been taking lessons on the pianoforte from her father since the age of five, but this was the first real job she had ever had. Under his tutelage she was becoming an accomplished voice instructor.

"It just seems unfair," said Susan, "that the only ways a woman can hope to acquire wealth in this world are through marriage or inheritance. I don't expect an inheritance and I don't intend to marry. I suppose I shall die penniless."

"Not that it will matter then," said Benjamin. "We all enter the grave as equals."

"But I would like to make a professional living," she said. "Voice teaching can supply a modest income, but not enough to keep me from poverty if you should die. A woman shouldn't have to depend so much on the health and good favor of men, both of which are likely to betray us when we need them the most."

"I suggest you have this conversation with Mary Wollstonecraft," said Benjamin, sipping his tea languidly. "I can guarantee she will enjoy it more."

"She's dead, father," said Susan in a tone of great aggravation. "Which, if you cared anything about the sufferings of women, you would know."

Benjamin raised his hands in mock surrender. "I haven't been keeping up. I'm sorry."

"She's been dead nearly twenty years."

"What do you think of Caroline Beaumont?"

It was an obvious ploy to change the subject, but Susan sat up eagerly at the mention of her young protégé. "She's delightful, really. Her singing is not remarkable, though I have hopes that it will improve with proper training. But how could one hold it against her? No one at Pennley has treated me with more kindness."

"And how have you been treated otherwise?"

Susan shuddered at the question and the air itself seemed to grow colder for a moment. "The young Duke of Engleton is as bad as they say," she said.

"Though I have had the good fortune not to experience his wickedness directly, as he has seen fit to visit the brunt of it upon his servants and others he considers his social inferiors."

"Given that he's a Duke," said Benjamin, "one would expect us to qualify."

"And yet I have been spared," said Susan in a perplexed tone. "I have a theory as to why. I think perhaps he's not so fearsome as his reputation suggests, or as he wishes to suggest. Certainly he has humiliated butlers and maidservants in my presence, but always with an elaborate show as though trying to impress me. Yet he has never shown the least hint of unkindness to me or his sister."

"Why do you think that is?"

Susan tugged at her loose hair thoughtfully, a gesture that reminded Benjamin irresistibly of his late wife.

"I think," she said in a hesitant voice, "because he genuinely cares about Caroline and her education. He has been most insistent that she receive the best schooling available. It was almost charming to see the attention he lavished on her, the diligence with which he interviewed me, when he has shown no such care for any other living creature. I think it means that, whatever he says to the contrary, his heart can be penetrated. There is one other person on this earth that he loves."

Chapter Two

His Grace Frederick Beaumont, Duke of Engleton, was seated in his study. Behind him the sun was setting, throwing splashes of pink light onto the desk before him. On top of the desk sat an open lamp, a ceramic bowl in which a wick floated like a drowning sailor. He reached for a match to light it. He was at once thin and round shouldered. His arms were scrawny for all their encasement in fine linen.

Frederick held up a sheet of brown paper to the dim light. It was postmarked from London two days previously. James was known for being a prolific writer, his words running in a thin scrawl all the way down the page and wedged into the margins. So the brevity of this message was unusual. It said only,

"Coming up by chaise. Expect to arrive at the Trenton Inn by nightfall on the day you receive this letter. Send a servant to fetch me."

The letter was unsigned.

Frederick set the letter down with a look of great impatience.

"Jeremy!" he cried.

There was an echo of footsteps in the hallway and a servant of average height, dressed all in black and with a black patch over the socket of his right eye, strode into the room. He was older than the Duke, but of considerably more vigour.

"My brother is on his way home," said Frederick. "Did you know about this?"

"I just learned the news, Your Grace," said Jeremy, "having just received a letter myself."

Frederick frowned, as if wondering why his brother was writing letters to multiple people in the same house.

"This was sent yesterday," he said aloud. "The roads from London are dangerous. Perhaps he didn't make it."

"I suppose one could hope that," said Jeremy.

"Perhaps he got a bad driver — someone very old or very young — and they drove the carriage into a ditch. Perhaps vines and ivy will grow over his body forever."

"There are worse ways to die, My Lord," said Jeremy.

"Don't interrupt." Frederick turned to face the window, running his fingers through his long hair. "It's a savage world outside Pennley. Especially during the summer. Especially in the south. Robbers and thieves guard the roads out of London. Highwaymen will take his purse. Murderers will poke at him with their long knives."

"Those are all things that could happen," Jeremy replied.

Frederick sighed and turned back around.

"You know how much I appreciate you, Jeremy…"

"I do, My Lord."

"Stop interrupting! I love you like my own brother, but you never contradict me. You agree with whatever I say, and frankly, it's exhausting."

Jeremy gritted his teeth as though wanting to admit that, yes, this was a problem.

"Why is everyone so afraid of me?" said Frederick, as much to himself as to his servant. "I've asked the entire household staff that question and still haven't gotten a straight answer."

"Not everyone fears you," said Jeremy.

"Name one person who doesn't."

"I can name two, My Lord. Caroline, your sister, and Susan Mowatt."

Frederick paused and looked at Jeremy for a moment with a perplexed expression, as though he had never heard that name before.

"The voice instructor, My Lord," said Jeremy. "The one who has been training Caroline for the past three months."

"Oh, right! What reason has she to be afraid of me? I've given her a steady job. After Father's death it was necessary for someone to continue with Caroline's voice and pianoforte lessons, and I wasn't the one to do it."

He paused again, as though struck by a new thought. "Why *isn't* she afraid of me?"

"Pardon?"

"Everyone else is so scared of me. What makes her different?"

"She's young and arrogant," said Jeremy. "A very proud creature. You should see the way she addresses the staff, as if she was their Queen."

"I remember being struck by her impertinence when I interviewed her," said Frederick. "It was delightful."

"I should think such a disposition would have been disqualifying, My Lord."

"Not in a girl like her," said Frederick. A smile transformed his face for a moment, making it almost handsome. "Pride and obstinacy are vices in a man. They will drag him down to ruin. But there was something in her eyes when I spoke to her. A fire. It invigorated my old bones."

Jeremy wondered, not for the first time, whether Frederick had fallen for the young woman. But he dared not ask. And why he referred to himself as having old bones while not yet having thirty years.

"Perhaps if your brother had been born a woman," said Jeremy, "relations between you wouldn't be so frayed."

"Perhaps," said Frederick. "And if he had not been born my brother." Silence fell between them for a moment. The sun had slipped behind the hills, leaving the room dark but for the lamp on the desk.

"You want me to go and pick up James, then?" said Jeremy.

Frederick stared at him incredulously.

"What? No. Of course not."

Jeremy stared back at him.

"But it's a forty-mile walk from the nearest inn, My Lord," he said. "You can't mean to make him walk all that way."

"It won't hurt him," said Frederick. "And if it does…"

He puffed out his cheeks, as though vainly wishing for something that he knew would never happen.

Jeremy waved his arms in a helpless fashion, like a windmill.

"But—"

"Don't contradict me, Jeremy," said Frederick, a scowl darkening his face.

"But just a moment ago you said—"

"I know what I said. Don't be impertinent. You know how much I hate impertinence."

Jeremy had never seen a man contradict himself so much in the space of a few sentences. It made his head hurt.

"Under no circumstances," said Frederick, beating his hand into his fist, "is anyone to fetch James. I want him to languish at that inn. I want him to pace his room miserably from morning to morning. I want him to suffer the indignities of the poor and helpless!"

"Very well, My Lord," said Jeremy, realizing that there was nothing more he could do. "But what will the people think of you?"

"The people?"

"The staff, the renters who rent your land, the surrounding villages who hold James in the highest esteem? If they learn that the son of the late Duke had to wade through dirt and mud in the hottest part of the summer because of his brother's refusal to assist him, it will create a scandal. Popular opinion will favor him, not you. You will be disgraced."

Frederick had been gritting his teeth since the mention of his father. Any reminder that someone else had once been the Duke of Engleton irritated him. Still more did it irritate him to be reminded that his brother was still beloved throughout the county while he languished in his study in isolation.

"I'm not trying to take sides," said Jeremy. "I just feel it would be in your best interest—"

"No need to say more," said Frederick with a wave of his hand. "I see that I have been betrayed on all sides. My own servants conspire against me in the daylight, hoping to raise up my successor. My rival. Answer me this — was this the first letter you've received from James in the past year, or have there been others."

Jeremy exhaled loudly.

"He has written many letters, My Lord. Not just to me but to the whole staff. Full of the soundest and most helpful instructions."

"As I suspected! He's not even here and still he undermines my authority. How much more so when he returns home, when he's once again living under this roof!"

"But perhaps if you would follow his advice," said Jeremy, his voice quivering slightly, "he wouldn't need to operate in secret."

"Follow his advice — follow your advice!" said Frederick. He paced back and forth in front of the fire, his hands behind him, looking indignant. "What can a man do when he is surrounded by traitors?"

"Am I correct in thinking you've torn up and burned every letter he's sent you, My Lord?" asked Jeremy.

"Of course I have!" said Frederick, flexing his jaw muscles menacingly. "All of them full of his 'wisdom.' 'Don't throw that party.' 'Don't hire more maids than you can afford.' 'Lower the price of rent to keep the renters happy.' As if he could run this estate better. He would do well to remember that I am the Duke — not he!"

Jeremy let out a loud and profound sigh. Keeping up with his master's changes in mood was exhausting. He could be spiteful and vindictive one minute, melancholy and self-pitying in the next. He was perpetually plagued by insecurities and self-doubts. Yet he seemed to regret his petty mistreatment of others even in the moment they were committed.

"You have spent," said Jeremy, bracing himself for the blow that was surely coming— "you have spent so much of your income since the late Duke's death. You have spent almost everything you own."

Frederick gritted his teeth, but said nothing.

"But you're not yet ruined," said Jeremy. "There's still time to right your course. I can help you. And your brother, too, if you would let him."

"Maybe I will," Frederick said sarcastically. "But first he'll have to find his way back here."

"Which he now has," came a powerful voice through the partially open door. A moment later the door swung open wide and the imposing figure of James Beaumont entered the room.

Continued……

Get

'The Duke's Nerveless Nemesis'

as soon as its released
(due Feb / Mar 2017)

Sign up for Alyce Healey's
newsletter at
www.alycehealey.com

ARIETTA RICHMOND, GRACE AUSTEN, ISABELLA THORNE,
KATHERINE KEATS AND ALYCE HEALEY

Other Books from Dreamstone Publishing

Dreamstone publishes books in a wide variety of categories, ranging from Romance to Kids Books, Books on Writing, Business Books, Photography, Cook Books, Diaries, Coloring books and much more. New books are released each month.

Be the first to know when our next books are coming out

Be first to get all the news – sign up for our newsletter at

http://www.dreamstonepublishing.com

ARIETTA RICHMOND, GRACE AUSTEN, ISABELLA THORNE,
KATHERINE KEATS AND ALYCE HEALEY

www.ingramcontent.com/pod-product-compliance
Lightning Source LLC
Chambersburg PA
CBHW071426190726
48292CB00001B/137